Give Fangs a Chance is an adul
adult themes, and adult scenes. Readers' discretion is advised.
This story takes place in America, in the 1970s. As such, attitudes of the time are reflected in this work. Please read all trigger warnings. The "dark" of this story is not in the romance itself, but surrounding it.
I hope you enjoy this book. If you're looking for a more teen friendly novel, or you just like my writing, may I suggest my book Branches. It's set in the same universe as this one.

TRIGGER WARNINGS

Inside of the romance/ main characters

Internalized homophobia, Grief, Discussion of child death, Emotional instability, Internalized Ageism, Blood play, Jealousy, Past abusive relationships mentioned/discussed, Past child abuse mentioned/discussed

Outside of the romance/side characters

Racism, Homophobia, Ageism, Misogyny, Mentioned Drug, Death, Murder, Mentioned gore, Mentioned/implied Child death, Stalking, Obsession, Mentioned animal death

Chapter 1	3
Chapter 2	21
Chapter 3	49
Chapter 4	69
Chapter 5	93
Chapter 6	116
Chapter 7	142
Chapter 8	169
Chapter 9	206
Chapter 10	233
Chapter 11	261
Chapter 12	280
Chapter 13	310
Chapter 14	328
Chapter 15	352
Chapter 16	374
Chapter 17	394
Chapter 18	408
Chapter 19	431
Epilogue	437

Chapter 1

The beeping of the alarm was akin to nails on a chalkboard. It was awful, but it woke Adelaide up. With a fist, she slammed the top of the screeching device. The noise stopped. The bed creaked as Adelaide sat up. She ripped off her bonnet. A cascade of black and gray curls fell around her. Decades of growing out her hair paid off in long looser curls. They were messy from sleep and fell into her eyes. She blew them away.

Adelaide slipped off the bed, her feet entered her worn slippers. She stretched up high, hearing a pop from her spine. It offered an instant relief. The room was dark, but Adelaide knew it well. She'd lived in those walls her whole life. All fifty years. She walked to the bathroom.

Decades ago, she'd sneak in there to steal a spray of her mother's perfume. She'd sit on the toilet top for hours as her mother tried to tame her hair. She'd do her makeup in the large oval mirror. The walls around her were soaked with memories and the scent of pomegranate. The perfume sat on the sink. It glittered under the yellow light. The deep red glass was mesmerizing. It reflected across the porcelain, painting it in a blood plum color. The bottle was from her great grandmother. It had been the first thing her great grandfather had bought with his new found wealth. The glass reminded her of church windows. When was the last time she'd been to church? Twenty, no, it was thirty years ago. Not since her mother's death.

    Adelaide looked into the mirror. Her eyes looked like black holes in the morning. The brown underneath wasn't visible, even with the light. Their abyssal darkness could rival a mirror in their reflectiveness. Her umber skin had softened over the years. A few dark spots littered it. There were wrinkles. Crows feet. Smile lines. Not as deep as some people her age, but still there. Adelaide wore it all with pride.

    To grow old was a privilege very few in her family got. When Adelaide was a child, women in her life warned her not to smile too much. Adelaide never listened. She smiled whenever she wanted, whenever life allowed. She lived through the depression. She lived through the second World War. She lived through the Civil Rights Movement. She lived through Vietnam. She'd smile when she damn well pleased. And if it showed on her face?

Good. Adelaide got more than anyone expected and was still getting.

She went through her daily motions. Fix hair. Wash face. Lotion. Deodorant. Brush teeth. Once finished, she walked out the bathroom and went to her closet. All her attire had been picked out by her girls. Their favorite thing to do was help Mama A look hip. Adelaide had been dragged to the mall and fabric stores more times then she could count. Fashion magazines and pattern books littered her sewing room and closet floor. Paisley prints and platform boots. Fringe jackets and bell bottoms. Adelaide had spent many nights customizing her girls' bell bottoms. Making them their dream dresses and shirts. Those were nights well spent. The screams of joy she got in return added years to her life.

Adelaide had a lovely side business of making custom clothes. Being in a college town had its advantages. A revolving door of kids wanting what stores didn't supply or things in sizes the stores didn't carry. 'Better than Sears!' one of the boys she sewed a jacket for had proclaimed. That was her favorite review. Over the years Adelaide had perfected her craft. Most of her clothes came from her own hands. Why bother paying for what you could make?

She threw on a pair of burnt orange bell bottoms and a yellow paisley button up. Adelaide adored the corduroy pants. The strange fabric had always been her favorite. The sun began to peak through her curtains. Adelaide hurried out of her room, past the multiple doors.

The house had been a plantation home. It had been left to rot after the Civil War. Adelaide's great grandfather had invented a seeding and irrigation system that had helped the dying farming community thrive once more. He'd turned around and bought the home his family had been enslaved under. He was the first free black man in town to own his own home. Adelaide's great grandfather had intended for his family to live in the walls for generations, as owners.

Now though, there was only Adelaide. She had wondered what to do with such a big house. Selling it wasn't an option. There was nowhere else for Adelaide to go. In the past, her mother would say to fill it with children. In a way, Adelaide had.

In the 1940's, the university came. The once small farming community exploded into a college town. Complete with streetlights, sidewalks, and stop lights. The downtown had been expanded into a full district in the 50s.

Adelaide watched as her world morphed and changed. Instead of resisting, she evolved alongside it.

Her home became a sorority. She became a house mother. Adelaide had a few bad apples at first. She noticed though, once education started, most girls became kinder. They'd learn the history of her family, of the home they lived in, those hateful eyes turned loving. She hadn't had to throw a girl out in over two decades.

The sun's light was beginning to flood the home. It was a honey glow that made the particles glitter. Adelaide made her way to the kitchen. There was a chill in the air. Winter was settling in. Cold crept through the windows and doors. Thankfully cooking would heat up the house.

The kitchen was spacious. A large oval table sat toward the wall. Twelve chairs encircled it. The door that led out to the backyard had some frost on it. Adelaide opened the curtain of its built-in window fully. More sunlight flooded in. The kitchen looked picturesque.

The counter spanned two walls and was perfect for an in-home buffet. A large sink sat under the window that faced the left side of the house. The oven was close to the sink. It wasn't the oven Adelaide grew up with. No, the old cast iron stove had to go with the gaudy wallpaper and ancient appliances. Adelaide clicked on the burner and placed a pan on top of the flame. She left it to warm and went to gather up her ingredients. There were two fridges. A community one and one where the girl's kept their personal items. The community one was always stocked. Adelaide took out what she needed.

All of her girls were at the top of their classes. Some were even in the running for valedictorian. Some of her girls had even been chosen, in the past. Adelaide did her best to nurture them to their fullest potentials. She made sure they studied. She made sure they were fed. She gave them shoulders to cry on and someone to lean on. The results spoke for themselves. Other houses in town called them the poindexters. They took it as a compliment.

Adelaide double checked the calendar. It was one of those huge ones that held every day on one piece of paper. It sat on the wall beside the table. Adelaide trailed her eyes over all of the crossed out dates. Soon, she'd have to say goodbye to 1977 and usher in 1978. That day's date, December 5th, was circled in red. All test days were. Adelaide normally wrote who had what, but today all her girls had exams.

She always made sure to fix breakfast on test days. Coffee was brewed before she started on the food. The smell of it would perk up her seniors. The first alarm went off upstairs. It was time to work. Adelaide started making breakfast. Bacon, eggs, pancakes, and sliced fruit piled up on serving plates. Adelaide was efficient. She had this routine memorized. Thirty years of practice was behind her. It was muscle memory at that point.

Wendy stumbled into the kitchen. Her cornflour hair was a mess, straying in all different directions. "Morning, Mama," she slurred, rubbing her eyes. She was ready to get her doctorate and sleep for a year before joining the workforce.

Adelaide snickered, "I need to get you a bonnet, baby." Wendy would be graduating in the summer. Majoring in chemistry. She was going to make an amazing chemist. She'd make change, good change.

Wendy mumbled something. Her stomach growled loudly, which woke her up fully. The blonde went to the coffee pot, pouring herself a cup. "You're too good to us," she whispered before taking a sip. Wendy sat at the table. "Better than my ma," she said, longing in her voice.

Adelaide smiled sadly. Most of her girls missed their mothers terribly or didn't have a good one. She saw them grow from children to adults. Exiting girlhood fully and entering womanhood without the support of the woman they needed most. Nights of crying over calculations, heartbreaks, and ruined friendships. Adelaide had seen it all. She'd experienced it herself, in many ways.

To some of her girls, she was a second mother. To others, she was their mother. Alumni came every Christmas to visit her. She'd been to dozens of baby showers, weddings, and had thousands of phone calls. Adelaide found belonging in the love she received. A vindication. It proved Adelaide was worthy of love, of people's time, of their smile, and their care. Adelaide's mother had loved her daughter, but never actually loved Adelaide. The woman swallowed her bitterness and flipped the flapjack in the pan.

Monica walked in next. Her afro was picked to perfection. Adelaide loved the style, though she didn't think it would look as good on her. It worked perfectly on Monica. She had a slim face and sharp features. Intense beauty some would say. Adelaide knew Monica would be an amazing doctor. She couldn't wait to visit her future practice.

"Morning, Mama." Monica got some coffee and sat down next to Wendy. "You ready?" she asked the other woman. Wendy groaned and let her head fall on the table. Monica giggled and patted her friend's back.

"You girls are gonna kill it!" Adelaide cheered. She set down serving bowls and plates, all filled with food. "Eat up. A fed brain is a working brain." Adelaide watched as the two began to make plates for themselves.

Tracey walked in next. "Breakfast!" she cheered. Her red hair seemed to shine in the sunlight. A mass amount of freckles covered her face. She hadn't bothered to change out of her pajamas. Tracey was a first year. Her tests were going to be a breeze, at least for her. Tracey sat and loaded a plate. "Can I have some juice, Mama?" she asked the older woman.

Adelaide giggled. Tracey was her youngest. The redhead had graduated early from high school. Only sixteen and states away from home. Tracey was the house baby and everyone doted on her. "Of course," Adelaide got out the orange and cranberry juice. She set them on the table along with a glass for the girl.

Tracey giggled and poured herself a glass. Mama was so kind. With a simple ask, she'd help! Tracey had never experienced such kindness before.

"Your first semester is almost done. How do you feel?" Monica asked as she buttered her pancakes.

Tracey's eyes lit up. Back home, she was so used to being ignored. "I'm excited to get into the hard stuff!" She didn't know what major she wanted to do just yet. Something in science though. She'd need to declare something soon. "Mama," she asked the older woman, "what did you study?"

Wendy and Monica frowned at the question. They looked at Adelaide with a pitying gaze.

Adelaide smiled sadly. A lot of her freshmen assumed she had gone to college. Everything she knew was through helping them study and after thirty years of doing that, most girls assumed she was a retired professor. Adelaide never had the chance to attend college. She'd admit she lived vicariously through every girl she accepted in her home and watched walk across the stage. "I've never been," Adelaide admitted. She watched as Tracey's eyes went wide. Comically wide.

"But you're so smart!" Tracey looked at Wendy and Monica. "She's so smart," she restated. The other girls gave her a gentle smile. The kind you'd give a well meaning child, which Tracey was.

"You can be very wise and never step foot in a college," Monica said sagely. Wendy nodded in agreement.

Tracey frowned till an idea made her face brighten up again. "Why don't you enroll, Mama?" she encouraged, "We could graduate together!"

Adelaide burst into laughter. "I'm fifty, baby. Too old to be going to college." She shook her head, "Besides, even if I graduate, what job would I get? If I got one, who would watch the house? Who'd make sure the next wave of scientists had a good breakfast before exams?"

Tracey thought. Her big blue eyes stared at Adelaide. "I mean. Maybe you wouldn't use the degree per se, but it'd still be something to frame on the wall. Something just for you."

Adelaide felt her chest tighten. Something for her. When was the last time she'd had something for her? "You're sweet, baby." She patted the girl on her shoulder, "Eat your breakfast." The other girls began to flood in. The quiet kitchen became boisterous as ten delightful women filled it with chatter.

Heather savagely ripped into her bacon. "If Mr. Finley puts that bullshit question on the final, I'm gonna-"

"You should count yourself lucky you got Finley!" Tina interjected, "I got Dobson. That creepy son of a-"

"Isn't he under investigation?" Dawn asked.

"He needs to be fired! He's groped how many girls now?" Monica sneered.

"Well, you're safe, Monie. He doesn't grab the dark ones," Nicole laughed. The others at the table burst into laughter.

Monica giggled, "Small blessings."

Adelaide sat at the head of the table. She looked up and noticed a face in the back door window.

It was Tony. The boy began knocking viciously at the door.

Adelaide sighed and stood. The girls all cried out.

"Leave him out there!" "Don't open the door, Mama!" "Boo!"

Adelaide would have left him out, if Tony wasn't a delivery boy for the college. She opened the door. "We have a mail slot," she informed him for the thousandth time.

14

Tony just smiled brightly. He was a handsome man. If only his personality wasn't so rotten. "I just wanted to check on the girls." He peeked over Adelaide's shoulder. The older woman moved to block his view. Not that he minded. "And you too, Mama," he said with a wink.

Adelaide hated how he said the title like the end of a dirty joke. Tony tapped the bundle of letters he had on her chest. She snatched them up. "Thank you, Tony," she hissed. The boy made to cop a feel but she quickly stepped back and slammed the door in his face, locking it.

"Aw, come on, Mama!" Tony called from behind the glass. "You're not too old for some action!"

Adelaide pulled the curtain on the window closed. She ignored Tony's still muffled cries. Adelaide held up the letters. "Mail!" she cheered.

All the girls laughed uproariously.

"Why's he such a creep?" Tracey asked. She was still innocent in many ways, still confused about sleazy men and shitty people.

"He wants to fuck, Mama," Monica informed.

"Some of the fraternities call her the forbidden chocolate," Heather snickered.

"Cause Mama has never put out," Tina teased.

Adelaide rolled her eyes. "I don't fuck kids," she grit out. The girls all giggled. She rarely cursed but it always tickled them pink when she did. Adelaide sat back down. The letters in her hands were thick. "Julia," she called out and handed it to said girl. "Mabel," she said and handed the letter off. "Heather," she teased the girl by pulling the letter away before handing it over. Adelaide watched them open the envelopes. Mabel had simple paper work for her payments. Julia got an acceptance to a class she'd been on the waitlist for. Heather however;

"I GOT INTO HARVARD!" Heather screamed. She jumped out of her chair and began running around the room.

Cheers erupted and bounced off the walls. Adelaide applauded and she gasped when Heather's arms wrapped around her. The girl shook her in joy. Adelaide giggled and kissed the girl's cheek. "I'm proud of you, baby!" she said.

"Thank you, Mama. Thank you!" Heather wept.

Adelaide's face softened. "Aw, baby. Look at me." She cupped the girl's face in her hands. "You did this baby. You did all of this. It was all you and I can't tell you how proud I am."

Heather wept and buried herself in Adelaide's chest. She remembered when her mother found her acceptance letter. How she had screamed and thrown things. How she'd thrown Heather out. Heather had come to this house a depressed girl and she'd be leaving a Harvard acceptee. She looked up at Adelaide. The black woman's soft smile and warm embrace had carried her through so many trials and tribulations. This woman had shown her and so many girls love. Selfless, kind, unwavering love. Heather would be honored to be one of the alumni who came back every Christmas. She'd be honored to take care of the woman when she got too old and needed someone to take care of her for once. "I love you, Mama," Heather said and she meant every word of it.

Adelaide walked down the aisles. She grabbed a brand of cereal some of the girls ate and put it in her basket. The fluorescent lights of the grocery store buzzed above her. Christmas was around the corner. Festive cheer was in the air and almost ready to ignite into an explosion. Adelaide felt giddy. She hopped on the end of her shopping cart, leaning over it and riding it down the aisle. It was fun and reminded her of childhood. Her mother never let her do it, she couldn't stop Adelaide now though.

    A sharp wolf whistle startled her off. She hopped off the cart and turned toward the sound and groaned. Tony came bounding down the aisle with some of his fraternity brothers. "Hey, Mama~"

    Adelaide rolled her eyes, straightened her back and started walking. She decided not to look at them. "Hello, Anthony." Some of the other boys snickered. "Shouldn't y'all be taking your exams?" Maybe they were skipping. Maybe Adelaide could slip a note to the dean. God, she hoped so. Foreman was a coward, but even he was tired of 'the boys in the little blue house'. Tony had turned his frat into a den of chaos. Adelaide didn't know what energy he had or what sway he used, but the boys had been worse since he enrolled. Adelaide kept telling herself she'd only have to endure it for two more years. Maybe less if Tony kept acting out and got expelled. Adelaide hoped he'd get expelled.

One of the boys muttered a 'ya'll'. He had come from up north, like Tony. They found her accent amusing. It hadn't been rare growing up, but since the college was built, it had become sparse. Now, only the elders in town had it. Tidewater was what one of the girls said her accent was. Had that been Heather? No, it was Tina. She was the linguist.

Tony moved closer to Adelaide. Pressing against her side and inhaling her perfume. The woman smelled divine. Most wore those floral scents that burned his nostrils, but not Adelaide. Her scent was sweet, fruity. Tony didn't understand why the woman wouldn't let herself have some fun. "Just finished them actually." He smiled. It would have been charming if the look in his eyes wasn't so lecherous. "I heard you're going to be home alone till the New Year." The woman still wasn't looking at him. It made his blood boil. He was a catch, dammit! How dare Adelaide not see that.

Adelaide scoffed. She'd heard this one before. Over and over and over. Year after year. "Not all alone," she said firmly. One of Tony's hands grabbed the side of her cart. Adelaide looked at it. The grip Tony had on it was turning his knuckles white. Finally, she looked at the boy. His face was red with indignation. Adelaide sighed, "Anthony. I'm old enough to be your mother. How would you feel if some little boy was coming onto her like some horny hound dog?"

Tony snorted, "My ma's a bitch. Maybe some good dick would actually make her bearable."

Adelaide's eyes widened in shock. Which caused all the boys to laugh. She quickly schooled her face. "You're a mess," she replied and tried to push her cart. Tony wasn't letting go though. She warned, "Anthony-"

"Tony," he said. "Come on, Mama. Call me Tony." The boy added, "You're always walking around, calling us 'baby'. Kind of sending mixed signals. Ya know?"

Adelaide huffed, "I call y'all baby 'cause you are babies. I'm too old for this." She got in his face. "Now you're going to let go of my cart and let me finish shopping or I will be going to the dean and maybe drop a line to the cops about all that grass in your house." That made Tony let go. The cops were lenient with alcohol, but not weed. Rick had a vendetta against reefer for years. Adelaide didn't understand why, but she wasn't going to question the sheriff.

The boy held up his hands in surrender. "Okay, okay, Jesus. Excuse me for trying to show your prude ass a good time."

Adelaide sneered, "I've heard the rumors about you. Your time is short and it sure as hell ain't good."

The other boys started laughing. Tony's face twisted in rage. He whipped around. "The fuck's so funny?!"

Adelaide took the opportunity to escape. It felt nice to bite back for once. She hoped it'd be the last time she had to see the awful boy. In her fantasies, Adelaide had bashed Tony's head in more times than she'd care to count. It was healthier than the alternative, still…An awful part of her hoped somebody would do it for real.

Chapter 2

Adelaide popped a bottle of champagne. Her girls cheered. Winter break had officially begun! Most of them were packing to go home or to take trips together.

"You sure you don't want to come, Mama?" Monica asked. The ski trip had an extra seat available, just for Adelaide. Just in case. The woman had barely stepped foot outside their town, unless one of her girls called her away.

Some people in town whispered Adelaide fled to New York in her youth. She had run away with the clothes on her back and went wild in the city. Parties, drugs, queers, chaos. Adelaide was apparently a lounge singer. To think the calm and motherly woman was once a heartstopping songbird was absurd. Monica found the tale hard to believe. .
"You never take vacations," Monica chided. "You deserve a break."

Adelaide chuckled, pouring glasses for everyone. "I'm fine, baby. I'm living the dream." She gave the girl a glass. "Besides, people get rowdy around here. I gotta hold down the fort." Adelaide handed another glass of champagne to Tina. "You better use that camera," she said with a wink.

Tina smiled brightly. "You didn't have to get me a gift, Mama." She took a sip of her glass. Adelaide had splurged on the good stuff. The woman always did. Tina would make sure to bring back some frameable photos.

Adelaide waved her off. "I got a bonus for churning out graduates. Might as well spend it on y'all." Adelaide gasped when

Tracey's arms wrapped around her. The girl almost made her drop the alcohol. "Now what are you doing?" she asked the excited teen.

Tracey was buzzing with energy. "Can I have a drink?" she asked, batting her lashes.

Adelaide pursed her lips. "I don't know," she drug out the sentence, just to tease the girl. It had the desired effect of making Tracey pout. Adelaide giggled at the sight.

"Oh, let her have a glass, Mama!" Julia urged.

"Yeah, Ma," Mabel joined in, chugging her glass.

"Oh, alright," Adelaide gave Tracey some champagne. The room cheered. The girls watched as Tracey took her first sip of alcohol. Better here than at some frat party. Adelaide sat in her chair. She sipped her drink as the girls mingled, sang, and danced. Their joy made her heart swell. Adelaide looked into the roaring fire. The flames danced and whipped around the cracking log. The gate was closed. Adelaide didn't trust the girls to not get too rowdy and accidentally land in the flames.

On the mantle were framed photos. Every year, Adelaide took a photo of her and the girls. The first frame was marked 1947. Adelaide had only been twenty at the time.

She'd come back to a house and a dying mother. The final frame was of this year, 1977.

Thirty years. Thirty years. Adelaide frowned. She had tried to get into college. She tried her hardest for years and years. Never got accepted. No matter how perfect her test scores, she only got rejected. The 40s and 50s were a different time. A black person getting in was rare, but a black woman?

Adelaide scoffed and chugged the rest of her drink. It wasn't until the 60s that more color got integrated into the halls. By that time, Adelaide felt too old. She'd already carved out her place. She might not have a degree, but she had love. Not the love she'd always craved or dreamed of, but the love she had now was no less important and real. She had decades of helping girls who would go on to change the world. Some in big ways, some in small, but all good. Adelaide didn't regret her choices. She tried not to regret her choices.

Adelaide looked into the fire. She thought of a girl from long ago. Her curly red hair and myriad of freckles. Adelaide wondered where she was now. Still in New York? Was she a wife now? Was she still living in a cramped apartment with five others? Did she still do drag or did she now have grandchildren. Tears flooded Adelaide's eyes. She'd tried to get the woman to come with her. Begged and pleaded. It was no use. Adelaide came back to town alone. The champagne in her hand was getting warm. Adelaide missed the woman's lips. She missed the chip in her tooth and the warmth of her hands.

Adelaide couldn't remember her name or full face.

The girls began screaming Bohemian Rhapsody. That snapped Adelaide out of her stupor. The sound made her jump. They were jumping and flailing, miserably failing at harmonizing with Freddie's voice.

"Oh, mamma mia!"

"Mamma mia!"

Heather turned to Adelaide with outstretched arms. "Mamma mia! Let me go!" She ran to the older woman and tugged her to her feet. "Come on, mama!"

Adelaide giggled and let herself be pulled into the group. She sang alongside them. All of them screamed, "For me! FOR ME!" Adelaide adored the chaos. Her girls made her feel young. She sang with them till the record stopped and they argued whether or not to put on the Bee Gees or Diana Ross.

Adelaide might not have reached the moon, but she had landed among the stars. It wasn't what she dreamed of having, but it was everything she needed. She could live without having a romance. She could live without a degree. She could live without a woman's touch. Adelaide wanted all those things, but she could live without. She'd done it for fifty years…and would probably only have to do it for a few more.

  The wind whipped, sending Adelaide's curls flying. The crisp winter air made it hard to breathe. Still, she pressed on. She'd gone out to grab a few things from the store, hoping to beat the setting sun. Just her luck to get caught up in the dark. Another gust of wind hit her. She pulled the coat around her tighter. It was fur lined and insanely warm, but did little to shield her face. The chill in the air sunk into the bone. Her nose was stuffy and her lips were chapped. Adelaide stopped walking to bury her face into the furs. It gave her a few seconds of relief. She really should have brought her scarf.
  The house was empty. Cold, dark, and empty. She always hated the first week of break. She was all alone in that huge yellow house. Adelaide tried to pretend the loneliness

didn't get to her. That she didn't feel empty and hollow inside without a constant stream of life echoing through her halls. Winter and summer brought in the dark reminder that her house would always be a temporary home. Hell, that's how she felt about it too.

    The moon above her was bright. The streets were deserted, not a soul around. Adelaide's footsteps echoed on the concrete. Winter and summer made everything silent. Too silent. A cold wind blew. Adelaide braced against it. She clutched her groceries tighter and walked faster toward home.

    In the distance, there was a thump of music. It made the hairs on Adelaide's neck stand up. One of the houses was having a party. Normally they waited a few days into break to start blasting music. Adelaide wondered which kids were having fun. The sight of the pale blue house made her grimace. It was Tony's frat. She braced herself. Adelaide clutched her coat tighter and pulled her hat down more. Maybe, if she was quick-

    "Hey, chocolate mama!" one of the boys called after her. Thankfully, Tony didn't seem to be on the porch. Small blessings. One boy, a brunet, pulled his friend by the collar, "Leave her alone, Benny."

Adelaide was surprised. She'd never seen the boy before. He smiled at her, a sorry on his lips. Adelaide returned the smile. She kept moving but watched the boy pull the other into the house.

Adelaide rolled her eyes. Boys. The music faded and silence surrounded her once more. The moon helped to light the way where the streetlights stopped. It was a beautiful night. Adelaide paused and looked up at the sky. The stars were glittering. They were so clear, unlike in the city, where smog and neon lights drowned them out. That was one thing Adelaide thought this town had on New York, a clear view of the heavens.

A shooting star flew across the sky. Adelaide gasped. A puff of air left her lips and crystalized. Adelaide couldn't help herself, she made a wish. Just a small one. A little selfish wish to keep near her heart.

THUMP

Adelaide jumped. She looked around in a panic. The sound echoed. Was it a firework? A bomb? Any noise seemed out of place in the dead of winter. Eventually, something caught her eye and made her freeze. In the church yard was a figure.

No, a woman.

She stood among the bulldozers and piled up dirt. Her slim frame looked so out of place. The poor thing must've been freezing. Her outfit was tattered. A dirty, stained, ripped dress. She had a large trunk by her side. Her hair was matted and covered in muck. It looked fair, maybe blonde? She was staring up at the cross on top of the church.

The church had been built back in the late 1600s. It was finally going through renovations after rotting for so long. The construction noise was annoying, but it was worth it for the dilapidation to be fixed. When Adelaide was a child, it was the only church around. The fire and brimstone preacher would scream so loud he'd rattle the stained glass windows.

Its rotten roof would leak in the rain. Drops of water would litter her Bible and soak the thin paper. As if God was crying onto his own words. The ink would bleed like the tortured Jesus that hung from the ceiling. Adelaide would look up and see his pleading eyes staring back at her. Adelaide could see the same desperate look in the woman's eyes. What could have happened to her? Was she all alone? Did she need help?

"Miss?!" Adelaide called out to her. The woman turned to her and Adelaide's breath hitched. The woman's eyes were a beautiful shade of green. Two gorgeous emeralds that shined like gems under the moonlight. Those pleading, lost eyes bore into her. They called to Adelaide, like the Jesus statue had. They beckoned her. They begged.

Adelaide went into the church yard. The gate was short. She easily stepped over it in her platforms. The woman walked carefully through the disrupted ground. They had been digging a new foundation to expand the church. Adelaide walked slowly, not wanting to frighten the girl. The woman was about a foot shorter than Adelaide. She reminded Adelaide of the ballerina that used to spin in her music box. "Are you hurt?" she asked the stranger.

Adelaide noticed that some parts of the tattered dress were completely gone. The bare skin underneath was covered in mud. The taller woman gasped. She dropped her groceries, letting them scatter on the ground, and stripped off her coat. "Oh, sugar." She didn't know how the woman wasn't shivering. Adelaide gently placed the coat over the stranger's shoulders. She buttoned a few of the buttons. So many questions raced through Adelaide's mind. Why was the woman so dirty? Why was her dress torn? "Do you understand me?" Adelaide asked softly. The woman nodded. It was a slow, jerky movement. As if her neck was stiff.

Adelaide noted the large leather trunk. It was heavily damaged, much like the woman's dress. "Okay, do you know where you're going?"

The woman shook her head.

Adelaide frowned. The poor dear. Lost and obviously in shock. Adelaide offered, "Why don't you come home with me? We can get you something hot to eat and a nice warm bath." The woman's eyes went distant. She looked at the church again, staring up at the cross on top of the spire.

Adelaide could see the cross reflected in the woman's green eyes. Those eyes turned back to her and once again, the woman nodded. Adelaide sighed in relief. She wouldn't have been able to leave the woman. At least, not alone in a cold and dark churchyard.

"Okay, come on, honey." She took the woman's hand and guided her out of the churchyard. The woman picked up the large trunk easily. It groaned in agony as it was lifted. How old was it? Adelaide was shocked how easily the lithe woman carried it, as if it weighed nothing. Maybe it didn't. Maybe it was empty or degraded enough to move with one hand.

The woman wound her arm around Adelaide's. She nuzzled her face into Adelaide's shoulder. The action was a shocking show of affection. Adelaide was happy the stranger felt safe with her. The immediate trust was odd, but the taller woman wasn't complaining. Adelaide would be the first to admit, she'd been feeling touch starved. She looked down at the woman and her breath caught. Those emerald eyes were staring up at her. The woman was stunning under the moonlight, even through dirt. Heat flooded Adelaide's cheeks, that wasn't good.

 Adelaide cleared her throat. "Come on, sweetheart." She guided the woman out of the churchyard. They walked the deserted streets. No music. No words. Silence. A comfortable silence. Suddenly, in the dark, came a lighthouse that guided them to safety. A pale yellow home that Adelaide knew too well.

 "Here we are," Adelaide opened the front door and went inside. She mourned the loss of her groceries, but it was a worthy loss. Adelaide kicked off her shoes. She turned to speak to the woman, but she wasn't there. Adelaide looked at the door. The woman stood before the threshold. The pair stared at each other. This had happened before. Some people needed to be told they could come in. Like little vampires. Adelaide giggled. What a silly thought. "You can come in, sugar," Adelaide beckoned her inside..

The woman walked across the doorway.

Adelaide closed the door behind the stranger. "You can leave your trunk here, for now. Let's get you a hot shower and some clothes first."

The woman let the trunk drop next to the front door. It landed heavily. A loud 'THUMP' that shocked Adelaide. Adelaide joked, "You got bricks in there?"

The woman tilted her head.

Adelaide frowned. The poor thing probably wasn't in the mood for jokes. "Come on, honey," she encouraged and took the woman's hand. She led her upstairs, past the multiple doors and into her room. Adelaide didn't know why she brought the woman to *her* room, but it was too late to turn around. The woman looked at her surroundings with awe. Adelaide turned on the overhead light and the woman gasped. The taller woman watched in amusement as the stranger stared at the lightswitch.

Adelaide was going to ask her something, but the woman started flicking the light on and off. It was as cute as it was unnerving. Adelaide wondered where the woman came from. One of the Amish communities? An overseas village?

Adelaide frowned at the mud covering her carpet. She really needed to get the woman cleaned. Adelaide walked up to the stranger. She started unbuttoning the coat on the woman's shoulders. Those green eyes watched her hands intently. Adelaide carefully guided the coat off the woman's arms. More dirt littered the floor.

"So, the bathroom is over here." Adelaide showed her the en suite. She turned on the light and the woman looked up. Adelaide frowned. "Sugar, don't stare directly at it," she lightly scolded. Adelaide gently took the woman's chin and tilted her head down. "It'll hurt your eyes," she explained. The woman blinked at her rapidly, then nodded.

Adelaide went to the shower and turned it on. The water rained down from the showerhead. A loud noise made her jump. Adelaide turned back. The woman had thrown herself against the door frame. The stranger's long, sharp nails were digging into the wood and making it creak in agony. Her green eyes were wide in shock, her mouth agape.

"It's okay!" Adelaide quickly reassured. She stuck her hand under the water. "It's just water. I promise." The woman's tense muscles slowly relaxed. Adelaide reached out her hand. The woman took it. "Feel," she instructed and brought the woman's hand to the water.

Those green eyes went half lidded.

"Does it feel okay?" Adelaide asked. The woman nodded. Adelaide smiled. She stood and went to the cabinet under the sink and got a washcloth and towel. "Here," she handed the washcloth to the girl. Adelaide then pointed out the soap, shampoo and conditioner. "Feel free to use those. I'll find you something to wear." Adelaide walked out of the bathroom and gently shut the door. She paused and listened. There was a rustling of clothes, the drawing back of the curtain, and shifting of how the water fell. Perfect, the woman got in.

Adelaide smiled and stepped away from the bathroom door. She got her handheld vacuum and got up the clumps of mud. Thank goodness it was dry. Adelaide heard the woman splashing around. It made her giggle. Adelaide hissed as she stood up straight again.

Now to find clothes. The woman was smaller than her. Too small to wear her clothes comfortably. Well, it was a good thing she had spares. Adelaide left the room and went downstairs. She looked at the decrepit trunk. Curiously, she went to it and tried to move it. It didn't budge. Adelaide stared at it in shock. She knew she was getting old, but her muscles hadn't given out yet. Adelaide pursed her lips. She decided to leave it alone and went to her sewing room.

The double doors that led into the room were mostly made of glass. A pair of windows into chaos. Fabric was draped across the couches and tables. There were multiple tables that held sewing machines. A large dresser drawer sat against a wall. Clothing was poking out of the drawers and hung from the handles. All her extra creations of varying sizes.

Adelaide opened a drawer and grabbed a pair of pajamas and underwear. Simple, solid colors. Hopefully the girl would talk soon. That way Adelaide could make her something to her taste.

The water cut off. The house was old and the pipes groaned in pain. Sometimes, like now, it was a blessing. Adelaide quickly shut the drawer as best she could and raced up the steps. A strange noise echoed through the hall. It sounded like tearing paper. A rough scrape. Adelaide walked into her room to find the woman was ripping her hair out with a brush. She was naked, sitting on the floor. A towel was under her and she savagely tugged at her hair. .

"Oh, honey!" Adelaide threw the clothes on her bed and kneeled next to the woman. "Let me help," she pleaded. Adelaide took the brush from trembling, pale fingers. She got behind the woman. "You have to start from the bottom." Adelaide gathered the matted locks and began brushing. "Gonna make yourself bald otherwise." The woman brought her knees up to her chest and buried her face in them. Was she in pain?

Adelaide's heart clenched. She kept brushing. Thankfully the hair wasn't matted beyond repair. The silence in the room eventually got to her. She began to softly hum. Adelaide watched as the woman relaxed. The stranger's shoulders slumped and her arms hung loosely. Adelaide kept singing. The urge to kiss the woman's shoulder washed over her. Adelaide blinked rapidly. What the hell was wrong with her? She tried to shake the thought from her mind and force herself to focus on her task.

The strawberry blonde hair became smoother. It was beautiful. A true peachy color that made Adelaide want to play with it. Maybe the woman would let her style it some day. For now, she'd work on untangling the waves. The loss of hair was minimal. Adelaide smiled, "I don't think we'll need to cut it." She ran her fingers through the light colored tresses. "I've only seen hair like yours in paintings," she mused. Adelaide went to stand. Her knees clicked loudly, which made the woman jump. Adelaide chuckled. "It's okay. I'm old, peaches." She walked to the bathroom and got another towel.

When she came back out, the woman was still sitting. The blonde was in awe again, but she was only looking at Adelaide. How odd. Maybe it was the towel? Adelaide kneeled down again, this time in front of the woman. She gently dried the waves. "I got you some clothes," Adelaide informed. "Are you hungry? I can make you some soup or hot chocolate?" The woman shook her head 'no'. Adelaide nodded. She grunted as she stood again. The clothes on the bed were crumpled now. Adelaide smoothed them out. The woman was still sitting on the floor, staring up at her. Adelaide filled the silence. "If you want a bra, we'll have to measure you. I hope the underwear fits. It was the smallest size I have-" Adelaide jumped as a pale hand picked up the shirt.

The woman was now on the bed in front of her. Somehow. Adelaide knew she was getting old, but she wasn't *that* oblivious, yet. "You're fast," she chuckled, a bit put off by the woman's speed and silence. Much like the trunk, Adelaide decided to let it go. Questions could be asked tomorrow. Now, they both could use some sleep. "Anyway, here," Adelaide handed the woman the other pieces of clothing.

"Misha."

Adelaide started. The woman spoke. She spoke! Adelaide placed a knee on the bed. She stared at the woman in wonder. Misha. What a lovely word. Adelaide tilted her head, "Misha?"

The woman nodded. "My name is Misha."

Adelaide let her hands rest on the bed. The woman, Misha's, voice was unique. It was rough. Smokey. Like she hadn't spoken in years. Deep and longing. It reminded Adelaide of an abandoned church. Dark, echoing, but beautiful. Misha had a thick accent. Something Slavic, but Adelaide couldn't place it. She took a guess. "Are you Russian?" she asked.

"What is Russian?" Misha rebutted. She slipped the shirt on.

Adelaide furrowed her brow. Misha seemed genuinely confused. "You sleep through McCarthy?" she teased. Misha didn't laugh. In fact, she looked even more confused. "That was probably before your time," Adelaide explained. She asked instead, "Okay, well, where are you from?"

Misha cocked her head to the side. She started off into space. "I lived in Menkerman for a time. I don't remember the name from before or what it is called now." Once again, Misha brought her knees up to rest her face on them.

Adelaide frowned. "I'm sorry." She reached out and touched Misha's hand. It was freezing cold. "Oh, peaches!" Adelaide stood quickly. She urged, "Put the rest of your clothes on. I'll get some more blankets. The heater too!"

Misha looked at the other clothing. She picked them up slowly, near reverently. Misha watched as the woman left the room. She slipped on the sleepwear. The fabric was soft. Well stitched. It smelled like the stranger. Pomegranates. Misha hated how that made her heart skip a beat. She tugged the shirt to her nose and inhaled deeply.

Adelaide went to the hall closet and got the softest blankets she had. They were a fluffy material that made you want to bury your face in them. Adelaide normally kept them for emergencies. A girl who wasn't feeling well or if one of her girls brought their baby over. She took the blankets back to the room. Misha was thankfully dressed. "Good." Adelaide smiled.

The taller woman set the blankets down on the bed. "Here, wrap yourself up." Next, Adelaide went to her closet and rifled through her belongings before letting out a triumphant, "Ah ha!"

Misha watched in wonder as the stranger brought out an odd box. The woman was mumbling to herself as she cleared off a space on a low dresser. It sat against the wall in front of the bed. The box was set down and made an odd metallic noise. The box had a tail that was placed behind the dresser. Misha watched as the woman bent over. She licked her dry lips. The woman had a lovely behind. It was too early to think about those activities. She shook those thoughts away, for now. Instead she caressed the blankets the stranger had given her. They were a material she'd never felt before. Everything was so new. A loud clunky sound made her jump in fright. The small box began to rattle and glow red. "What is that?!" she scrambled back toward the headboard.

Adelaide turned to the woman. "It's a heater. Like a fireplace, but electric."

Misha frowned, "What is electric?"

Adelaide's eyes widened. She furrowed her brow in thought. "Electric is…" Adelaide pursed her lips. The light switch caught her eye. "It's what makes this," she shut the lights off and on, "work."

Misha hummed. She crawled to the foot of the bed again. The box was steady now. Its awful death rattle had ceased, now it hummed. Misha liked it. It was soothing. She could almost feel the heat. "Why have you done this?" she asked the woman.

Adelaide sat on the bed. "You're cold." She took the woman's pale hand.

Misha frowned. "What is your name?" she asked.

Adelaide blinked for a moment. "Oh my god!" she gasped. "Where are my manners? If mama was alive, she'd have tanned my hide!" Adelaide laughed. She saw how perplexed Misha was. "Sorry, sorry. I'm Adelaide," she introduced. "You can call me Mama or Mama A. Most of you young things do."

Misha frowned, "Young?"

Adelaide sighed. She never understood why young people sneered at their youth. "Yes, young. What, you're twenty-three, twenty-four?" She stood from the bed and went to her closet. Adelaide closed the door a bit to change into her own pajamas. "I'm double that!" she announced. Adelaide then thought about it, "Actually, a little more than double." She reentered the room with her nightgown on.

"You're a spring chicken compared to me, peaches."

Misha frowned. "You are very young, Adelaide." She looked the woman up and down. "Did you make that?"

Adelaide looked down at herself. "Sure did!" she said with pride. "I make most of my clothes." Adelaide gestured to Misha's outfit, "Made yours too."

Misha looked down at the clothing. That explained why they smelt like the woman. The clothes she wore were obviously not Adelaide's size. The woman was taller than Misha, much more shapely. They used to say a mother's body. Soft and curved. "You are very talented," Misha complimented. The stitching was expertly done. "Do you do it professionally?"

Adelaide shrugged. "It's more for my mad money. I mainly run the house. Make sure the girls are in order and that they're safe." She shut off the light. The space heater illuminated the room with a fiery glow. Adelaide crawled onto the bed, sitting against the headboard. She grabbed the fluffy blankets. Adelaide patted the space beside her.

Misha crawled up the bed to sit next to Adelaide. This woman was so talented. So Kind. Why? She'd taken Misha from the cemetery. She'd offered her home, clothes, warmth, and food. Yet no thought of gains crossed Adelaide's mind. The woman just wanted Misha to be safe, to feel safe. Misha couldn't remember the last time someone had been so selfless. Tears pricked her eyes. She needed to distract herself. "This is an orphanage?" Misha asked.

Adelaide chuckled, "No, peaches. It's a sorority." Those green eyes blinked owlishly at her. Adelaide explained, "It's a place for girls to live while they go to college." That caused a light to go off in Misha's eyes. A spark of recognition.

"I see," Misha said. She looked at the metal box. Its hellfire glow was enchanting. More enchanting than a true fire. "Are you free now?" she asked.

Adelaide furrowed her brow. "Free?"

Misha nodded. "Your people. Are you still enslaved?"

Adelaide frowned. The woman knew about slavery but not electricity? Adelaide shook her head. "Been legally free since the 1860s. Just got Civil Rights a little over ten years ago."

Misha mumbled, "1860s." She bit her lip. Staring into the box. "What year is it?"

Adelaide's chest clenched. The woman's question sounded so sad. Forlorn.

Mournful. Adelaide almost didn't want to answer. She did though, "It's 1977."

Misha fell back against the headboard. She laid there in shock. "I see." Her green eyes stared up at the ceiling. With her head tilted like that, it kept the tears at bay.

Adelaide brushed against the woman's arm. It was still cold. "Oh, peaches." She covered Misha in one of the blankets. It had been warmed by the space heater. Adelaide noticed how Misha pointed her toes. "Were you a dancer?" she asked, hoping to distract the sorrowful woman.

Misha blinked the tears back. She looked at Adelaide. How could the woman know? "Why do you ask this?"

The taller woman shrugged. "The way you walk," she gestured to the woman's feet, "That. Also how lean you are. Muscular, but not bulky. You're graceful. Also you're fast as hell and silent!" Adelaide chuckled. She looked at Misha. Those green eyes shimmered in the heater's light. "I used to want to be a ballerina," Adelaide admitted.

"Why did you not become one?" Misha turned her body toward the woman. Adelaide had examined her effortlessly. She'd picked up on Misha's ways and understood them.

Adelaide scoffed, "Look at me, peaches." She'd heard it all. Too tall. Too fat. Too dark. The disgusted eyes of the dance instructor would never leave her mind. They'd stain her memory forever. Adelaide bit her lip to keep it from quivering. It was stupid that something said to her when she was seven could hurt her now at fifty.

Misha furrowed her brow. "You are a beautiful woman, Adelaide," she took the woman's warm hand. "I would have been honored to share a stage with you."

Adelaide sniffled. God, why was she crying? The woman's words were so sweet. "Thank you, Misha." She looked at their clasped hands. "I bet I could make you some slippers." Adelaide beamed, "Maybe you could teach me a few moves."

The thought of dancing used to make Misha nauseous. It used to make her want to scream. Rip her hair out. Curse god. Now, at this moment, she was excited. She wanted to dance. She wanted to dance with Adelaide. "I would be honored to teach you." Misha's heart fluttered, "I would be honored to have anything made by you."

Adelaide squeezed Misha's hand. Tears flooded her eyes. She wiped them away and forced a smile. "I'd...I." She took a deep breath and pulled her hand away from the blonde's. "Here, let's snuggle up and go to bed," Adelaide suggested. She scooted down to lay on the bed. It was a blessing her skin was so dark. The beautiful blonde couldn't see the heat in her cheeks. Adelaide noticed Misha struggled with the blankets. She sat up again and helped the blonde get comfortable. "Here, peaches."

    Misha relaxed against the mattress. She let Adelaide tuck her in. It was something she hadn't had done to her in… She couldn't remember how long. Misha nuzzled into the blankets. A metamorphosis took place. Misha was in a fuzzy little cocoon, safely tucked into a lovely bed with a lovely woman. She used to have dreams like this while at the academy. Locked in that freezing tomb and only seeing- Misha stopped her thoughts. She refused to linger on the past. The blankets were warm. The room had light. The person beside her was someone she actually wanted to sleep with. Misha shimmied in excitement.

    Adelaide watched the woman wiggle. It was adorable. Too adorable. She wanted to lay a kiss on Misha's forehead. She abstained. It wasn't clear whether or not Misha would appreciate the gesture. Adelaide also didn't know if she could keep herself from kissing the blonde's lips. She got under her covers and snuggled up as well. Everything was so warm. Misha had the blanket pulled up and over her nose. Those green eyes were staring at Adelaide. There was a shimmer of amusement in them. Adelaide giggled, pulling her blankets up as well. "You a lil snuggle bunny?" The statement made Misha giggle and duck her head under the blankets.

A cool hand tugged at Adelaide. She ducked under the covers as well. Misha was waiting for her. The blonde scooted closer. "What?" Adelaide let a teasing tone enter her voice, "You want to cuddle?"

Misha raised an eyebrow. "Cuddle?"

Adelaide explained, "It's like hugging while sleeping."

Misha's eyes widened in wonder. "Yes, let us cuddle!" She moved closer and wrapped her arms around Adelaide's waist.

The taller woman didn't think the blonde would agree so quickly. Adelaide wasn't complaining though. She wrapped her arms around Misha. The woman was still cool, but had definitely warmed up. Adelaide let her nose rest against Misha's strawberry blonde hair. It smelt like pomegranates. Adelaide's eyes widened. Misha had used her perfume. Once again, Adelaide's face heated up. The gorgeous blonde would be the death of her. "G'night, Misha," Adelaide whispered into the peachy hair.

Misha snuggled against Adelaide's chest. She replied, "Good night, Adelaide."

Chapter 3

Sunlight streamed in through the window. The room was hot. Adelaide groaned. Curls tickled her nose. What? She cracked open her eyes. Her purple bonnet hung on her bedpost. In the chaos of last night, she forgot it. Adelaide huffed. She needed a shower anyway, so it wasn't that much of a loss. The sunlight flooding her room was new. When was the last time she woke up after the sun? When was the last time she slept so hard she woke up aching? The alarm by her bed had been blissfully silent. Which was odd.

In big white letters, it read 9:10 AM.

Adelaide sighed and stretched. Well, she tried to. Something was laying on her chest. Something cool and soft. She looked down. Misha was on top of her. The woman was nuzzled into the valley of Adelaide's breasts. Those strawberry blonde waves were messy and tickled Adelaide's chin. Misha looked serene under the morning light. The woman was wrapped around Adelaide like ivy. As if she was afraid Adelaide would try to escape.

Why would she want to? Adelaide couldn't remember the last time she'd slept with someone in her bed. It was definitely in her twenties. Jesus, had it really been thirty years? Adelaide never let any students sleep in her room. That was a line she refused to cross. The girls in her house were her children. They were children.

Misha was an exception though. Well, she felt like one. Something about her was different in a way Adelaide couldn't articulate. Which was a problem. Not being able to name the feeling made Adelaide doubt herself. How could Misha feel different when by all accounts she seemed to be the same age as Monica or Wendy? Adelaide would put her at twenty five, at most! Still, Misha was odd.

How could she not know about electricity and running water, but did know American history? She obviously spoke English but didn't know the name of her own country? She was willing to follow a stranger home but was frightened by a heater? Something about Misha was off and Adelaide wanted to pry. She wanted to ask question after question.

Misha stirred, rubbing her face against Adelaide's chest. The older woman felt her face heat up. Guilt riddled her. Why hadn't she insisted Misha sleep in one of the empty rooms? Misha let out a soft noise, Adelaide felt awful for basking in the woman's arms. It was foolish to want, foolish to dream. *I'm too old*, Adelaide scolded herself, *Far, far too old!*

Adelaide wouldn't indulge. Wouldn't fantasize. Adelaide had never had this problem before. Why did she struggle so much with this stranger? That was a whole other can of worms. Misha was a stranger. Adelaide didn't know her! The woman could be faking everything, or on the run for tax evasion, or murder! Adelaide warred with herself. She laid out the facts as best she knew them. One, she was old enough to be Misha's mother. Which, gross. Two, even if that wasn't an issue, if the college found out she'd lose her sorority. Three, she wouldn't risk scaring a woman who was already traumatized.

The last thing Misha needed was an old lady chasing her skirt. Adelaide would be content with this one morning, this one embrace. It was enough. It'd be enough. Adelaide was good at finding happiness in her limitations, and this was no different. She decided it was time to get up. Adelaide gently ran her fingers through Misha's hair. It was softer than the night before. The straw like waves were now gentle wisps. Adelaide wondered what combination of products the girl had used to make that happen overnight. Misha smelt like Adelaide's perfume. The woman tried not to let that knowledge warm her core.

Misha's green eyes opened. The heartbeat under her ear had shifted. A little faster now. There was a sweetness in the air. Misha turned her nose toward Adelaide's skin. She inhaled deeply.

Adelaide jumped. Her face went hot. She looked down at the other woman. Misha's emerald eyes looked brighter in the sunlight. Adelaide swallowed, her throat audibly clicked. "Mornin'" Adelaide whispered. It felt illegal to be louder than a whisper. Misha smiled at her and Adelaide's chest clenched. Her heart stopped. Her breath caught.

"Good morning, beloved," Misha greeted back. Her lips were pressed against Adelaide's sternum. The woman shuddered underneath her. Misha smiled. She nuzzled back into Adelaide's chest. Yes. This would do, this would do just nicely. Misha hummed, rubbing her cheek against umber skin. It was so warm.

Adelaide's face felt like it had been pushed into hot coals. Beloved. Oh, out of every nickname Misha could have chosen. Adelaide tried not to dwell on it. It might be the equivalent of calling someone 'darling' or 'dear' where she's from.

It was fine. The nickname was fine. Adelaide would ignore how her face was aflame. That wasn't good. Adelaide coughed, trying to clear her tight throat. "I think we should get up." She tried to wiggle out from under the other woman. Misha groaned and the noise made Adelaide want to scream. Her mama always said the devil would be pretty. Adelaide had always thought her mother was exaggerating, till now. "I'll make you breakfast." Adelaide hoped the promise of food would get the woman moving. Hopefully before Adelaide exploded. She pushed at the woman's shoulders.

Misha giggled. She could smell the hormones in the air. A sweetened spice that tickled her nose. Misha licked her lips. It would be best to rise. She'd eventually lay a kiss on the black woman's lips. Not now, but hopefully soon. Misha allowed Adelaide to move her. "I do not eat," she announced, stretching her limbs.

Adelaide frowned. It wasn't her first time hearing that. Too many girls had passed through her threshold with that mentality. "Food is important," Adelaide said firmly. She sat up, resting against the headboard. Her childhood had been spent living off the land. They planted and picked their meals for decades. Her family had been luckier than most. Fertile soil had once surrounded the house. As the town was built up, the need for a garden shrank.

Now there was so much food. Yet so many, women especially, starved themselves. On purpose no less! And for what? Beauty? Adelaide didn't get it. Misha was already tiny. Not in an unhealthy way, like some. She was built like a ballerina. Lithe but most certainly muscular. Especially since Misha had been able to carry that heavy trunk.

Adelaide wondered if the woman had come to the college to dance. There were far better schools for it, but maybe this was the one that accepted? Maybe that was why Misha was here. Adelaide decided to accept her own theory, for now. "Your body needs food to thrive, peaches."

Misha heard the genuine concern in the woman's gentle tone. She racked her brain for a more valid excuse. "I have…um," Misha pursed her lips. The word had escaped her mind. "I can not eat most things," she groaned. What was the word? "It upsets my body."

Adelaide sighed in relief. That was far better than personal starvation. "You have food allergies?"

Misha lit up. "Yes! Those. Allergies." She nibbled at her finger. "I can only eat one specific thing."

Adelaide frowned, "Oh, peaches. I'm so sorry." She stood from the bed. Her back was killing her. Adelaide stretched, hearing the satisfying 'pop' that brought instant relief. "What is it?" she asked the woman, "I can go out and find it for you."

Misha smiled. "It is not something you must worry about, beloved." She slipped off the bed as well and mimicked Adelaide's stretch. Unlike the other woman, her back didn't pop.

Adelaide giggled. "Oh, to be young." The comment was forced, it sounded forced. Normally, that kind of teasing rolled off her tongue without a second thought. With Misha though, it had felt wrong. What was wrong with her? Maybe she just slept for too long. That must be it. She sighed and rubbed her face. "I need to shower," Adelaide announced. Her head gestured to the door and looked at Misha. The blonde didn't seem to get the message.

Misha instead sat on the bed. "I will wait here." She had no intention of leaving the woman's side. Besides, she didn't know the layout of the home. No use wandering by herself when she could get the grand tour.

Adelaide teased, trying her best to keep her tone carefree, "If you want. I don't know many that want to risk seeing a grandma naked." She had thought the mention of her nudity would chase the woman off. Instead it only made Misha settle in more.

"I would not mind seeing you nude."

Adelaide felt her face heat up again. She laughed, trying to hide her embarrassment. "Your eyes, your funeral." There wasn't any use dwelling on the comment. It wouldn't do any good to. Adelaide grabbed some sweatpants, underwear, and a t-shirt. Maybe after breakfast they would go out and she'd get dressed up, but something comfortable would be best for now. "I'll be back in a bit," she told the still sitting blonde. Misha only nodded in acknowledgement. Adelaide escaped into her bathroom. She could feel Misha's eyes on her back. Adelaide was tempted to leave the door open.

No.

The older woman shook her head. Misha was just a flirt, many young people were. It wasn't a true interest. Much like Tony, Misha was just teasing. They wanted to get a rise out of Adelaide, or they had a fetish. For her skin or her age, it didn't matter which. She'd ignore it, like she always had.

Adelaide brought the shower to life and stripped off her nightgown. She combed out her curls under the spray, washed herself and then basked in the heat. The warm water was comforting. A hug that covered her entire body. Misha then popped into her mind. No, no, no!

Adelaide tried to bat the idea of the woman away. She hated how the thought of the blonde made her cheeks burn. Adelaide hadn't had a crush in twenty years. Women like her were hard to find. Even harder to find ones who'd date her. Not to mention if it got out she was queer.

Adelaide didn't want to think of the possible scorn her girls would have for her. She didn't want to think about how the college may come down on her. Dobson would have a damn field day. All the gossip and hate. Adelaide let her head rest against the tiled wall. Despair filled her.

Stonewall was still fresh in her mind. The riot made her sob. Both with pride and shame. She remembered how one of her girls, Beatrice, had complained about the Lavender Menace in her feminist circles.

The campus wasn't in San Francisco. It wasn't in Provincetown. It was a college carved out in the middle of nowhere Virginia. Sure, some of the kids may be open minded, but that meant nothing in the face of the board.

There was too much to lose on a crush. Adelaide shut off the water and stepped out of the shower. She dried off and lotioned herself before slipping on her lounge clothes. The pomegranate perfume sat on the back of her toilet.

Adelaide debated putting some on. She didn't really need it yet. Misha may not want to even go out later. Still, Adelaide remembered how Misha smelled her. How the strawberry blonde buried her nose in Adelaide's chest. An awful want tugged at her heart. What would the harm be? She'd smell nice? Misha might compliment her? The older woman bit her lip. She spritzed herself with the perfume before leaving.

Misha was still on the bed. In her hands was a book. Adelaide snickered, "So you found one of my Harlequin's?" She noticed the cover. The cartoonish vampire and scandalized maiden made Adelaide giggle. "Oh, that one's my favorite."

Misha looked up from the words. "Why is that?" The book wasn't well written, in fact, it was awful. The main character was annoying and the strange man was deranged.

Adelaide shrugged. She shut off the heater. The room was stiflingly hot. "I like the idea of vampires." She noticed Misha's wide eyes and continued to explain, "Just. The idea of your lover being kept alive by you. Or living together forever. As a young thing, I thought it was so romantic."

Misha teased, "So it has nothing to do with the sex scenes?"

Adelaide snickered. "Well, they're very funny, in an inaccurate way." The older woman opened her door and shivered at the rush of cold air. "Guys with twelve inch pricks and petite women with breasts the size of watermelons." Adelaide remembered a particular scene and giggled. "It's just unrealistic and that's what makes it funny." Adelaide gestured to herself, "Everyone knows big breasts and ass have to come with some tummy." She walked out of her room, hoping the blonde would follow.

Misha tilted her head, gazing at the woman. Her eyes roamed over Adelaide's body. "Yes, they do." She let the book drop on the bed and stood. Misha trailed the woman. The doors they passed were closed with plaques on them. Strange. "What are these for?" she asked, pointing to a name plate.

"For the girls," Adelaide explained. "When a girl moves in, I make her a little sign. I got a whole box full of 'em!" Adelaide laughed. It sounded sad when she said it out loud. Lord. She needed to change the subject. "I'll make up a room for you and help carry that trunk up." Adelaide descended the stairs. "Then, we can talk about getting you some food. Maybe there's something here you can eat. Also about enrollment. We'll need to see if you're on the list or-"

"I can't sleep with you?" Misha asked forlornly.

Adelaide stopped. She turned back to the woman. Even on the steps, Misha was still shorter than her. "Well..." Adelaide trailed off. The temptation was back. Like a serpent curling and writhing in her gut. "You should have your own room," she said firmly. Misha's green eyes dimmed. A frown formed on those petal pink lips. Oh. Adelaide bit the inside of her cheek. What could be the harm with letting Misha sleep in her bed every once in a while? Maybe it would do them both some good. "I mean, a woman needs her own space," she started, "but, you can always come to sleep over, if you want?" A compromise. A very good compromise that hopefully wouldn't end in disaster.

Misha's lips twitched into a small smile. She had no intention of keeping to her own room. "I would like that," she said sweetly.

Something about her voice made Adelaide's knees knock. She clutched the banister. Thankfully, she could blame her unsteadiness on her age.

Misha got closer to Adelaide, not wanting the woman to fall. "Are you alright, beloved?" She placed her hands on Adelaide's waist. The woman was so warm. She wanted to slip her hands underneath Adelaide's shirt and touch that fiery skin again. Sleeping on the woman's chest had been heaven. The steady heartbeat and the sweet smell of her flesh had soothed Misha into a restful slumber. She couldn't imagine going back to the cold of sleeping alone.

Misha felt like a moth. A lucky one that found a light which didn't burn. She was safe to bask in its warmth. Safe to enjoy its shine. Just safe. Misha wanted to kiss her new found light. She wanted to make it quiver, and flicker, and shake. Explode the bulb and make it spark. Misha sighed, those were dangerous thoughts.

Adelaide tried to not take the nickname seriously. She likened it to her own use of nicknames. 'Baby' and now 'peaches', thanks to Misha's hair. They could be used romantically, but also be platonic. Beloved though. Beloved seemed so romantic. Especially since Misha was staring at her like she was the moon and the stars. No. Adelaide pushed that idea away. Misha was just…European. That's what Adelaide would cling to when her mind wandered in certain directions. "I'm fine," Adelaide croaked out and tried not to focus on Misha's steadying hands. "Just a little weak in the mornin'."

Misha's smile turned suggestive. "That is good to know."

Adelaide swallowed audibly and turned around. "Alright! I'm going to make some coffee," she informed, hopping off the last two steps and quickly sprinting to the kitchen. No time to unpack all of that. In fact, Adelaide would store it in her chest and throw it all away.

Misha followed slowly. She stopped to look around the foyer. It wasn't anything grand, but it was cozy. There was a wall covered in strange paintings. They were expertly done. A hyperrealism that Misha had never seen before. They must have cost a fortune. Especially since their size was so small. Each painting was in a frame. They had a little plaque, showing the date. Some dated back decades. Some were even a century old. The worn, leather trunk was still by the front door. Misha left it, not knowing where Adelaide would want her to take it yet. To her right was a living room.

It had a large couch, and a few chairs. In the upholstery, she smelled alcohol, sweat, and clashing perfumes. This was where the girls of the house congregated. There was a large fireplace with a black gate. On its mantle was another line of paintings. Thirty of them in fact. They were packed on the mantle. Four stood out, closer to the edge.

The frames surrounding the paintings were bright gold. The morning sunlight made them beam and drawed the eye. These ones were dated as well. The first one on the edge read 1947. Misha easily picked out Adelaide. She was the only black woman in the photo after all. Misha tilted her head. Younger Adelaide was just as beautiful as current Adelaide.

In 1947, Adelaide was a girl. Young, with a wide, bright smile. There were five white girls beside her. In 1957, there were more girls, still

63

all white. Once again, Adelaide stuck out among them. She was dressed in more mature clothing. Her smile was just as wide and bright. In 1967, Adelaide had a few gray hairs. The smile lines on her face were permanently there. The girls in the photo now came in more colors. Some had flowers in their hair. Some were putting flowers in Adelaide's hair. It was a very cute photo. Misha came to the last photo. 1977. Adelaide looked as she did now. Beautiful, wearing her life on her face.

Misha touched the glass. She wanted to take the painting and cut Adelaide out, keeping that piece for herself. Maybe she could ask Adelaide to get a painting done with her.

"Those are of me and all my girls," Adelaide informed. She had a mug in her hand and was leaning on the frame that led to the kitchen. "They're my favorite to take." At the start of every school year, she gathered the girls in the front yard to take a photo. Adelaide had more in her scrapbooks, but those photos were worth displaying.

Misha furrowed her brow. "Photo?"

Adelaide blinked. Misha made the word seem foreign. "That's what we call these." She walked over, pointing at the pictures, "These are photos. From a camera."

Misha was even more perplexed. "What is a camera?" Was it the name of her painter?

Adelaide tapped her finger against the side of her mug. Much like allergies, camera was probably a word Misha didn't know in english. It would be easier to just show her then explain with words. "Here," Adelaide handed her cup of coffee to the woman. "I'll go get one."

Misha stood by the mantle as the other woman disappeared to another room. She looked at the substance in the mug. The coffee did not look the same. It used to be pitch black, a bitter smell to it. Comforting but odd. This version was a lighter color and had a sweeter scent. How strange.

Camera. Misha rolled the word in her mind. She looked at the small paintings again. Misha noticed another strange white peg on the far wall. She flicked it up. The room illuminated. Misha giggled. A child-like wonder took over. She flicked the peg down and up a few times. Footsteps echoed through the hall. Misha flicked the peg down and went to stand by the mantle again.

Adelaide entered with her polaroid. "This!" she announced, lifting the device a bit. "This is a camera."

Misha's face scrunched in confusion. "That makes your paintings?" She stepped closer. The device was stranger than the metal fire box. This thing was white and brown and had a strange eye.

"They're not paintings, peaches," Adelaide took her coffee back and set it on the mantle. "Here, smile!" Adelaide encouraged. Misha went stock still, a small smile on her face. Adelaide took a photo.

Misha jumped, scrambling back. The bright light the camera emitted reminded her of an explosion. She flew to the other side of the room, clinging to the wall.

Adelaide quickly set the camera down. "Oh peaches, I'm sorry!" She raced over to the woman. "I thought-" Adelaide scolded herself. She should have warned Misha about the flash. Bright green eyes were wide and looking around the room in terror. Adelaide pulled the woman close. "It's okay, Misha. It's okay. You're safe. You're safe, peaches. I promise," she reassured and smoothed out the woman's frazzled hair.

"Why did it explode?" Misha asked timidly. She blinked her eyes rapidly. "Did I break it?"

Adelaide frowned. "No, no, peaches." She explained, "That's the flash. It makes sure the picture comes out clear." Adelaide kissed Misha's forehead. "I didn't mean to scare you, sweetheart. I should have warned you."

Misha hugged the woman. She nuzzled into Adelaide's shoulder. The burst of fear was worth it to be wrapped in Adelaide's arms. "It is okay." Misha nuzzled into Adelaide's chest. She wanted the woman to kiss her again. Those lips were so soft and made Misha yearn. She noticed the strange paper on the floor. "What is that?" she asked, pointing to the piece of white on the ground.

Adelaide looked back. "Oh! That's the photo." She leaned down and grabbed the picture. "Here, it's still developing." The picture was only half finished. "See, that's you!" she giggled.

Misha looked at the partially developed photo in wonder. She hadn't seen herself in so long. The woman watched as the picture became clearer and clearer before her eyes. Photo. She wanted to take one of Adelaide! Misha went to the mantle and picked up the camera. "Show me how it works?"

Adelaide smiled. The blonde was no longer frightened. That's all that mattered. Adelaide walked over to the woman. "Well, it's pretty simple." She pointed at the button. "This one takes the picture." She then pointed to the lens, "You look through this to see what you're photographing." Adelaide then pointed to a knob, "This is a timer."

Misha nodded, taking in the lesson. She then took a few steps back, aimed the camera at Adelaide. "Smile!"

Adelaide giggled as her photo was snapped.

Misha watched in wonder as the strange paper slowly slipped from the little slot on the front of the camera. She took it. The paper was milky. She frowned. "Where are you?" she asked Adelaide.

The woman's giggle turned into a full laugh. "It's got to develop, peaches." She took the photo. "You need to place it down and wait a couple minutes." Adelaide set the photo Misha took next to the other one Misha left on the mantle. "There used to be a legend that if you shook 'em they'd develop faster, but that's not true." She smiled sadly, "In fact, it can ruin them." Adelaide turned back and gasped when Misha took another picture. The flash made her blink rapidly. "Misha!" she scolded with a smile. The strawberry blonde giggled behind the camera.

"You're adorable, beloved." Misha wiggled the camera. "I want to take a picture of us together. How do I do it?"

Adelaide smiled, "That's what the timer's for." She took the camera and placed it on the mantle. She set the timer for ten seconds. The click started. "Okay, line up with the lens." Adelaide leaned into Misha. The other woman wrapped her arms around Adelaide's waist. Strawberry blonde waves tickled Adelaide's chin. The black woman put her arm around Misha's shoulder. That seemed to make her melt against Adelaide. "Smile!" Adelaide cheered as the camera got closer to going off.

"Why?" Misha asked. The camera was making little clicks. It reminded her of a metronome. All of a sudden the tempo picked up. She squeezed Adelaide tighter and prepared for the flash.

Adelaide mumbled, "'Cause, you're beautiful when you smile." She rested her head on Misha's soft hair. The camera stopped clicking.

Misha smiled brightly, looking up at Adelaide's beautiful face.

The camera went off with a click.

Chapter 4

Misha watched Adelaide cook. The woman was so confident in the kitchen. She walked with a gentle authority Misha had never encountered before. It was intoxicating. The woman was currently at the stove, leaving the blonde to explore. Misha opened and closed the strange cold boxes that sat against the wall. There were all types of food inside. Fruits, vegetables, things Misha couldn't name. More food than most noble families had. "What happens to the light when you close the door?" she asked, closing the boxes again.

Adelaide informed, "It goes off. Only comes on for us to see inside." Misha was still wearing her pajamas. "I'll need to find you something to wear out. We can get you an outfit or two this afternoon." She made herself a plate. Misha had insisted she wasn't hungry and she would eat later. Adelaide didn't like it, but she didn't push. Pushing only brought out rebellion. Food finished, Adelaide went to sit at the table. When she sat, she jumped at the sight of Misha sitting across from her. Adelaide looked at the fridges, where the woman once stood, and then the woman again.

Misha asked, "Why do you have two?" She pointed to the boxes and then asked, "Why does one have names on the food?"

Adelaide took a sip of her coffee before answering. The woman had asked her how the fridges worked. That was a lengthy conversation that went into electricity then closed systems then coils. Adelaide had to stop Misha from taking the refrigerator apart. Those green eyes were sparkling with curiosity. "Well, ten girls live here. One fridge is communal. The other is for what they buy themselves."

Misha tilted her head. "You buy them food?" The woman nodded. Misha's long nails tapped on the table. Adelaide was so kind. When was the last time Misha had met someone so selfless? The girls were not Adelaide's by blood and yet she treated them better than most kin would. The blonde watched Adelaide eat. The food was at least familiar. Eggs, bread, bacon. There was also a bowl of colorful sweet smelling cubes. The smell was delicious, though Misha preferred Adelaide's sweet scent above all others.

They fell into silence. Misha looked at Adelaide's half finished plate. She could feel how uncomfortable Adelaide was with Misha not eating. There were those that starved themselves. Misha was not one of them, but without proof… a demonstration would be needed to ease Adelaide's mind. "I have never had that," Misha pointed at the sliced fruit.

Adelaide's eyes went wide. "It's mango." She picked up a cube for Misha. "You wanna try a piece?"

Misha nodded. "I hope it does not make me sick." It would. She ate the fruit and tasted nothing. It was dust. The same curse God gave to the serpent was on her tongue. Misha swallowed and waited. The churn in her stomach began. She took an unneeded breath. She hadn't eaten in so long, so this would be bad.

Adelaide jumped when the woman raced to the sink and began to vomit. "Oh, Misha!" She ran to the vomiting girl's side. Whatever allergies she had were most certainly real and restrictive. Adelaide grabbed a towel and patted the girl's back. She saw the crimson in the sink and gasped in horror.

Misha stopped throwing up, standing unsteadily. Adelaide noticed that blood was coming from Misha's eyes as well. "Oh my god!" She turned the sink on and wet the towel, wiping the woman's face. Misha hiccuped and let herself be cleaned. "Oh, sweetheart. I'm so sorry." She finished cleaning Misha's face. Adelaide went to the phone. "I'll call for help!" Before she could get the operator on the line,

Misha stopped her. A pale hand wrapped around her wrist and forced the phone back on the hook.

"No, no," Misha shook her head. She noticed Adelaide's confusion. Misha forced a smile, "I am okay." She joked, "I suppose I can not have man-go."

Adelaide frowned, brow furrowed. "Are you sure?" She'd never seen an allergic reaction like Misha's. "I can drive you to the hospital." Misha shook her head. Adelaide bit her lip. Fear was making her shiver. Only one girl had ever died under Adelaide's roof and that was something she never wanted to happen again. At least this one wouldn't be by Misha's own hands. God, that was so dark. Too dark. Adelaide tried to calm down. Misha seemed calm. She seemed fine. Adelaide took a deep breath. "Are you sure? I can take you to the doctor."

Misha shook her head. "No, no, please." A part of her felt terrible for scaring the poor woman. It was necessary though. Unfortunately, now she was *starving*. Misha shuddered. The hunger shakes were the worst. She looked down at her bloody shirt. "Can I have new clothes?" Misha batted her bright green eyes and watched Adelaide melt.

The black woman nodded. "Of course, peaches. I'll go find you something." Adelaide kissed the woman's forehead and left. "Call me if you need me, peaches. Okay? Don't hesitate." She quickly went to the sewing room to piece together an outfit.

Misha nodded and watched the woman go. Throwing up was a bad idea. Her stomach screamed in agony. A knock came against the back door. Misha could smell the man on the other side. Greasy, sweaty, hormonal. His thoughts were loud. Disgusting. Lecherous. He wanted Adelaide. He knew she was alone. He hoped to be invited in. Misha's fangs dropped. She stalked to the door, that was still being incessantly knocked on, and ripped it open.

Tony jumped back in shock. "Oh shit!" He smoothed his hair back again. "Who are you, toots?" He looked the strawberry blonde up and down. She was beautiful. A bit too petite for his taste, but still poster worthy. He guessed she was one of the alumni or a new student who was there early for the spring semester. Tony noticed the red on the front of the girl's shirt. Adelaide made wonderful jams and juices, but they stained like a bitch. "Victim of mama's cran-pomegranate juice, huh?" he teased.

Misha looked down at the stains on her shirt. She looked at the man again. "Yes," she answered simply. "What are you doing here?"

The man pursed his lips. "You a russki?" Tony asked, a bit of venom in his voice.

Misha tilted her head and glared at the man. "I do not know what that is."

Tony huffed, "Whatever, chick. Go get Mama. I came here to see her." The 'Not you' wasn't said aloud but was heavily implied. He wanted to see Adelaide in her lounge clothes, which was normally sans bra. He'd brought a bottle of bubbly with him. A little apology gift. He'd say how sorry he was and how she was right. He was a selfish boy whose mother was mean to him. Tony needed someone sweet and nurturing like Adelaide. God, Dobson was a genius, helping him come up with the plan. She'd feel obliged to let him in. Probably comfort him. If Tony could squeeze out some tears maybe she'd hug him. Give him a kiss. Maybe make him a hot breakfast. Maybe let him bend her over and-

The door slamming made Tony jump. The strange woman's eyes were filled with rage. "The fuck's your deal?" he spat. "Listen, little commi, I'm trying to get laid." The girl was glaring at him. It was pissing him off. Who the hell was she to judge? "Could you kindly, fuck

off?!" Tony tried to move the girl but she didn't budge. Not even an inch. She was like a stone statue. What the hell?

Misha looked at the bottle in the boy's hand. She snatched it, making the boy's eyes widened in disbelief. Misha set the bottle on the step. There might be a struggle and she didn't want it to break. It was a very pretty bottle and she wanted to see Adelaide's eyes sparkle when she was gifted with it.

Tony stepped back. He sucked in a cold breath. "Hey, you can keep it," he offered. The girl had moved fast as lightning and quite frankly, he was terrified. He hoped the offer would placate the strange girl. It didn't. The woman stepped onto the frozen ground. Not even flinching at the ice on her bare feet. He wondered why she seemed so menacing. So unnatural. Tony huffed out a shaky breath, it crystalized in the winter air. Then it hit him, she wasn't breathing. She hadn't been breathing. Not a single puff of frozen air. The hairs on the back of his neck stood up. Tony stumbled back, tripping over his feet and landing in the yard. The cold penetrated his clothes and chilled him to the bone. "Listen, I'll leave-" The words died in his throat. Fear took his voice.

Misha smiled. In a blink, she pressed the man's shoulders into the frozen ground.

The boy cried out and began to struggle. Misha wrapped her hand around his neck. The boy choked. His eyes widened in shock. Misha giggled, "I can hear your thoughts, rotten boy." She saw the reflection of her fangs in the boy's wide eyes. Misha pressed her nose against the boy's and hissed, "She's mine."

    Adelaide collected an outfit. She hoped Misha would like it. A knock made Adelaide groan. It was probably Tony. She decided to ignore it. Eventually he'd leave. The pants Adelaide found were corduroy. Soft but would keep Misha warm. The shirt was a simple turtleneck and Adelaide added a sweater for good measure.
    "Here we go," she mumbled to herself. Adelaide then pouted. Did she have any shoes that would fit the woman's small feet? Adelaide wondered if adding a couple pairs of socks would remedy the size difference.
    "Beloved?"
    Adelaide jumped, nearly dropping the clothes. "Jesus, Misha!" She chuckled, "I'm an old woman. You can't sneak up on me. Might give me a heart attack."

Misha pouted, "You are very young, Adelaide." She noticed the clothes. "Are those for me?"

Adelaide nodded. She couldn't stay mad at the girl. "Here. Get changed. I'll find you some shoes too." She handed Misha the clothes. Adelaide went to her sewing closet. She parsed through the shoes. The smallest size she had was an eight. Adelaide hummed. The shoes would have to do. She grabbed some socks.

Thankfully Misha was fully dressed by the time she came back out. The sweater was two sizes too big. The sleeves had to be bunched up to not cover Misha's hands. It was adorable. Adelaide couldn't help but smile. The blonde looked happy and cozy. There was a warmth in her pale cheeks. Adelaide realized, despite the cold from last night, Misha never looked flushed. The winter air caused no pink to paint her nose and cheeks. Strange. Adelaide shook her head. There was no reason to focus on something she probably just overlooked. "Does everything feel okay?" she asked.

Misha nodded. She hugged the woman. "Thank you, beloved." Misha nuzzled into Adelaide. "You are very talented."

Adelaide coughed and gently pushed the woman's head away from her chest. Misha pouted up at her. Oh. That made Adelaide second guess herself. Maybe Misha really was just flirty and sweet and didn't know about American culture. Those green eyes were pleading to her again. Adelaide leaned down and kissed the top of the woman's head. It was too late to stop now. "Thank you, peaches." Adelaide revealed the shoes and socks. "Here, let's try these on." Adelaide cleared off a chair and offered it to the woman. She patted the seat.

Misha sat. She pulled on the two pairs of fluffy socks and then the boots. The shoes were big but thanks to the garments they fit comfortably. Adelaide knew her body and how to work with it so well, despite never having it. Misha wondered if Adelaide would let her know her body in turn. "They are perfect, beloved." Misha stood and spun in her outfit.

"You're beautiful," Adelaide whispered. She hadn't meant to say it out loud. The blonde looked at her with those shimmering eyes. The joy in them was palpable. Those eyes then roamed over Adelaide's body. It made a shiver run up her spine. Maybe she hadn't been wrong.

Misha smiled, "Thank you, Adelaide." She walked up to the woman. "May I pick out your clothes?" Misha ran her finger down Adelaide's arm. She then pouted, "It is a shame it is winter. I would adore to clothe you in silks."

Adelaide's knees felt weak. She bit her lip to keep a whimper at bay. "I suppose." Maybe Misha just liked fashion and dress up. Most girls did! Adelaide did. It was stupid to read into the comment. Very, very stupid. Adelaide gasped when Misha grabbed her wrist and led her up toward her room. The blonde was radiating a giddy energy. It infected Adelaide too. The two women giggled their way down the hall. She felt like a teen again.

Misha raced to Adelaide's closet. The array of clothing was mind boggling. All sorts of colors, patterns, and fabric surrounded her. How did the woman not get lost in such a mess?

Adelaide sat on her bed. Misha was ripping through her clothes. The girls would do this. This was normal. Misha was normal, and Adelaide was normal about Misha. It was fine. It was fun! They were being young and having fun.

Young. Adelaide couldn't remember the last time she'd felt young. Sure, some said she looked young or dressed young, but she'd never felt young. Adelaide had always had to be the responsible one. The voice of guidance and reason. Even as a child, she was made the take charge when her mother was on a date with Mr. Jim Beam. Adelaide batted those memories away. No use dwelling on that woman and her liquor. Especially since there was another woman now battling for space in Adelaide's mind. A woman who was probably destroying what little organization her clothes were in.

  Adelaide wondered if Misha's flirting was superficial, like Tony's. Was it all a childish game? It wouldn't have been the first time. Adelaide would wait for the boot to drop. The curtain would eventually close and the actor would take their bow. They always did. The thought of Misha being like the others stung. It ached in a way Adelaide had never felt before. It was easy to ignore the boys. It wasn't easy to ignore Misha.

  Pretty, pretty Misha. Adelaide groaned. She covered her face with her hands. Misha was so beautiful that she'd be hanging off a man's arm in a week. Hell, a day, if she wanted! She'd have her pick of the litter. No man could ever deny her. Adelaide would be forgotten. Left in this house. Just the strange black woman that refused to leave her small town. Old Mama A in her little yellow house.

That would be her legacy.

Misha burst back into the room. "Here!" she excitedly tossed the clothes on the bed.

Adelaide looked at the ensemble. It was impressive. She was happy Misha seemed to grasp color theory. A pair of brown corduroy bell bottoms and a matching vest. A forest green turtleneck and a newsboy hat. Adelaide had to admit, it was a good outfit. "This is adorable, peaches!" she praised. The blonde was beaming.

Misha sat on the floor, looking up at Adelaide. She was overjoyed. The woman liked the clothes she chose! "Put it on!" Misha encouraged. She was practically vibrating with excitement.

Adelaide giggled. "Alright, alright." She stood, then paused. Misha was still sitting on the floor. Her green eyes were shimmering. Oh, the sight of Adelaide's body would snuff that light out. There was a time when her body was beautiful. Those days were long past. Now she was covered in stretch marks and cellulite. "Do you mind?" she teased. The woman didn't budge. Adelaide frowned.

The blonde shook her head, "Not at all."

Adelaide burst out laughing. She supposed she'd already seen Misha naked. It was only fair. Maybe it would make Misha give up her act sooner. To hell with it. Adelaide shook her head and stripped off her lounge clothes. Those big green eyes never left her. They roamed her body. It was like Misha was examining every pore on her body.

Adelaide didn't make a show of getting undressed or dressed. Wasn't like she'd offer a show anyone would find appealing. Adelaide tried to shake the disparaging remarks from her own mind. Especially with how Misha was reacting. The strange woman seemed hypnotized. That couldn't be good.

Misha bit her lip and lightly swayed. She sat on her hands. Not wanting her fingers to wander where they weren't wanted. This was a sweet torture, to have something you wanted so close but so far. Misha could feel vibrations running through her veins. Oh the hunger in her was roaring. Thankfully the agony didn't last long. Adelaide was fully dressed in minutes. She looked beautiful. Misha swelled with pride at the sight. She'd never dressed a lover, potential lover, before. Misha cheered, "Oh, beloved! You are stunning."

Adelaide felt her face heat up. Damn that nickname. She looked down at her outfit.

Mostly to escape those glittering eyes. Misha had said it so sincerely, so sweetly. Praise like that was dangerous. Adelaide shook off her longing. No use dwelling. No use. Distraction. She needed a distraction. "Okay, let's move that trunk!" Adelaide declared. She practically ran out of the room.

Misha shot up and scrambled after the girl. "I will get it!" Adelaide would not be able to lift the case. It may hurt her. Misha got ahead of the woman in the hallway.

Adelaide frowned. A pout formed on her lips. "I can help," she insisted. "I know I'm old, but I'm not that old." She followed after the woman.

Misha rolled her eyes. As if Adelaide knew anything about age. "No," Misha said firmly. She turned and laid a hand on the woman's shoulder. It stopped Adelaide in her tracks. Those beautiful doe eyes looked down at her. Oh the pout on those plush lips was adorable. "It is my trunk and must be moved in a certain way," Misha lied. "It is my cross, let me bare it, beloved. There are many things inside I treasure deeply."

Adelaide sighed. She understood. Still, she wanted to be useful, but there was no use fighting the blonde. "Okay, I'll open your room up for ya." Adelaide watched as Misha descended the stairs. She looked up and down the hall. There were two empty rooms. One close to the stairs and one right across from Adelaide's. Which to choose?

An awful selfishness filled Adelaide. A sort of possessiveness she'd never felt before. She didn't want Misha too far. A logical argument could be made that Misha needed help. She was all alone in a new country. She didn't grasp technology and she trusted Adelaide. It made sense for her to be near Adelaide. If she ever needed help.

That's how Adelaide rationalized unlocking the door across from hers. She'd make a name tag for it later. The room was smaller than Adelaide's. It held a full bed and vanity. There was an adjoining bathroom and closet. The bare cream walls and shiny wood floor shined in the sunlight. Adelaide opened the window.

A crisp winter breeze pushed out the must. Adelaide took a deep breath. She looked at the bare bed. That would need to be fixed. She went to the hall closet for a set of sheets and a spare comforter. She made the bed and fluffed the pillows. It looked cozy. The thought of Misha sleeping in the bed made Adelaide's heart ache. What was wrong with her?

Adelaide sat on the bed and waited for the other woman.

Misha walked in, effortlessly carrying her worn trunk. She set it on the ground. "How lovely," Misha whispered, looking around the room. When was the last time she had such a spacious room? She looked at Adelaide, who seemed to be glowing in the golden light of the sun. Misha couldn't help herself. She cupped Adelaide's face and kissed the woman's forehead. "You are too kind, beloved." Misha rubbed her forehead against Adelaide's. She went to her trunk. It opened with a scream of protest. The lid smacked against the wood floor and caused some dust to fly.

Adelaide leaned back on her hands. Dazed by the interaction. When was the last time she was kissed by someone she wanted? The reality of wanting Misha made a pit open in Adelaide's stomach. The older woman had never been attracted to a student, even when she was close to their age. She'd never been attracted to any girl that had lived in her house. What was wrong with her?

There was something different about Misha. Something that made the blonde alluring. Adelaide didn't even know how old Misha truly was. She acted and spoke with an air far beyond her years, but that meant nothing. There were professors who everyone knew had wandering eyes for younger people. Men who took advantage of the fact students knew so little about the world. Just because the students were adults didn't make it right. Adelaide now found herself wanting. A want that she had to ignore. She had to. Not just for her own safety, but Misha's.

Misha huffed. She bit her tongue and dug through her trunk. The woman was a well of confusion. Why couldn't Adelaide just- Misha sighed. No. Courting. She just needed to keep courting. Finally Misha found what she was looking for. A gift. The first of many she planned to give. Misha turned to the conflicted woman. "Here, beloved!"

Adelaide's eyes went wide. A necklace dangled from Misha's fingers. It was a string of pearls. Adelaide had never seen a pearl necklace in real life. She used to dream of having one, but never had an excuse to spend the money. It wasn't like she had anywhere nice to go anymore. Pearls always reminded her of Betty Boop. She was driven to sing by the little cartoon. The idea of being on stage had driven her up to the city. Her voice could never go as high as Betty's, but the soldier boys liked it all the same. "Where did you get this?" she asked the woman.

Misha beamed. The wonder on Adelaide's face was worth every pearl in the sea. She stood and climbed on the bed, sitting behind Adelaide. "It is from my family." Misha looped the necklace around Adelaide's throat. The pearls contrasted beautifully with the woman's umber skin. Misha clicked the necklace in place. "It is passed down to the woman of the house." Misha took the opportunity to smell Adelaide's dense curls. Pomegranates and a hint of hormones. It was a sweetness she wanted to sink her teeth into. Heavens above. Misha wanted to bury her nose in Adelaide's hair. The woman would be the death of her.

Adelaide let out a shuddering breath. She reached up and touched the pearls. The smooth gems spun on the thin string connecting them. She stood abruptly. "I can't accept this!" she declared, "I- This should be a gift for your wif-" Adelaide closed her mouth. She corrected, "You should be wearing this. When you get a husband."

Misha huffed and rolled her eyes. Not this again. How many times had she heard that? Misha waved her hand dismissively and told the woman, "The necklace is yours, beloved. I will not accept it back." She laid sideways on the bed. Her bent arm was propping up her head. "You may sell it if you wish. Either way, it is yours."

Adelaide's lip quivered. Tears pricked at her eyes. "Misha. You could use this for money. This could go toward your tuition! One necklace could probably pay it!"

The strawberry blonde chuckled. She rested against the bed, laying on her back. "I have silver and gold for that, beloved." Misha waved to her trunk. Money hadn't been a concern for…Misha pursed her lips. She didn't even know how long.

Adelaide pursed her lips. She looked at the open trunk. Sure enough, one of the compartments had a horde of silver and gold coins. That wasn't what truly captured her attention though. The largest compartment held books. Adelaide kneeled down. They looked ancient. Possibly first editions. "Can I pick these up?" she asked Misha. The blonde was staring at her with a Cheshire smile.

"All that is mine, is yours, beloved." Misha waved her hand toward the trunk.

Adelaide swallowed. The words sounded like vows. She took one of the books. It was made of worn leather. "Where did you get *these*?" she asked, sitting criss-crossed. Adelaide opened the book to see the title. **The Odyssey**. Adelaide carefully picked up another. **Faust** was written on the cover in gold. She grabbed another. **The Bible**. Those were the only titles in English. All the other books were in languages Adelaide didn't know. They also varied. "How many languages do you speak?" she asked Misha.

The woman was letting her head hang upside down from the bed. Misha counted on her fingers. "I believe my mother tongue is called Ruthenian. English. French. German. Italian. Greek. Turk." Misha looked at her fingers. "Seven!" she declared with a smile.

Adelaide was amazed. "Incredible," she looked at the books. "Well, at least you won't need to take any language courses," Adelaide giggled. "You should talk with Tina. She's studying to be a linguist. She'd probably love to pick your brain."

Carefully, Adelaide placed the books back in the trunk. The silver and gold coins caught her eyes. She frowned. The coins were stamped, definitely foreign, but they also looked incredibly old. "We'll need to see who can convert those for you."

Adelaide grabbed the Faust book again. She wondered if the story was just as good as she remembered it. The first time she read it was under her covers in the dead of night. It was the perfect setting to read as God's favorite man was dragged into temptation. The gold intricate pattern on the thick leather book was flaking. The spine creaked when Adelaide opened it. Pages shifted, hanging loose. Some of the stitches had come undone. It was more worn than the other tomes. Well read and well loved. Adelaide looked at the still staring woman. Those green eyes seemed enchanted with her. Adelaide couldn't help but tease, "Are you Mephistopheles or Faust?"

Misha tilted her head. It was an odd quirk from her childhood she never lost. She slipped off the bed. The movement had the smoothness of a snake and the elegance of a cat. Misha's nails tapped on the wood floor. She crawled over to the other woman. The slow deliberate movements were as mesmerizing as they were menacing. Her green eyes seemed darker, despite the sunlight shining on them.

Adelaide felt like a gazelle in the savanna. Stuck in the headlights of a lion's gaze. It froze her. She was too shocked to move, but also too curious to see what would happen. Most likely, like the gazelle, she'd end up being eaten alive. Adelaide bit her lip to hold back a whimper. Pale, cold fingers took the book from her hands.

Misha placed the book back with the others in her trunk. She didn't want it in the way. "Who do you think I am?" Misha touched Adelaide's knee. She let her fingers lightly trace the seam along Adelaide's thigh. Misha continued, "Am I the scholar or the devil?"

Adelaide smiled slyly. "Well, you are the one that followed me home." She curled one of Misha's locks around her fingers. She teased, "And you'd make a cute poodle."

Misha's eyes widened in shock. She then snorted and laughed uproariously.

Adelaide watched her. Misha's laugh was deep and rich. The room seemed to brighten at the sound. The sun's honey glow turned bright yellow. The off white walls shined. Particles danced like fairy lights. The center of her world was Misha. Beautiful Misha. Her Misha.

Adelaide's eyes widened in horror. She scrambled to her feet. "We should head out!" she announced. "Before the shops get too crazy." Adelaide let out a nervous laugh and quickly left the room. "Come on, peaches!"

Misha pouted. She crossed her arms and huffed. So close.

Chapter 5

Misha was wandering the store with a twinkle in her eye. Adelaide watched as she brought night gowns to her cheek. Nuzzling each one. Some Misha stuffed into her basket, Others she scoffed at. The strawberry blonde dangled items in the light and examined shoes. Her pale fingers skittered over leather bags and traced the brim of hats. Adelaide took note of what Misha liked and didn't like.

Misha loved silk, velvet, cotton, corduroy, and anything plush. She hated denim, satin, chiffon, and fleece. Whenever her finger grazed the materials she disliked, they twitched in shock. Misha would then wipe her hand on a fabric she did enjoy. It was as endearing as it was odd.

Adelaide looked down at the woman's overflowing cart. They still hadn't gone to the bank or whoever they were supposed to go to to turn gold coins to cash. Adelaide sighed. The strawberry blonde's smile was worth every penny. Besides, Adelaide still had some of her bonus left. A treat couldn't hurt. Especially since Misha had been so generous.

Adelaide touched the pearls. A part of her had wanted to rip off the necklace and firmly tell the blonde no. That seemed too rude. Besides, lady of the house would be an accurate way to describe Adelaide. It didn't mean Misha saw her as a wife. Adelaide was just a lady. The mental gymnastics were giving the woman a headache. Well, not a traditional headache. It didn't hurt per se, just a random pressure behind her eyes, but she'd never experienced it before. It had been happening on and off all day. Maybe she was getting a cold?

    Misha looked at the shiny piece of jewelry behind the glass. "Beloved!" she called to Adelaide. The blonde was bouncing up and down on her toes. Adelaide snapped out of her head and looked at Misha. The blonde smiled, waving the taller woman over, "Come here!"

    Adelaide relaxed. This was supposed to be fun. Shopping was meant to be fun. Why was she focused on nonsense? Adelaide went to Misha's side. The blonde was adorable when giddy. Well, Misha was always cute. Not in the childlike way her girls were, but in the way Marilyn Monroe was. God, Adelaide tried to banish those thoughts. Comparing her new crush to her celebrity one would cause nothing but trouble. Instead, she looked down at the necklace Misha was pointing out. It was a large emerald on a gold chain. "Oh, it's pretty,"

Adelaide praised. The gem would compliment Misha's eyes. Hopefully it wasn't as expensive as it looked. There were little engravings on the gold holding the jewel. Adelaide leaned on the counter, trying to get a closer look. It was something her mother would've scolded her for doing. Adelaide hated how her mind drifted. Too many memories. She tried to focus in on the necklace. A part of her wished to have it.

"Do you want it?" Misha asked. Before Adelaide could lie, Misha flagged down a worker. "Excuse me!" The attendant was a fine woman. In all black, with a tight skirt, and her blonde hair was slicked back into a bun. It reminded Misha of the ballerinas she used to dance with. Nostalgia filled her chest. Ballet was one of the blessings of man. The shoes were creations of Satan, but the art itself was captivating. Misha would always treasure its creation.

The sharply dressed attendant walked behind the counter. Rachel looked between the women. Such an odd couple, especially on a weekday afternoon. She remembered the kids were on break. Even still, it was strange. "May I help you?" The peachy hair girl was beautiful. The old woman leaning on her counter looked familiar. Rachel had definitely seen her before. A teacher? Maybe an old townie? Who could say? The woman's wrinkled face was looking intently downward.

"Yes," Misha pointed at the emerald. "I want that necklace." She noticed a pair of golden rings, "Those as well, please." Misha missed her rings. Gold and silver used to adorn her fingers. When had she lost them? Paris? Italy? Somewhere in this huge country? It didn't matter. Misha would make a new collection and give Adelaide some as well.

The worker chuckled. Rachel wondered what Russian mob boss had allowed his daughter overseas. The girl was either filthy rich or bluffing. Rachel set out the rings. "Here you go." She slipped one of her hands under the counter, finger resting on the panic button. Just in case the girl decided to run. She'd told Max they needed locking doors, but the old man refused to listen. Rachel didn't know why she wasted her time with the man.

Misha eyed the items. They were real. She'd seen fools gold too many times in her day. Now it was second nature to spot it. She took one of the rings and turned to Adelaide. "Look, beloved. Is it not beautiful?" Misha put her own ring on. "We will match!" She slipped the ring onto the taller woman's finger.

Adelaide's eyes softened. She giggled. The ring was pretty. Gold and glittering under the fluorescent lights. Adelaide had never had a ring before. Her own or from someone else. Adelaide heard a disgruntled noise. That broke through her happiness. In her moment of bliss, she'd forgotten that they weren't alone. She looked at the attendant, then back at the ring. Oh. The well dressed woman's face was twisted in disgust. Adelaide's heart sank.

Rachel chuckled. "I'm sorry." She quickly snatched the necklace off the counter before the other women could touch it. "Those are engagement rings," she explained. The foreigner didn't even flinch. Nothing. Rachel's frown deepened.

Misha rolled her eyes, "Obviously. They are being used as they should." She took Adelaide's hand. "Gold truly is your color, beloved," Misha mused. She looked at the counter and wondered what other rings to get.

Adelaide's eyes widened in horror. "Misha," she warned with a hiss. What the hell was she doing? God, did Misha even know what engagement meant? Perhaps she thought it meant something platonic. Like friendship rings. Adelaide didn't even know if those were a thing. She knew about friendship necklaces and bracelets. Adelaide felt the weight of the pearls around her neck again.

'For the woman of the house' Misha had said. Lord, Adelaide could only deny so much.

Rachel's lip quivered. A shiver ran down her spine. "I need the rings back." The worker glared at Adelaide. A filthy older woman taking advantage of a younger woman? At least older men doing it was understandable, was natural, unlike this. This bastardization of lust. Rachel noticed the peachy haired woman didn't seem to hear her or didn't care. Those green eyes were scanning the jewelry case. The foreigner probably barely understood english. No wonder the old woman was able to trick her. Rachel repeated, louder, "I need the rings *back*!"

Misha ignored the woman. She looked up at Adelaide. The woman seemed terrified. Why? Misha examined the ring. It was a perfect fit. Did it hurt? No, that wasn't it. Misha tried to find an answer but got distracted. The pearls around Adelaide's neck were mesmerizing. The blackness of her eyes, the rich brown of her skin. Misha got lost in the woman. "Oh, beloved," she sighed in wonder. What a vision. Misha wanted to adorn her with precious stones and metals. She wanted to wrap Adelaide in silks and lavish her with affection.

Rachel's face turned red with indignation. "Excuse me!" she hissed, "I need you to give the rings back!"

The shout made Adelaide jump. Panic gripped her. She chuckled, trying to defuse the worker's rage. Adelaide knew the look of judgment well. The look of prejudice. The look of hate. She tried to explain, tried to find an excuse, "She's from Europe. They express things differently-"

"I know what you are," the attendant hissed. "At least the professors pay for their little girls' things." Rachel couldn't believe this woman not only had the gall to flaunt something so terrible in public, but to also be a welfare queen? "Too broke to sugar on your own dime," Rachel snapped. She watched as tears welled in the woman's eyes. Good.

Adelaide froze. The words felt like a smack to the face. All her insecurities about Misha were spat at her so plainly. Tears rolled down her face. Adelaide was a silent crier. She'd picked up the skill when she was young and never broke it. In times like this, it was a blessing.

Adelaide wept. All the awful things she'd been thinking about herself were suddenly true. A dirty old woman. That's all she was. An awful, sick, dirty old woman. Adelaide looked down at the ground. Shame overwhelmed her.

Misha's head snapped in the worker's direction. "**Apologize**," she hissed with more force than necessary. The rage she felt was palpable. How dare this woman. How dare this awful woman and her fake blonde hair disrespect her love. How dare she make Adelaide doubt her beauty, her worth, her self image. Misha would rip the woman's throat out.

Adelaide was surprised by the tone. Misha sounded enraged. The blonde's voice was also odd, like there was more than one. Maybe it was a trick on old ears. Adelaide looked at Misha. Those green eyes were glaring daggers at the attendant. Adelaide spared the woman behind the counter a glance. She watched in confusion as the attendant's face went from wrathful, to placid. She looked at Adelaide.

"I apologize." Her voice was flat. Robotic.

Misha ordered, "Give me the necklace." She stuck out her hand.

Rachel got the emerald necklace out of the case and handed it to Misha. Her movements were jerky, unnatural.

"Now, leave us," the strawberry blonde hissed. The worker walked off. Her gait was strange. Too stiff for comfort. Misha huffed and looked at Adelaide. The woman's coal black eyes were wide. Misha cooed. She took the taller's face in her hands. "I am sorry, beloved. I should have sent her away sooner. Such an awful being, daring to question your character. You are too beautiful and kind to deal with such slander." She stood on her tiptoes and kissed Adelaide's cheek. Misha then hooked the emerald necklace around the taller woman's neck. "Oh, my beauty. The emerald makes your eyes shine." She touched the gem and giggled.

    Adelaide shuddered. What the hell. She wiped her face dry. "Misha, peaches. I know you're not from America, but-" She didn't want to accuse Misha of doing something she wasn't. 'You can't act like you're in love with me' could be met with rage. Adelaide knew the woman was just flirty and didn't mean to come off the way she did. God, denial usually worked. Why wasn't it working?

    Adelaide took a deep breath and collected herself. "Some people don't understand being kind to people of different colors or the same gender. They get mad. They yell." Adelaide licked her lips in worry. "I need you- you can't call me beloved in front of others," Adelaide whispered.

Misha frowned, "Why not?"

Adelaide sighed, "Misha. We could get in trouble. *I* could get in trouble. This isn't the city. There may be a college but there are still small minds here." Why didn't the blonde understand? Did she not know how dangerous it was to act the way she did? Two decades ago Adelaide would've been hung from a tree for this, hell, it might still happen! Panic was making her pant. She wanted to go home. The terror of being found out was making her nauseous.

Misha pouted. The woman was much more distressed than Misha had anticipated. Maybe the hesitation wasn't solely due to Adelaide, but outside factors. No matter. Misha could best all, if it meant keeping Adelaide safe. "I have no time for small minded fools." She hugged the woman. That seemed to calm Adelaide. That was good. It meant, even if it was subconscious, Adelaide found safety in her arms. Misha was impatient, but she could work with that. Her girl wanted to go home, so they would. Misha picked up her overflowing basket then took Adelaide's hand, "I only have time for you." She left off the 'beloved', not wanting to stress the woman further. Instead, it would be their private name. Only for her to say and for Adelaide to hear. Misha kissed the woman's knuckles and then led her toward the register. "Come, I am finished."

Adelaide let herself be walked to the check out. She was too dazed to fight the hold or argue a case. Misha was an unstoppable force. Once she got going, she was gone. Adelaide just hoped they made it home before gossip started. The person at the checkout smiled at them. A sweet girl who looked to be in her teens. She began ringing up Misha's items. The number climbed and climbed, from double to triple digits.

Adelaide swallowed thickly. That was a number she couldn't pay for. She sighed and wondered if she could give the necklace back.

Misha took out a hoard of silver and gold from her pocket. "Here you go!" She handed the treasure to the shocked girl.

The girl looked at the heavy coins, then Misha. "Uh, I don't know if I can accept these?," she looked around in confusion.

Misha smiled. "Call your boss," she instructed. Misha rested her elbows on the counter and her chin in her palms. The child didn't protest. She was a kind girl, unlike the awful attendant.

The girl picked up the phone. She spoke over the intercom, "Max, can you come to the front?"

Misha watched as a man lumbered out from the back of the store. Her lips curled. The man smelt of sweat and cheese. His gray hair was slicked back and the suspenders on his shoulders were too tight. Misha put on her prettiest smile as he approached. "Hello," she batted her eyes.

The man, Max, smiled at the sight of Misha. She was a beautiful girl. "Well, hello there. How can I help you?" He noticed the older woman. She had quite the figure. She looked oddly familiar too.

Misha pouted, "I am new here." She showed her coins. "Could I please pay with these?"

Max looked at the coins. It was probably worth more than the items she had on the counter. Hell, it could probably buy the whole store! "Of course!" Max cheered. "Janet, cash this little lady out, please."

The young girl behind the counter nodded. Janet bagged the strange peachy haired woman's items. Max seemed enthralled with her. Janet noticed the nervous black woman behind the blonde. She looked a bit like a deer in headlights. Janet squinted her eyes. "Wait, aren't you Mama A?" she asked.

Adelaide was surprised. She knew some kids talked about her, but this girl seemed to be in high school. "I am," Adelaide answered.

Max knew Adelaide was ten years younger than him. He'd heard of her through the kids that had worked at his store. She looked great for her age. "Well, well, you're the famous Mama A?" He walked up to her. Max noticed the emerald necklace and string of pearls. "Those yours?" he asked.

Adelaide shrugged, "Now they are." The jewelry definitely clashed when worn together. She touched the necklaces.

Misha huffed. She didn't like the way the man seemed to be creeping closer to Adelaide. "I'm paying for the necklace too," Misha told the girl.

Janet nodded. She wrote that on the receipt. The teen looked at Adelaide. "I hope I can get into your sorority!" she said. That seemed to make the woman's eyes fill with warmth.

"I hope so too, baby," Adelaide smiled, a little giggle in her voice. Seeing a girl excited to join her house made her heart swell with pride. "I'd be happy to have you."

Janet beamed. "Is it true you cook and make clothes?" she asked.

Adelaide nodded, stepping away from Max. She got closer to the counter, less nervous than she was before. "I do. I can make almost anything." She gestured to her outfit, "Made all this," she gestured to Misha's, "and hers."

Janet's eyes seemed to sparkle. "Really, that's incredible!"

Max chuckled, "No wonder I've never seen you in here." He tugged at Adelaide's vest, "You really made this?"

Adelaide didn't like the man casually touching her, but she answered honestly, "Yes."

"Could you tailor my graduation dress?" Janet asked. "The one I got is a little too loose, but it's so pretty!"

Adelaide giggled, "Of course, baby. Just bring it by my house, I'll mend it for ya."

Janet's smile was wide. "Oh, thank you! You live in that big house right? The pale yellow one?"

"Sure do!" Adelaide answered. "Stop by after the Holidays. I'll fix it up for you."

Janet beamed, "Oh, thank you!"

Misha bit the inside of her cheek. A nasty gnat of jealousy was buzzing around her head. Adelaide's black eyes were shimmering in delight. The little girl behind the counter had innocent eyes but Max was currently staring at Adelaide's ass. The woman didn't even realize the show she was giving, leaning on the counter while she spoke to the teen. The arch of her back was tantalizing. The pants she wore slid down a bit, showing a sliver of dark skin.

Misha loudly coughed. A hacking thing that startled the three. "I am sorry," she said, wiping her eyes. Adelaide's face twisted in worry. "I think I am still getting over this morning," she pouted.

"Oh, peaches. I'm sorry," Adelaide went to the blonde's side. "I haven't even thought about it." She started taking bags off the counter. Here she was chit chatting and lollygagging while Misha was silently suffering.

Adelaide was usually so good at caring for her girls. Well, Misha wasn't really one of her girls. Adelaide couldn't see her as a girl. She should. Adelaide should see Misha as a girl, but she couldn't. Regardless. Misha needed some love and care and Adelaide was happy to provide. "I'll carry these," she insisted when Misha tried to take a bag.

"She okay?" Max asked. He took a step back, "Can't afford to get sick."

Adelaide shook her head, "No, no she had an allergic reaction this morning. Nothing contagious, I promise."

Janet frowned, "Oh, I'm sorry." She finished bagging the final items, handing them to Adelaide. "Do you need any help?"

Adelaide shook her head, "No, baby. Thank you though." She looped her arm with Misha's. "Come on, peaches, let's get you home."

Misha nodded and demurely tucked her head against Adelaide's shoulder. She hacked out a cough again. It was worth the discomfort to have Adelaide's protective arm around her shoulder. It was a bit manipulative and conniving, but Misha had done worse.

Misha opened the bottle that foolish boy had so graciously left behind. "Here, beloved," she poured some of the sparkling liquid into Adelaide's flute. She poured one for herself next.

Adelaide giggled, "Thank you, peaches." Once they got home, Misha seemed to perk up again. They'd organized the blonde's room and Adelaide fixed herself some dinner. Apparently Misha had eaten earlier, but wouldn't disclose what it was. Adelaide would push later, but not now, not with Misha getting sick so fresh in her mind. "Where'd you get this?" she asked. All the champagne in the house had been drunk before the girls left.

Misha set the bottle down on the low table. She sat next to Adelaide on the couch. "Consider it a thank you gift," Misha sipped her glass. The none answer didn't satisfy the taller woman. However, Adelaide let it go. Misha kept drinking.

Adelaide rolled her eyes, "So one of your safe foods is alcohol?"

Misha shrugged, "Small blessings." She bit her lips as Adelaide laughed uproariously. The sound was like music to Misha's ears. More beautiful than the toll of church bells or a heavenly choir. Misha would chase that laugh for the rest of her days. She placed her elbow on the back of the couch, resting her head on her hand. Her whole body was facing Adelaide. "Cheers, beloved." She offered up her half full glass for a toast.

Adelaide finished her laughter and clinked her flute with Misha's. "Cheers," she mirrored and took a sip of the champagne. "This is good stuff." The bubbles slipped down her throat and warmed her belly. It bloomed through her. Loosened her tongue and relaxed her body. Adelaide drank more. Misha's green eyes looked dark again, staring at Adelaide's throat. With a little liquid courage, Adelaide asked, "Why do you call me beloved?"

Misha's eyes snapped back to Adelaide's. "Because you are. You are my beloved." It was nice to admit. Maybe it was too soon. Time was a fickle thing that Misha barely paid attention to. Too soon. Too late. Too- who gave a shit. She wanted Adelaide. The woman wanted her. Why wait?

Adelaide shuddered. The blonde had said it in such a low, dangerous tone. Adelaide downed the rest of her glass, then set it on the table. "Misha, you know that," Adelaide sighed, "you say things like that come off as…" She trailed off, heat burning her cheeks.

Misha set her glass down and moved closer. She gently took Adelaide's chin and turned the woman's head. "Beloved," she cooed. Misha pressed her thumb against Adelaide's lips. They were so soft and plush. Misha had never seen lips like hers before. Two toned. A dark upper lip and a pink bottom one. "You are so beautiful," Misha whispered, breathlessly. She put a hand on Adelaide's thigh. The woman was staring at Misha's lips. Those pretty black eyes reflected the flames of the fireplace. The light gave Adelaide's skin a golden hue. A royal woman. An idol meant to be praised and worshiped. Oh, how Misha wanted to kneel in prayer to a goddess.

Adelaide could blame the alcohol. She would blame it. Her caution was to the wind as she leaned forward-

"HEY MAMA A!" A voice screamed from behind the front door. A loud pounding followed. Multiple knocking hands and calls.

Adelaide jumped up. She stumbled a bit, bumping into the table. "Sorry, I need to-" she couldn't say an excuse and raced to the front door.

Misha sighed and rolled her eyes. So close. She poured herself another glass and downed it.

Adelaide collected herself before opening the door and saw the gang of boys behind it. "What's going on?" They all looked at her then each other.

"Have you seen Tony?" A blond asked.

Adelaide shook her head. "No, I think he knocked on my door this morning but I didn't answer. Was busy." She leaned against her door frame, "Why?"

The boys all looked between each other again. "He went out to see you but hasn't come home since."

Adelaide frowned. She turned and looked at the living room. "Misha!" she called.

The strawberry blonde calmly walked into view. "Did you answer the door this morning?"

Misha made herself look nervous, rubbing one of her arms. She lied, "No. There was banging, but I was too scared to answer."

"Who's that?!" one of the boys asked. The rest of the boys seemed to get giddy at the sound of a new girl.

Adelaide grabbed her door. A flash of jealousy burning through her. "None of your business!" she hissed. Adelaide began to close the door. "Goodnight boys."

Some of the boys pouted. A few awed. A few whistled, "Bye, Mama A!" "When you gonna let me fuck, mama?" "That outfit looks hot!" A few blew kisses.

Adelaide slammed the door and locked it. She hated winter. Most of the boys stayed behind and made themselves a nuisance. She turned to Misha. The woman's face was twisted in rage. Her fists were clenched tight.

"How dare they! How can you stand it?" Misha hissed. "Insolent, crude, little bast-"

Adelaide soothed her, "They're children, peaches. It's just teasing."

Misha huffed, "They are not. They-" She paused, fully soaking in Adelaide's words. "Children...They are children to you?"

112

Adelaide nodded, "Yes, they're kids. They like to mess with me. I've been dealing with it for thirty years." She ruffled Misha's hair. "They just need to get it out of their system." Adelaide went back to the living room. She sat on the couch and poured herself another glass of champagne. Adelaide downed it and then set the flute on the table. She closed her eyes and let her body melt into the couch. Her head hung back, resting on the back of the couch. Adelaide opened her eyes and saw Misha staring down at her. She jumped in shock. God, the blonde was too quiet when she moved.

"Am I a child to you?" the blonde asked. Misha's voice was weak. Hollow. As if she was expecting something devastating.

Adelaide was surprised by the question. "What do you mean?" She moved to sit up, but Misha's cool hands buried themselves in her hair. They lightly led her back down. Those fingers wound through her curls. A shiver went down Adelaide's spine. Those green eyes were dark. It made her swallow in worry…and arousal.

Misha asked again, hurt in her voice. "Do you see me as a child too?"

Adelaide frowned, "No, Misha. That's the problem." She gripped the couch cushion under her, nails biting into the fabric. God, she was just like the attendant said. A perverted old woman. Taking advantage of a young beautiful girl like Misha.

Misha leaned down, burying her nose in the woman's black curls. "Why is it a problem?" She let her hands slide down Adelaide's neck, over her shoulders, and down her arms. Misha whispered in the woman's ear, "We're both adults."

Adelaide whimpered. Her hips wiggled involuntarily. A shot of arousal ran through her. This wasn't how she expected the day to end. The furthest thing from her mind in fact. Misha's hands began to wander. Slipping from her arms to cup her breast. Adelaide gasped. Her legs spread unconsciously. "Misha," she gasped. Was this really happening?

Misha was purring. She leaned forward, lips brushing Adelaide's neck and inhaled deeply. The sweet scent of hormones and the salty twinge of sweat made Misha's mouth water. She squeezed Adelaide's breasts. "Beloved." Her fingers wandered down, across Adelaide's stomach. She rubbed the hem of the green turtle neck. Misha slipped her hands under the fabric. Adelaide's stomach was on fire. Hot and soft. Misha wanted to bite it, and

Adelaide's thighs, and her neck. "Let me taste you."

Adelaide was about to nod.

Suddenly there was banging on the front door. "HEY MAMA A, CAN YOU MAKE US DINNER?!"

Misha screeched, flying away from Adelaide and ripping the front door open, nearly off the hinges. "GO AWAY!" she roared. The gang of boys fled in terror. She cursed in every language she knew as she chased them off the property. They scattered, fleeing down the road. Misha stalked back into the house and slammed the door behind her. She rubbed her face and tried to quell her rage. Misha went back to the living room, finding it empty. She frowned. The shower in Adelaide's room turned on. The house groaned, pipes crying in the walls.

Misha sighed and raced up the steps. They needed to talk. Misha needed to finish their conversation and maybe fall into bed with the woman. She turned Adelaide's door knob. It was locked. Misha frowned. A deep hurt ripped through her. Tears pricked her eyes. Misha sucked in a shaky breath to keep from crying. Rejection wasn't something she'd experienced before. It was horrible. It was painful. She went to her room across the hall and slammed the door.

The ache in her chest wasn't stopping. The rage in her veins was flowing freely. She wanted to scream, to break things, and curse god. She needed to do something. Tear into something. Misha looked at the window. The moon was shining. Her throat felt dry. She tore open the window and jumped into the night.

Chapter 6

Max counted the gold and silver coins. They were stacked in lovely little towers. Today's haul was good. The Christmas crunch seemed to get better every year. Max stacked the money and fibbed on his reports. Slipping some of the cash into his pocket. Rachel was closing up the jewelry counter. Janet had clocked out long ago. Max chuckled to himself, chewing on his cigar as he moved the coins into a box. He'd have to go to a friend to turn the metals into money. It was worth it though. That stupid foreigner had just set him up for life and then some!

His store did well. Little college girls loved to spend their daddy's money on little trinkets and clothes. With these coins though, he could shut down. Maybe he'd kick his feet up at some nice beach somewhere. Sell his house and get out of town. As long as his pockets were full, his wife would follow quietly. The woman was a doormat as long as she had a fur and her quaaludes. She'd overlook embezzlement. She'd overlook lies. She'd overlook extramarital affairs. Speaking of affairs. Where was Rachel?

A loud pop echoed through the building.

Max jumped. What the hell was that? A blown fuse? He called out, "Rachel?!" Max stood. The noise was strange. Now that he thought about it, Rachel was normally finished by now. Max was used to having his massage on time, dammit. Max opened his office door. "Rachel?"

The store was pitch black. Max huffed. Just his luck, it was a blown fuse. Not the first time, but it was still annoying. Max grabbed his flashlight. "Rachel?" he called again. "This isn't funny, cutie pie." A crash made the man grip his chest in terror. He hated the dark. Max shined his light around. "Rachel!" he screamed. He walked deeper into the blackness. A couple of mannequins were knocked down. Clothes were scattered. Max roared, "This mess is coming out of your check, Rachel!"

A wet sound made Max jump. A shudder went down his spine. Oh god. What the hell was that? He looked around. The sound reminded him of when his wife squeezed a chunk of gelatin between her tear soaked hands. The squishing and wet sounds got louder. Max shuddered. He gagged as a foul smell hit him. Ammonia and something metallic.

Max walked around. There was a harsh smack of a heel on the ground. He saw Rachel's feet sticking out from behind the jewelry counter. Her heels clacked against the floor again. "Rachel!" Max raced over to the woman. Was she having a seizure? Did she hit her head and fall? Did a light fall on top of her?

Max shined his flashlight on what he thought would be a comatose woman. Instead he saw someone on top of Rachel. The wet sounds were coming from her. Max recognized that peachy hair. Another horrid wet sound. Like taking a knife out of a juicy piece of meat. The strawberry blonde sat up, her back to Max.

Her head slowly turned toward him. Max gasped. Oh god. Her mouth was crimson. She had been eating Rachel. Jesus Christ! What the hell was this thing?! Max wanted to check on Rachel but he was too terrified to take his eyes off the monster on top of her. Max raised his free hand in surrender. "T-take whatever you want," he begged, "please. Please don't hurt me."

Misha smiled. The sight of her bloody fangs made the man scream.

Max ran. Fight, flight, freeze. He'd always chosen flight. Always running. Always fleeing. Max didn't hear the girl chasing him. Maybe she had run after being caught. He could hope. Max could prey. A gust of wind blew past him, but he ignored it. Max made it to the warm glow of his office. He practically threw himself inside, throwing the door closed and locking it. Max wheezed, coughed, and rested against the wall. He hadn't run that fast in years. The cops. He needed to call the cops! Max looked at his desk. He noticed his chair was facing the wall. Was it like that when he left? Max jumped when one of the gold coins flipped in the air.

The chair turned around to face him. Slowly, teasingly. There, the monster sat, playing with a coin. Max looked at the locked door, then the woman shaped thing. "What do you want?" he wept.

Misha twirled the coin along her knuckles. She stood, floating to stand on the desk. The man wet himself. Pathetic. Misha saw the safe. That would be useful. Less work for her and Adelaide. "Open it," she ordered.

Max nodded. He nodded so hard his neck ached. "Of course! Of course," he quickly went over to the metal box and turned the combination. The heavy door opened. "All yours!" he declared, hoping to appease the beast.

Misha hopped off the desk and looked at the piles of money. She nodded, "Wonderful." Maybe a new gift would make Adelaide reconsider her apprehension. Misha thumbed through the bills. Money looked so strange. The paper was so small and thin.

Max sniffled. He pressed his back to the wall and slowly tried to follow it to the door. The creature was examining the cash. Running her bloody fingers along bills and coins. Was that older woman a monster too? No. Janet said Mama A was a sweetheart. Was that poor woman dead? Did this awful thing eat her like she did Rachel?

Adelaide was such a beautiful woman, especially for her age. A little too plump for his liking, but he could have overlooked that. With a perm and some makeup, the woman could have been a bombshell-

Max gasped as the back of his head was slammed into the wall. He choked, a small hand gripping his throat impossibly tight. Max tried to punch and scratch at the woman. Nothing. She didn't even flinch.

Misha smiled, "She's alive."

Max's eyes went wide. He couldn't even let out a scream as the woman ripped his throat out.

Adelaide tossed and turned. She was too conflicted to sleep. She'd cried in the shower. She'd pulled at her hair and wrote a pros and cons list. She'd paced her room until she collapsed on the bed. Adelaide rubbed her face raw and screamed into her pillow. Even though she was exhausted, she couldn't sleep.

She'd been trying for hours. That terrifying want she felt earlier was still in her. That 'awful perversion' her mother would say. New tears flooded to her eyes. God, why couldn't she have been born a boy? Why couldn't Misha be a boy? Why was what she wanted *always* wrong? It wasn't fair. None of it was fair. She'd been content. Her whole life she'd been content!

Then this woman. This strange woman ruined everything. Adelaide beat at her pillow and felt like a toddler. She was throwing a tantrum. God, she was being childish. It wasn't Misha's fault. None of it was. Adelaide had been thrown in the closet. She took up a shovel and dug even deeper.

Adelaide had only been with a woman once. She was eighteen at the time. Wide-eyed and new to the city. That woman had broken her heart when she was twenty. Back then, she made a promise. Never again. Never a real person again. She'd live in her fantasies and she'd be content. She had to be. Especially now. Adelaide was old. Who the hell would want her?

Misha.

Adelaide sniffled. She sat up, giving up on rest and wiped her eyes. What a mess. Adelaide turned on the lamp that sat on her nightstand. The list she made was there, waiting for her. Adelaide's shaky fingers picked up the paper. She read over the page. Her eyes scanned the cons then the pros. The final pro read: **I could be loved.**

Adelaide's lip quivered. She wept and pressed the page against her chest. When was the last time she'd been loved? Loved like the women in her books and movies. Not just as a mother, but as a partner. Why couldn't she be loved? Just because some awful people wanted to be in her bed and her business? Screw them. They already took thirty years. Adelaide wouldn't give them any more. She was done with only being content.

Adelaide shot up, throwing off her blankets. She tugged off her bonnet. Adelaide was fifty. Fifty and life was short. With her family's history, she'd be lucky to get ten more years. Adelaide took a deep breath and ripped open her door.

Misha's door was shut. No door in her house had ever looked so daunting. Adelaide licked her lips. It was past midnight. She hoped Misha was still awake. Her fist was raised to knock. It shook. Adelaide forced herself to move. The sound rang out in the dark hallway. It echoed throughout the house. Bouncing off the walls and rattling her nerves. Adelaide forced herself to say, "Misha, peaches?" God, her voice was wrecked. Why couldn't she stop shaking? What if Misha didn't answer? Adelaide sniffled and tried to stop her blubbering. God, her mother would have had her by the hair if she could hear her. Probably drag her to the yard and make her pick a switch. Adelaide wondered if Misha had already decided to throw in the towel, just as Adelaide decided to give it a try.

Like an answer to her anxious mind, the door creaked open. One of Misha's green eyes stared up at Adelaide. "Yes?" Her accent was thicker.

Adelaide swallowed. "I...I've been thinking."

Misha pursed her lips and opened the door wider. "About?"

Adelaide licked her suddenly dry lips. "I'd like to talk to you about," she gestured between them, "this."

Misha huffed and crossed her arms over her chest. "What is there to talk about? I want you. You want me. It is simple."

Adelaide's eyes widened. She hated how easy Misha made it all sound. Would it be that easy? Adelaide shook her head. "No, it's not that...simple." She pinched the bridge of her nose, "Can we sit down?" Fatigue was weighing her down. She'd cried herself weak and needed to get off her feet before she passed out.

Misha nodded. She turned and walked into the room, taking a seat on the bed. Her arms were still crossed. The nastiness inside the attendant's mind weighed heavy. The nastiness inside of the shop owner's mind made her stomach turn. Was that why Adelaide feared so much? People like them? Misha moved her jaw side to side.

Adelaide nearly collapsed onto the edge of the bed. She gave Misha a few feet of space. Just in case. She didn't want to pressure the blonde. Although Adelaide wanted to touch her. To hug her. To kiss her. Adelaide shuddered, "Misha, it isn't you-"

"But it is. For some reason it is," Misha interrupted. "You want me. I want you. I do not understand why you seem so..." She covered her face. She did understand, it just didn't make sense. This new society was an enigma. What was open was now taboo and what's taboo is now open? Misha and Adelaide could share a meal but not a kiss? There was no rhyme or reason.

Adelaide rubbed her face. "Misha, I just met you." That was why it was so frightening. One day, hell, one night and this woman ripped Adelaide out of her hole and dragged her into the light. The blonde made Adelaide want to be in the light. The worst part was Adelaide wanted to be out. She wanted to be loved. Wanted. Wanting was dangerous. It had always been dangerous and Adelaide was terrified how Misha made it feel safe. That didn't even touch on the largest elephant in the room. Age. God, why her? "This isn't normal," Adelaide whispered.

"But we still *both* want each other," Misha countered. Frustrated tears pricked her eyes. Why did time matter? Who was time to judge, when it stole all the beauty in the world for itself. Misha sniffled. She couldn't cry, not yet, but she wanted to wail. Why could she never have what she wanted? It wasn't fair.

Adelaide gripped her pajama pants. She rambled off in a panicked tone, "Misha, if the school finds out we're together, they could take away my sorority. We could get in trouble. My girls would lose their second home. We could go to jail!" She hoped she was making Misha understand.

The blonde huffed, "I would not let that happen." Misha crossed her leg. Closing in on herself as she ground her teeth. "I do not understand your country's ways, but I would not let anything happen to you." How could Adelaide not see that Misha would protect her. Had she not shown that already? Misha debated revealing her nature. It might be wise to. The woman would find out eventually. Better now than later.

Adelaide sighed. It was scary how easy she believed the blonde. "I do want you," she admitted. It felt good to admit it. It felt good to say it out loud. "I want to be with you," Adelaide whispered. She was scared Misha wouldn't hear her, but the blonde's head snapped to her. Misha definitely had sensitive ears. Those green eyes were longing.

It gave Adelaide the strength to continue. "I've only had one relationship before. It was…" Adelaide didn't even know where to begin with her city fling. "Listen, the point is I haven't dated since. I've always been too scared to. That being said," Adelaide turned her body toward the other woman, "I need you to understand some things."

Misha nodded. Her body language became open. Arms and legs uncrossed. She moved closer to Adelaide. The woman had said. She said it plainly. Oh, what a joyous day.

The taller woman went on. "I'm fifty, Misha. I am an old woman. I can't go clubbing. I can't go joy riding every weekend. I'm not out. We can never be out here. This would have to stay between us and-," Adelaide paused. She knew what she was going to say next could make or break them, "I need you to understand that people in my family rarely make it to sixty. If we do this, you'll at most be in your thirties when I die. Still young. You'll still have so much life ahead of you, Misha." Adelaide licked her lips nervously and took Misha's hand. "I need you to understand all of this. I don't want to keep you from finding a love who can grow old with you, not die before you."

Adelaide rubbed her thumb along the back of Misha's hand. She caressed the gold ring Misha wore, it mirrored her own. Despite all of her doubts, she couldn't find it in herself to take the band off. "If this is just a fling, just a bit of fun, I don't want a part of it. There's plenty of girls who'll gladly play with you. I won't." This was one of the reasons Adelaide hadn't had much in her life. She wasn't flippant with love. She couldn't be casual, no matter how hard she tried. Adelaide saw the blank face Misha wore. Adelaide's heart clenched. So, it was a game. She tried to slip her hand away.

Misha held her fast. She looked Adelaide up and down. Misha entwined their fingers. The realization she'd misread Adelaide's hesitation was weighing heavy on her heart. It wasn't just society. It was also that Adelaide hadn't thought Misha's intentions were pure. Well, they weren't pure in a sexual sense, but they were true. She looked at their hands. The contrast of their skin was even more evident in the moonlight. Misha then looked up into Adelaide's coal black eyes. Her green eyes were reflected in them. They were beautiful black mirrors that held the same want Misha had. Pale fingers squeezed Adelaide's. "I am obsessive," Misha admitted. "I will not let you go." The blood she'd fed on made her heart pump faster. Her stomach fluttered. "I am jealous," she warned, "I am possessive." Misha leaned forward, "This will not be a 'fling', Adelaide. I will want you till we are both dust. When the world collapses around us, I will hold you, beloved."

    The confession made Adelaide shiver. The logical side of her told her to run. Statistically, a relationship like theirs would end in disaster. That needling voice screamed that she was in danger, that she would lose everything she fought so hard to force and maintain. However, another part of her was delighted. She had never been the center of someone's world before. She'd never been an obsession. She never had someone vow to follow her to the end of time and hold her as it all faded to black. Adelaide looked into Misha's eyes and realized, it was worth it. Potential fall out be damned. It was worth it. Time wasn't on her side, but Misha was. A tear rolled down her cheek. "Okay," she nodded, "Okay." Adelaide sucked in a shaky breath. "So…" she looked at Misha, "I'm willing to, if you are?"

The unneeded air Misha took in, caught. Oh, her girl was so lovely. It wasn't fair. She clambering into Adelaide's lap. The woman gasped. Those big doe eyes stared up at Misha. She could see her reflection in them. She looked as crazed as she felt. Misha tangled her fingers in Adelaide's curls. "I want to kiss you. Please, beloved. Can I kiss you?"

Adelaide swallowed thickly. She noticed that Misha's face didn't have a single pore. Only smooth pale skin that looked radiant in the moonlight. Adelaide nodded. Lips were on hers in a blink. Adelaide had never believed in the fireworks people described when being kissed. It seemed too Hollywood, too movie magical. Adelaide had never been so happy to be wrong. Misha's lips were soft. Adelaide tilted her head to deepen the kiss. A tongue swept over her lips. Adelaide shivered and parted her lips.

Misha moaned. Her tongue caressed Adelaide's. The woman's responding moan made Misha's legs shake. She leaned in harder, finally managing to get Adelaide to collapse back on her bed. Blood was rushing through Adelaide's veins. It flooded in her cheeks, pounded through her heart, and heated her skin. Misha pulled back, gasping. She'd just fed yet she still felt *thirsty*.

Adelaide looked up at Misha. She panted out, "Peaches." Cool hands went under her shirt. Deft fingers traveled up her stomach and over her breasts. "Fuck, Misha," Adelaide gasped. The blonde shuddered above her. "Come here, peaches," Adelaide urged. She grabbed the front of Misha's shirt and dragged the woman down to her.

The blonde went without protest. She kissed Adelaide with reverence. Like one would kiss a god. "My beauty," Misha whispered against the woman's plush lips. "My Aphrodite." A kiss. "My Demeter." Another kiss. "My Hestia." A final kiss. Misha sat up. Her fingers rolled Adelaide's nipples. The reaction was immediate. Adelaide's back bowed. The moan she let out made Misha's mouth water. Her fangs dropped. Misha panted, "Beloved. Please." Her hips rolled against Adelaide's. God she was starving.

Adelaide mewled, "Anything, peaches. Anything you want." She'd never been so sensitive. Granted, she was used to her own hand. No wonder most people preferred a partner. It was electrifying. Adelaide grabbed Misha's ass. It was a lovely little handful that Adelaide squeezed. The blonde moaned. "Come on, peaches," she whispered, "take what you want."

Misha growled. The hormones in the air made her salivate. Pomegranate, salt, iron- Misha sank her fangs into Adelaide's neck. The woman gasped under her. Adelaide's hands clutched at Misha. The blonde expected to be pushed away. Thrown across the room. To her shock though, Adelaide held her *closer*. Those warm arms encircled her.

Misha moaned. She wept. Acceptance. Love. All the feelings her beloved held for her were in the hot blood that now slipped down Misha's throat. She swallowed mouthful after mouthful of ambrosia. Her hips ground against Adelaide's. The woman returned the undulations. Adelaide's hand traveled up her back and to her hair. Misha could hear Adelaide's heart beneath her fingers. The pulse made her eyes roll back in ecstasy.

The heat inside of Adelaide was slowly being drained. Her toes and fingertips felt tingly. That couldn't be good. "Misha," Adelaide whispered weakly. "Stop."

The blonde pulled back. It took all her strength to pull away. Her mouth was covered in blood. It dripped down her neck. The heat of the nectar made her shiver. Misha looked down at Adelaide. The woman was panting. Oh, what a vision. "Forgive me," she whispered, descending for another kiss. "Forgive me, my love."

Adelaide moaned. The taste of copper should have disgusted her. It didn't though. A hunger rumbled through her. A want. An eye for an eye. Adelaide bit Misha's lip. Hard. The blonde quaked, moaning loudly. Blood. New blood. Adelaide gasped as Misha's blood hit her tongue. A spark. A fire. Adelaide shot up. She nearly crushed Misha against her. Her arms trembled as she squeezed the woman. Adelaide asked breathlessly, "What are you?" Her hands slid down and rubbed Misha's thighs. Oddly warm. Oddly softer. Was that because of her? Her blood?

Misha pressed kiss after kiss on Adelaide's face. The warmth of the woman under her was intoxicating. "I am yours, beloved," she whispered against Adelaide's lips. Misha nicked her lip with her fang. She swiped the blood on her tongue and kissed Adelaide. The woman gasped. "I am only yours."

Adelaide grabbed Misha's shoulders. She pushed the woman away. "Don't try to distract me," she slurred. Why did she feel high? "I need to know what I'm getting into. If you want me, answer me." Adelaide cupped Misha's lovely heart shaped face. She placed little kisses on the blonde's pouting lips, "I want to adore you, Misha. Can't adore what I don't know."

Misha whimpered. Tears pricked her eyes. Blood rolled down her cheeks. "I am not human."

Adelaide giggled, "Obviously." Holy shit. She was high, like she just took a tab of molly. Light and wonderful. She wanted Misha to be honest, to tell her, so she could kiss the strawberry blonde more. Kiss her pretty little freckles and pink lips. "Just tell me."

Misha let out a shuddering breath. "I'm a vampire." She'd never confessed it to anyone before. Well, no one she planned to keep alive.

Adelaide giggled. The high was climbing. She was like the Apollo 11, going to the moon. "No," she kissed Misha's nose, "you're a cutie pie."

Misha's eyes widened. Her green eyes sparkled. She giggled, rolling into a full laugh. She dove in to kiss the woman. The blood in her veins was Adelaide's. The warmth inside her was Adelaide. The light inside her was Adelaide. The joy inside her was from Adelaide. "Oh, beloved!"

Adelaide giggled and kissed Misha back. The woman was flying. She'd say it was love, but it wasn't. Something was off. It was unlike anything she'd ever had before. Everything felt more. Pleasure was more. God, Adelaide wanted to fuck. "I feel…strange." Adelaide gasped as Misha placed kiss after kiss on her neck. "Did you give me something?" she giggled. Fangs scraped her skin. Teasing. God, Adelaide wanted Misha to bite down again. How many nights had she fantasized about this? How many dirty dreams? A beautiful vampire stalking through her window and-

Adelaide gasped when Misha sucked a hickey onto her neck. The buzz was wearing off. Her mind was clearing but her body still felt hot.

Misha placed a kiss on Adelaide's cheek. "It is my blood, beloved. I should have warned you." She nuzzled the woman's cheek. "I'm sorry."

Adelaide nodded. She hugged Misha tight. "It's okay, peaches." A vampire. Misha was a vampire! She sighed and nuzzled into the pale woman's neck. Adelaide wondered what could have possibly drawn such an amazing woman to her. What could she possibly offer such an ethereal being? What could she give? Adelaide wasn't sure why Misha would waste her time with an old woman like her. "Ah!" Adelaide jumped as fangs pricked her skin. Not sinking in fully but definitely giving her a shock.

"Do not speak of yourself so cruelly." Misha growled, "I want you because you are unlike any other I have ever met." She nuzzled into Adelaide's shoulder. "You are warm. You are kind. You are beautiful." Misha placed kiss after kiss along Adelaide's neck. "I want you," she whispered in the woman's ear, "because you are mine."

Adelaide shuddered. She licked her lips. "So what now?"

Misha pulled back. She looked Adelaide up and down. "Well, we could-"

Adelaide rolled her eyes. "Never mind. Bed." She lightly pushed at Misha's hips. The strawberry blonde pouted but moved off her lap. Adelaide groaned as she stood. She noticed that Misha's trunk was still on the floor. There was now a mountain of cash sitting in it. Adelaide pointed at the suspicious money. "Where'd you get that?"

Misha pursed her lips. She could lie. She should probably lie. Misha saw the amusement in Adelaide's eyes. A full confession would snuff that adorable look out. "Stole it," Misha settled on. It wasn't an outright lie.

Adelaide put her hands on her hips. "Misha, you can't steal. You have a whole trunk of gold." She looked at the cash. Well, it wasn't like either of them knew how to turn it into cash. Hell, they would probably get robbed anyway with an exchange. There were more evils than theft. "Was the guy you stole from at least an asshole?" It would make Adelaide feel less bad about not caring about the crime.

Misha nodded vigorously. "He was a disgusting man," she seethed. His blood had the audacity to taste disgusting as well. "Greasy fingers and wandering hands," Misha ranted. The man was practically drugging his wife into compliance. Both giving her the powder and forcing pills down her throat. Misha hoped the woman would get sober.

Adelaide frowned, "I see." She looked at the money then back at Misha. The venom in the woman's voice spoke volumes. Adelaide should have been concerned. She doubted the man was still alive. The realization that Misha probably killed someone didn't hit her as hard as one would expect. Adelaide's lips pursed. Murder was a sin. She looked at the blonde. The vampire's face was still twisted in rage. The dangerous air that swirled around Misha was palpable. This was a monster. A hunter.

Adelaide huffed. She was already sinning. Might as well enjoy the ride while it lasted. Hopefully Misha knew how to clean up after herself. That settled that. Adelaide didn't care. It was actually frightening how little she cared. She let her hands drop off her hips. Her mother had always said there was something wrong with her. Guess the drunk was right. "Come on," Adelaide urged. Those green eyes went wide in surprise. Adelaide smiled, "Unless you'd rather sleep here tonight."

Misha immediately stood up. She took Adelaide's warm hand, dragging the woman out the door and across the hall. "Can we turn on the fire box?" the blonde asked.

Adelaide giggled. "It's called a heater," she informed. The little box sat on the table. Adelaide went to it. She stopped short. "You want to turn it on?" she asked the blonde. Adelaide pointed to the knob, "You just turn this to the right."

Misha walked cautiously up to the box. The white piece Adelaide pointed to didn't look like it could be moved. Carefully, Misha turned it. The knob did move! It made a click and then the orange light began to grow. Misha smiled brightly. The hum from the heater reminded her of a cat's purr. "Can you show me how the stove works tomorrow?" she asked Adelaide.

The taller woman was smiling down at her with the kindest eyes. Misha wanted to kiss the other woman again.

Adelaide giggled. "Of course, peaches." She leaned down and laid a kiss on Misha's forehead. "I'll show you all the modern wonders of the world," she teased. Adelaide climbed into bed. "Actually, speaking of modern," she asked, "how old are you?"

Misha pursed her lips. "I believe it was 1345 when I was turned." She climbed onto the bed, taking a seat next to Adelaide at the headboard. "I went to sleep after the revolution ended."

Adelaide's eyes widened in shock. "The revolution here?" she asked in astonishment.

Misha nodded. "My maker…" she trailed off, staring into the glow of the heater. Misha tucked her legs up and rested her chin on her knees. "Things happened," she said simply. Adelaide wanted to ask more but didn't. Misha appreciated that. Adelaide didn't demand her attention. Didn't demand her time or a body. Adelaide was longing, but never commanding. Misha looked at the woman, who was thoughtfully waiting. Listening. Attentive. The blonde looked down at the bed. She didn't know what to say next.

Adelaide relaxed against the headboard. She asked, "Do you want a hug?" Those green eyes were glassy when they looked at her again. Adelaide opened her arms. Misha climbed into them. The blonde's body was cool once again. Adelaide pressed her nose into Misha's hair. Blood. Misha smelt like blood, but also something sweet. It was her pomegranate perfume. Adelaide felt her cheeks warm. Misha wanted to smell like her. The blonde wanted to be marked as hers in one of the most primal ways.

Misha kissed Adelaide's neck. She nuzzled into the taller woman's dark skin. The warmth of her was intoxicating. "Oh beloved."

Adelaide relaxed into Misha. "I haven't done this in thirty years," she whispered. "I don't remember much, aside from the heartbreak." Adelaide laughed sadly. "So, I hope I don't disappoint you too much."

Misha shifted, looking up at the woman. "You could never disappoint me, beloved." She laid her hand over her lover's heart. The beat of it was rapid. Misha bit her lip. Honesty was owed, was needed. "I have been with…others."

Adelaide chuckled, "Well, you've lived at least 5 lifetimes. I expected that." She nuzzled into the peachy hair under her nose. "No shame in that, peaches."

Misha frowned. It was deep enough to be felt. "Even if it was a man?"

Adelaide's eyes widened. She pulled back and noticed the tears rolling down Misha's face. "What do you mean?" She placed a hand on Misha's cheek. The woman wasn't looking at her. Those green eyes were staring at her chest.

"Would you be ashamed of me if I have been with a man?" Misha was too wrapped up in her own mind to read Adelaide's. "Would you still want me if I was tainted?" The words burned like acid in her throat. Past rejections filled her mind. Women who refused her for having laid with a man. It was frightfully common. Misha had no want of a man, but she was curious. Why did curiosity always get met with scorn? Misha hoped Adelaide wasn't like those women. She prayed her lover was understanding.

Adelaide's brow furrowed. "Misha. Just because you've slept with a man, and I haven't, doesn't mean you're 'tainted'." That made the woman finally look at her. There was disbelief in those green eyes. Adelaide said firmly, "I mean it. Just because you've had sex with a man doesn't mean anything. Whoever came before," Adelaide's voice strained, "whoever comes after," she let out a shuddering breath, "They don't matter. They don't matter to me. They don't matter to us. This," She gestured between them, "is just us."

Misha was dumbfounded, "Us?"

Adelaide nodded, "Us." She kissed Misha's forehead. "Men, women, whatever's in between, whoever you've had or will have after me, don't matter. Right now, it's just about us."

Misha pulled Adelaide to her. Hugging the woman tight. "There will be no 'after you', beloved. There will only be us."

The words made Adelaide's heart clench. It brought tears to her eyes. She hugged Misha back, squeezing her tight as well. They rocked back and forth and the heater hummed.

Chapter 7

A week went by in a blink. Adelaide learned a lot in those seven days. Mostly about Misha.

One, Misha was clingy. Adelaide woke up everyday wrapped in the vampire's arms. She stuck by Adelaide's side when they went out. She was constantly holding, touching, or grabbing the taller woman.

Two, Misha was a fast learner. All it took was one explanation. One tutorial. Next thing Adelaide knew, she was being served breakfast in bed. Misha now knew every electronic inside and out. Literally. She'd taken apart multiple devices. The camera. The toaster. The television. The blender. Adelaide had found the blonde multiple times surrounded by scattered metal parts. A manual in one hand and a screwdriver in the other. Adelaide had helped her put things back together too.

Three, Misha was jealous. She was a vicious thing. Snapping at and glaring at anyone who dared to even glance at Adelaide. It should have been exhausting or concerning, but Adelaide didn't hate it. She was so used to being bothered by people that it was nice to be left alone. The fraternity had started calling Misha Adelaide's 'Russian wolf'. They howled when the pair passed by, but scattered when Misha glared at them. It was fun.

Four, Misha was obsessed with her. Once again, it should have been concerning. Should, but wasn't. Misha loved everything about Adelaide. Her body. Her voice. Her hair. Her smell. Her *everything*. Adelaide had never been wanted for every part of herself before. Most only wanted pieces of her, snippets, but never the whole. Misha didn't see a single fault in Adelaide. Nothing made her think twice.

Adelaide also learned some things about herself. For one, she didn't mind that Misha was a monster. Well, what society would deem as a monster. Adelaide didn't see her as one. Vampires being real still hadn't settled in. Mostly because real world vampires weren't like the books. Sunlight didn't hurt Misha. It made her weaker but didn't burn her. Misha mentioned when she was first turned, the sun made her ill. Blood was needed, but Misha could survive off of little sips of Adelaide everynight. Apparently blood had different flavors. Which shouldn't have surprised Adelaide, but it did.

Misha could read minds, which was concerning. All vampires apparently could after their first year. Misha also had a form of telekinesis and or maybe electrokinesis? Misha could make things move and mess with electronics. The blonde had turned the TV on with a glance. Had changed the radio station from across the room. It was startling at first, but now it was a neat trick. Vampires also had enhanced speed and strength. They could also compel people with their voice. Those were things Adelaide had expected.

Adelaide giggled to herself. Carmilla was far closer to real vampires than Dracula. Adelaide dipped her paint roller into the tray. She rolled it onto the wall. They had gone to the hardware store and Misha had grabbed a can of paint and wouldn't let it go. It was called 'Peach Pink'. The vampire was apparently very fond of the nickname Adelaide had given her. In fact, Misha had asked her to eat some peaches so she could taste them in her blood. Adelaide giggled at the memory of Misha's green eyes widening in wonder. The color looked nice on Misha's wall and made the room feel more alive.

Adelaide looked at the vampire, who was painting along the baseboards. The precision of her strokes was enviable. They were both in old pairs of overalls. Misha's had to be gathered in the back and made into a bunny tail. Otherwise they would have swallowed her smaller frame. They were three sizes too big. It was precious.

Adelaide's own overalls were also too big and covered in paint. It wasn't her first rodeo customizing a room. They were almost done. After that they'd just have to wait for the walls to dry. The sunlight bounced off the paint and made the room brighter. Warmer. Homey.

A knock at the door made Adelaide nearly fall off the step stool. She let out a sharp cry.

Misha caught her. "Careful, beloved." She helped the other woman down.

Adelaide giggled, "Thank you, peaches." She kissed the vampire's cheek. The knock came again, firmer. Adelaide sighed. "I'll get it," she told Misha, leaving the room. As she trotted down the steps, Adelaide noticed the figures behind the frosty glass of the door were broad shouldered and tall. She opened it slowly. Just as she feared, cops. Even worse, it was Rick, the town's sheriff and some fresh faced boy Adelaide had never met before. "Can I help you?"

The men looked Adelaide up and down. "Yes, ma'am," the younger officer said, "We're investigating a few missing persons reports."

Adelaide's eyes widened. "Missing persons?" That was news. Despite being a college town, not many went missing. Well, not a few people all at once.

The older, Rick, officer nodded. He explained, "Max Holden, Rachel Martin, and Anthony Romano."

"Anthony is still missing?" Adelaide asked, looking between the pair.

The officers shared a glance. Rick nodded. "He is, how did you know?" Adelaide had always been a strange woman. She was quiet. Kept to herself and minded her girls. Rick didn't know how the woman stayed out of trouble for multiple decades.

"Some of the boys came by and asked if I'd seen him," Adelaide explained.

"Why would you have seen him?" the younger one asked, his eyes narrowing.

Adelaide frowned, "Tony had a...he delivered letters for the university. He liked chasing skirts and teasing house mothers." It wasn't the whole truth, but also wasn't a complete lie. "He sometimes would knock at the back door, but I didn't answer that day. I got a new student and was preoccupied."

Rick frowned, "I see." He looked Adelaide up and down. The woman appeared to be in the middle of renovating. Adelaide wouldn't have been strong enough to take down the boy or Max. He had no doubts about her story. Still. "A new student?"

Adelaide nodded, "For the spring. She came early. Good for me. Otherwise I would have been all alone for a while." She chuckled, hoping to get the officers to smile. It didn't work. "Did you check with Anthony's mother?

He may have gone home. I know he's from New York."

The younger officer scoffed, "Of course we called his mom." He placed a hand on his hip. "Can we please speak with this new student? Just to check your alibi?"

Rick bumped his partner's side in warning, "Mike," he hissed. The boy was too ambitious for his own good. Rick tried to tell him 'you catch more flies with honey', but the man simply replied 'you could catch even more with traps'. Mike reminded him of himself, when he was young. That was why Rick tried so hard to reign him in.

Mike noticed the paint stained woman was eyeing him suspiciously. He cleared his throat. "We're just covering all our bases." Her shoulders relaxed a bit.

Adelaide frowned, but nodded. "Of course, I understand." She turned around to call Misha, but the vampire was already there on the bottom step. "Oh, peaches. These men are looking for Tony, did you see him?" Adelaide frowned. A pit formed in her stomach. She had a feeling Tony was in some shallow grave.

Misha walked to the door. She wanted to snap at the officers. Their eyes held suspicion. They were right, but that didn't mean

148

she liked it. "I did not see him," she lied simply. "I heard the door but did not answer."

Mike's eyes narrowed, "You didn't answer?"

Misha shook her head, "Mother said not to talk to strangers." She rested her head on Adelaide's shoulder. It made her look smaller. She looked at the men through her eye lashes. "It scared me and I ran to find Adelaide." Misha pouted, "If I had known he would go missing after, I would have-" She sniffled.

Both officers relaxed their postures. "Oh, cutie, it's not your fault," the older officer cooed.

Adelaide wrapped a protective arm around Misha. "Do you think Tony is linked to the other disappearances?"

The younger officer huffed, "We're still investigating." Their one lead had been a dud, damn. Mike wanted to scratch his head but knew that would only make the woman's glare worse. Instead. he looked to Rick.

The older officer took control. "We were told Tony may have come here, so we wanted to follow up," he explained.

Adelaide nodded, "I understand. I hope he just ran off with a girl for a holiday trip."

"That's most likely what happened," Rick mused. He addressed Misha next, "Don't worry, they always turn up eventually."

Misha nodded and retucked her head into Adelaide's chest.

The older officer tipped his hat. He addressed his partner, "Come on, Mike. Let's leave these little ladies alone. Probably scared them enough for one day."

Mike frowned. Rick made being charming and a cop seem so simple. A part of him wanted to rip into the women's stories, but there were no grounds to. Still, he looked at the pair with wary eyes. Something felt off about them. Something strange. Maybe his breakfast hadn't settled right.. "Keep safe," he said and tried to force a smile before walking off the porch.

Adelaide waved at the pair and closed the door. She pressed her forehead to it and turned to see Misha had fled to somewhere in the house. The sound of tinkering made Adelaide head to the kitchen. Misha was fiddling with one of her creations. Some amalgamation of wires and metal that Adelaide didn't understand. It was scattered across the dining room table. The blonde's back was to her. Shoulders hunched as she screwed something into place. Misha created and fiddled when stressed. Which told Adelaide all she needed to know. Still, she wanted to hear it from the vampire. "Misha." Her voice was firm and made the blonde pause.

"Yes?" Misha carried on with her device. Not that she was making any progress. It was mindless fidgeting. A distraction. A very needed distraction. Shame overtook her. Misha had to block out Adelaide's thoughts and feelings. Otherwise she'd cry. Shame was more painful than any hit or the flame. It was an ache with no end. It was a burn that could not be soothed. She hoped the other woman would just drop the topic. Adelaide already knew. Why did she have to say it?

The lack of a 'beloved' made Adelaide's lip curl. "Misha. What did you do?" The blonde shrugged, refusing to look at her. Hurt curled in Adelaide's chest. "Misha. What did you do?" she practically growled. The woman kept her back turned. It was childish. Did the woman not know how much trouble she could get in? No, Misha wasn't stupid. Just reckless. "Misha!" Adelaide said louder, trying to get the woman's attention.

The blonde slammed the screwdriver on the table. "You already know!" she snapped. Misha curled in on herself. The disappointment Adelaide was giving off was suffocating. It made her throat tighten and her eyes leak. "I don't understand why you want to humiliate me!" He used to do that. He would force her to confess her 'sins' so he could berate her. He'd replay the deaths he caused in her mind. For hours, he'd make her listen to the final words of the people she dared to attach herself to. The memories came flooding back. The wails of her friends, of her lovers, of her children. If Misha needed to breathe, she would have been hyperventilating. Instead, her body vibrated.

Adelaide rubbed her face. "I can't read your mind, Misha." She buried her hands in her hair. "I can only assume. I want to hear it from you. I want you to be honest."

Misha laughed hollowly. "Of course. Of course!" What an excuse! The same one he used. She stood, whipped around to look at Adelaide. "You want me to be honest?!" She threw the chair into the wall, it shattered and tore the large calendar upon impact. Blood was streaming down her face. Why was she so mad? She felt awful. With pain in her heart, she roared, "I killed them! Obviously. I ate them. There is your truth!" She hissed, "Satisfied?"

Misha looked at the ground. Her hand's looked blurred with how fast she was trembling. It wasn't stopping. Why wasn't it stopping? She tried to will her body to cease, but it refused to listen. Nothing ever listened when she begged it to stop. That thought made her hysterical. She hiccuped and tugged at her hair. The pain helped her mind go blank. A momentary relief.

Adelaide pressed her back against the wall. Fear practically punched her in the face. Adelaide's heart picked up. Stay still, stay quiet. That's what she'd learned to do. It was what kept her safe. How many chairs had been replaced in her youth? At least a dozen.

Adelaide sniffled. She tried to make herself see reason. Misha was upset, but Adelaide wasn't a little girl anymore. She was okay. It would be okay. Tears blurred her vision. The panic in her chest exploded like the chair. Adelaide bit her lip. Stifling herself, as she always had. Only pathetic little whimpers managed to escape. She cried a lot as a child, but never loud enough to wake her mother. Never loud enough to draw attention. Why didn't Misha understand her fear? Did she really think disappearances just went away? Maybe in her time they did, but not now. Adelaide hiccuped and wiped at her face. She covered her eyes with her arms. She felt like she was ten again. She was even in the exact same place.

The noise made Misha look up. Her heart broke. Like when she'd shattered her glass figurine. The little unicorn had snapped at the neck. The body had crumbled into chunks. Once again, her awful hands had ruined something one of a kind and beautiful. Here she was, repeating the same mistake, but with something that was far more precious. "I am sorry," Misha hiccuped. What had she done? She'd made her angel cry. Of all of her sins, this was her worst. "I am so sorry, beloved." She fell to her knees in front of Adelaide. "I...please. I am sorry. You can...I-" Misha clutched at Adelaide's legs. "Please, forgive me. Please." She buried her face into Adelaide's warm thigh. The woman was so warm. Light incarnate, like the sun that brought life to this world. "Forgive me," Misha wept.

Adelaide shuddered and gasped. The vampire's face was a mess. Blood marred her skin. The blonde was smearing it onto Adelaide's overalls. Misha was crying harder now. Poor thing was going to make herself sick. "Misha, get off the floor." She tried to tug the blonde up, but the vampire wouldn't budge. Adelaide decided to just collapse alongside her. "Misha-"

"I will leave," Misha sobbed. It hurt like hell to say. "I will leave, beloved. If you wish." She knew love between a human and vampire was a tightrope. There were so many places where a misstep could lead to disaster, so many chances to fall. It was, after all, a hunter trying to keep its prey. Misha took life, Adelaide tended to it. The vampire wanted more than anything to keep the little life they were forming. She wanted to wipe the woman's mind and go back to their painting. That wouldn't be right. She wouldn't be like her maker. Adelaide was precious. Her mind was precious. The woman deserved her autonomy.

Adelaide took Misha's face in her hands. "Misha, I don't want you to leave. I need you to understand, disappearances don't go away. People investigate, sometimes for decades! I need you to understand that you have to be careful!" Those green eyes filled with remorse, but Adelaide knew it wasn't for the murders. "I don't want you to leave," she repeated and rested her forehead against the vampires.

"You…" Misha sniffled, "You are not mad at me?" The vampire managed to reign herself in. She scanned her girl's mind. Oh. Her lover's heart was darker than she had initially thought. Such a strange woman, so kind and yet murder was not what upset her, but Misha's recklessness in who she chose.

Adelaide sighed, "I'm mad you killed people who could easily be tied to us. We're a common denominator, Misha. We literally saw all of them on the day they disappeared!" The vampire pouted. Adelaide hated how cute it was. "I need you to tell me if you're going to or if you have eaten someone. Luckily, I didn't know shit, and we had good alibis." Adelaide stood. She was too old to stay on the hard ground with her knees. "Where are they?" she asked and went to get the broom.

Misha took it from the woman. "It is my mess," she mumbled and went to clean up the chair's remains. "I buried them," she answered.

Adelaide sighed, "Where?"

Misha bit her lip, "The woods, outside of town."

Adelaide nodded. "Good." She made herself a glass of water and downed it. "Misha, this isn't the city. People will notice folks going missing." She thought about what Misha said. How the vampire was apparently old enough to only need sips to survive. "Why did you kill them?"

Misha opened the back door and put the shattered wood in the metal can. She then walked to Adelaide. "The boy was planning to seduce you with cheap champagne and I was starving after getting sick. The shopkeeper thought lowly of you and was drugging his wife. The jewelry girl," Misha's face twisted in disgust.

Adelaide nodded. Well, it was good to have an explanation. "I don't want you hunting anymore. Maybe if we move to a city, someday, but not here."

Misha was amazed. "You do not want me to leave?"

Adelaide huffed. "Misha, I've waited thirty years for someone like you. You could kill Carter for all I care, just don't connect it back to here, or me." She explained, "You can get away with a lot, but I can't." Adelaide held up her hand. "Black, remember? I've seen people like me being used as scapegoats for things less terrible and with no evidence." She refilled her glass and chugged it. "We're lucky Rick genuinely cares about doing his job or I'd be in a damn cell just for admitting Tony stopped by, and there ain't a Finch here, who'd represent me, either. I'd be fucked." She pulled her curls out of the messy bun she wore. The tension and situation had given her a headache. Adelaide leaned over the sink. The old drip from the faucet reminded her of a metronome. It helped her calm down. The pain in her head eased. The strange pressure was back. Adelaide looked at Misha. "Is that you?" she asked.

The vampire nodded and finished soothing the ache. Whatever deity she had pleased had given her a love like no other. She slipped her arms around Adelaide's waist. "I will not take without asking, " she vowed. The woman practically melted into her arms. Her early histrionics now felt silly.

"Why did you react like that?" Adelaide asked.

Misha frowned and held the woman tighter. "My maker used to…" she pressed her lips against Adelaide's shoulder. The words were there but they refused to be vocalized. "He likened himself to a priest," Misha managed to get out. Once the words started, they tumbled. "When he would find me, he would make me confess my sins. He never laid a hand on me, but he still took." The feeling of her maker raking through her mind and memories made her shudder. It would have hurt less if he had ripped off a limb. Misha looked up at Adelaide, those doe eyes were so soft. "I am sorry," she said again, "I should not have yelled at you, beloved."

Adelaide accepted the apology. She would have forgiven, even if Misha hadn't said anything. There was a part of her that just wanted to roll over. Normally, that was what she did. Instead, Adelaide said, "Don't break things."

Misha saw the flashes in the woman's mind. Bottles and chairs broken near her head and over her body. Misha's lips quivered. "I will not," she vowed and kissed over the woman's heart. The vampire wondered how such a kind woman could be forged from such violence. Misha mused, "I would have eaten her for you."

Adelaide was so surprised, she burst into laughter. The woman had to hold the edge of the counter to keep herself up right. Misha giggled as well. Adelaide captured the vampire's lips in a kiss. "Let's go finish your room, peaches," she said and nuzzled her nose against Misha's. The blonde looked up at her with those big emerald eyes.

"Yes, beloved," was all the vampire said in reply.

Mike chewed his pen. "I don't trust them."

Rick sighed. He looked at the photos of the missing people. When was the last time a missing persons case lasted more than two days? Five, maybe ten years? Most 'missing people' were just kids who ran off with a lover or forgot to tell someone they were heading home. It was simple miscommunication or misunderstanding. These three though, they were truly gone. Max and Rachel were most likely dead. The store had been ransacked. There was blood behind the jewelry counter. Max was a large man, but he wasn't violent. He preferred pacifying over hitting. God, poor Janet. That woman had stumbled in with her furs, slurring about Max not coming home. Rick rubbed his eyes, "Adelaide has been in the town her whole life. Don't think that woman could swat a fly."

Mike huffed. He was young and didn't put anything past anyone. Too much true crime had told him to never trust a book by its cover. The book he was fixating on was the strange peachy haired woman. Something about her was…off. "That girl sounded foreign."

Rick chuckled, "Here I was thinking the red scare was dying. You really think a girl her size could take down Max and this Anthony boy?" No, the redhead or blonde? Whatever, the peachy girl probably didn't have the strength to carry her own shopping, much less take down two fully grown men. "That girl was obviously inspired by Brigitte Bardot." He pulled out a book and kicked his feet up on his desk. "Or Twiggy."

Mike pursed his lips. "I guess without help…" he drifted off. The feeling in his gut was still gnawing at him. He looked out the window. Mike frowned. There was a strange figure moving from around the building to the entrance. The guy was dressed sharply. A high collar, three piece suit. Black leather gloves covered his hands. A wooden cane was hooked on his arm. Obviously the man came from money. His hair was red. One of those deep, fiery shades. It was long and slicked back. His eyes were a piercing blue. When they locked on Mike, it made the man shudder. Something about those eyes wasn't right. Something about the man wasn't right.

Mike immediately became uncomfortable. He didn't know why. Something about the man made the air shift. Mike sat up straighter. He looked at Rick, the older officer seemed to be in the same disturbed state.

"Gentlemen," the man began. His voice was thick with an accent. Deep and rough.

"Can we help you?" Rick asked. The man looked to be in his 30's. Obviously foreign.

"I am looking for someone. I am hoping you will know where she resides," the man explained.

Mike frowned. He nervously asked, "Do you have a name?" Mike locked eyes with

Rick, raising his eyebrows in a bewildered manner.

"Margosha is what I named her. I do not know if she is using a new one though." The man saw the officers' worried eyes. He added, "I know that our languages are different and you may struggle with her given name. I think she has changed it for your tongue's sake."

"Right," Rick drawled out. He sighed. "Do you have a description?"

The man nodded. "About this tall," he brought his hand to his chest. "Pale, green eyes, red hair."

"She your daughter? Sister?" Mike asked.

The man pursed his lips, "In some ways." He looked at the billboard. He noticed the missing persons posters. "Only three?" he commented.

"Excuse me?" Mike glared at the man. The guy had the audacity to shrug.

"I hear places of learning normally have more…lost children."

Rick cleared his throat. The way the man said 'children' made his stomach turn. Who the hell was this creep? "Alright, listen, Mr…"

"Vladan," the man said.

Mike scoffed, "Like Dracula?" He looked the guy up and down. The man smiled. It made Mike's skin crawl.

"I was named before him," Vladan laughed, "Quite the coincidence, in all honesty." He walked closer to the men. "Have you seen her?"

Rick frowned, "Sorry sir. Lots of little girls here fit that description."

Vladan frowned. "I see." He sighed, "I suppose I will just have to look." He turned and slipped out of the office.

Mike blinked his eyes rapidly. The man had practically floated out. His movements were so smooth it made Mike's head spin. "Jesus Christ."

Rick frowned. "We need to keep an eye on him."

Mike scoffed, "Yea, no shit."

Adelaide and Misha laid on the floor. Surrounded by records. They took turns placing one on the turntable. Evening had brought its golden light through the windows. The sound of Ella Fitzgerald echoed off the walls. Adelaide normally kept her old records to herself. Most of the girls didn't like her slow old music. Misha was sitting up, looking down at Adelaide. Her heart shaped face was resting on her knees. The red in the blonde's hair was set alight by the sun's dying rays.

Adelaide turned to her side. They had stripped out of their overalls. Relaxing. Basking. She looked at Misha's feet and noticed the deep arch. "How long did you dance?" Adelaide asked.

Misha looked down and relaxed her feet. She had unconsciously curled them. "Centuries," she answered.

Adelaide smiled, "So you're a master?"

Misha chuckled. "I have not done it for two centuries."

Adelaide shrugged, "I would think it's like riding a bike. I haven't ridden one in decades, but I know if I hopped on one, I'd still be able to." She laid on her stomach. "Muscle memory and all that. Same with swimmin'." Adelaide reached out, touching Misha's ankle. "I wanted to dance," she confessed again.

"Why didn't you?" Misha stretched her legs out.

Adelaide chuckled. "Small town." She gestured to herself. "Black girl." Misha tilted her head in confusion. Adelaide sighed. "The only dance teacher in town was racist." That made green eyes widen in understanding.

"Oh," Misha frowned. Sometimes she forgot. It seemed foolish, but she genuinely did. "I would have taught you," Misha said. She imagined a little Adelaide in a pink tutu. It brought a smile to her face.

Adelaide giggled, "Still could." She knew that would be foolish. Adelaide was too big and old to really learn, but it was a nice thought.

Misha blinked. "Yes, I could." She stood. "Up, beloved."

Adelaide looked at the vampire's outstretched hand. "Why?" She let Misha guide her to her feet.

"We will have a dance lesson," the blonde said simply. She cleaned up all the records in a blink. Setting the stack on a table, out of the way. "Here," Misha offered her hand again. "A simple two step."

"Two step?" Adelaide chuckled, "You plan on taking me somewhere fancy?"

"Of course," Misha answered. "I will take you to the most beautiful places in the world and dance with you in every single one of them." She placed her hand on Adelaide's hip. "Mirror my arms," Misha instructed.

Adelaide did. She watched as Misha used her telekinesis to place a new record on the turntable. Brass blared. Kitty Kallen began to sing. The pair began to sway. "I like this song," Adelaide whispered. It was the type of song that made you feel at home. The brass and strings made Adelaide's ears pur. She hummed to the song, letting Misha lead them in the dance.

"Sing for me," Misha whispered. "Please." She loved Adelaide's voice. Female altos were uncommon to her. She'd been surrounded by sopranos in the academy. They were song birds. Like violins or the hum of crystal. Adelaide though, she sang like the cello, or the roll of far off thunder, or Notre Dame's bells.

Misha laid her head on Adelaide's chest. The woman began to sing along with the record. She listened as that lovely voice hummed through Adelaide's bones. God, how had she lived so long without her beloved's voice? How had she survived without her? Misha's eyes fluttered. Her body melted into Adelaide's. Their steps became sloppy. The pair just swayed.

The record died. Fuzz filled the air. Adelaide buried her nose in Misha's hair. Her cheek pressed against the top of the strawberry blonde's head. She kept singing. Song after song, till her throat began to strain. The golden light of the evening turned into moonlight. Eventually, Adelaide went silent. They moved their arms to hug one another.

Misha hummed. She rested her chin against Adelaide's chest. Those coal black eyes stared down at her. They reflected hers. "My eyes make yours appear green," she whispered, laying a kiss over Adelaide's heart. "Living mirrors."

"Well, someone needs to reflect your beauty," Adelaide teased.

"I can think of no one more worthy," Misha whispered. Adelaide leaned down and kissed her. Misha had never seen heaven, but she imagined it would be like this.

Adelaide asked, "Are you going to enroll?" If Misha was going to go in the spring, they'd need to sign her up soon. Adelaide could probably pull some strings and lord knows Misha could use her compulsion to get in. Still, they'd need to get the paperwork filled out.

Misha hummed. She blinked her tired eyes and looked up at Adelaide. College. Misha had never been before. She'd seen female scholars before. They were very appealing. Misha nibbled her bottom lip. Adelaide would make a beautiful scholar. The woman's mind was so bright, she'd easily pass any course and help Misha along the way. The blonde giggled. The thought of going to school together made her heart skip a beat. "Will you enroll with me?" she asked.

Adelaide chuckled, "Oh, peaches. I'm too old." She was having Déjà vu. Every girl that came through her household always asked her.

Misha frowned. She stopped swaying with the woman. "I am far older than you, Adelaide." The woman's doe eyes filled with sadness. Misha couldn't understand why Adelaide was so hesitant to learn.

"I know," Adelaide tried to explain, "I just mean, you don't look old. I do, I am, in human terms." She sighed. "People won't look at you like you're some old fart who missed the bus decades ago." Adelaide looked at the ground. "I mean, even if I get the degree, what the hell would I do with it?" Adelaide forced a laugh. "Not like I could get a job anywhere. Why get it?"

Misha frowned. Her poor love. Her sweet, sweet girl. Misha gently rubbed her hands up and down Adelaide's arms. "It would make you happy," she whispered.

Adelaide finally looked at the vampire. She moved her jaw side to side. The vampire wasn't wrong, but still. Could Adelaide go? She knew her girls would support her, but god, the professors, the dean. What would they all think? Adelaide was so used to being a shaper, not the one being shaped. She bit her lip. "Maybe," Adelaide whispered.

Misha smiled. She hugged the woman. Adelaide chuckled and the sound rang in Misha's ears. The vampire placed a kiss over Adelaide's heart. The woman gasped above her. Misha looked up, Adelaide's eyes were heady. The vampire stood on her tiptoes and captured the woman's lips in a kiss.

Chapter 8

Adelaide rolled out the dough. Misha was sitting at the table, sorting through different cookie cutters. Adelaide waited for Misha to make her choice. The blonde enjoyed helping. She liked being able to join in on Adelaide's activities. Sewing. Cooking. Cleaning. Being offered to be included or just being able to be there was enough to make Misha smile. Holding thread. Fetching a sanitizer. Mixing some ingredients. So many simple things made the blonde beam. However, Misha sometimes overthought things. What fabric to use? What speed worked best? What cookie cutter was perfect? Other people may have lost their patience with Misha, but not Adelaide. Adelaide would wait for hours just to see Misha smile.

The blonde decided on the tree cutter. "Here, beloved." Misha handed the strange plastic to Adelaide. "When did you have your children?" she asked, to fill the silence.

Adelaide giggled. "They aren't my blood, peaches." She turned the dough into little Christmas trees. "Just sweet girls who still visit their old house mother. Patricia is bringing her baby." Adelaide was excited to see little JJ again.

Misha smiled. "How old?"

Adelaide thought, counting in her head. "I think he's a year old now," she whispered in wonder. Adelaide chuckled, "Time flies." After a few trees she asked, "What next?"

Misha nodded, "It does." She picked up a cutter that looked like a bird. "Here, this one," Misha watched Adelaide work. "Will they be spending the night?" The blonde picked up a man shaped cutter next. She hoped the women wouldn't stay. Misha knew she was being selfish. The women had once lived here for schooling. Speaking of schooling. The papers on the table's edge sat dauntingly. A stack of drivel she had to fill out to start at the college. It was tedious. Why did the modern age use so much paper? What was the point?

"No. They got a hotel. No room here," Adelaide chuckled. Her girls never spent the night. It used to make Adelaide sad, but now with Misha here, she didn't mind. There were enough dough birds on the cookie sheet. "What next, peaches?" Adelaide asked.

Misha handed the taller woman the man shaped cookie cutter. "So it is Patricia and her child?"

"And her husband," Adelaide added. She went on, "Also Cathy and Joyce are coming. So five total."

Misha nodded, five. That wouldn't be too much to handle for a night. When was the last time she'd seen a baby? The vampire shook her head and decided to grab the stack of papers. They'd been vexing her for hours. She looked through the forms. Adelaide finished her shaping and went to put the cookies in the oven. The words became a jumbled mess for a moment as Misha tried to ignore Adelaide's lovely ass. The blonde sighed wistfully. Misha scolded herself. She refocused on the forms. Last name? Misha rolled her eyes. Why did they need to know that? What does sex have to do with education?

Adelaide set the pot holders on the counter. She looked back and noticed Misha's face. It was pinched, furrowed brow and disgust on her face. The papers were clenched tightly in her pale fist. "You okay, peaches?" she asked.

Misha let out an exasperated sigh. "Why do they need to know these things?!" She dropped the papers on the table. "What is S-S-N?"

Adelaide frowned. This would definitely be a challenge. She set the timer and went back to the table. Some scraps of dough littered the cutting board. She scooped it up and ate it. Flour got on her fingers and lips. It was worth the mess.

"Is that safe?" Misha asked. Raw dough in her time could lead to death. Was it still the same now?

Adelaide shrugged. "It's worth a little tummy ache," she giggled. Adelaide took the papers. "I'll fill these out for you," she said. She was well versed in them at this point. Three decades would do that. Of course she'd have to make up most of it. It was a good thing Adelaide was a pretty decent yarn spinner.

Misha pouted, "I can do it."

Adelaide smiled. Those big green eyes made her heart skip a beat. "Let me help you this time, honey love," she insisted. Misha's cheeks pinkened. She licked her pretty lips and looked Adelaide up and down. Butterflies took flight in Adelaide's stomach. That look was back in Misha's eyes. Hungry. Wanting. Adelaide slowly backed up. Her face flushed.

Misha slowly stood, prowling around the table to get to Adelaide. Her footsteps didn't make a sound as she stalked the taller woman against the counter. Cool fingers found their way under Adelaide's sweater. Misha held onto the woman's waist. "Honey love," the blonde echoed. She began to sway, Adelaide followed her movements. "Such a sweet nickname," she whispered.

Misha loved that Adelaide was taller than her. She could look up at her gorgeous woman. Sometimes a light would be over Adelaide's head and give her the most enchanting halo. Misha tucked her face into the taller woman's chest. She kissed over Adelaide's heart. An angel. Her own beloved angel. "Peaches, honey, sugar. You always connect me to sweetness."

Adelaide smiled. "You are sweet," she whispered into the blonde's hair before laying a kiss on the top of Misha's head. "When you're not being a fucking menace," she teased. Adelaide tickled the vampire's sides.

Misha giggled and nipped at Adelaide's sweater.

"Ah!" Adelaide squeaked. She lightly swatted at the blonde's butt. "Oh, stop it you." A devious smile spread across Adelaide's face. She wrapped her arms around Misha and swung the girl around. The blonde let out a screech. It was the cutest sound Adelaide had ever heard. Misha was rarely caught off guard. Adelaide counted every surprise she gave Misha as a blessing. The vampire was surprisingly light. Adelaide plopped Misha on the counter. She placed her hands on Misha's bare thighs. The woman had stolen one of her sweaters and a pair of shorts. Adelaide wondered if Misha couldn't feel the cold. The blonde could definitely feel heat. She loved taking Adelaide's or sitting in front of the fire.

Adelaide teased her fingertips under Misha's long shorts. Flirting was still new to Adelaide, but she was learning. It helped that she'd witnessed a lot of it over the years. "Whatcha you gonna do now, peaches?"

Misha bit her bottom lip. "I seem to be trapped, beloved." She wrapped her arms around Adelaide's neck. The woman's curls felt so soft against her skin. Misha had missed being able to *feel* something. Two centuries of laying in the dark gave her a whole new appreciation for sensation. Misha looked into Adelaide's black eyes. They were deep pools of ink that Misha wanted to dive into. When lights reflected on those black mirrors, they became a star filled sky. Adelaide's thoughts were always so gentle. So loving. "What will you do with me?" she asked, leaning forward. Their lips were only inches apart.

Adelaide moved closer, pressing her forehead against Misha's. "Keep you," she replied before kissing the blonde. Misha's giggle made her lips tingle. Adelaide had meant to keep the kiss chaste. Misha had other ideas though. The blonde swiped her tongue across Adelaide's bottom lip. Adelaide moaned, letting her in. Kissing was new. So very new. It was wonderful. If Adelaide could have spent the rest of her days kissing Misha, she would.

Misha tangled her fingers into Adelaide's ebony curls. "Oh beloved," she whispered against the woman's plush lips. "How you tease me," she giggled, rubbing their noses together.

"I'm teasing you?!" Adelaide pinched the woman's side. Misha squeaked and pulled her into another kiss. "You're a menace."

"I am your menace, beloved," Misha kissed the woman's cheek.

The timer went off and the pair separated. Adelaide got the cookies out and set them on the stove top. "Can you get out the icing, sweetheart?" She began putting the cookies on the cooling rack.

Misha jumped off the counter. "Yes!" She went to the fridge. Misha didn't understand icing. The French seemed to like it on their cakes. She'd never seen it on cookies. Granted she'd never had gingerbread. Misha got out the frosting and brought it over to the stove.

Adelaide got the piping bags. "Here, take the spatula," she demonstrated filling the bag. "Just scoop it in and move it down." Adelaide watched as Misha quickly followed her lead. The blonde smiled up at her. "Good job, peaches." She twisted the end of the bag. Adelaide tapped the cookies. They were cool enough. "So, you can't pipe on hot cookies."

Misha tilted her head in confusion. "Why not?"

Adelaide explained, "The icing will melt and make a mess." She began drawing on a cookie. She drew some frosting fangs and angry eyebrows. It was stupid, but it made Adelaide giggle. "Here we go! A lil gingerbread vampire," Adelaide showed the cookie proudly.

Misha's green eyes were alight with amusement. That look would be the death of her. It was precious.

Misha giggled, "I will do one!" She drew on her own cookie. Giving the featureless figure a turtleneck and some curls. "Look! It is you," she held up the cookie. Adelaide laughed. It was Misha's favorite sound. Adelaide's voice was so smooth. There was an edge of age seeping in, but not overpowering. Like a crackling of a long burning fire. Soothing like the rolls of ocean waves. An accent that made Misha melt. She wanted to know how It'd sound while gripped with ecstasy.

Adelaide went back to decorating. She felt those green eyes still on her. Staring. Always staring. Adelaide was getting used to it. Slowly, people, trees, and birds all got dressed for winter. Adelaide finished and set down the icing bag. She looked at Misha. The woman was still staring. "You gonna finish your cookies?" she teased. That snapped the blonde back.

"Yes!" Misha turned back to her own treats.

Adelaide giggled. She leaned over and kissed the other woman's cheek. "Good job, peaches." That made the blonde's face pinken. It was adorable. A knock at the door made

Adelaide's face brighten. "They're here!" she announced, running to the front door. Adelaide stopped, took a deep breath, then opened it. Five beautiful faces stared back at her.

"Hi, mama!" they all screamed, even little JJ.

Tears flooded Adelaide's eyes. "Oh, hi babies!" She ushered them all inside. "Come in! Come in!" They all walked through the threshold. Adelaide shut the door behind them. "Oh, I'm so happy to see you!" she wept. Joyce and Cathy wrapped her in a tight hug. Patricia came next, JJ on her hip. The little boy grabbed Adelaide's hair. She laughed as everyone gasped.

"JJ," Patricia scolded, untangling her son's little fingers from Adelaide's hair. "I'm sorry, mama," Patricia said.

"Oh, he's fine, Pattie!" Adelaide smiled. "Can I hold him?" she asked.

Patricia didn't hesitate to hand off her son.

Adelaide took the boy into her arms. "Hello, little stranger." She lightly pinched the boy's cheek. His big blue eyes stared into Adelaide's "How was your trip?" The baby tucked his head into her shoulder. Adelaide laughed, as did everyone else.

"Do you want me to put the cookies out?" Misha asked. She looked at the new people. They seemed harmless. They all looked at Adelaide with the eyes a child would their mother. Misha didn't understand how they weren't Adelaide's children. The small boy on Adelaide's hip was quite cute. His small hand was in Adelaide's coils. His big blue eyes stared at Misha in wonder.

Everyone turned to her. "Oh, I thought all the girls were gone?" Joyce looked at Adelaide. The older woman was normally so good at informing them. The small woman in the living room seemed... off? Nothing physically was wrong per se, but the air around her was strange. The woman's green eyes sent a chill down Joyce's spine. She looked at Cathy and Patricia, they seemed to feel it too.

Adelaide chuckled, trying to think of an excuse. "Yes well, Misha is here for the spring semester! Poor dear got here early." She watched as her girls immediately relaxed. Adelaide walked into the living room. "Take off your coats and shoes, babies. Stay a while," she urged the group.

Tim, Patricia's husband, asked the strange woman. "Where are you from?" Those green eyes bore into him. He suddenly felt unsafe. It was like staring at a wolf from across a clearing, or a bear from across a river. This girl was a predator. Tim swallowed audibly.

"I am from…" Misha paused, "Russia?"

One of Tim's eyebrows rose in confusion. "You don't know?"

Misha pursed her lips, "I am unsure if it is pronounced that way in your language. I speak more than two."

Tim then nodded, "Oh, sorry." He stripped off his coat and hung it up. Tim gave Patricia an unsure look. His wife returned the wary gaze. That eased him a bit, knowing he wasn't alone.

Adelaide sat on the couch with JJ in her lap. "You can set the cookies on the table, peaches," she told Misha. The strawberry blonde nodded, sparing another glance at the others before going back into the kitchen.

"Peaches?" Cathy sat, "never heard you call a girl that."

Adelaide tried to not show her embarrassment. She laughed it off. "Well, Misha doesn't like 'baby'. You know I don't call people things they don't like. Besides, look at her hair. It's peachy!" She stood JJ on her lap. The little boy smiled and began jumping. "Such a big boy!" Adelaide cheered. "Let's get this coat off, sweet heart," she cooed.

Patricia smiled. She noticed that Adelaide had placed the gate on the fireplace. Trinkets that JJ could have grabbed were now on higher shelves. It was a small thing to do, a consideration, but it meant everything. Patricia sat by her Mama A. JJ was overjoyed. He was normally shyer. He was a sweet little boy that stole her heart and her sleep. "Do you ever regret not having kids, mama?" Patricia asked. The woman had never had a man in her life. Too preoccupied raising other people's kids to have her own. Patricia thought it was so sad.

    Adelaide paused bouncing the little boy on her knees. JJ didn't seem to mind. He still giggled. Adelaide looked at him. Those big blue eyes were alight with amusement. She went quiet and thought. Did she regret it? Adelaide thought about went into making and having a baby. No. No, she didn't regret it.

    "Adelaide does have children," Misha declared. She set the plate of cookies on the coffee table. The adults were all looking at her in confusion. "Did she not care for you?" Misha looked between the three women. "Do you not see her as a motherly figure in your lives? An addition or even a replacement?" She looked at Adelaide, "She may not have given birth, but she is most certainly a mother." Misha gestured to the photos on the mantle. "A mother to many," she sat on the other side of Adelaide. Misha looked at the little boy. "He is plump, that is good. Skinny ones do not survive winter." She cooed and rubbed one of JJ's chubby cheeks with her finger. The baby giggled and reached out to her. "May I?" she asked Patricia.

Patricia nodded dumbly. Too stunned to deny the girl. When the stranger walked past, she smelled like Adelaide's perfume. It was strange. Mama A rarely shared it with others. Patricia supposed it was for the occasion. She watched as the strawberry blonde gently took her son. The woman at least knew how to handle a baby.

"You are very warm," Misha told the boy. There was none of the high pitched tone most took when talking to children. She began to bounce the boy again. "Your legs are strong. You will be walking soon." Misha looked at Patricia, "You should prepare, he will run soon as well."

Patricia chuckled, "Oh lord." She looked at Tim. "You ready?" she teased. Tim shrugged and tried to not snatch his son from the strange woman's grasp.

Cathy and Joyce watched the woman play with the baby and relaxed. She seemed more human and warm now. "What are you studying?" Cathy asked.

Misha thought for a moment. "I like technology. Adelaide helped me dissect the television. I enjoyed the wires." She looked at the two women. "What degree encompasses that?"

Joyce laughed, "Lord, another Kelsey!"

Patricia and Cathy laughed as well.

Misha pursed her lips and looked at Adelaide. The taller woman was also laughing. "Who is this Kelsey?"

Adelaide explained, "She works at NASA now. She loved taking things apart and figuring out how they worked."

"She helped make the spaceship that landed on the moon," Joyce said. "What was that one?"

"Apollo 11," Adelaide said.

Cathy giggled, "You're so smart, mama. You should go to school."

Patricia nodded, "You should! You could be a professor. I wouldn't have been able to pass without you." She told Misha. "If you ever need help studying, ask her. She's a wiz!"

Misha raised an eyebrow, "What is a wiz?" She looked at Adelaide.

The taller woman explained, "A wiz, like a wizard. It means that you're so good at something that it's practically magic."

Misha nodded. She looked at JJ. "You will be a wiz at walking." Everyone, including JJ, laughed. She stood the boy up again. "Now, we bounce, little stranger." JJ giggled and began jumping again with Misha's help. "Very good."

Adelaide watched the blonde with JJ. The little boy was enchanted by Misha. The woman in turn had such a gentle authority about her. It warmed Adelaide's heart.

Tim sighed in relief and placed his head on Patricia's shoulder. Cathy and Joyce began chatting with Adelaide. JJ continued his giggles. Gingerbread was eaten and drinks were drunk. It was a lovely night and the fire crackled.

Christmas was settling in.

Vladan looked at the box. The hotel in town wasn't as grand as the others he'd stayed in before, but it would suffice. It was a strange machine that gave food for money. He did not need it, but it was fascinating and kept his mind off his pearl. The chill in the air caused some frost to form on the glass. Vladan scraped it off with his claw. Winter was so alive now, it used to bring a deathly quiet. Now, the world continued its lively hum in spite of the cold. Vladan did not care for humanity, but even he had to respect their ingenuity.

"It stuck?" a voice asked. Tim noticed the man's stillness. He wondered if the guy was on something. Tim tried to cut through the oddity with levity. "Hotel ones have a tendency to do that," he chuckled. "Money racket, some say."

Vladan looked at the man. His blood was tantalizing, but Vladan wanted to familiarize himself more with this strange town before eating. If he was lucky, Margosha already had some morsels waiting for him. The girl had always struggled with solitude, she never took to it. Maybe ripping apart her latest lover or friends would get it through to her that he was all she needed. Vladan had thought eating her children would have made the point clear, but his pearl was headstrong. She had run across the ocean to try and get away from him. Vladan huffed. Did the foolish girl not realize they were tied? When her eyes opened, so did his. "No, I am just deciding," he said, finally answering the man.

Tim chuckled, "You're the second person I've met today with that accent." It was strange to hear it so close in such a southern town. "Mind if I get something?" he asked the stranger.

Vladan stepped back. "I am the second?" This man's mind was preoccupied with his offspring. Vladan mused. He hadn't had an infant in a while. They drew too much attention to consume regularly, but their blood was so sweet.

Tim nodded. "Yeah, my wife's old house mother has a new girl with your accent." He put some quarters into the machine and typed in B4. The candy bar fell into the trap below. He squatted down to get it. When he stood up, the strange man was terrifyingly close. "Uh?"

"What was this girl's name?"

Tim tilted his head. What was her name? He'd been so scared of her holding his son that he hadn't paid that much attention. Didn't help that he was bad at names. All he could remember was the nickname Adelaide gave her. "They called her peaches."

Vladan's mouth twisted, "Peaches?"

Tim nodded. "I wasn't really listening to why."

Vladan huffed. "I see. Thank you." He turned and left the hall.

Tim took a sigh of relief. He hadn't realized he'd been holding his breath. The man had been so close. Tim realized, to his shock, the man hadn't had a single pore on his skin. Tim tried not to dwell on it. Maybe fear just blurred his vision. The father opened his candy bar and quickly walked back to his hotel room. He felt like he'd stared death in the face twice in one day.

Adelaide groaned as she looked over the forms. Paperwork was the worst. Most of the questions had to be filled in with lies. Misha didn't even remember her parents' names. Of course she also didn't have an address. Adelaide just wrote that she was from the Soviet Union. It was easier to paint Misha as an escapee that came with the clothes on her back in order to obtain the American dream. It wasn't a complete lie.

Adelaide groaned and leaned back against her headboard. The glasses perched on her nose were large and round. She only needed them when she read for long periods. Otherwise, she got a splitting headache. The papers were scattered on her sheets. Adelaide nibbled at her pen. The clipboard she was using was perched on her thigh. Adelaide sighed and rested her head back. She bit her lip, the stretch of her neck caused the bite Misha left to ache. The memory of Misha's lips. The kisses. The fangs. It was mostly healed now, but the ache remained. Adelaide touched the two marks. "Fuck," she hissed as she pressed down.

A spark of arousal went through her. It was a fiery heat that started in her stomach and spread through her entire body. Adelaide didn't know what was wrong with her. Why was she so riled up? Was it from earlier? The shower stopped and Adelaide looked at the closed bathroom door. The visit had been nice, but Adelaide was happy to be alone with Misha again. Especially now.

When was the last time she'd taken care of herself? Not since finding Misha. Two weeks? Adelaide whined. God, she needed to calm down. Adelaide wiggled her hips. The friction both eased her aching and made it worse. She sighed and rubbed her face, trying to quell her arousal. Why did it have to hit now?

Her pants were getting wet. "Jesus christ," she gasped. Adelaide stood and began to pace around her room. What had set her off? Was it kissing in the kitchen? Was it seeing Misha act so well with JJ? Was it Misha's smiles across the dinner table? Was it just Misha?

It was probably just Misha.

Adelaide organized the papers, hoping to distract herself. It wasn't helping. She kneeled on the bed, squeezing her thighs together. Adelaide sighed and bounced a bit on the mattress. "Knock it off," she scolded herself. When was the last time she'd felt so ravenously horny? Her cheeks were burning. Her palms were sweaty. Adelaide wondered if she should leave and escape to the unused room down the hall and take care of herself.

That would probably be for the best. Yes, Misha loved Adelaide but loving someone didn't mean you wanted to fuck them. God, would Misha recoil at the sight of her naked. Adelaide tried to push her insecurities away. No, Misha had seen her naked, more than once now. Still. Adelaide set the papers on the nightstand to be safe and tried to think of an excuse to leave for thirty minutes to fix herself.

Misha threw open the bathroom door. It slammed into the wall and made Adelaide jump in shock. Before the woman could speak, Misha pounced. She moved as fast as lightning to drag the taller woman down onto the bed.

Adelaide yelped when her back hit the mattress. She was laying width wise, her hair was hanging off the edge.

Glasses askew, Adelaide looked up at Misha. The vampire looked crazed. Adelaide felt herself get wetter. Jesus, what was wrong with her? Adelaide wiggled her hips again. She felt like a teenager. Hot and bothered with no immediate cause, just randomly horny. She would have been more embarrassed if Misha didn't look like she wanted to eat her alive.

Misha had her hands on Adelaide's thighs. The woman's legs were still closed, but Misha looked like she wanted to pry them open. Those pale hands were shaking with restraint. Misha's nails were clipped down, no longer the claws she normally had. Even though they were trimmed, she still dug them into Adelaide's thighs. The slight pain was titilating. Her clit pulsed with excitement. Oh, god. Adelaide whimpered, "Misha."

"You are doing it on purpose," the blonde hissed. Her hips wiggled as well. God, the friction! Misha ran her hands up and down Adelaide's hot thigh. She could hear the blood rushing through them. She could smell the arousal in the air. It was all for her. All for Misha. "You know I can smell you. You know I can hear your mind. You're torturing me, beloved." Misha's hands shook. "Please, please," she mumbled against Adelaide's knee. An animalistic want took over her. Misha rubbed against Adelaide, like a horny dog. Dear lord, this beautiful woman had brought her low. Her base desires howled inside her. "Please, beloved," she whimpered, moving against the woman. The feeling made Misha's eyes roll back. She kissed Adelaide's knee again. "Let me have you, beloved. Let me know you. Let me taste you."

Adelaide shuddered. She spread her legs, Misha immediately settled herself between them. Hands grasped at each other. Adelaide moved to take off her glasses but Misha stopped her.

"Keep them on, please," Misha asked. The spectacles made Adelaide look distinguished. Learned. Which the woman was. Misha had always had a thing for scholars.

Adelaide chuckled, "Okay, peaches." She sat up, planning to throw off her clothes. Thankfully her pajamas were easy to strip off.

Misha helped Adelaide. She practically tore off Adelaide's underwear. Her eagerness made the taller woman laugh again. Thankfully, Misha didn't need to strip. The call of her siren made her race out of the bathroom without clothing. She'd clipped her nails in a blink and prayed that she could use her fingers. Misha was still damp, but she didn't care. She planned on making a mess and getting wetter.

Adelaide gasped when Misha slipped between her thighs again. The blonde's skin was cool. It made Adelaide shiver. Before she could ask Misha for a kiss, the blonde ducked down and latched onto her nipple. "Ah!" Adelaide cried out. Her thighs jumped against Misha's flank. More kisses followed. Teasing fingers groped her chest and rolled her nipples. Adelaide's toes curled, catching the sheets. "Peaches!" Adelaide cried. "Please." Misha's mouth was on her in a flash. Adelaide gasped, giving Misha an opening to deepen the kiss. She buried her hands in the blonde's hair. Teeth and tongue. It wasn't conquering, but consumption. Their bodies moved against each other. The undulations caused them both to moan. "I love you," she whispered against the blonde's lips.

Misha gasped. Tears pricking her eyes. She took an unneeded breath. "Oh, beloved." She moved, kissing along Adelaide's jaw and down her neck. "May I?" she asked. Her last bite was still healing. Misha licked it. The faint taste of blood was there. Her fangs scraped against Adelaide's skin. Not piercing, just teasing.

Adelaide nodded. "Anything you want, peaches. Anything."

Misha debated. Where to bite? Where to start? Her sinful mouth trailed down Adelaide's stomach. She couldn't resist nibbling on the fat she found there. Misha traced her tongue over the adorable little lines on Adelaide's skin. Stretch marks? Was that the name? She nuzzled against the soft tissue. Misha shuddered, grinding against the sheets. She couldn't remember the last time she'd felt so excited to have someone. Misha began to cover Adelaide's hips and thighs with hickies. "My beautiful girl." The rush of blood under Adelaide's umber skin made Misha's mouth water. Misha raised Adelaide's thigh. She sank her fangs into the juicy vein hiding inside.

Adelaide gasped. She gripped at the bedding. Fingers and toes tugged at the sheets. "Misha!" she moaned. Adelaide gasped, "Oh god." The feeling of blood being pulled from her was riveting. It was so incomprehensibly hot. "Peaches, Mimi, sweet heart, please!" She needed stimulation. Something on her clit or inside her.

Misha moaned loudly. Her eyes rolled back. The ambrosia from Adelaide's veins burned her throat. It heated her core and pumped through her heart. Misha pulled away.

She gasped and panted. Blood trailed down her chin, she licked it up. She whimpered, "Beloved. Beloved."

Adelaide reached up and pulled the woman to her. "Come here, peaches." She kissed the woman's forehead then her bloody lips. An iron kiss that made her head spin. Misha's cool fingers slipped down her body. Over her chest, stomach, and finally between her legs. Adelaide hissed as a cool fingertip circled her clit. She gasped, "I haven't-" Adelaide hadn't fucked in decades. She wanted to warn the woman she'd be rusty, at best.

"I know," Misha answered. She shuddered as hot slick covered her fingers. "So wet for me, beloved. I have barely begun," Misha teased. She kissed along Adelaide's neck, smearing blood along the way. Her first bite hadn't fully healed. The idea of reopening it was intoxicating. Misha slipped a finger into Adelaide. The woman jumped. "My pretty girl," Misha purred, "so sensitive for me." She used the heel of her palm to stimulate that little bundle of nerves that made Adelaide moan. When was the last time she'd had the pleasure of making a gorgeous woman arch her back? It didn't matter. Now, she had Adelaide. A beauty that could rival Aphrodite. An angel. Misha nibbled on the other woman's ear. "My love. My beauty. More?" She quickened her finger, curling it, making the woman below her jump. Misha smiled when she found the spot inside of Adelaide that made the woman scream in pleasure. The vampire's finger made sure to stimulate the spot until the woman was incoherent.

    Adelaide gasped and squirmed against the bed sheets. Her thighs spread wider. Little punched out moaned left her as she tried to move with Misha. Thighs tensed then relaxed and tensed again. "Fuck," she gasped, "Misha. Mimi-"

    Misha growled, "I love that." She kissed Adelaide. A feral thing with teeth and tongue. A sharp bite to her lip made Misha shudder. "Your little names for me," she moaned.

    Adelaide moved her leg, placing it between Misha's pale thighs. She managed to wrangle her hand from the sheets and laid it on the small of the smaller woman's back. Misha was on her thigh. The blonde began to rock against it. Little gasps left her pink lips. Adelaide wanted more of those noises. More. Louder. Adelaide shot up, teeth finding Misha's neck. The blonde quaked, chin falling on Adelaide's shoulder. Misha's finger left her then came back with a friend.

Adelaide's breath hitched as the two fingers stimulated the sensitive parts inside her. Her head lolled back. Her hand pressed down on Misha's back. She tried to move her leg back and forth. The blonde let out little moans against her skin. Those nimble fingers sped up. Thrusting deeper into her. The soft heel of her palm pressed harder against Adelaide's clit. It was ecstasy. Adelaide let out a scream. Her legs shook. "Fuck, Misha!" She reached lower and grabbed a handful of the blonde's ass.

Misha chuckled, kissing Adelaide's clavicle. The warm hand was trying to get her to move. She rolled her hips, rocking against the thigh between her legs. Misha bit her lip. A small bead of blood formed. "Lover." She grabbed a handful of Adelaide's curls. Those silky strands were framing the woman's face like a black halo. Misha licked up her own blood, leaving it on her tongue. She offered it to Adelaide. Those coal black eyes stared into hers. They were filled with such a heat that Misha could feel it in her bones.

Adelaide sucked in a breath through clenched teeth. She slipped the hand on Misha's back down to the vampire's thighs. The blonde began to pant over her. Adelaide leaned up, licking the blood off of Misha's tongue. She then captured those pink lips in another searing kiss. The blood made her shudder. The high creeped in. It was like cracking a popper. "Fuck, fuck!" She moaned and shuddered around Misha's fingers. Her orgasm hit her like a freight train. Misha wasn't stopping her fingers and Adelaide didn't want her too. Overstimulation passed quickly and the build up began again. "Mimi, Misha!"

    The vampire purred. Adelaide coming onto her fingers was unlike anything she'd felt before. She redoubled her efforts, making Adelaide moan into her mouth. How many times could she make Adelaide fall apart? Misha gasped. Her eyes rolled back as scorching hot fingers found their way inside her. Misha barely needed any stimulation. She was already on the edge and Adelaide was about to throw her off. Misha pulled back, sitting up. "Another!" she demanded. Adelaide didn't hesitate to comply.

    Misha began to ride those lovely fingers. They were bigger than her own and so hot. So very hot. Misha mewled, she pulled her fingers out of Adelaide. Too afraid that she may accidentally hurt the woman in her own throes of pleasure. Misha grabbed Adelaide's thumb, guiding it to her clit. "Circles, circles," she instructed. Adelaide listened. She always listened. Misha moaned, "Press harder, beloved." Without hesitation, Adelaide complied. The wet noises coming from Misha's cunt made her ears burn. "Yes!" Misha cried. Her thighs began to shake. The twitch in them was rhythmic.

Adelaide gasped. Just watching Misha was enough to make her wetter. "Mimi," she tried to move her fingers the same way Misha did. The blonde's back arched beautifully. "Prettiest little peach," Adelaide moaned. "You almost there?"

Misha nodded. She felt like an animal. Bouncing on Adelaide's fingers and needlessly panting. "Beloved. Beloved. Beloved!" she cried, "Adelaide!" Misha shuddered. She grabbed the woman's wrist. Using the poor girl for her own pleasure. "Oh god!" Misha wailed. She jumped and shook, cumming for the first time in centuries. Bloody tears rolled down her face. She felt reborn. Resurrected. The high after the fall was so intoxicating.

Adelaide bit her lip. She reached her unoccupied hand down to her dripping cunt. This part was familiar. She focused on Misha's blushing face. Those soft pants that echoed off the walls. The grip Misha's hand on her wrist. Adelaide's toes curled in the sheets. She was close.

Misha noticed Adelaide's hand. She hissed and moved off the other woman's leg.

Adelaide squeaked as Misha grabbed her ankles. They were thrown over the vampire's shoulders. Adelaide sat up on her elbows. "Misha?" The vampire licked a stripe up her pussy. Those crimson lips wrapped around her clit and sucked. Adelaide screamed. Her body jerked. She tangled her hands in Misha's hair, gripping it like a vice. Her mind went blank, head falling back in ecstasy. "Misha!" she cried out. The vampire kept sucking her clit. Fingers slipped back inside of her. They were plunging deeper now, faster too.

Adelaide's hips jumped and bucked. Her legs were around the blonde's head, squeezing, humping. Adelaide used her hold on the blonde's hair to press the vampire closer. She was riding Misha's face. Adelaide managed to look down her body and saw green eyes staring back. They were dark. Heady. Wanting. They looked like they were fighting the urge to roll back into Misha's skull.

Tears beaded in Adelaide's eyes. "Misha. Peaches. Mimi!" Her thighs squeezed harder. They jumped, tightened, flexed, shook. Adelaide screamed. Another orgasm rocked through her. This one hit harder than the last.

Her toes curled and her back bowed. The grip she had on Misha's hair must have been painful. It would have been painful to a human. Misha probably would have suffocated, had she been mortal. Thank god Misha was a vampire. Adelaide's vision went fuzzy. Her legs fell open, sore and exhausted.

Adelaide felt fangs puncturing her thigh again. The pull of her blood caused a shiver to run down her spine. Adelaide sighed. Her body melted against the sheets. Muscles relaxed. Darkness crept around the edges of her vision. She passed out as her lover drank.

The soft sloshing of water was hypnotic. The mirror was fogged. The fan was left off. The low light of the candles gave the bathroom a golden glow. Pomegranate and honey floated through the air. A tart sweetness.

Misha used the strange mesh ball to spread the soap along Adelaide's back. Figure 8's then ups and downs. The mesh left Adelaide's skin soft. Misha cupped some water and washed the suds away. She kissed the freckles on Adelaide's shoulder. The woman's dark skin looked ethereal in the candle light. Misha then settled back against the edge of the tub. She gently took Adelaide's shoulders and pulled her. "Come here, beloved," Misha encouraged, "lay against me."

Adelaide sighed and let herself be led against Misha's chest. She moaned. The bath was hot. She was already tired and Misha's ministrations weren't helping. Adelaide couldn't remember the last time a bath had left her so boneless. "Want me to wash you?" she asked sleepily. Misha's hands were running along her body. Those talented fingers were finding every sore spot and soothing them.

Misha kissed Adelaide's cheek. "No, my love," she nipped at the woman's neck with her blunt teeth, "This is about you." The strands of gray in Adelaide's curls looked silver under the low light. They glittered. Misha couldn't remember the last time she'd been so satisfied after sex. It was no use to think of those that came before. Most were dead or better left forgotten. A hole had been in her chest and it finally felt full. Her heart had been ripped out and it was finally back.

Adelaide mewled. She was going to turn into a pile of goo. The draw to sleep in the warm water was intoxicating. Adelaide blinked her eyes rapidly. "Okay." She sat up, water shifting and falling. "We need to get out," she informed, "Otherwise I'm gonna pass out again."

Misha pouted. "I can carry you to bed, beloved." She wanted to stay in this strange space where time slowed. They had their own sweet smelling world in here. The lights were low and the water was warm. But, if her beloved wanted to leave, she would follow. The vampire helped Adelaide stand. The woman's legs were still weak. Something that Misha took great pride in. Misha grabbed the towel hanging from the wall and wrapped it around her love. "Careful, beloved," Misha warned, helping Adelaide over the edge of the tub. The idea of the taller woman falling made her blood run cold.

The taller woman chuckled. "I ain't that old, peaches," she teased. Adelaide stepped onto the bathmat. She grabbed another towel and wrapped it around Misha in turn. "Come on you," Adelaide guided the shorter woman into the bedroom. The heater kicked on and Adelaide jumped. She looked at the blonde, who was smiling slyly. "My girlfriend is Carrie White," Adelaide chuckled and began drying herself off.

Misha frowned. The title made her stomach twist. "I am not your girl friend." Had their love making meant nothing? It wouldn't have been the first time she'd taken a woman to bed only to have her feelings be belittled as flights of fancy. Still, this stung worse. Adelaide had said she loved her. Misha knew the woman meant it too. It wasn't just the winds of passion. Friends weren't lovers. The title was demeaning. Misha crossed her arms and sat on the edge of the bed. Tears pricked her eyes. An ache bloomed in her chest.

Adelaide frowned, "What do you mean?" She took her hair down from the messy bun she had it in. Did Misha not want her? Did she regret everything?

Misha huffed. She tossed the towel into the hamper. "We are not just friends, beloved. Do not use such a flippant term as 'friend'." The blonde crawled into the bed, preferring to sleep in the nude. She was hurt, but she couldn't bring herself to leave. Adelaide's purple sheets. They were silky and felt wonderfully on her skin.

Misha smashed her face into the satin pillows. The scent of their love making lingered. It made the sting worse. She wanted to sulk. An awful, pathetic part of her knew that she wouldn't be able to stay angry at the disrespect. Misha knew she'd roll over eventually. She couldn't help it. Adelaide was kind to her. Far better than the others. Adelaide wasn't selfish in bed. Adelaide wasn't intentionally cruel. Adelaide could call her anything she wished. It hurt, but Misha would swallow her angst after a pout. Misha at least now knew Adelaide wasn't one to scream when Misha voiced her displeasure. A warm hand touched her shoulder.

"Misha," Adelaide started gently. She laid on her stomach. There was a space between them, an arm's length. Enough to not be suffocating but not too distant. "Peaches, girlfriend isn't the same as a girl who's a friend."

Misha turned her head, squinting at the woman. "What? They are the same words!" She sat up on her elbows. "Do not deceive me!"

Adelaide sighed. "Misha, peaches. It can mean that, but it also means a girl you're seeing. A girl who you love and want to marry someday. I meant you're my lover." She slipped her hand off of Misha's cool shoulder and let it fall to the bed. "If you still want to be," Adelaide whispered, newly insecure.

Misha frowned. She squeezed the pillow under her. "I am sorry." Misha took Adelaide's hand. Those coal eyes were glassy. Filled with tears. Misha felt awful. What a demon she was, in an angel's guise. The purest being she'd ever met was in tears because of her. Again. "I am sorry, beloved," Misha scooted closer. "I am cruel-"

Adelaide chuckled, one of her tears escaping. "You're not cruel, Misha. You just misunderstood. All our brain chemicals are out of whack because we had good sex. Being hormonal is normal. It's fine. We talked about it. You understand now, right?" The blonde nodded. "Good. You still want to do this?" Adelaide asked, pointing back and forth between them. Misha nodded eagerly. Adelaide smiled, "Okay then." She pulled Misha closer. "Can I kiss you?" Misha smiled, nodding again. She pulled the blonde into a kiss. It was a chaste thing. Simple. It was something to bring them both back to center.

Misha was bewildered by how easy it all was. There obviously had to be more. That couldn't be the end of it. "What do you want me to do?" she asked the woman. Adelaide seemed confused. "How do I amend this?"

Adelaide blinked owlishly at the blonde. "Peaches, there's nothing to amend. We talked about it. I'm not mad. Are you?" Misha shook her head. Adelaide relaxed. She kissed Misha's forehead. "Okay then." Adelaide lifted up the blankets and pulled them over them. "Let's get some sleep."

Misha's mouth twitched downward. She whimpered. It was a sound she hadn't meant to let slip. She was normally better at hiding distress, but Adelaide made all of her masks fall. "You are not mad?"

Adelaide frowned. "Peaches," she kissed the woman. "I'm not mad. We're okay." She wrapped her arms around the blonde. "Do you wanna go to the Christmas parade tomorrow?"

Misha melted against the other woman. She nuzzled into Adelaide's chest. The rhythmic pace of Adelaide's heart was like a lullaby. A steady thump. Thump. Thump. Misha wanted to bury herself next to it. Keep it beating for eternity. "I am short," she mumbled into the woman's soft skin. "We will need a high point to see."

Adelaide slyly suggested, "Maybe I could put you on my shoulders." She felt Misha's laugh against her skin. It was the best feeling in the world.

Chapter 9

The Christmas lights reflected beautifully in Misha's eyes. It was a hypnotic sight. Adelaide held the strawberry blonde's hand as they stood in the cold. They'd been out for over an hour. They walked to house after decorated house. Misha would stare at the intricate displays for five minutes. Those green eyes took in every adornment before moving next door.

They were at the end of the neighborhood. Adelaide had let the vampire take it all in. The blonde was obviously having a good time, in her own strange way. "I love you," Adelaide whispered. She hadn't meant to say it out loud but it was worth it. Misha's face made it worth it. For the first time in a while, Misha gave Adelaide her full attention. The Christmas lights made the vampire glow. She looked heavenly.

"I love you too," Misha said slowly. She hooked her finger around Adelaide's belt loop and tugged the woman closer. "My beautiful girl." Misha smiled mischievously. She pressed her body against Adelaide's. More blood rushed to the woman's face. Misha wanted to kiss those burning cheeks.

Adelaide shivered, only slightly from the cold. "We should head back." She didn't move though. Misha pressed against her. Adelaide bit her lip and looked at the houses around them. Most of the windows were dark. Adelaide had waited for the dead of night to come out for this reason. Misha wanted to flaunt them. More than anything, Adelaide wanted to give that to her. They couldn't have the day, the sun scrutinized and scorned. The night was kinder, it both hid and freed. The moon lovingly embraced them. It allowed them to steal kisses and interlock their fingers.

"Beloved."

Adelaide looked down at the woman. Those green eyes had gone dark again. Hungry. That was the word to describe the look. It was hunger. Adelaide met Misha halfway. The pair shared a kiss. Probably one of the most scenic kisses that could be had in a small town. The Christmas lights gave the world a dream-like quality. Fuzzy and shimmering. It was like a movie. By some miracle, Adelaide had gotten the girl and her happy ending. It was a fairytale. Between kisses, Adelaide's hot breath crystalized in the air. Not a puff came from Misha. Adelaide knew Misha's nature, but she still got surprised by every reminder.

Misha deepened the kiss. Chasing Adelaide's tongue with hers. Gripping the woman's soft body. "Mine," she mumbled against the plush, warm lips.

"Yours," Adelaide bit Misha's bottom lip. "All yours, peaches." It was embarrassing how easily they fell into making out like teenagers. On the sidewalk of a neighborhood no less! At least most kids had a car to hide in and fog up the windows of. Oh, that was an idea. Car rides and kissing. Could Adelaide convince Misha to have sex in the back seat?

"Hey!" A man from across the street called out. "Get a room, you crazy kids!" He couldn't make out the necking forms, but he knew a couple kissing when he saw one.

Adelaide's eyes widened in shock. She tugged her beanie down tighter. Hopefully the man assumed she was a man. Just two college kids enjoying the lights, not an old woman and her vampire lover who couldn't keep their hands off each other. Misha grumbled something in a language Adelaide didn't know. "Come on!" Adelaide tugged Misha out of the neighborhood. The pair took off down the street. They were giggling like newlyweds.

After a block, they slowed down. Misha huffed. It was a crime that they were unable to savor their kiss. Granted, Adelaide said she had some lights at home. Maybe they could string them up in Adelaide's bedroom. They could kiss for as long as they wanted there. Still, the interruption was rude. "You should have let me eat him," Misha casually said.

Adelaide chuckled. It shouldn't have been funny. It should have terrified her. It didn't though. Misha was a monster, but she was Adelaide's little monster. "He doesn't deserve that just for being a prude."

Misha rolled her eyes. She tucked herself against Adelaide's side. "I have killed for less."

Adelaide frowned, "You should be more discerning." She kissed the top of Misha's head. "We can kiss more at home." Misha nuzzled against her, stealing Adelaide's warmth. It was worth it. It always was.

The pair walked down the block. Music pounded from one of the fraternity houses. A little blue house. Shit. Adelaide grimaced. Lord, help her.

"HEY! THAT YOU MAMA?!" one of the boys screamed from the porch. The boy's hair was shaggy, brown. A crooked smile and freckles. "Hey mama's dog!" the boy laughed, targeting Misha. "Taking her for a walk, mama?" one of his friends asked.

Adelaide glared at them. "You need to learn some manners!" The boys jumped. She rarely raised her voice. Their shock quickly morphed into defiance.

One of the boys giggled, "You gonna teach us a lesson?"

"Yeah, mama, come here and spank us!" Another teased.

"Guys, leave them alone," one of the boys groaned. He looked at the pair. "Sorry, they're drunk!" the boy excused.

"Aw, come on, Jamie. She's hot in an exotic way," the brunet laughed.

"Even the little ruskie is cute," the other boy chugged his beer.

"Got to be careful though, might go missing like Tony," the brunet snickered and the other boy joined in.

Jamie sighed, "You guys are pigs." He looked at the pair. The redhead looked pissed. Adelaide just looked disappointed. The same looked he'd seen on his own mother's face one too many times. "Have a good night!" he waved to them, hoping that his frat brothers hadn't ruined the girls' entire night.

Misha huffed, tugging Adelaide along.

"Be safe!" Adelaide called back. She'd recognized the corralling boy. He'd been the one from the night Adelaide met Misha. One of the rare boys who scolded his fraternity brothers. It warmed her heart. Maybe Tony's awful influence was fading.

Adelaide frowned. She should have felt worse. She should have felt guilty about Tony being dead. She felt nothing. Adelaide hated to admit that she was relieved. Was she a bad person? Probably. Definitely. Adelaide never claimed to be saintly. If she had the power Misha did, she'd probably swat a few pests too. God, that was awful. Adelaide shook her dark thoughts away. Misha and her fell back into a walking pattern. "Boys," she sighed, just to fill the silence. Misha gripped her arm tighter. "Peaches?"

Misha bit her lip. "I hate them. I want to kill them all." It was a childish rage, but she couldn't shake it. Their lecherous eyes and snide remarks. Oh how she wanted to drain them, like she had the boy who'd dare try and woo Adelaide with a cheap bottle of champagne.

That made Adelaide pause. "Misha, they're just dumb kids," she wrapped an arm around the blonde's shoulders. Adelaide explained, "It's always been like this. They come and go. Some even come back and apologize for being a little shit."

Misha tasted bile in her mouth. Adelaide was too forgiving. Too kind. "I do not accept the apologies of cockroaches."

Adelaide's eyes widened in shock. She abruptly laughed. Misha's mean streak was always striking to witness. Adelaide wished she had that fire. Their pale yellow house came into view. She led the other woman inside. They took off their coats and hung them by the door. Misha still seemed miffed. That wouldn't do. Adelaide decided to distract the woman. "What do you want for Christmas?" she asked.

The blonde paused her pouting. "What do you mean?"

Adelaide shrugged, "Well, you get people you love presents for Christmas." She made her way up the steps. Misha was behind her. Adelaide bit back her smile. "Is there a gadget you want to dissect or something you want me to make? I know it's only a few days away but…" She entered her room and started to peel off her clothes. "Maybe a new dress for the spring or-"

"Sit on my face!" Misha blurted out. Embarrassment flooded her. If she had fed, her cheeks would have been scarlet. Speaking of feeding, she'd need to eat soon.

Adelaide burst into laughter. She was kicking off her pants and fell over. Thankfully the bed was there to catch her. Leave it to Misha to knock her off balance. Adelaide laughed uproariously. She managed to detangle her legs from her bell bottoms and sit up on the bed. "Okay!" she snickered, "Anything else?"

"I want Christmas lights in the bedroom!" Misha added. She quickly shucked off her own clothes. Adelaide's mirth was infectious. She giggled as she placed her clothes in the hamper.

Adelaide nodded. "Okay." She scooted up the bed to sit against the headboard. "Anything else, love?" Adelaide stretched her legs. They were sore from walking around town. Her toes were cold. She tried to wiggle more blood flow into them.

Misha pursed her lips. Adelaide's discomfort would not be tolerated. With a look, the heater kicked on. Its rumble filled the room. She crawled onto the bed. "No. That is all." Misha sat next to Adelaide. The woman hissed when their thighs touched. The blonde frowned. Was she that cold?

"You're freezing, peaches!" Adelaide tugged the blankets up. Misha was practically a block of ice. Normally Misha was room temperature. Had the cold really affected her so much? Adelaide noticed Misha had bags forming under her eyes. It reminded the woman of when she and the vampire first met. After Misha was buried for two hundred years…Realization dawned on Adelaide. The vampire hadn't drank from her in a few days. "Misha," Adelaide started slowly. She laid a hand on the blonde's thigh. Who in turn melted against her heat.

"Yes, beloved?" Misha asked. She laid her cheek against the headboard. Adelaide's face was twisted in concern. Misha frowned. What could possibly be plaguing her love?

"When did you last eat?"

Green eyes widened in shock. Misha's lips parted then closed. There wasn't a satisfying answer to that question. Atleast, not one Adelaide would take. She shut her mouth. Adelaide sighed. Not a frustrated sigh, nor a condescending sigh. It was a warm sigh. One you would give to a fool you adored.

"Okay," Adelaide crawled away from the headboard and sat on the edge of the bed. She lifted her hair up and snatched her bonnet from the bedpost. She tucked her curls into it. Her hair being out of the way would make everything easier. Adelaide looked back at Misha. Those green eyes were glittering in the warm light of the heater. "Well, come get your supper, peaches." Adelaide tapped the side of her neck.

Misha gripped the sheets, her nails making a harsh sound against the fabric. "Beloved," she tried to warn, but Adelaide wasn't having it.

"Misha," the taller woman said firmly. "Come eat."

The blonde bit her lip. She crawled to the woman. Her mouth watered. The smell of Adelaide, the blood in her veins. Misha deeply inhaled. Her eyes rolled back, fluttering in ecstasy. The blonde opened her mouth. Fangs elongated and itched to bite. Adelaide tilted her head to the side, giving Misha more space. It was an open invitation. An offering.

Adelaide whimpered as she was bitten. It reminded her of getting vaccines. Then a wave of bliss washed over her. The pain faded into a lovely ache. Adelaide's head rolled back. Her lips parted and she gasped. Misha moaned against her skin. Adelaide swore she could feel the vampire's fangs vibrate inside her. The feeling of her blood being pulled from her veins was exhilarating. Adelaide's thighs spread unconsciously. A dizziness was setting in and left her feeling high.

Misha felt Adelaide's body going more and more lax. She forced herself to pull away.

Her fangs retracted. A bite to her own tongue and a lick healed the puncture wounds. Adelaide sighed in ecstasy. The taller woman was practically putty in her hands. Misha inhaled deeply, smelling the hormones in the air. The blonde slipped a hand down Adelaide's warm shoulder, over her breast, and down her stomach. "Beloved?" she touched the waistband of Adelaide's panties. They were a pair Misha had picked out. They were an orange that contrasted beautifully with the woman's dark skin. It truly wasn't fair how gorgeous Adelaide was. It was even more unfair how weak Misha was to her wiles. The vampire began laying kisses along the woman's neck.

    Adelaide blinked the dizziness out of her eyes. Her vision cleared again. The kisses Misha was laying were lovely. Those lips were warm with her blood. Stone-like flesh was now malleable, because of her. Her blood made Misha alive.

    Adelaide moaned. She looked back at Misha. Despite just eating, the vampire looked hungry. The flush was back in the blonde's cheeks. She was warm. Warmed by Adelaide. Oh god. The arousal that swirled within her would have made the little ladies at church faint. Pale fingers were circling the little bow on her underwear. Asking permission. "Fuck it," Adelaide turned and pushed Misha onto the bed. The vampire went down without resistance. In fact, the blonde looked elated! Adelaide threw off her panties. She ducked down to kiss Misha. The vampire giggled against her lips. "My turn," Adelaide whispered, laying a kiss on Misha's throat. The blonde tilted her head to the side. Offering her neck to her beloved.

Misha was accepted.

Adelaide had no doubt she would be. Especially since Misha went into the office and used her strange ways on the people. The pair were in the bookstore. Textbooks Misha needed and also just wanted were piled in a basket. "Peaches, you don't need that." She frowned at the psychology book. Misha was majoring in computer science. It wasn't surprising. Misha was obsessed with technology and especially computers, the 'strange boxes' as she lovingly called them. They'd snuck into the computer lab and Misha had a field day examining everything.

"But I want it," the blonde answered simply. She plucked another book off the shelf. It was an anatomy book. She put it in the basket.

Adelaide shook her head and chuckled. She was weak to Misha's joy. The extra books would only hurt the blonde's bank. Maybe learning about modern day psychology would be helpful for Misha. The woman was socially…not inept, but most definitely lacking in finesse. Maybe Adelaide should get a book too. There had been one she'd been wanting for awhile. "I'm going to look for something," Adelaide announced.

Misha's face brightened at the declaration. "Of course, beloved. Get whatever you wish!" She loved when Adelaide took. The woman so rarely allowed herself to have things she wanted. Too selfless to be healthy, in Misha's opinion.

Adelaide smiled and went off. The bookstore was sparse, thankfully. The sun was shining. Its persistent rays broke through the winter gray that had been covering the town. Some of the snow was melting, but more was forecasted to be on the way. They'd have another white Christmas. Adelaide wondered if Misha's family had celebrated the holiday. Christmas as Adelaide knew it was fairly new in the grand scale of time. Maybe Misha had a tradition she wanted to partake in.

    Adelaide finally found the poetry section. She scanned the rows with squinted eyes. Why did the print have to be so small? There, she found it. Adelaide slipped the black book out and took it in hand. She hadn't read it in over a decade. One of her girls had bought the book back in the 60's. She had been majoring in women's studies and ancient history. Adelaide's heart clenched at the memory. Deep seat guilt and grief filled her.

    Barbara had confessed to Adelaide she was queer. It wasn't the first time someone had come out to Adelaide and it most likely wouldn't be the last. Oh, Barbara. The name itself made Adelaide want to weep. The poor girl hadn't survived her first Christmas home. She'd found herself at college and that self wasn't one her family would accept.

    Adelaide had read some of the poems with Barbara. The pair would sigh wistfully and giggle at the innuendos. Adelaide would always remember the call. Barbara's mother blamed her. Barbara's father threatened to sue. Neither were in their right minds at the time. They did try to sue the college, claiming it had turned their daughter 'sinful'. They said their little girl's head was filled with nonsense from the book. Barbara had written her suicide note in the cover. Adelaide wished she had snatched it. Barbara's parents had burned it after the funeral. Adelaide looked down at the book. Her eyes reflected the cover.

<u>Poems by Sappho</u> was typed in white on a black background. It was thin and unassuming, much like the other poetry books. Still, holding it in her hands again made Adelaide want to weep. Both in pain and in joy. Maybe Misha would read it with her. Did Misha even like poetry? Adelaide wondered, but she'd soon find out. The woman opened the book to a random page. She began to flip through. Even though she hadn't read it in years, she remembered most of the poems.

Adelaide smiled, pressing the book to her breast. A melancholy happiness filled her. More memories flashed in her mind. Barbara had written a note just for Adelaide. Her handwriting was so flowing that it looked like art. Barbara's mother had smashed the letter into Adelaide's chest at the wake. The pain in the woman's eyes was the only reason Adelaide hadn't snapped. Adelaide had waited to get home before reading the note. Barbara had said that the sorority was the only true home she ever had and she loved everyone…and that she was sorry. Tears pricked at Adelaide's eyes. Her grip on the book tightened and made the glossy cover creak.

A surprisingly chipper voice cut through her grief, "Oh, it's you!"

Adelaide sniffled. She wiped her eyes with her sleeve and looked to see a boy. He had brown hair and blue eyes. It was the young man from the night before. The one that was willing to chastise his catcalling friends. "Oh! Hello, baby." Adelaide hated that her voice was unsteady. How embarrassing.

Jamie's cheeks went pink. When was the last time someone had greeted him so warmly? He chuckled, "Jamie. Jamie Alder." The boy noticed the tears in the woman's eyes. "Are you okay?"

Adelaide forced a smile. "Oh yes, yes, I'm sorry." She wiped her face dry. "Just, memories. Have too many. The joys of old age." Adelaide felt ridiculous. Crying in the book store while holding a queer author's poems.

Jamie snorted, "Can't be that old. You look younger than my ma."

Adelaide loved this part. "I'm fifty." The look of shock that spread across the boy's face was priceless. It was the same reaction a five year old had to a twenty year old. Someone being decades older was incomprehensible.

"No way!" Jamie looked the woman up and down. The boys in the frat would talk about Mama A. Jamie had assumed the woman was in her late thirties, mid forties at most. He hadn't been lying when he said Adelaide looked younger than his mother. The woman's black hair only had a handful of silver strands. His mother was fully gray. Granted, he'd never met an older black person before. The few he'd seen, he hadn't asked their age. How old had they been?! "Black really doesn't crack, huh?" he joked, hoping it would cheer the woman up. It did.

Adelaide laughed, "No, it doesn't!" This boy was cute. Cute in a way most boys lost when they went to college. There was still a kindness in him that hadn't curdled into cruelty. It was so refreshing.

Jamie beamed. Her laugh was beautiful. A warm and welcoming sound that felt like a hug. "What book you getting?" he asked, trying to distract from the blush in her cheeks.

Adelaide's eyes went wide. She looked at the book then up at the boy. "Just poetry," she answered, it was true.

Jamie nodded. "I always liked Dickenson. She's got that…quiet melancholy about her." The woman's face didn't turn. There were no pursing lips of distaste or narrowed eyes of judgment. In fact, the woman seemed enraptured. Those big doe eyes sparkled in recognition. Jamie was so used to older people telling him that poetry wasn't worth the paper it was printed on.

Adelaide was surprised. Her body relaxed, shoulders untensed. It'd been so long since she'd had a literary mind to bounce off of. Most of her girls were science focused. Adelaide couldn't help herself. "I felt a Funeral, in my Brain," she recited.

Jamie's eyes went wide. He answered, giddy with acceptance, "And Mourners to and fro." His own mother wouldn't engage with poetry. Too much emotion, she'd say. His father was always furious at his love of literature. They had compromised with Jamie playing baseball. A small sacrifice to be let loose in the library uninterrupted. He continued the poem, "Kept treading - treading - till it seemed."

Adelaide smiled, "That sense was breaking through." The pair stared at each other, before a shared laughter erupted. It was nice.

Jamie felt how warm his face was. Geez, he was a mess. A little poetry and he was puddy in the woman's hands. He needed

224

to get them on another topic. Jamie cleared his throat. "So...All the frats think you ate Tony, black widow style. Did you?"

Adelaide snorted. "If I was a black widow, I would've had to marry him first." She rested her shoulder against the bookcase. The boy chuckled at her answer.

Jamie scratched the back of his head nervously, "Touche." He looked Adelaide up and down. She didn't seem like the killing type. Too kind. Jamie didn't miss Tony. The guy was a prick. Still, someone going missing was a big deal, especially if they lived with you. Jamie hated that he got dragged to the fraternity. He'd come on a sports scholarship and got corralled in with the other baseball kids. The house was always a mess and loud.

Adelaide noticed the boy was in his head. She went on, "I don't know where Tony is. I won't say I'm sad he's gone though. That boy was a damn menace." She looked at the shelves and decided to grab a book of poems by Emily Dickenson. Jamie reminded her how much she adored the woman's work.

Jamie frowned. He'd heard Tony and other boys complaining about Adelaide. How the woman wouldn't fuck them. Jamie thought it was pathetic, especially now. What about the woman made them act like mindless horn dogs? He didn't get it. "Why do they pick on you?" he asked. Maybe Adelaide had fucked a student before and became a legend? Even then, that wouldn't excuse anything, but it would make sense why so many boys were adamant about sleeping with her.

Adelaide paused. What a question. There wasn't an easy answer. "When I was younger," she began, "It was just racism, I think. I was exotic and new. Over time, it turned to fetishism. The older I got, the more taboo. I was the hot mom who never slept with anyone. A prize to be won." Adelaide noticed how bewildered Jamie looked. She finished, "I've been doing this for three decades. It's always been the same. The tone is different, but the roots haven't changed."

Jamie's face fell. "I'm so sorry, Miss Adelaide."

It was sincere. A sincerity Adelaide wasn't used to hearing. "It's not your fault, baby." She smiled gently. "You're a good boy, Jamie." Adelaide gently cupped the boy's cheek. "Thank you for giving me some hope."

Jamie's mouth twitched. A pang in his chest bloomed. God, human decency shouldn't be praised like an act of heroism. Jamie shrugged. "Don't mention it," he tried to say casually, but it came out strained. Adelaide stepped back. Her gentle smile was still there. It was warm like the sun and just as bright. Jamie wanted to hug her.

The woman added, "Also, just Adelaide is fine. No miss required for you, baby."

Jamie felt his heart melt. He chuckled and bit his lip. "Well, don't mention it, Adelaide." God, could he ask her out for coffee? Was that allowed? Was it too cliche? He didn't think it'd be appropriate, but he'd clarify it was just to cheer her up, not a date. Jamie would want to know her longer before asking that. A woman like Adelaide deserved to be wooed and courted. Jamie rubbed his face. God, his cheeks were burning. He'd never been smitten so quickly before.

"Beloved?"

Adelaide looked back, seeing Misha at the end of the book cases. "Oh, there you are, peaches!" Misha looked beautiful in the sunlight. Her strawberry blonde hair gave her a fiery halo. She looked holy. Adelaide knew the vampire didn't like the sun. It would sometimes make her lethargic, but god, Misha looked gorgeous in the light. Ethereal. There was no other word for it.

Adelaide walked to the other woman. The basket at the blonde's hip was practically overflowing. She took some of the books. "Oh, peaches. You're gonna break the basket," Adelaide laughed. She looked to see that Misha was glaring behind her. Jamie was just standing there, staring at Misha. Adelaide knew that look. Knew it too well. She'd seen it on some many men's faces, especially toward Misha. Poor Jamie. Poor, sweet poet Jamie. "Oh, Misha," she pointed to the boy, "this is Jamie." Adelaide looked back, "Jamie, this is Misha!"

Jamie waved awkwardly, taking a couple steps forward. "Hi, there. We saw each other the other night."

Misha sneered. "Yes. One of the disrespectful, rowdy little boys," she spat. The blonde looked up at Adelaide. "I am ready to leave." She lifted the basket.

Jamie frowned. "Here, let me carry those for you. To make up for those assholes."

Misha smiled cruelly. "Of course." She handed the basket over and watched as the boy nearly collapsed under the weight. He grunted, huffing and puffing to keep himself upward and the basket in his arms. "Do you have it?" Misha asked with a too wide smile.

Adelaide frowned. "Misha," she scolded.

The blonde pouted. She snatched the basket from the boy. "We will not need your help, thank you." Misha turned to Adelaide,

"Come, beloved. We will be late for our movie." Misha took Adelaide's hand and guided her through the book cases.

Jamie gasped. Not only was the girl strong, she was also insanely fast! "Hey, I'll see you around?" he called after them.

Adelaide looked back "Of course, baby," she said as she was pulled around the corner.

Jamie smiled. He leaned against the bookcase. He rolled his shoulder, hissing at the ache. The pair had looked so strange in the shadows of the night. Like two stalking monsters. In the sun though, they looked like angels. Beings of warmth and fury. Jamie couldn't wait to see them again.

Misha was strange, probably due to whatever culture she came from, but Adelaide. Oh, Adelaide. What a woman. Jamie wished he'd been born sooner or Adelaide born later. His mother would have a cow if he brought back a black woman, but it would be worth it. The woman was so- Jamie rubbed his face. He felt like Romeo, a lovesick fool.

Once they were out of Jamie's sight and ear shot, Adelaide asked, "Misha, what's wrong?" The vampire was gripping her tight. It wasn't unusual but the rage that seemed to be radiating off the woman was.

Misha stopped in her tracks. She turned and hissed, "That boy wants you." The basket on her arm dropped to the ground with a loud THUNK.

Adelaide looked at the basket, some of the books were now on the ground, then back at the vampire. Misha's face was red with indignation. Adelaide snorted out a laugh. She hadn't meant to, but she couldn't help it. "Misha, he was looking at you."

"No, he wasn't," Misha growled. She stalked forward, backing Adelaide into a shelf. "I can hear his mind, beloved. I *read* his mind." The ones that looked at Adelaide normally saw her as a piece of meat. A conquest to have. Not a person. Not a woman. That boy though. That boy saw her not only as a woman, but a beautiful smart woman. A woman worth marrying, spending a life with. All those things were true of Adelaide, but they were not for the boy to have.

The rage inside of Misha was spilling out into subtle tremors. She wanted to rip his throat out. How dare he fantasize about taking her beloved, noble, kind, beautiful- Misha had to stop herself. She grabbed Adelaide's hips. "He wants you," Misha seethed. Tears pricked her eyes. This new century wasn't fair. It wasn't fair she couldn't flaunt her love. It wasn't fair the foolish boys thought they had a chance.

Adelaide looked around. They were alone among the books. Dust danced in the sunlight. The soft noises of others lost in the aisles seemed far away. Misha was looking up at her with glassy eyes. Adelaide could see the red gathering in the corners. Those bloody tears were ready to spill. It made Adelaide's heart clench. The fear in those green eyes seemed genuine. Did Misha really think a frat boy could hold a candle to her? Did she really think Adelaide would leave her for someone who was still, in so many ways, a child? No, that wouldn't do. Doubt like that wouldn't do at all. She cupped the vampire's face in her hands.

Emerald eyes were glassy and shimmered under the afternoon sun. They were filled with insecurity. Adelaide leaned down and kissed Misha. She tried to pour all of her devotion into it. Misha moaned against her lips. Adelaide kissed her until her neck screamed in agony. When Adelaide pulled back, Misha tried to follow her lips, even standing on her tiptoes. Adelaide giggled, laying another kiss on her forehead. "Too bad for him," Adelaide whispered against the vampire's skin, "I don't like boys."

Misha wrapped her arms around Adelaide's neck. She stared into the woman's eyes. "You enjoyed his company," Misha whispered. She rested her cheek against Adelaide's chest. The woman sighed and Misha felt it against her ear.

Adelaide rubbed the vampire's back. "I can enjoy someone's company and not want to be with them,Misha." She asked, "Do you really think I'd leave you for a child?"

Misha frowned. "He is kind," she whispered. Her nail caught Adelaide's flannel. The boy would be a far better partner. They could be seen together. They could openly share a bed and have a wedding. They could grow old together. All the things Misha could not give.

Adelaide laughed. "Misha, I don't want kind." She turned the woman's face up to look at her. "I want you, peaches. Meanness and all," she teased. Adelaide wiped the escaping bloody tear with her sleeve. "I'm not a good person," Adelaide admitted. "In fact, if I could get away with half the things you do…" Adelaide trailed off. She looked out the window beside them. "People are complicated. We can be as bad as we are good." Adelaide stared back into the vampire's eyes. "You're mean," she started, "and a brat, sometimes. You get really emotional and struggle to communicate." Adelaide gripped the woman tight when Misha tried to pull away. "But," Adelaide began, "You're also sweet and affectionate. You find wonder in the mundane and your curiosity knows no bounds. You're smart and talented and beautiful and I love you, Misha."

The vampire didn't understand. She buried her face in Adelaide's chest. The woman wasn't lying. That was what hurt the most. Adelaide was being completely honest. "How can you love something so broken?" she asked, voice muffled in the fabric of the woman's shirt.

Adelaide chuckled, her own tears forming. "I'm just as broken, Misha. My cracks might be different, but they're still there. You love me in spite of my flaws, why would I not love you the same?"

Misha hiccuped and clutched the woman. She pressed her ear to Adelaide's chest and listened to her heart beat. The woman wasn't lying.

Chapter 10

It was another cold night. The motel offered little in the way of entertainment. In fact, the entire town seemed dormant. Vladan strolled down the empty streets. No matter the era, there'd always be a small town to get lost in. There was a ruckus coming from down the block.

Vladan made out the sounds of cheerful boys. Rowdy. Drunk. They were out late. They were playing in the churchyard. Some were on top of the large vehicles. They took turns jumping into piles of snow. All cheered when one descended. Humans were still humans. Foolish, simple things. Vladan stopped to watch them. They reminded him of monkeys at a zoo. Hooting and hollering as they mindlessly played. One of the boys called out to him.

"Hey, mister, got a smoke?!"

Vladan tilted his head in confusion. What a strange question. The brunet ran over to him and Vladan noted that he had freckles like his Margosha. "A smoke?" he asked.

"Wow, town's getting full of you slavs huh?" the brunet laughed. "A cig, cigarette." He mimicked smoking.

Vladan grimaced. "What do you mean 'getting full'?"

The brunet shrugged, "Between you and Mama A's little wolf, there's two of you now." A blond came over and chimed in, "Also you're both redheads!" "Nah, little wolf has more pink hair." "Peachy." "Isn't that why Mama called her peaches?"

Vladan's eyes widened. "Where is this Mama A and wolf?"

The boys muttered amongst themselves till the burnet piped up, "What do we get in return?" "Yeah, what'll you give us?" the blonde asked. The other boys came over and began blathering about bargaining. It was childish.

Vladan grinned, "I will not kill you." The boys all oohed and awed. They made wild gestures and taunted the man. Vladan shrugged. He was hungry. His fangs elongated. All at once the boys fell silent. They backed up into the churchyard.

"Hey now," the burnet laughed nervously. He knew the guy hadn't had fangs just a second ago. The cold air seemed to be even colder now. He looked back at his friend but a scream made him whip around. The guy's nose was pressed into his. The boy froze. The smell of decay hit him. The man's face was twisted and wrong. His pupils swallowed the ice blue of his eyes. "They-" the boy stuttered, "They live in the yellow house. Big one. On Belle road."

Vladan smiled, "See how easy that was?" He lunged forward and buried his fangs into the boy's neck. The others screamed and scattered. Vladan didn't worry though. Their heartbeats were loud.

He'd find them.

Misha sat by the window. She watched as the sun set over the horizon. It set her room ablaze. Speaking of her room, it felt more 'homey' as Adelaide would say. There were a few posters, a nice rug, and a record player with a leaning stack of albums beside it. One was spinning on the table. Misha was too preoccupied to pay attention to the tune. It would be Christmas tomorrow. The smell of cold and pine she once knew this time of year was now replaced by sugar and warmth. The source of that change was currently napping. Which gave Misha ample time to enact her plan.

Well. It wasn't a plan. More of a full hearted attempt. It was going well so far. Adelaide was slumbering and Misha was almost done. The woman had asked Misha to pick up a few things for dinner. That trip had been speedy, leaving enough time for Misha to finalize her gift and hopefully sneak it under the tree. Along with the other things she had bought.

    The blonde was never good at mending or sewing, but she wanted to give Adelaide something crafted by her own hands. Misha looked at the pattern slices on the floor. The flimsy paper was difficult to use, but by some miracle, she managed not to tear it. Misha thought of crafting the piece in the sewing room, but didn't want Adelaide to notice. Besides, The speed she possessed made her faster than Adelaide's machine. Her little gift was going to be a surprise.

    Misha finished her stitch and tied off the thread. The garment was modeled after the diamond woman's gown. Gentlemen Prefer Blondes was a fun film. The music was lovely and the leads were lovelier. Their outfits though! Oh the outfits. Adelaide went on and on about them. How much she loved them. How she'd always wanted the bejeweled orange gown. That was all Misha needed to hear. Whatever Adelaide wanted, Adelaide would get.

    Misha smoothed out the fabric, making sure there were no loose threads or misstitches. She folded the dress and placed it into a box, gently laying tissue paper over it. The lid fit snuggly and Misha topped it off with a bow. "Perfect," she whispered, a childish glee in her voice. Misha took the package and the other gifts into her arms. She opened the door a crack. Adelaide's door was still closed.

Good.

Misha snuck down the stairs. A noise in the living room made her pause. Who was there? Misha inhaled deeply. She smiled. Her beloved was clever. There in the room was Adelaide. The woman was kneeling by the Christmas tree, arranging presents. "Well, well, well..." Misha took on a teasing tone.

Adelaide jumped. She looked back at Misha. "Oh! I thought you were still out." It didn't matter, but Adelaide was hoping to surprise the other. It had been hard enough to sneak gifts in the first place. Adelaide had only managed by sending the strawberry blonde out on errands. Well, Misha would have found out tomorrow anyway. "Surprise!" she giggled, "I made you a few things."

Misha noticed the boxes. Her eyes went wide. When was the last time she'd been given handmade gifts? Not since her children. Misha's heart ached at the memory. That wouldn't do. There was a spark of joy from

Adelaide's thoughtfulness, Misha clung to that. "For me?"

Adelaide smiled, "Of course, peaches." She patted the floor next to her. The sun was setting. The room was alight in a golden glow. "I see you got me a few things too," Adelaide gestured to the presents.

Misha nodded. She came closer and kneeled on the floor, setting her boxes next to the tree. "I would give you the sun and the moon, beloved."

Adelaide felt her heart skip and beat. "Oh, Misha. All I want is you." The strawberry blonde's eyes went glassy. Bloody tears welled in the corners and spilled over. Even Adelaide was surprised by how heartfelt she'd sounded. God, what had this woman done to her? Melted her to her core and revealed the devotion she'd been begging to give to someone. Well, she couldn't have picked a better someone to give it to. Adelaide grabbed one of the presents. "This one first," she said.

Misha took the wrapped box. She moved to sit cross legged. "Aren't we supposed to open them tomorrow?" she asked with a teasing tone in her voice. The wrapping paper Adelaide had chosen was a glittering red. Like fresh blood. Oh, her love was funny.

Adelaide shrugged. Memories came back like a flash bang. She hadn't thought of her childhood Christmases in…decades! Adelaide laughed, "Actually, I used to open one on the eve and the rest in the morn'." She blushed, her accent had thickened. Adelaide cleared her throat. "Anyway, mama said that's what she used to do so…" God, her mother. When was the last time she'd lingered on that woman?

Misha looked at the boxes she'd brought down. Tradition had always seemed foolish to her, but this one, she would happily share and indulge in. Misha took one of the gifts and handed it to Adelaide. "Here, beloved."

Adelaide took it easily. The pair opened their packages. Misha had wrapped Adelaide's gifts in gold. It was precious. Misha seemed to like ribbons and bows. Not that Adelaide could blame her, they were nice. The vampire meticulously opened the wrapping paper. As if trying to preserve it. It was adorable. Adelaide opened her gift with the savagery of an excited child. She couldn't help it. The books that sat in her lap were all pulpy harlequin romances. Adelaide burst out laughing.

Misha looked up from her gift extraction and laughed as well. "I thought you would like them."

Adelaide reigned in her giggles. "I love them, peaches." She noticed all the books had a vampire love interest. Adelaide smiled slyly. "You looking for date night ideas?"

Misha scoffed, "Of course not, beloved. Maybe some bedroom ones." That got a shocked look from Adelaide before the woman laughed again. Misha finally got to her present and neatly placed the red wrapping paper on the ground beside her. She opened the lid of the cardboard box and found a pair of ballet shoes.

"I thought maybe you'd like to dance again," Adelaide explained. "I understand if you don't want to, but I wanted you to have the option-" She gasped when Misha practically tackled her to the ground. "Misha!" she scolded with a laugh. Kisses were being laid across her neck and face. Adelaide giggled and captured Misha's mouth for a proper kiss. "What got into you?"

The blonde kissed the taller woman again. "I do not deserve you, my love. My beloved."

"I just made you some shoes, Misha. Jesus!" Adelaide laughed and pushed herself up. "Actin' like I proposed!" Misha's eyes went wide. Adelaide blushed. It's not like she wouldn't propose. If times were kinder, she would in a heartbeat. Adelaide gasped when her face was covered in kisses again. "Misha!" she giggled, gently pushing the blonde away. "Jesus, peaches!"

Misha shuddered against her. "Can I have my present early?" She slipped her hand down Adelaide's side and down between her legs. "Please, beloved?"

Adelaide gasped. Her head thunked against the floor. "Jesus Christ, Misha." The heat in her cheeks could have rivaled the flames in the fireplace. "Do you really want to-"

"Yes!" Misha slammed her hands on either side of Adelaide's face. She straddled Adelaide's waist.

Doubt crept in. Adelaide didn't want to hurt Misha. She was twice the other woman's size. "Misha. I could smother you."

Misha smiled. "Oh, beloved. That's what I'm hoping for." She noticed the shock in Adelaide's eyes. "I am a vampire, my love." Misha let her fangs drop. "Have you forgotten? I do not need to breathe. You can not crush me. You can not hurt me." The blonde leaned down. "I want to feel your warmth around me. I want to taste the ambrosia between your legs. I want my beautiful sun goddess to sit upon her throne and take her pleasure." Misha pressed her forehead against Adelaide. Their lips brushed as she spoke, "Please, Adelaide?"

Said woman felt her brain flat line. She was dead. This was heaven. This beautiful angel. This fallen angel had decided to take pity on her poor mortal soul and declare her divine. Adelaide whined. God, Misha on top of her wasn't helping. The heat in her core was growing. "Misha, I'll only last five minutes."

The blonde pressed her nose against Adelaide's. She whispered hotly against those plush lips, "Then what a glorious five minutes it'll be."

Adelaide leaned up and kissed the blonde. "Fine."

Misha squealed in excitement. She stood quickly and picked up Adelaide bridal style, carrying the woman upstairs. The taller woman laughed in her ear.

Mike ate one of the over sugared cookies. He normally stayed clear of the sweets, but it was Christmas. Rick had already had three and two cups of coffee. Mike laughed as Nancy danced to jingle bells. "Go, Nan!" The woman spun, the bell necklace she wore jiggled.

Rick laughed and a few other deputies whistled.

Jamie walked into the station. He noticed the festive air and felt awful that he was about to ruin it.

Mike sat up straight. "Can I help you, son?"

Jamie nervously rubbed his hands together. "I uh…I think my friends are missing."

Rick raised an eyebrow. "Think?"

Jamie nodded. "They went out last night and never came home." He quickly added, "They didn't take their cars…and I called their moms already." Jamie's lip quivered, "No one's seen them." He went on, "Tony disappeared and now the rest of the frat is gone and I'm just freaked out." Jamie felt like he was hyperventilating.

Rick stood from his desk and went to the boy. "Hey, hey, it's alright, son." Rick put a hand on the boy's shoulder. "Let's get your statement and a warm drink." He looked at Nancy, "Can you get him a hot chocolate?" The woman nodded and went to the kitchen. Rick looked at the now crying boy. "What's your name son?"

It was Christmas! Misha woke up and shaked Adelaide's shoulder. "Beloved!" the woman cheered. Adelaide's eyes snapped open. Misha smiled down at her. "Presents!" The vampire had never felt so giddy. Christmas was such a bland affair in her past. It was pageantry and church going. Dull. Now, it was a celebration! "Come, come!" she urged.

Adelaide watched as the vampire hopped off the bed and bounded down the hall. It was precious. Adelaide groaned. Her thighs were killing her. She stood with a hiss. The ache in her cunt made her stumble. The vampire had eaten her out for hours. Adelaide sucked in a breath and limped to her closet to get her robe. She threw her bonnet off and went out the door.

Adelaide walked down the steps and heard the giddy movements of the vampire. Misha had lit a fire and sat by the Christmas tree. A hot cup of coffee sat on the table. Adelaide giggled, she collapsed onto the couch. She took a few sips of her drink before saying, "Go ahead, peaches."

Misha cheered and stacked Adelaide's presents on the table. All in order of how they were to be opened. The vampire then grabbed her own presents. Misha waited for the woman to grab the top box before opening her own presents. She carefully peeled off the wrapping. The paper was too pretty to rip. Adelaide slipped to the floor and took her gifts. She tore them open. There was a gorgeous pair of orange heels. Next was a pair of pearl earrings. There were two presents left. A medium and large box. Adelaide took the medium one. She opened the lid to reveal a lingerie set. Adelaide blushed. "Misha!" she teasingly scolded.

The blonde giggled. She opened her first gift. It was a pair of handmade mittens and a wool hat. Misha slipped the gloves on. Next was a ballet leotard. The fabric was soft. Misha rubbed it against her cheek. She looked at her final gift. "Shall we open our last ones together?" she asked.

Adelaide nodded. She took the dress box and slowly opened it. She gasped, "Misha!" Tears welled in Adelaide's eyes. She stood, holding up the gown. The orange dress glittered in the morning light. "Oh, peaches! I love it." Adelaide hopped over the table and kneeled beside Misha. She pulled the woman into a hug. "Did you make this?!" she asked.

"Yes!" Misha kissed the woman. "I am glad you love it."

Adelaide pushed Misha's gift to her. "Open it! Open it!" she urged.

Misha lifted the box's lid. "Oh, beloved!" she cheered. "This is exactly like the pretty blonde's dress!"

Adelaide giggled, "Marilyn Monroe, peaches."

"Yes!" Misha pressed the dress to her chest. "Oh, beloved." She stood and twirled. The fabric was perfect!

Adelaide asked, "So, why the whole outfit?" She gestured to the rest of the gifts. "Planning to take me somewhere special?"

Misha smiled mischievously. "Oh yes, my love. I plan to take you to the city of your past. I plan to take you to the finest restaurants and see the greatest shows. I will take you to exhibits and dance with you in exclusive lounges. Finally, I will lay you on the softest bed and peel you out of your clothes." Misha pressed her lips against Adelaide's. "Then I will make you see stars as you're bathed in the neon lights. From our window."

Adelaide shuddered, "Misha." She kissed the vampire. The idea of going back to New York made her heart swell. She would love to live there again. Adelaide now had enough money for a brownstone, instead of a roach infested apartment. The idea of moving away elated her, until reality came crashing. She couldn't leave the house.

"Why not?" Misha asked. Adelaide blinked at her owlishly. "Why can we not move? Why not leave and start anew?" she asked. Misha moved closer, "We could build a home together. One that is all ours."

The idea was sweet. Adelaide bit her lip. "Misha, the girls-"

The vampire huffed. "Adelaide. You deserve a life too." The woman looked at the floor. Misha frowned and took the woman's hand. "Beloved," she turned the woman's chin, "could you at least consider it? Our future?"

Our. Adelaide shuddered. What a word. Not mine, not yours, but ours. Adelaide took Misha's hand and kissed the vampire's pale knuckles. She pressed her forehead against Misha's. "I'll think about it."

A knock at the door made the pair start. Adelaide looked at the front door. She stood.

Misha whined, "Leave them, it is Christmas,"

Adelaide chuckled. "That's exactly why I should check. It means its something big." She went to the door and was shocked to find Jamie there. "Oh, Merry Christmas, baby." Adelaide noted that Jamie was fidgety. His eyes were red. Had he been crying? What did the other boys do to him? Did he get bad news?

Jamie frowned. "Yeah," his voice broke. The boy covered his mouth and stared at his feet. God, he'd probably interrupted Adelaide's Christmas. What a way to make a second impression. "I'm sorry, I shouldn't have come. I just-" Jamie finally glanced at Adelaide and what he saw took his breath away. Her eyes were gentle. Her arms were open. Jamie sobbed and went to the woman, hugging her tight. "I'm sorry," he wept. "I'm so sorry."

"Shh," Adelaide soothed. She pet the boy's hair. "Come in, baby," she pulled Jamie inside. The poor boy was shivering, and not just from his distress. "What happened, sweetheart?"

Jamie hiccuped and tried to fruitlessly wipe his eyes. "The guys. They're all missing. I should have gone with them!" Jamie wailed. "They probably got drunk and lost or whatever got Tony got them." Jamie hugged Adelaide. "I don't want to be alone," he cried.

Adelaide rubbed his back and looked at Misha. The vampire seemed just as confused. Adelaide glared at her. The blonde put her hands up and shook her head. Adelaide sighed in relief. "Come on, baby. Let's sit you down and get you something hot to eat."

Misha huffed and went to the living room. By the time Adelaide sat the boy down, the gifts were all in Adelaide's room.

The boy collapsed onto the couch. "I'm sorry, Adelaide," he wept. "I didn't know where else to go."

"Nonsense, baby." Adelaide smoothed out the hair sticking to the boy's face. "I'll make you some soup."

Jamie smiled. He wiped his face dry. Jamie noticed the blonde was glaring at him. "Sorry to you too, Missa."

The vampire growled, "It's Misha."

Jamie blushed, "Oh, sorry." The blonde huffed and followed Adelaide into the kitchen. She then came back in and turned on the TV for him. Misha tossed the remote to his side. Jamie watched as she retreated back to the kitchen. "Thank you," he called after her. The woman waved her hand dismissively and didn't look back. Jamie felt like he interrupted something, but at least the women were kind enough to have him.

Adelaide giggled at the description. Her novels were ludacris and pulpy, but they were fun. The vampire was currently hiding as a bat in the main character's nightstand. Adelaide snorted at the wild descriptions and flowery language. She was laying on the couch, the afternoon light illuminated her terrible novel.

Misha was out on business, finally giving Adelaide some space. The vampire had been even more clingy. She'd been cagey since Christmas. Paranoid in a way Adelaide hadn't seen her be before. It was like Misha knew something Adelaide didn't. At first, Adelaide chalked it up to Jamie coming over on Christmas, but after three days…

Adelaide tried to put the odd behavior out of her mind. She wanted to ask but didn't want to interrogate the woman. The blonde had taken a sack of gold with her, so maybe she was just getting it converted. That didn't explain the clinginess, but it was some form of an answer.

This morning, Misha had left Adelaide to her own devices. It was a breath of fresh air. Adelaide loved Misha but the blonde had even been following her into the bathroom. It was getting concerning. Adelaide was enjoying her book. Misha hated them, which made her buying them funnier. The blonde would roll her eyes whenever Adelaide read an inaccuracy. Misha never failed to voice her disapproval.

'We do not become bats!' 'Having sex while flying is insane!' 'We do not walk with our hands out. This book is ridiculous!'

Adelaide giggled. Her poor little vampire. Adelaide found the woman's exasperation very entertaining. A particular line made Adelaide snort. She had to set her book down on a cushion as she laughed.

A knock at the door made Adelaide sit up. Was Misha back? Adelaide got up and went to the door. The man on the other side was odd. That's what immediately hit Adelaide. His hair was a deep red and slicked back. His eyes were a piercing blue. The man was younger than her. He was sharply dressed. Adelaide wondered where he came from. "Can I help you?" she asked.

Vladan tilted his head. The woman was odd. He wanted to grab her hair and caress her skin. Maybe later. "Good day," he greeted, "I am looking for someone. I was told you may know where she is." The woman tilted her head, but like MArgosha always did. How adorable.

Adelaide stood straighter and opened the door wider. She was weary but remained cordial. "I suppose I could point you in the right direction. What's her name?"

Vladan smiled. He appraised the woman. She was taller than most. Her dark skin shined in the sunlight. He could smell the blood under her skin. It was just as mouth watering as the sweet perfume she wore. If he had not stuffed himself on those boys, he would have taken a sip. "Her name is Margosha."

Adelaide thought. She'd had a few Margo's over the years, but never a Margosha. "I don't have any Margosha's. I'm sorry, honey."

Vladan tilted his head in confusion at the name. When was the last time someone addressed him so warmly? Such a sweet woman with a lovely voice. Vladan would have to visit her again. She'd make good company or at least good food. He knew the woman wasn't lying. That was a good sign. Honesty was hard to find in the modern age. "I see. I feel quite lost." He looked at the woman, "Do you have any ideas?"

Adelaide pursed her lips and thought. "Admission keeps records of everyone that's come and gone. You may be able to find her there."

"Come and gone?" Vladan tilted his head straight again.

Adelaide chuckled. "Well, most only stay here for school before moving on. My girls only live here till they graduate. All the Margo's I've ever had have flown the coop years ago." She noticed the crestfallen expression on the man's face. "I'm sorry, honey. I wish I could have been more help."

Vladan forced a smile. "No, no. You were very helpful, my dear." He took a bow. "Have a good day."

"You too," Adelaide replied. Before he turned around Adelaide added. "Wait." The man stopped. "She might be going by Margo or Margot or Margaret. Most people here don't go by Margosha."

Vladan nodded. The woman was far more helpful than he had originally thought. "I will keep that in mind, thank you." He bowed again and left.

Adelaide watched the man walk off the porch and down the street. She shut the door and pressed her back to it. Her hand shook as she bolted the door. What the hell was that? The man's aura was suffocating. Terrifying in a primal way. 'Dear lord, thank you for my poker face,' Adelaide thought. She stood on her shaky legs and went back to the couch.

    Margosha
        Margosha
            Margosha

The name was foreign, obviously. Adelaide went to her bookcase. She scanned the titles and found her baby name books. Adelaide sat on the floor. She opened them and went to the M's. It took two books before she found it.

Margosha, Russian name meaning Pearl. A simple definition. Adelaide frowned. Russian. She gathered the books and placed them back on the shelf. Well then. Adelaide laid on the floor. She stared up at the ceiling. There was a crack there. It had formed after an earthquake. The house held, but the crack remained. A symbol of strength, like a scar.

Now that Adelaide thought about it, the man had obviously been after Misha. Thank god fear wiped her mind of everything except what she needed to survive. Adelaide sighed. So a strange guy with an awful aura came to the door calling Misha by another name. That couldn't be good. It most certainly could not be good. She rolled on her stomach.

Why would he be after Misha? A friend? No, Misha had never mentioned friends. Or even other vampires. No, that wasn't true. Misha had mentioned one other vampire- The back door opened and closed. A loud thump made Adelaide shake in fright. Had her thoughts lured the man back? "Peaches?!" she called. Adelaide scrambled to her feet and ran into the kitchen. The blonde had a suitcase on the table. A new suitcase that Adelaide had never seen before. Black, leather, sleek, it was lovely. It made Adelaide narrow her eyes. "What you been doin'?" she asked.

"I have converted my coins!" Misha announced. There were pounds of paper in the suitcase. The money man had been shocked by her gold. His face was quite funny. Buggy eyed and mouth opened wide. Misha was glad to be home though. She went to hug Adelaide, then paused. A faint smell was rolling off of the woman. Far off, distant, but there.

It was a smell Misha terrifyingly knew. "What..." She looked the woman up and down. Adelaide wasn't harmed. No smell of blood. No obvious signs of trauma. By some miracle, Adelaide was intact. He was lurking. Maybe even watching. Misha screamed to him in her native tongue and then roared, "Where are you?!" Misha began tearing through the house. The smell of him lingered by the door but hadn't entered the house. Misha was confused. How could he hide his scent? Why wasn't he attacking as he always had? Had he not gotten into the house? She would rip the place apart and make sure he wasn't lurking in some dark corner.

Adelaide jumped in shock. She watched as Misha turned into a blur. A raging tornado that tore through the halls. Screaming and slamming doors. It was terrifying. Something needed to be done. Adelaide could barely comprehend what was going on. "Misha?!" She couldn't even grab the woman. "Stop!" she demanded. To her shock, the blonde did.

"WHERE ARE YOU?!" she screeched at the ceiling. Her voice rattled the windows. Was she going insane? Was this another tactic of his. "I WILL NEVER BE YOURS!" she screamed. They needed to leave. Needed to run. Before he struck. Misha wouldn't be foolish, like last time. She wouldn't lose anyone else. She refused to lose anyone else to that bastard! Misha went to Adelaide. She took the woman's hands. "We need to go. We need to- Pack, beloved. We have to go. Before he comes back and-" Her nerves were on fire. Sparking in all different directions.

"Misha, calm down," Adelaide placed her hands on the blonde's shoulders. "Talk to me, please." She guided the vampire to the couch. "Sit down and breathe." The blonde was crying. Her green eyes were wide and scanning around the room. "Peaches, please." Adelaide held the woman's face. That seemed to calm Misha down.

The blonde sucked in a breath. It wasn't needed but it did make her feel better. "Beloved. I smell…my maker." Misha sniffled. Her body was shaking. "He…he will kill you, beloved. He kills everyone I love" Misha hiccuped. She wept. "I thought he would finally leave me alone. It's been 200 years!" Misha reached out and grabbed Adelaide's shirt. "Beloved, we must leave. I can't lose you. Please, beloved. Come with me."

Adelaide's eyes widened. Dear lord. She'd heard of stalkers, but this was ridiculous. Whoever this creator was, he most certainly wasn't driving them out of her home! She kneeled in front of the vampire. Her knees would scream later, but that was a price she'd willingly pay. "Misha. Honey." The blonde was crying harder. "Did…" Adelaide licked her lips, "did he ever call you Margosha?"

Misha's eyes widened. "You spoke to him?" Adelaide nodded. Misha slipped onto the floor. "How…how are you alive?" She held the woman's face. "You are a wonder. A miracle." Misha kissed Adelaide. Once, twice, more and more. Misha felt hysterical. "I shouldn't have left you alone! I will not make the same mistake. I swear to you! In our next home, I will not leave your side!" she vowed.

"Misha!" Adelaide grabbed the blonde's arms. "There isn't going to be a next home!" The vampire looked shocked. Hurt filled her eyes but Adelaide quickly explained, "Peaches. He came. I talked to him. He left. We don't need to go anywhere. Not right now anyway." She relaxed, leaning back on her hands. "He asked for a Margosha. I told him I didn't have a girl by that name. He's probably bugging admissions. Probably going to harass every Margot that ever attended this place."

Misha frowned, "He…" Oh course he hadn't smelt her. She was doused in Adelaide's scent. "Oh, beloved." The vampire began to laugh, and laugh, and laugh. "My beautiful angel. My love!" Misha let her body fall back against the couch. Her head fell on the cushion. "You have sent him on a- a-" Misha giggled, "What is it called when you go on a journey fueled by foolishness with no end?"

Adelaide snorted, "A wild goose chase?"

Misha laughed anew. "A wild goose chase!" The expression was so fitting. The girls Vladan would find would not be her. Chasing his tail before giving up. Granted, Misha had hoped after 200 years he would leave her the hell alone. Reality set in. Adelaide had come so close to death. If Vladan had smelt her. If he had- Misha was snapped out of her thoughts

259

by Adelaide's warm hand on her cheek. She turned and kissed Adelaide's palm. "Beloved?"

"It's okay," the woman reassured. Misha had gotten lost in her head and Adelaide needed to pull her out. Otherwise, the poor thing might spiral into another running fit. A peachy tornado. The thought made Adelaide giggle. She leaned forward and kissed the blonde. Adelaide stood. Her knees screamed, but she ignored their crying. "He'll be running around all over God's creation for who knows how long." She looked down at Misha. "Come on, peaches." Adelaide held out her hand for the vampire. The blonde took it and easily stood up. Adelaide envied her joints. "Want to hear about my book?"

Misha rolled her eyes, but couldn't hold back her smile. How could a woman so well read enjoy such drivel? Misha would listen though. She'd make Adelaide laugh and correct the awful depictions of vampires. They'd both giggle at the awful sex scenes and make fun of the bad anatomy. Misha stood on her tiptoes and gave the woman a kiss on the cheek. "Of course, beloved." Adelaide began talking about her novel. How the vampire climbed into the protagonist's room at night to watch them sleep. Misha wrinkled her nose. "No class," she spat. Adelaide laughed and

Misha's anxiety melted away. Her maker was forgotten.

Chapter 11

Jamie stepped up on the front porch. He smoothed his hair back. The flowers in his hand were yellow and white. He hoped Adelaide appreciated the colors. They reminded Jamie of her.

The bouquet was a way to apologize for intruding on her Christmas. The woman had been so kind to him, even giving him some handmade clothes. Jamie was wearing the fringe jacket she'd gifted him. None of his fraternity had come home yet. The cops had called in some dogs to hopefully find them. They would be in town in a few days. Jamie hoped the boys were okay. Jamie pushed away his anxious thoughts and knocked on the front door. To his delight, Adelaide answered.

"Oh! Hi, baby!" Adelaide greeted. She noticed the flowers. White lilies and yellow daisies. "Oh, those are beautiful," she whispered in awe.

Jamie's eyes lit up. "They're for you!" He practically pushed the bouquet into the woman's hands. "I mean," Jamie chuckled nervously. "I feel bad that I crashed your Christmas, so…" He frowned. "I just wanted to give you those, as a sorry."

Adelaide looked at the flowers then Jamie. "Oh, thank you, baby!" She opened her arms and the boy hugged her. "You didn't need to apologize, though. We were happy to have you." Adelaide ruffled the boy's hair.

Jamie laughed. A blushed spread across his cheeks. God, the woman was so warm. Jamie scratched the back of his head. "I was happy to be here." Adelaide smelled her flowers and her doe eyes fluttered. Jamie bit his lip. He tried to mentally bat away his dirty thoughts. Geez, what was wrong with him? Jamie cleared his throat, "Well, I'm gonna head out. Have a good day!" He ran off the porch and down the street.

"Oh! Bye!" she called after him. Adelaide watched him go jogging down the road. She snorted out a laugh and closed the door. The flowers smelled wonderfully. Adelaide went to get a vase. Misha was sitting at the table, fiddling with her computer.

"Who was that?" the blonde asked.

Adelaide smiled, "Little Jamie. He brought me some flowers." She set the bouquet on the table. The vase was in the low cabinet under the toaster. She retrieved it and turned back to the table to see Misha gripping the flowers in a vice. That jealousy was back. "Peaches," Adelaide placed her hand on her hip. "They're just flowers."

"This is a courting gift," Misha seethed. She slammed the flowers on the table. She wanted to burn them. Nasty little blooms. They were colors that complimented Adelaide perfectly. Sunshine. It made Misha sick. How dare this boy. This awful, romantic boy. Misha huffed. She'd get a better bouquet. A bigger one. A beautiful one.

Adelaide poured some water into the vase and set it on the table. She picked up the flowers and placed them inside. The vampire was practically vibrating in rage. Adelaide smiled softly. "Peaches," those green eyes looked up at her, "He's a child." That seemed to calm Misha down. Adelaide sighed, "Besides, flowers are nice, but I'd prefer a kiss." She leaned down. Misha immediately met her lips. Adelaide giggled at her eagerness. "I love you," she played with one of Misha's curls. Adelaide looked at the pieces on the table. "So, how's the building going?" she asked.

Misha smiled brightly. "I am almost complete!" she cheered. The processor was almost finished. She just needed a few more components. "I can't wait to use it!"

Adelaide pursed her lips. "Actually. Do you want to do something fun?"

Misha looked up. "What kind of fun?" she asked with a sly smile.

Adelaide rolled her eyes. "I haven't shown you video games yet, have I?"

Misha sat back. "Video games?"

Adelaide giggled. "Come on, let's get dressed. You're going to love this!" She excitedly ran out of the kitchen. Misha followed close behind.

"Welcome to the arcade!" Adelaide announced. Thankfully they were the only ones there. Misha looked around at the lights. It reminded Adelaide of when they went Christmas light looking. Those big green eyes were shimmering in amazement. Adelaide giggled. She looked at the poor man behind the counter. Adelaide remembered when the boy was a child. "Hello, Jake."

The man looked at the woman, then his eyes lit up in recognition. It was the same woman who would feed the kids on the street.

The same one who handed out full size candy bars every Halloween. "Oh! Hey mama A." He noticed the girl staring at all the arcade cabinets. "New girl?" he asked, pointing to the short woman. The strawberry blonde was cute. She seemed new to the arcade scene. "Here!" Jake grabbed some coins. "On the house!" he explained. "Show her circus."

Adelaide smiled, "Aw, thank you, baby!" She took the gold coins. "I appreciate you."

Jake blushed. "Aw, no problem, foxy mama!" he said with a wink.

Adelaide giggled and walked back to Misha. "Come on, peaches." The blonde was still staring at the lights. Entranced. Adelaide guided her to one of the cabinets. "Let's start with pong. It's probably the easiest." Adelaide placed in a coin. "Watch."

Misha peaked around Adelaide's side. The small dot bounced back and forth. Adelaide was manipulating the two knobs on the face of the tall box. Misha noticed the lines on the screen moved with Adelaide's movements. "Are you doing this?" she pointed at the lines.

The taller woman nodded. "It's like tennis. You need to keep the ball going back and forth and you earn points."

Misha tapped one of Adelaide's hands. "Can I try?" That warm hand moved away and let Misha take control. The pair stood, passing the ball back and forth.

"Aw, shit!" Adelaide said as her paddle missed the ball.

"Yes!" Misha cheered, jumping up and down in delight.

Adelaide giggled. The blonde's delight was infectious. "Congrats! You won your first video game."

Misha tugged Adelaide's arm. "Let us play more!" She went to another colorful box. There was a steering wheel on the front of it. A car game. Racing. "This one!" Misha declared, pointing at the screen.

Adelaide chuckled and placed the coins in. "Have at it, peaches."

Misha squealed in delight.

Adelaide watched as the vampire maneuvered and managed to get first place. Misha cheered. Adelaide giggled. She clapped for the vampire. They'd definitely need more coins. Adelaide got a few dollars worth. She had to explain that this money could only be used on the games. Misha wrinkled her nose in confusion but quickly got distracted by a flashing animation on a cabinet screen. The pair went from game to game. Misha wanted to play every single one. The gold coins overflowing her pocket jingled when she bounced in triumph.

    Adelaide played a few games but mostly watched Misha. She was worried the vampire would try to take apart the cabinet. The vampire's curiosity knew no bounds.

    "I want one!" Misha declared after she finished the final game. "How do we get one?" she asked Adelaide. The taller woman laughed. Misha took no offense. Adelaide's mind and face were radiating love.

    "They're pretty costly, peaches," Adelaide explained. "There are a few at home consoles you can play." She looked at the cabinets. "I'm sure there's someone selling them. We could maybe get a broken one for you to fix up."

    Misha beamed. Her love was so thoughtful and wonderful. Misha couldn't wait to find a game to take apart. Adelaide would probably help her too! Oh, Misha was so lucky to have the love she did. She looked around and wondered which game to choose. Her green eyes landed on one of the posters adorning the walls. It showed a happy couple playing one of the games. The large letters on it read **Why not a date to the arcade?**. A date. That was what Adelaide said courting was called now. Misha realized Adelaide had taken her on a date. They were on a date. It seemed ridiculous that she'd only just noticed.

Misha looked at the bored man sitting behind the counter toward the front. Misha led Adelaide behind one of the cabinets. She pressed the woman's back against it. Adelaide looked at Misha curiously. The blonde looked around. They were out of sight of the windows and single attendant. She pressed herself flush with Adelaide's front. The taller woman was biting her lip.

"What are you doing?" Adelaide asked. She noticed Misha's pupils were expanding. Oh. That meant she was either hungry or-

"Adelaide," Misha whispered, standing on her tiptoes and silently beckoned the woman to kiss her. She placed her hands on Adelaide's hips, squeezing the soft skin there. Those plush lips opened, letting out a shuddering breath. Misha whined, "Beloved."

"What got into you?" Adelaide asked. Her voice was barely a whisper. She was afraid that Jake might see them. The poor boy wasn't paid enough to deal with that. Not to mention them being caught could cause all sorts of chaos. She went to look around the corner of the cabinet. Misha took her by the chin and turned her back to look into those green eyes. "Peaches?"

Misha pulled the woman into a kiss. She balanced on the toes of her shoes. It was similar to being en pointe. It made it easier on Adelaide's neck and that was worth it.

Adelaide shivered. Misha's lips were so soft. The vampire's fangs nipped her bottom lip. Adelaide hissed at the pain. She cupped Misha's ass. The blonde was wearing bright red hot pants. It was absolute torture watching her walk around in them.

"There's a yellow pair for you," Misha said against the woman's lips. The idea of Adelaide in the shorts made her mouth water. Of course Misha would have to fend off the hordes of hungry eyes, but it'd be worth it to see Adelaide's plump ass shake as she walked. Misha groaned, "I can't wait for summer."

Adelaide pressed another kiss on Misha's lips. "You're lucky people don't question pretty girls wearing things out of season." She lightly slapped the blonde's ass. Misha moaned and pressed herself closer. Those room temperature hands slipped under Adelaide's shirt. "Misha," she tried to scold the vampire, but it came out breathless. Adelaide slipped her hands into Misha's back pockets. "We're in public."

Misha chuckled. "Jake has gone to the back room," she said and nibbled on Adelaide's neck. "He is eating his lunch. We can have some fun." Misha slipped her hands under Adelaide's bra. She rolled the woman's nipples. Adelaide gasped. Misha licked her lips. "Beloved."

Adelaide groaned and used every ounce of self control she had to push the blonde away. "Oh, you're the devil," she huffed, straightening her clothes out. "I ain't risking this," she said firmly.

Misha pouted. She was going to argue but Adelaide grabbed her wrist and pulled her through the arcade. Misha was confused till she saw the neon sign of the bathroom. The vampire almost squealed in joy.

Adelaide knew it was a single use. She pulled Misha inside and pressed the blonde against the door. Adelaide clicked the lock in place. She held Misha's face in her hands. "Too horny for your own good." Adelaide hissed and kissed the blonde.

Misha purred. Oh, her Adelaide was a gift. A precious gift who was currently tugging down her tight pants. Misha giggled and helped the other slip her shorts and underwear down.

Adelaide took off her coat and laid it on the floor. She kneeled in front of Misha. The blonde looked down at her in shock. "Here, pretty girl," she took one of Misha's legs, "put this on my shoulder." The vampire did. Adelaide scooted closer. She pressed a kiss below Misha's belly button. Adelaide looked up at the blonde. The vampire's pupils nearly swallowed all the green in Misha's eyes. "Want my mouth, peaches?" Adelaide asked with a tease in her voice. The shudder she received in turn was delightful.

Misha groaned when Adelaide's scorching hot mouth latched onto her inner thigh. The woman left hickey after hickey on her. Misha cursed her nature. Those marks were worth keeping. Misha wanted to wear them forever. She wanted to flaunt them to the masses and show off she was Adelaide's. Curse this day and age. Adelaide's teeth dug into her thigh. Misha moaned. It echoed off the bathroom walls. Misha slammed her hand on the switch by the door and turned on the fan. "Beloved, please!" Misha begged, "your mouth. Give me your mouth!"

Adelaide giggled. She hadn't given the blonde oral yet. Now she got to give it her all. The vampire's folds glistened with slick. "Poor thing," Adelaide teased, "no wonder you always want to fuck. Pretty girl can't keep it in her pants." Adelaide broadly licked up Misha's pussy. The blonde moaned and it spurred Adelaide on. She shuffled closer and sucked on Misha's clit. Licking the swollen nub and swirling her tongue around it in slow, tight circles.

Misha's head snapped back and cracked against the door. The thunk on the wood sounded harsh, even to her ears. She covered her mouth and tried to stifle her moans. Her leg shook. Misha buried one of her hands into Adelaide's curls. That hot tongue thrust inside her then returned to her clit. Misha moved her hips.

Adelaide groaned. Her eyes fluttered at the taste of Misha on her tongue. Adelaide was feeling light headed. Oh. The metallic taste made sense now. There wasn't any water in Misha. Every fluid was tinged in blood. The high from Misha's slick was less than when Misha gave her blood, but it was a nice buzz.

Adelaide gasped as Misha tugged her curls. She moaned against the vampire's cunt. Adelaide unbuttoned her pants and stuffed her hand inside them. She moaned anew as she touched herself. Adelaide used her free hand to stuff two fingers inside of Misha. Curling them up as she sucked Misha's clit harder.

The vampire jumped and shook. She screamed behind her hand. It was incredible. Misha was tugging Adelaide's head closer. The woman's fingers undulated inside her, pressing into her most sensitive spot. It made Misha's knee buckle. Adelaide pulled her mouth back. "You can put it on my shoulder," she panted out. That unsteady leg was placed on her other shoulder. Adelaide went back to eating the woman out.

Misha whimpered, bloody tears running down her face. She pulled her hand out of Adelaide's curls and clawed the back of the door. Her hips wiggled and she used her legs to grind into Adelaide's face. God, she'd forgotten how wonderful a mouth felt. "Fuck, fuck, fuck!" Misha bit her hand. Her fangs dug into her skin.

Adelaide whined as her face was ridden. She pressed hard onto the vampire's clit. Her fingers became faster. Her eyes rolled back and moaned. Her knees ached and her neck screamed, but it was worth it. Misha losing herself in pleasure was worth any physical discomfort. Adelaide quaked. The fingers she was using on herself quickened their pace as well. Her peak was approaching and she was going to go over the edge. Pale thighs were squeezing her head and shook. Misha was close. Adelaide doubled her efforts. She wanted the vampire to fall apart. Adelaide came, moaning loudly against Misha's clit. The vampire tightened around her fingers.

Misha's hips stuttered. Her eyes rolled back. She gasped and tried to remember how to speak. "Beloved," she warned. "Beloved, I'm -" she tried to warn her love but had to cover her mouth again to muffle her scream as she came. It felt like being struck by lightning. A choir of angels sang in her head. She would've collapsed if Adelaide didn't have her legs on her shoulders. Misha inhaled. The scent of Adelaide's spend filled her nose. Misha looked down, pupils wide. The taller woman's hair was a mess. Curls were flying in all different directions. Misha's legs relaxed

Adelaide pulled back and sat on her heels. She pulled her fingers free from the vampire's cunt. The ache in her knees turned into an inferno. She pulled her hand out of her pants and sat on the floor, hissing in pain. Misha's legs fell off her shoulders. Adelaide felt like a mess. They were a mess. Adelaide grimaced. The smell of their pleasure would be stuck on them. Jesus, they were in a public bathroom! One of Misha's cool hands cupped Adelaide's chin and raised her face.

"Beloved?" Misha sank to the floor. She bit her own tongue and pulled Adelaide into a kiss. The taller woman moaned at the taste of her blood. Misha chuckled and kissed her deeper.

A knock at the door made the woman start.

"You two okay?" Jake asked through the wood.

Adelaide and Misha stared at each other. The vampire quickly said, "I GOT MY PERIOD!" Adelaide covered her laugh.

Adelaide towel dried her hair, scrunching it. The shower had been nice, but now It was time to oil her scalp and detangle her curls. Misha was getting dressed behind her. The vampire had never been in the room when Adelaide did her routine. The woman sat on the edge of the tub and could feels Misha's eyes roaming her body. "Peaches, I ain't young," Adelaide teased. She placed the towel by her side and reached back for her comb.

Nothing.

Adelaide looked back, confused. All the products she had meticulously laid out on the toilet lid were gone. Adelaide turned around.

Misha had everything on the sink. The wide tooth comb was in her hand.

Adelaide pursed her lips. "Peaches, what are you doing?" The vampire came closer.

"I want to help," Misha answered. She lightly touched Adelaide's curls. "Please?" Adelaide's hair was unlike any she'd ever seen. Dark as night and soft as silk. Some of the girls she met had curls, but Adelaide's were tighter, thicker. Misha knew their upkeep was far different from her own. Adelaide would come out of the bathroom sore after taking care of her hair. It was apparently a very involved and long process. Misha knew having someone do your hair was far simpler than doing it yourself. What kind of partner would she be if she didn't offer to help?

Adelaide thought for a moment. It would definitely spare her body any more aches. Besides, it's not like Misha was wielding a pair of scissors. Combing and integrating some creams was simple, just tedious. However, Misha didn't seem to find anything concerning Adelaide boring. The blonde even seemed excited. The comb in her hand was being gripped tight. As if Adelaide would take it and banish the vampire away. Adelaide smiled, "Sure, peaches."

Misha squealed in joy. "How do I start?" she asked.

Adelaide instructed, "We need to section my hair." She traced lines over her hair. "Four sections." Misha used the comb and parted her hair. "Okay, now get the blue bottle." The blonde had it in hand in a blink. Adelaide explained, "Now run that through each section with your hands first then comb it." Misha's cream covered hands ran through Adelaide's coils. The taller woman's eyes closed. It felt wonderful. She relaxed back into Misha's fingers. Adelaide moaned.

Misha swallowed audibly. What a lovely noise. Too lovely. The blonde distracted herself with Adelaide's hair. She went section by section. Finally, when she finished, Misha asked. "What is next, my love?"

Adelaide blinked her eyes open. "Oh," she looked over her shoulder. "Get the green bottle." It was in Misha's hands in a flash. "That's oil for my scalp. So, take the dropper and just put drops around then massage it in."

Misha nodded. The steps seemed simple enough. She set the glass bottle aside and rubbed the oil into Adelaide's scalp. The taller woman melted under her touch. Her head fell back and tried to follow Misha's hands whenever the blonde moved away. There was a temptation to go on for longer, but Misha didn't want to risk ruining Adelaide's grooming process. "What next, beloved?" she asked in a whisper. Adelaide's doe eyes opened and stared up at her. She smiled dreamily and Misha's knees felt weak.

Adelaide cleared her throat and put her head level again. "Okay, get the red spray bottle." She didn't need to check if Misha had it. "Now take that and spritz it around." The sound of the nozzle spraying made a shiver go down Adelaide's spine. She swayed a bit, too relaxed. A part of her wanted to lay down and just let Misha play with her hair.

"I'd be honored." The vampire placed a kiss on Adelaide's cheek. "There is no greater joy than worshiping you. Especially the pieces of you, you see as mundane."

Adelaide shuddered. She turned her head and captured Misha's lips. The kiss was quick, chaste. It was something Adelaide needed to do to expel the overflow of love in her chest. Oh, how Misha made her weak. "I want to do your hair too," she whispered against cool lips.

"I will cry," Misha whispered back. She pressed another kiss to Adelaide's lips and stood up again. "What is next?"

Adelaide smiled softly, "I normally braid it. Just a simple two strand one."

Misha parted Adelaide's curls. Misha was well versed in these braids. Her sisters had always asked for them. It made making a bun easier. A memory made her pause. She quickly blinked her eyes, trying to expel it. Misha swallowed the ache in her throat. The longing had slapped her in the face. A tear rolled down her cheek. Misha quickly wiped it away. This moment was pure. It was gentle. Her mind's wicked machinations would have to wait.

Adelaide needed pampering.

Vladan licked her fingers clean. The woman's remains were scattered around the room. He looked through the files in the cabinet. So many Margots and Margarets. Vladan sighed and pulled out the folders. There was a nice stack.

Vladan opened the manilla folders. Some of them had photos attached. That made it easier for him. He tossed those files aside. Vladan looked at the briefcase the admissions woman had. He took it and shook out the contents and placed the folders inside the case.

"Well," he looked at the mangled remains of the office woman, "It was a pleasure meeting you." The woman had been particularly unhelpful and nasty. Her twisted frown and refusal to give him the file resulted in his temper flaring up.

Vladan had to wait post Christmas to come here. Honestly, he should have just broken in and started his search sooner. Vladan took the woman's car keys and headed out of the office. The office worker drove a car that was serviceable enough. Vladan would make a road map. Start with the closer girl and work his way out.

Vladan tossed the briefcase into the passenger seat and got into the driver's side. The vampire started the car and sped to the motel. He had the map of the country. The vampire was going on a little road trip.

Chapter 12

Adelaide sat against the headboard. The book in her lap shook with her laughter. The vampire man had just broken into the main character's room and was now having very funnily described sex with her. Lengths were thrusting into flowers and causing worlds to shatter. Adelaide snickered and buried her nose in her book, trying to stifle her giggles.

Misha pursed her lips. She looked over at Adelaide. "Beloved," Misha set her own book on the nightstand. Dostoevsky would have to wait. "That filth can not be good for you."

Adelaide rolled her eyes. "It's funny, peaches!" She read aloud, "He rode me like a stallion, except I was a woman and he didn't sit on a saddle, I sat on his-"

Misha groaned, but a smile was on her lips, "Enough!" She kneeled on the bed and plucked the book away from the woman. "Reading pornography beside your lover should be counted as a sin."

Adelaide huffed, "You bought 'em for me." She bit her lip. "I also think you're the one who mentioned 'ideas'" Adelaide wiggled her eyebrows. She didn't have to work hard for a little play. Misha was always up for a round of fun. The right look could get the vampire's motor running. Adelaide watched as Misha's put out face morphed into a smug smile.

The vampire chuckled. "Oh beloved, I will show you true pleasure." Misha scanned the book. Her nose wrinkled. She would make it work. The book landed somewhere on the sheets. "My beautiful girl," Misha recited, that caused Adelaide to giggle. The vampire tried to ignore the absurdity that made her want to laugh as well. "You have bewitched me with your womanly wiles and supple…" Misha tried to hold back her giggles, "rump."

Adelaide burst out laughing. She covered her face with her hands and looked away.

Misha groaned, "Beloved!" How could she act under these conditions?

Adelaide snorted, "Sorry, sorry. I can't."

Misha huffed, "You have to play along, Adelaide Freeman."

Said woman gasped, "Don't scold me while using my government!" She teasingly pinched the vampire. The pouting woman didn't react. "Such a theater kid," Adelaide sighed, a smile still wide on her face. "Listen, those lines aren't gonna work on me. I've read them." She gestured to the book, "Besides, they aren't good lines." Adelaide smiled deviously. She let one of her hands run up Misha's thigh. "Maybe we can take the bones and go off script?"

The vampire purred. She leaned forward, pressing her forehead against Adelaide's. "I will give you the performance of a lifetime." Misha captured Adelaide's lips. "I'll be back soon." With that, Misha was gone.

Adelaide blinked and she was alone. Her mouth fell open in shock. She looked around the room. A whine escaped her and a pout formed on her lips. Rude. She contemplated getting herself off, but decided to read instead. The vampire had said she'd be back, Adelaide could wait. After a couple chapters, Adelaide looked around, even more confused. She huffed. Well then. If Misha wanted to run off instead of fuck, then Adelaide would at least finish her book in peace. She found her place again and kept reading.

The clock ticked on and eventually Adelaide's eyes grew heavy. She yawned, stretched and decided to shut off the light. The room was now only illuminated by the heater's orange glow. "Misha?" she called out. Nothing. The house was silent. Adelaide frowned. She turned to grab her bonnet off the bed post, but it was missing. Adelaide didn't know what the hell Misha would have needed that for. She shrugged and got under the covers. The bed felt strange without Misha in it.

Adelaide wanted to call out to the vampire again. Instead, she tried to get herself to sleep. All of a sudden, there was pressure in her head. It wasn't painful, but it was definitely present. It felt like someone had their fingertips resting between her eyes. What the hell?

Adelaide whined. She couldn't relax. There was no comfort to be found in her lonesome. She'd gotten so used to being cuddled to sleep. She missed Misha's room temperature body and strong arms. There was a shift in the air. Adelaide furrowed her brow. Had she left the window open? No, there was no way she would have, so what was it? She turned on her back and opened her tired eyes. Adelaide startled.

Green eyes stared down at her.

Adelaide's face softened at the sight of Misha. She wondered if her love had heard her longing for snuggles. Before Adelaide could greet her, the vampire ripped the blankets down. Thankfully there was no chill in the air. It still made Adelaide gasp in shock. She opened her mouth to speak, but a pale finger pressed against her lips.

"Hush, my beautiful girl," Misha purred. She leaned closer. "I've been watching you, lovely little thing." Her pointer finger trailed down. Her sharp nail grazed along Adelaide's sternum. It eventually caught on the edge of the woman's nightgown. Misha's grin turned devious.

The sound of ripping silk made Adelaide jump. She looked down and watched in awe as Misha sliced through her clothes. Adelaide whimpered as heat pooled in her stomach. She tried to sit up on her elbows, but the vampire pushed her back down. Misha was staring at Adelaide like she was an oasis and the vampire looked thirsty. The blonde licked her lips. Misha smiled and Adelaide let out a shaky breath at the sight of her fangs. Adelaide rubbed her thighs together, trying to quell the arousal coursing through her.

Misha noticed the movement. She smiled devilishly. "Oh, what a naughty girl." Misha pressed her hand against Adelaide's hot stomach. The blood under her fingertips made her throat burn. "Here I was thinking I would need to woo you." She hooked her finger on the corner of Adelaide's cotton panties. "I knew you were lonely, but never imagined you would be a slut."

Adelaide's hips bucked as Misha cut the side of her underwear. The vampire ripped the other side, throwing her ruined panties into the dark of the room. Adelaide tightened her legs together. She looked up at Misha through her eyelashes. If they were doing this, she'd need to do her part. "Wait," Adelaide whined, "I don't even know your name."

Misha's smile widened. It had been a while since she'd been able to play with a partner. "Oh, my pretty girl." The claws on her left hand had been filed down. She played with the little curls that littered Adelaide's mons pubis. "I suppose you need a name to scream as you come for me," Misha teased. She kissed the woman's ear then caught it between her teeth. It turned burning hot against her tongue. "You may call me, Misha."

Adelaide gasped. Misha's accent was thicker, voice deeper. It was making Adelaide lose her mind. Her thighs quaked, toes flexing. Misha nibbled on her ear then trailed her blunt teeth down her jaw and along her neck. Adelaide's legs fell open. Her hips twitched as Misha's deft fingers rubbed the lips of her pussy.

"Misha," Adelaide gasped. She could feel the mess between her legs growing. Misha seemed to know exactly how to pull her strings. Adelaide wanted to tell the vampire to get on with it, but Misha captured her mouth in a kiss. That inhuman tongue dominated hers. Usually their kisses were shared, a dance. This one wasn't. Misha was ravenous. Adelaide whimpered as those fangs nipped her tongue. The vampire purred at the taste of her blood. "Touch me," Adelaide begged, "Please!"

Misha let out a shaky breath, "Oh, my pretty girl. So sweet for me." She sucked on Adelaide's bottom lip. "You're so warm," Misha growled against Adelaide's plush lips. "Will your pretty cunt be just as hot?" She nipped the woman's bottom lip. It was so plump and felt divine between her teeth. More blood rushed to the area. It was temptation incarnate. She ran her tongue over it. Misha spread Adelaide's labia. "Oh, would you look at that?" The vampire chuckled. "You're soaked," she teased.

Adelaide moaned. Misha's cool finger tip circled her clit. Her hips jumped off the bed. Tight, slow circles made Adelaide's eyes roll back. Her thighs quivered. It was incredible. Something about the strange scenario was making her go insane. Adelaide wanted more. She needed more. "Misha, I-"

"Shhh," the vampire shushed. Adelaide's face was scorching hot now. Blushes didn't show on Adelaide's umber skin, but Misha didn't need them to. She could see and smell the rush of blood underneath that lovely flesh. Those pretty apple cheeks were just as hot as Adelaide's ears. So much blood was rushing and running next to Misha's lips. "Oh, beloved," Misha groaned.

A cool tongue licked Adelaide's face. It was strange but also arousing in a primal way. Adelaide never thought she'd be into that sort of thing, but here she was, moaning like a porn star. Two fingers pushed inside her. The sudden intrusion made the woman's back bow. Adelaide let out a scream. The pads of those fingers were rubbing against her walls. Misha really had memorized her weak points and used them to her advantage. The noises her pussy was making were obscene. Wet and loud as undulating fingers played with her insides. The vampire hadn't been exaggerating, Adelaide was soaked. "Oh, yes," Adelaide moaned. Misha's fingers began to thrust inside her "Oh, fuck!" she wept. Her legs spasmed violently. "Fuck! Fuck! Fuck!" she screamed. Her stomach tightened and her hips shook. She was already close. Adelaide couldn't believe it.

Misha growled and pinned Adelaide to the bed. The woman gasped. Those pretty doe eyes were wet and filled with lust. The smell of sex made her feel high. Adelaide's loud moans were making Misha wet. "Do you hear yourself, beloved?" Misha licked up Adelaide's neck and to her ear. "Listen," she whispered. The blood rushing inside of Adelaide was tantalizing. Misha had to stop herself from biting. She'd wait for Adelaide's climax. Hell, maybe Misha could cause more than one.

That idea made the vampire moan. Adelaide could handle coming more than once. It would be worth it too. The blood would become ambrosia. Endorphins were unmatched in their taste. They made the blood sweeter, smoother. Misha's fangs itched. "Such a naughty little girl. My pretty girl." Adelaide tightened around her fingers. Misha groaned, pumping them faster, "Such a slut. Do you like that? Do you like the feeling of me inside you?"

Adelaide could only cry out. The sounds of Misha panting in her ear was making her stomach flutter. It was like the vampire was getting fucked as well. The pressure in her head was back. Was that Misha? It had to be. Another wave of slick spilled from her. Misha's thumb had now joined the fray and circled her clit. Adelaide screamed silently, mouth agape in ecstasy. Her leg kicked out uncontrollably. Adelaide wanted to give up and drop their game, but where was the fun in that? "I'm not-oh god" Adelaide whimpered, "I'm not a slut." The moan that followed made the words even more false.

Misha hissed, "No lying." She pressed her fingers in deeper and ground against Adelaide's sensitive walls. "I'm in your head, beloved. I hear every pretty little thought in there." Misha mockingly laughed, "I know you've always wanted to be taken like this." Misha could hear Adelaide's heartbeat pick up. The woman was close. "You read your silly little books, always disappointed because it's not a man you want inside you." Misha growled, "it's me."

Adelaide screamed, her climax taking her by surprise. She gripped the sheets and let her body shake and shiver. Adelaide tried to let her muscles relax but Misha's fingers were unrelenting. She tried to squirm away from them. "I came!" she cried, "I came." Adelaide knew Misha had felt it. The vampire obviously knew, but simply didn't care.

Misha giggled, "You think I'm done with you?" She kept up the same pace. Adelaide's scream reminded Misha of a viola. The pair were making a lovely little symphony. A concert of sex echoed off the walls. Misha, the player, and Adelaide, the instrument. An instrument who was currently pleading to god for mercy. Unfortunately, the maestro had no intention of stopping.

"Oh, god!" Adelaide tried to scramble away from the vampire's hands. The ache in her cunt was pulsing hot. Overstimulation was something she knew well, something she played with often. That strange state of wanting it to end but also wanting it to keep going. Adelaide could feel her slick running down her ass and thighs. The sheets would be ruined. Her face was on fire. The heater wasn't helping with her own internal inferno. "Misha," she whined. Adelaide didn't know what she was whining for. To stop? To keep going? Who could say?

"Such a messy girl," Misha cooed. She licked the side of Adelaide's neck. The vampire moaned, riding the waves with Adelaide till the woman once more stabilized. The arousal lowering from a roar to a rumble. Those screams turned to whines. Misha panted against Adelaide's neck. "More," she said, "You can give me more." Adelaide shook her head, but her mind screamed for Misha to keep going. The vampire obliged.

Misha's fingers left her. Adelaide wanted to sigh in relief and also cry out for the vampire to return. Why was Misha moving away? Was she done? She'd said more, right? Before Adelaide could ask what the vampire was doing. She was flipped onto her stomach.

Adelaide let out a surprised yelp. She tried to get on her elbows, but Misha pushed her head down. Her nose was buried into the bedding. The hand in her hair played with her curls.ABails lightly scratched her scalp. Adelaide moaned, her eyes fluttering as little shivers ran down her spine. Misha nuzzled her cheek. Those cool lips laid kiss after kiss on her face. The vampire lifted her hips up. "Misha," she mumbled into the bedding, "Please." Adelaide wiggled her hips.

Misha growled, slapping Adelaide's plump ass. "Now, now, naughty girl, be good for me," she purred. Misha squeezed Adelaide's ass before giving it another spank. Adelaide's fabric muffled moans made Misha groan. She knocked the woman's knees wider.

Adelaide jumped in shock as Misha's fingers slipped their way back inside her. "Oh, fuck," Adelaide gripped the edge of her bed. The game was long gone from her mind. "Wait, peac-" Misha pushed her face into the bedding again.

"Hush, beloved girl," the vampire growled. Misha pulled her fingers out of Adelaide's hot cunt. The woman was less slick than before. That wouldn't do. The vampire pricked her tongue on her fang. Misha spat blood and spit onto her fingers. "Here we go," she giggled, "now let's make you scream again."

Adelaide furrowed her brow. Misha was in her mind again. Adelaide whined, knowing round two was coming. On cue, the fingers pushed back in. It was different though. "OH FUCK!" Adelaide screamed into the sheets. Blood. Misha had put in her blood. Adelaide melted into the bed. A new wave of slick gushed out of her. Heat coursed through her veins. The blood was like an aphrodisiac. "I need to come!" Adelaide cried in urgency. "I need to, I need to!" She rubbed her cheek against the sheets. The fabric felt good, so fucking good. It was glorious. She was higher than the empire state building. Flying toward the moon on a rocket of pure pleasure. The fingers inside her rubbed rapidly at her walls. Adelaide gasped wetly as tears fell from her eyes. She caught the sheets between her teeth and gnawed on them. Her eyes rolled back in ecstasy. She'd never been so sensitive before. "More. More. More!" she moaned through her teeth. Adelaide moved her hips back, chasing her next orgasm.

The vampire chuckled. Adelaide's cunt was drenched. She buried her nose in the woman's neck. The sweet scent of Adelaide's blood made her inhale deeply. "Pretty girl, naughty girl, good girl. My sweet slutty girl and her slutty cunt." She shifted her hand and rubbed her thumb against Adelaide's clit. The little nub felt as hot as the tips of Adelaide's ears. "So warm for me," Misha slurred. The smell of Adelaide's blood and the shadow of the woman's pleasure made Misha feel divine. "I want you," Misha whined, "I want you. I want you. I want you!"

Adelaide planted her hands on the headboard. Her nails dug into the wood. Her toes caught and slipped on the bedding. Another orgasm rocked through her. "Misha!" she screamed, legs spasming. The heat in her stomach didn't subside though. If anything, it grew white hot. Adelaide's back bowed, her hand slapped against the headboard. "Oh god, oh god!" She rocked back on Misha's fingers. "Faster, oh please, faster!"

"Such a good pet," Misha moaned. "Pretty girl. My pretty girl." She sped up her thrusts. "How many will you give me?" Misha asked. She sucked a hickey into Adelaide's neck. Oh the blood. That sweet, succulent blood. So close. Misha was panting, drooling. She felt unhinged, a wild animal. The reflection of Adelaide's pleasure was driving her mad. She pressed her cheek against Adelaide's. The heat against her skin made Misha shudder in euphoria. Her eyes rolled back as another orgasm washed over Adelaide in waves.

"Misha!" Adelaide wept. She'd never been so high before. The edges of things around her wobbled. Colors seemed more vibrant. Everything had a glow to it. It was a gorgeous halo that made her room seem holy. "I wanna-" Adelaide's tongue refused to heed her. She projected her wants loudly in her mind. The need to see Misha. The need to kiss the vampire and look into those intense green eyes as she screamed through a final orgasm.

The vampire forced herself to stop fingering Adelaide long enough to turn the woman on her side. She placed an arm underneath the woman's head. Those ebony curls were wild. Misha smoothed them from the woman's face. The vampire then tugged at the coils, making Adelaide gasp and wiggle her hips. Misha pulled one of Adelaide's legs over her hip and replaced her fingers back inside the fluttering heat of her love. She pressed her forehead against Adelaide's. "Is this what you wanted, beloved girl?" Misha kissed the woman before teasing, "I can feel how close you are to release. Do you want it?"

Adelaide nodded. Misha's beauty became ethereal. Not just holy, nor simply angelic, but godly. A fiery goddess of lust and blood. Misha was panting, cheeks red and a line of drool rolling down the corner of her mouth. Green eyes were staring at her throat. Pearly white fangs glimmered in the hellfire light of the heater.

Misha watched in wonder as Adelaide offered her neck. "Come," Misha begged. Her fingers sped up. She buried her nose against Adelaide's neck. The woman was close, so close. The wet sounds of Adelaide's cunt echoed off the walls. The woman's moans and screams made Misha almost weep with want. Her throat was so dry. Unbearably dry. The smell of endorphins in Adelaide's blood made Misha's fangs itch in anticipation. She needed to bite. "Please, beloved," she begged, "I need you. I need it. I need you to come. I need it. I need it-"

Adelaide screamed. Her legs jerked in shock. Instead of closing her eyes, she kept them on Misha. Adelaide came so hard her body seized and curled in on itself as she shook apart. Misha's fangs were in her neck in an instant. The shot of pain made another wave of euphoria wash over Adelaide. The high reached its peak. Everything glew and glew until her vision whited out.

Blackness.

Slowly, the void faded. Everything was hazy and sounds were muffled. Adelaide blinked rapidly, till she could see once more. The woman groaned, every muscle in her body felt sore. The heater was off. Misha was wiping her down with a warm rag. "Peaches?" Adelaide slurred out. Her throat felt like sandpaper. Those green eyes flickered up at her.

The vampire paused her task. "Yes, beloved?" she asked.

Adelaide smiled. She let her head fall back against the pillows. "How long was I out?"

Misha mused, "A few minutes." She finished wiping down Adelaide and threw the washcloth in the hamper. "I need to change the sheets," the vampire announced. The woman whined. Misha chuckled. "I will not force you to get up," she said and gently rolled Adelaide this way and that to get the fabric off then swiftly replace it.

Adelaide made grabby hands at Misha. "Cuddle me," she mumbled, cheek pressed against the fresh sheets. The vampire smiled brightly. Adelaide sighed in relief when Misha wrapped around her. The blankets were pulled up and the pair snuggled together. "I love you," she whispered into the dark of the room..

"I love you too," the vampire whispered back.

Mike frowned at the mangled body. The admissions office was a wreck. "Like a fucking tornado," he whistled in shock.

Rick rubbed his face as the dean rambled on and on.

"We need to keep this quiet. The kids will be back soon," dean Foreman rambled. "We haven't had a murder in a decade, much less in the damn building!" Justin Foreman had taken the title of dean because it was easy. Well, it was pitched to him as easy. He wrung his tie in his sweaty hands. Oh, poor Teresa. That sweet woman didn't deserve to be ripped to shreds. "They stole so many student files! This can't get out!" Justin begged.

"We'll keep it under wraps," Rick said. He sighed. For better or worse, Teresa didn't have any family. She'd outlived everyone. Of course it'd take a monster to bring her down. The woman was practically decapitated. Her head was only hanging on by a few muscles. No one deserved to die like that.

Mike coughed, trying to keep his vomit down. The poor woman was splattered across the walls. "Alright…how the hell do we process this?" he asked Rick.

"Gotta call in the city boys," Rick said. He quickly turned to Justin, feeling the man's anxiety spike. "They'll be discreet!" The older officer rubbed his temple "What files did they take?"

Justin tried to stop his shaking. He sucked in a deep breath. "They took some files with the first names Margot and Margaret. Left behind all the ones with pictures"

Rick pursed his lips. "So he's obviously looking for someone."

Justin nodded solemnly. "All were alumni. Those were our only records. God, I hope they aren't living at the same addresses!"

Rick watched as the skittish man looked around wildly. Seeking an exit or answer, Rick couldn't say. The man was acting like a snared rabbit. "Justin," Rick put his hand on the man's shoulder. "Calm down, bud." The other man looked into Rick's eyes and took a deep breath then blew it out.

"Thank you, Ricky," Justin whispered. The officer patted his back.

Mike cleared his throat. They needed to get this show on the road. Before poor Teresa became ingrained into the hardwood floor. "I think we should call the boys...and the cleaners." He directed Mr. Foreman, "You need to make sure this section is closed off."

Justin nodded, "Of course. Of course!" He looked between the cops. With a sharp nod, he skittered out of the room.

Rick placed his hat back on. "Well, come on," he urged Mike. The younger officer followed him out.

"Do you think..." Before Mike could voice his thoughts, Rick agreed with a nod.

"We need to put an alert out on that Dracula guy," Rick said and climbed into the cop car.

Mike quickly got in. "Do you think he's still in town?"

Rick gripped the steering wheel. "I don't think so, but maybe someone knows where he's going next." The radio came to life. The panicked voice on the other end made the hair on the back of the men's neck raise.

"Rick, Mike, we got a situation at the old church!" Nancy frantically said. "Eight bodies!"

Mike and Rick's eyes widened. The older officer turned on his sirens and sped down the road. What the hell was happening to his town?

The girls would be back in a couple days and Adelaide wanted to have everything stocked for them. She pushed her shopping cart. Giddily, she stepped up on it and rode it down the aisle. A whistle made her head snap back.

Misha stood at the aisle entrance, holding a can of coffee. "What a wonderful sight, beloved," she teased.

Adelaide rolled her eyes, a smile on her face. She watched Misha put the coffee in the cart. The blonde made the most mundane of activities seem enchanting. The way she moved. The way she talked. God, Adelaide was so in love. Misha's eyes snapped up to hers.

"I love you too," the vampire whispered. Misha tapped the side of the cart. "Can I stroll?"

Adelaide giggled and moved so Misha could push. She looked over her list and crossed off a few items. "All we need is some orange juice." The pair moved through the store.

"You have so much food," Misha mumbled. In the past, if she had said there would be overflowing shelves of food in the future, she would have been called insane. Probably burned at the stake. The idea made her giggle.

Adelaide smiled. It wouldn't be a shopping trip with Misha if the vampire didn't marvel at modern abundance. "Alright," she grabbed a jug of orange juice, "Let's check out." The pair made their way through the process of paying and bagging their items.

Misha carried most of the paper sacks. Adelaide had huffed, but the vampire was stronger. Besides, Adelaide's faux annoyance was so delightful. The woman carried so much, everyday. The least Misha could do was help with the burden on her lover's shoulders.

The walk back home was nice. The streets had a few more people in them. Some of the kids had come back early from break. New Years would happen in a couple days. The last hurray before school began. "You excited to start?" Adelaide asked the vampire.

Misha smiled and practically skipped down the sidewalk. "Yes! I want to take apart a spaceship. Like your NASA child."

Adelaide snorted and rolled into a laugh. "She doesn't take them apart, peaches."

Adelaide explained, "She uses math in order to calculate how the craft will fly without-" Adelaide made an explosion sound. It made the vampire giggle. "Besides, you'll be building more than taking apart. Should've gone into forensics if you wanted to cut things up, or demolition."

Misha's eyes became alight. "Demolition?"

Adelaide had to stop walking to laugh again. "Jesus, peaches!" she tried to catch her breath. "It's people who tear down buildings," she explained. "Like with cranes and wrecking balls."

Misha was in awe. She thought for a moment. "Wait, are those the things in the churchyard?"

Adelaide pursed her lips, "Kind of?" She began to walk again. "The machines in the church are more for digging than knocking things down." They were going to walk past the church. "Here, I can show you-" Adelaide stopped in her tracks.

Misha furrowed her brow. She looked at the church. It was swarmed by police and bystanders. The machines were covered in yellow tape. The weight of Adelaide's eyes weighed heavily on her shoulder. Misha looked up at her. "It was not me, beloved. I swear!"

A heartbreaking scream made the women jump. Jamie wailed in horror. He pushed through the crowd and saw his friend's dismembered corpses. "NO!" he screamed, falling to his knees. "TOMMY!" he cried, "ADAM!" He dug his nails into the cold dirt as another grief filled wail left his throat. His vision blurred with tears. His throat felt like he'd swallowed glass. Everything was numb. The world around him was muffled. Jamie kept screaming. Broken, pained cries rang out in the winter air, like soul crushing church bells.

The agony in his voice brought tears to Adelaide's eyes. The boy was dry heaving, coughing and sputtering. He vomited, even that didn't stop his screaming. A couple people were trying to get him to stand, but he batted them away. Adelaide set down her bag of groceries and jumped over the short fence. "Jamie!" she called out to him. The boy looked up at her. His eyes were red, face ruddy.

Jamie coughed, spit and snot flying. God he was a mess. Still, Adelaide kneeled next to him. Her warm arms enveloped him. She smelt so good and she felt better. Warm. Warm like the sun. Her hand covered his eyes.

Adelaide glared at the cops, who seemed to be in a trance at the pile of bodies. "COVER THOSE UP!" she screamed. That snapped the men out of it. Someone offered a tarp from the construction site and laid it over the pile of boys. Adelaide whispered into Jamie's ear. "Baby, I need you to stand. Okay?" The boy was shaking violently in her arms. "Come on," she urged, pulling the boy to his feet.

Jamie staggered and let out another wail. He'd never cried like this before. He'd never had to confront death like this. The world was spinning. All he knew was the warmth of Adelaide. It was the only tangible thing he had, so he followed it. The sights and sounds around him were muted. Was it shock? Was he in shock? Probably. Jamie's mother had told him about how shock makes you a zombie. Wandering. Aimless. Thankfully, Adelaide was there. She was guiding him. She was helping him. The woman was so kind. So warm.

"Jamie!" a light slap to his cheek snapped him out of his stupor. The boy blinked rapidly. He looked up at Adelaide's concerned face. "I-" he closed his mouth. What was he going to say? What could he say? Jamie looked around. They were inside a house. Jamie realized Adelaide had taken him home with her. Probably for the best. There was nobody left at his house.

Adelaide wrapped a blanket around the boy. She asked, "Do you want some hot coco?"

Jamie thought for a moment. His hands felt stiff. He looked at them. Blood and cuts littered his skin. When had that happened? He sniffled and nodded. "Yes," Jamie answered aloud. Adelaide nodded, a sweet smile on her face. She rose and went to the kitchen. Jamie's lip quivered. He snuggled deeper into the blanket Adelaide gave him. It smelt like the woman. His mind calmed at the scent.

Adelaide walked into the kitchen. Misha was putting the food away. The vampire was moving on autopilot, much like Jamie had been. "Peaches," she said to get the woman's attention. Those green eyes came to life again. "Are you okay?" Adelaide asked. She knew Misha despised the boy, but there was no way Adelaide was going to leave him in the church yard.

Misha shut the fridge. She stood there, mind racing. "This is my fault," the vampire whispered. A crimson tear rolled down her cheek. "This is all my fault."

Adelaide frowned. "Misha, I need you to hold it together," she begged. The blonde nodded slowly. Adelaide asked in a whisper, "I'm guessing this was your maker's doing?" The vampire nodded again. Adelaide sighed and rubbed her face. At least she got that awful man away from town. "Misha," she slowly placed hands on the blonde's shoulders. She kept her grip light. "Jamie needs help," Adelaide explained, "He needs someone around. Are you going to be okay with him staying here?"

Misha snapped out of her misery. She nodded, "Yes. Yes." She may not like the boy's advances but he didn't deserve to be left alone after seeing the bodies of his friends. Misha looked up at Adelaide. "I am sorry," she whispered. "I am sorry how-" she didn't have a word other than 'broken'. Misha gestured to her head with shaking hands.

Adelaide frowned. "Misha," she pulled the woman into a hug. "I need you to remember, I love you." Adelaide placed a kiss on Misha's lips. A quick one. Enough to hopefully soothe the vampire's nerves.

Misha frowned when Adelaide walked past her and began to make the boy a drink. She swallowed thickly and walked to the living room. The boy was sitting stock still, staring at the dead fireplace. She knew that mourning look too well. Winter was still in the air and the boy was shivering like a leaf in the wind. Both from his nerves and the cold. Jamie's mind was going a million miles per hour. Thoughts scattered and flashing. Memories and missed opportunities.

Misha went to the fireplace. She stacked some wood inside and lit it. The warm glow of the flames made Misha feel at home. The last moments she shared with her mother had been surrounded by flames. Her mother's body grew colder as the fire melted her plague riddled flesh. The warmth was so lovely. The heat wasn't overwhelming, not yet. Just an orange glow and her family all around her. Misha was ready to join them on the other side. All of them in the pyre. She should have. But a hand dragged her out. Fangs dug into her bubo covered neck. Nails clutched at her. Misha was supposed to die, instead she was reborn.

"Thank you."

The meek voice made Misha stop her reminiscing. She stood up and noticed Jamie's empty eyes on her. "You are welcome," Misha replied. It sounded hollow. She sighed and took a seat on the opposite end of the couch. There was a space for Adelaide between them. Misha couldn't hate the boy anymore. He was now a kindred spirit. "I am sorry," she whispered, but the boy heard her. "I know how painfully losing people you love can be."

Jamie frowned. No wonder the woman was such a hard ass. No wonder she was so protective of Adelaide. He sniffled. "I'm sorry…" Jamie noticed her confusion, "For your losses too," he clarified.

Misha nodded. "Thank you." She looked at the fire and focused on the crackling.

"Is it bad I'm only mourning two of them?" Jamie asked out of nowhere. He felt guilty that only Tommy and Adam's deaths were making him spiral. It's not like he hated the other boys, but they were just…there. God, that sounded so awful. Jamie rubbed his eyes. They felt raw and it burned to touch them.

Misha shook her head. "It is not your fault that the others had no ties to you." She glanced at the boy. His thoughts were so loud. Guilt was an awful burden. "You could not have changed it." Jamie looked at her in shock. "If you had been there, you would have died too," Misha informed. "Do not hate yourself for being spared their fate. You could not have known." She looked back at the fire.

Jamie's brow furrowed. The woman sounded cold, but her words were comforting, or at least trying to be. Jamie nodded. He looked at the fire. "I can't call my mom. She'll have a cow."

Misha snorted, the smallest smile on her lips. "Humans can not have cows, silly boy."

Jamie smiled in shock. He chuckled. "So you can make jokes," he teased, relaxing into the couch. The heat of the fire was lulling. His muscles untensed and his mind mellowed.

Adelaide came into the room. She noted the fire and gave Misha a kind smile. 'Thank you' she mouthed to the woman. Adelaide sat in between them. She offered the mug of hot chocolate to Jamie. "Here, baby." The boy took the cup and had a few sips. Adelaide asked, "Are you hungry?"

Jamie nodded. The mug warmed his hands. His fingers felt alive again. Adelaide went back to the kitchen. He looked at Misha. The blonde stared at Adelaide. Her green eyes held so much love in them. Jamie remembered the book Adelaide had gotten. Something clicked in his mind. "Oh."

Misha's head snapped to the boy. There was a dopey smile on his lips. "What?"

Jamie chuckled, "Nothing." He drank his drink and mused about his romantic rival.

Chapter 13

Mike vomited into the bowl. His booted feet scrambled on the tiled floor. Tears ran down his face. He sniffled and spat. Mike flushed the toilet and tried to regain his senses. He looked at the door. Rick was standing there with a damp washcloth. "Thanks," Mike said, taking the rag and cleaning his mouth.

"You gonna be okay?" Rick asked his partner. The man coughed. It was a rough, horse noise.

Mike nodded. "Yeah, just…" the man sighed and leaned on the toilet. "This ever happened before?" he asked. The old man standing above him squatted down. A calloused hand rubbed his shoulder.

"No," Rick said. He stood and offered his hand to the younger man. Mike took it and he helped the man to his feet. "Hey," held Mike's shoulders. "It's okay."

Mike nodded. All of those books on serial killers, all that research, paled in comparison to the real thing. He sniffled and nodded again. "I'm okay," he said.

Rick smiled. "Come on. Greg is done with the examination." He led the other out of the bathroom and down the sterile hall of the medical examiner's office. Greg was waiting for them. Even he seemed a bit pale from the state of the bodies.

"Gentlemen," Greg greeted. He sighed and looked down at one of the boy's torn open torso. "I found something interesting," he said. Greg went to his table. "These wounds were made by claws and canines." He passed on his notes to Rick. Mike was leaning on the wall, sweat on his brow and he had a sickly look. Was a shame the boy's constitution wasn't stronger. Greg sighed and explained, "Saliva was found."

Great. Some beast and a mad man. Maybe the murders of Teresa and the boys weren't connected. Or worse, they were, and a man was using some creature to rip people apart for him. Rick hoped it wasn't a bear. "What animal are we dealing with?" Rick asked, looking over the notes.

Greg swallowed audibly, "Human."

The pair of cops went silent. Mike staggered off the wall. "Wait a minute, human?" He looked over Rick's shoulder. "You're telling me a human with fangs did this?"

Greg nodded solemnly. "All of them. Teresa, the boys, all have traces of it." He looked at the eight bodies in his office. "There was also this," Greg showed the man a clear bag. It contained a single strand of red hair.

"Jesus, Joseph, and Mary," Mike whispered in horror.

"At least we know who that probably belongs to," Rick said gruffly.

Mike scoffed, "Probably?!" A rage bubbled inside him. The man had been so close. So damn close. If they had held him up. If they had called in a watch on him, make him lag around for a bit more, maybe those boys-

Rick frowned, "Mikey." That snapped the boy out of his guilt. Rick looked at Greg. "Thank you," he took the bag. "If you find anything else, give us a call."

Greg nodded, "Of course." He looked at Mike. The young man was holding back tears. "We'll catch him," Greg swore. That made the boy's frown lessen. It was a small thing, but it was something. "Have they notified the families?" he asked Rick.

The older officer sighed, "Yes. We'll have a wave of wailing mothers on our hands." God and so close to the new year too. Rick grimaced. Eight closed casket funerals. Eight lives snuffed out, and for what? Did the bastard want to get his rocks off? No, he'd been looking for someone. Another redhead. Rick thought, frown deep on his face. There weren't many redheads in town, especially with an accent. Well, there was one. He turned to Mike. "After the New Year, we need to talk to that new girl Adelaide has."

Mike huffed, he'd been wanting to do that for days.

Jamie moaned around a spoonful of macaroni. "Adelaide, this is incredible." His mother's food was always bland and light. Something about staying thin in her 'old age'. Leafy greens with raisins. Thin spread tuna fish on white bread. Cottage cheese with peaches. She had a strange gelatin phase for the last three years he was home. Memories of the dead fish staring at him through green slime made him shudder. Thankfully, his mother's molded abominations couldn't follow him here. The frat house mostly lived on junk food and beer. Here though, Adelaide had blessed Jamie with a real home cooked meal. Macaroni, cornbread, ribs, green beans. God, Jamie hoped he could eat with the woman more often. This meal was fit for a king. Jamie grabbed another slice of cornbread. Adelaide looked at him with adoring eyes, like him eating her food like a wild animal was the greatest compliment in the world. It made Jamie's cheeks pinken.

Jamie took another bite of bread and looked at Misha. The woman sat to Adelaide's side, but she didn't have a plate. He furrowed his brow. Did Misha not like the food? How could she not like the food? It was incredible! Was she trying to look like Twiggy? Jamie didn't know why someone would starve themselves. He was a guy though, so maybe it was different.

Adelaide noticed the boy's confusion. She looked at Misha's missing plate. Adelaide swallowed her mouthful of greens. "Misha has some severe allergies," she explained. That smoothed the boy's furrowed brow.

Jamie's eyes widened. "Oh, shit." He looked at Misha, "I'm sorry." The blonde merely tilted her head. There was tension in the air. Jamie pursed his lips. How to break the ice? "So," Jamie tapped his finger on the table, "are you really from Russia?"

Misha's eyes narrowed, "What do you mean?"

Jamie shrugged, "You just sound like my grandma." Oh, that was a glare. A full on death glare. Jamie quickly explained, "I mean! You have the same accent. She was from Kiev." His grandmother was a sweet woman. She cooked like Adelaide. Hardy, hot meals that put Jamie to sleep. God, he missed her. He missed

Tommy. He missed Adam. Tears welled in Jamie's eyes. When he went back home, the house would be empty. Cold and empty.

Misha's shoulders relaxed. The sorrow rolling off the boy was palpable. She couldn't stay mad at him, even if she tried. "I do not know what my town is now called. I put Russia because it is what most people assume."

Jamie sniffled, wiping his eyes. He took a bite of bread to give him some time to gather himself. The women were looking at him with compassionate eyes. God, he felt stupid. "Sorry," he swallowed his food and took a drink of water. "Yeah, a lot of people can't tell the accents apart. At Least here." Jamie pressed his back into his chair. "Do you like it so far? America?"

Misha shrugged. "I have lived in many places." She copied Jamie's posture, back against her chair. "Paris, Sicily, Athens, London," Misha waved her hand in a motion to convey etcetera. "People are people."

Jamie smiled, "What's Paris like?" He leaned in, elbows on the table. "I've always wanted to go abroad but…" he also waved his hand.

Misha pursed her lips. "It is a city." She picked at the fabric on the table. "Dirty, many people, rats."

Jamie snorted out a laugh. "Sounds like New York."

Misha tilted her head. "New York?" It was the city Adelaide had lived in for a short time. Had the boy been?

Jamie nodded, "Yeah, one of our most famous cities. It's full of cool stuff, but also crazy people and rats." He chuckled, "They have rats the size of cats." Jamie showed the size with his hands. It was a bit of an exaggeration, but it was worth it to see Misha's green eyes go wide. "They steal babies."

Adelaide rolled her eyes with a good natured smile, "No they don't!" She looked at Misha, "Big ones like that are very rare."

"How do you know?" Jamie asked.

Adelaide huffed, "I lived in New York. Went there thinking I would be a lounge singer." Both Jamie and Misha were shocked. Adelaide explained. "It was a long time ago. Only did a few shows." If almost a hundred could count as 'a few'.

"You were a singer?" Jamie smiled brightly. Of course Adelaide had been a starlett, she probably still could be.

Misha was beaming. She'd known about the city, but not the singing! "You were! Why have you never told me?" She knew her lover's voice was too good to not be heard from a stage.

Adelaide shrugged, "It was a long time ago, peaches." She moved her food around with her fork. "I was young. Went up there just before the war ended and thought I could make it. Shows didn't pick up till after it was over. All those boys coming home wanted to hear a pretty voice and see a pretty face." Memories of stage lights and whistling men made her smile. "I was a little thing back then. Only lasted three years."

Jamie tilted his head. "Why'd you come back?"

Adelaide looked at the boy. He had a little pout on his face. As if he couldn't comprehend why Adelaide would come back. "My mother died."

Misha covered Adelaide's trembling hand with her own. The woman looked at her. Those big doe eyes were glassy.

Adelaide sniffled. "It was a long time ago," she restated, a bit firmer. Yes, she missed it. Her little hole in the wall apartment. The queer friends she found. Angel and his bright blue glass eye. They'd write songs and sew clothes together. Marta and her makeup collection. They'd spend hours putting paint on their face just to not go out. Frances and his dancing. They'd make people in the club whistle and clap. For three years, Adelaide got to live out of the closet. It had been hell, but also bliss. There was her love, who she couldn't even remember the face of. That one hurt the most.

    A cool hand wiped her cheek. Adelaide pulled herself out of her head. Misha was cleaning the tears off her face. Jamie was crying at the end of the table. Lord, what had the day done to them. Adelaide sniffled. "I made some chocolate cake!" she announced, standing. "Chocolate makes everything better!" Adelaide got the glass container from the counter and cut two thick slices.

    Jamie smiled through his tears. "It releases endorphins," he said and Adelaide set a piece in front of him. "More than kissing does."

    Misha huffed. She looked at Adelaide. The woman was washing something at the sink. Misha let her gaze move up and down the boy. "You have never been kissed properly," she teased the boy. Who in turn, choked on his forkful of cake. She smiled wickedly, making the boy shudder. Whether fear or arousal, Misha didn't care to find out.

    Jamie licked his lips and looked at Adelaide. The woman was placing stuff on the drying rack. He looked at Misha. "Maybe I will be," he teased back. The fire in the blonde's eyes burned brighter than the sun. Pissed. No better word for it, the woman was pissed.

Misha wanted to snarl. "You will lose your hands."

Adelaide set her slice on the table and looked between the pair. "What are you two whispering about?"

"Nothing," the pair said in unison.

Adelaide didn't believe them, but she still sat and ate her cake.

Margot Sherman folded the last of her son's clothes. The boy was a mess and still too little to do it by himself. The toddler was running through the halls. His little feet thunking against the carpeted floor.

"Mommy!" He held up a chewed up Lincoln log.

"Terrance!" Margot lightly scolded. She crouched down and took the wood toy away. "No bite!" she said firmly. The little boy giggled, not understanding why he was being scolded. It didn't help that Margot couldn't wipe the smile off her face. Anything her son did was a delight.

She scooped the boy up. Frederick would be home soon. They'd sit down for a nice dinner then watch The Mod Squad after Terry went to bed. Margot kissed her son's cheek. "Let's make some dinner!" she cheered. The pair went into the kitchen.

Thankfully, Frederick made enough to let Margot take a few years off to raise Terry. She never thought she'd be a mother, but she didn't regret it. Margot paused at the wall of pictures. A wave of nostalgia washed over her.

Mama A and her sorority sisters stood in front of their house. God, those four years had been incredible. Margot looked at the photo from last Christmas, Mama A holding a baby Terrance in her arms. The older woman's umber face littered multiple photos. She needed to call the woman soon.

Pat had told her Adelaide had a foreign girl now. She was apparently cold, but good with kids. A little Russian, Cathy gossiped. Only Mama A would take in a foreigner most would reject.

Terry wiggled in his mother's arms. That snapped Margot back to reality. "Okay, honey, okay." She placed her son into his high chair. "Let's get you some snackies," Margot cooed.

She got some chopped strawberries and bananas.

Terrance cheered, "Nanas!"

"Yes," Margot giggled, "Nanas!" She waited for Terry to take his first bite before going to the stove. Pots and pans were pulled out. She got out her ingredients. Meatloaf, veggies, and mashed potatoes were on the menu. It was Frederick's favorite meal. He'd just gotten a promotion at work. It was time to celebrate. Margot pulled her hair back into a ponytail.

A knock at the back door made Margot pause. She thought she'd misheard it and turned to go back to her work. The knock came again. A chill ran up Margot's spine. No one used the back door. They had a fence around the property. The sun was setting. Darkness was encroaching in. The silhouette behind the back door's curtain showed a shadow of a man.

"Door!" Terry pointed at it, "Daddy, door, mama!"

Margot frowned. For the first time, she wanted her son to shut up. The knock came again. Margot swallowed thickly. She walked to the door and cautiously pulled the curtain back. The man on the other side stood tall. Piercing blue eyes and fiery red hair. "Can I help you?" she asked through the glass.

The man leaned in closer. "Pity," he said.

Margot furrowed her brow in confusion. "Excuse me?"

"I had hoped this one would be right," Vladan chuckled, "wishful thinking." He tapped his finger on his lip. A rage was bubbling up inside him. Where the hell was she?! How dare she hide from him. Two hundred years. Two hundred fucking years! She'd slumbered and hoped he would forget? Foolish girl. Foolish, foolish girl! He knew as soon as she awoke. Felt her in the air. Smelt her on the wind. Heartbeat in his ears. Vladan felt his fangs lengthen.

Margot watched in horror as the man's face twisted in rage. He no longer looked like a man, but a monster. There were deep lines on his face as he snarled. Margot stepped back, letting the curtain close. Her heart was beating out of her chest.

Terry could feel his mother's distress. "Mama?" he asked, squishing a strawberry between his little fingers. Margot whipped around to her son and put her finger to her lips, "Shh!" The little boy giggled and copied her.

Glass shattered. Margot screamed. The man had blown out the window. She quickly ripped Terry's high chair tray off and unbuckled her son, trying to get him out as quickly as she could.

The man wasn't breaking down the door. He didn't even reach his hand in to unlock it. He merely said, "**Let me in**."

Margot stopped her frantic movements. Her eyes turned glassy. Terry looked up at his mother. Mama?" he tilted his head and reached his arms up to her. Margot stood up straight. She walked over to the door and unlocked it.

"Mama?" Terry called after her. Margot opened the door. She nodded to the man, moving to the side to let him in. Terry whimpered. His stomach felt wrong. It hurt. Mama was screaming. It hurt his ears. The man came to him. Covered in red. "Mama?" Terry called, but she was on the floor.

Vladan got eye level with the child. His mouth dripped with the woman's sweet blood. "Will you be just as sweet?" he asked, unbuckling the boy.

Terry began to cry. His little fingers went to his mouth, trying to soothe himself. The man picked him up. "Mama?"

Adelaide made up the bed for Jamie. Thankfully the room by the stairs wasn't a complete mess. She smoothed out the blankets. Jamie was waiting in the doorway. "The bathroom is down the hall," Adelaide explained. "I'll get you some clothes," she said, "I think a nice hot shower will do you good." The boy nodded. Adelaide rubbed his shoulder, moving past him to go to her sewing room.

Jamie walked into the sparse room and sat on the bed. He looked around, till his eyes landed on Misha. The woman was in the doorway, her face pinched. "Hi?" Jamie gave her a lame wave. The blonde walked into the room. Her hands went to her hips. Jamie's mouth turned into a line. He looked away from her. "So…" where to begin? "You and Adelaide are close."

"She is mine," Misha said firmly. Social norms be fucking damned.

Jamie pursed his lips. He gestured to the door with his head. "She know that?"

Misha's eyes narrowed, "She does." The blonde sighed. "I have marked her in more ways than one."

Jamie swallowed thickly. The idea of the women together. He shook his head. That was a thought for when he was alone. Jamie rubbed his eyes with his palms. "I get it," he said. He looked up at the blonde. Her arms relaxed. "I can't help it," Jamie explained, "Can you blame me?"

Misha sighed. She sat next to the boy. "No, I can not blame you." The vampire could hear the boy's heart beating rapidly. How strange. When was the last time she felt at ease near a man? The boy had taken the news well. He respected it. What a nice change of pace. Misha smiled, "Let us be friends." She offered her hand.

Jamie looked at the limb then back to Misha's emerald eyes. He smiled and shook it. The hand was cool. Strangely cold. Jamie looked at it and pulled his hand back slowly. "Should let her warm you up," he quipped.

Misha tilted her head. A smile spread across her face. "I will."

Adelaide came back into the room. She frowned at how close Misha was to Jamie. It wasn't jealousy per say, but wariness. The vampire looked at her, a grin on her face. Adelaide rolled her eyes. She handed the clothes and towels to Jamie. "Here, baby. Go wash up."

Jamie nodded and took the items. He walked out the room and down the hall.

Adelaide waited for the bathroom door to shut before asking Misha, "What are you doing?" She crossed her arms over her chest. "The boy's been through a lot today." The vampire looked up at her innocently. A cheeky little smile was on Misha's lips. "Peaches," she scolded.

The vampire leaned back. "I have made peace with him." Misha stood and wrapped her arms around Adelaide's waist. She swayed with the woman. "He knows you are mine," Misha rested her chin on Adelaide's chest. Her fingers slipped under the woman's sweater.

Adelaide frowned. "Misha, you-" The vampire's lips pressed against her own. The scolding on her tongue was halted, for now. Cool fingers trailed up her spine. Misha bit her lip. Adelaide groaned in pain. She dug her nails into Misha's sides. The vampire sucked the blood from her lip. When the vampire pulled away, Adelaide sighed. "You can't be tellin' people," she whispered.

Misha mewled, "He already knew." She pressed herself closer to Adelaide's warm body. "Come to bed with me," she urged.

Adelaide tried not to smile. Tried, being the key word. She huffed and tugged the woman down the hall and to their room.

Chapter 14

Vladan licked his fingers clean. He sat on the scratchy couch, placing his feet on the coffee table. The fire before him crackled. Bodies laid on the floor, their blood shimmered in the orange light. His rage had subsided after tearing out the throat of the large man. Who'd had the audacity to fire at him.

Vladan pulled out his list. Crossing of Margaret Phillips. How many had he eaten? At least ten, probably more. He tipped his head back, resting against the couch's edge. The blood on his mouth was drying. "Oh, Margosha," he whispered into the night.

His beautiful girl. His sweet pearl. Vladan groaned, relaxing into the upholstery. The woman had been molded to be his. From childhood, he had reared her to be perfect. The perfect height. The perfect body. The perfect voice. Perfect. He'd sculpted his own David in Aphrodite's visage. Vladan was not a creature who felt guilt. Why would he?

Rage though, rage was a feeling he knew all too well. Vladan had felt rage as he ripped his other little dancers apart. Some had laid with his pearl. They kissed the lips he was denied. Tasted the fruit he'd tended to so lovingly. He felt nothing as he strung them up. They made such lovely decorations, adorning the stage. Margosha's cries of anguish were more heavenly than the choir. Did she really think he'd let her leave?

The girl then had the audacity to set the academy ablaze. She had the audacity to run. The wretched little thing. Thankfully, the flames never found him. He'd found refuge in the basement. The thick black smoke did nothing to his dead lungs.

His little pearl ran home to her mother and sisters. Their sad little cottage on the outskirts of the village. It took Vladan time to put himself back together. He needed a home to bring her back to afterall. Vladan came with a bouquet and gifts. The ungrateful whelp spat in his face and barred him from the home.

Finally, the plague came. Once again the plague came. It ravaged the village. Vladan, in his pettiness, released a rat into his Pearl's house. He waited by her window each night, begging her to come to him. The women inside withered. Margosha was the last to fall ill. Even as she laid in her bed, covered in sores, she refused him. The little monster.

The men from the city came. They loaded all the bodies into a pyre. Vladan refused to let the fire take him, like hell he'd let it take Margosha. Vladan had to preserve her. Over a decade of hard work couldn't end in flames! He had to keep that perfection for eternity. The woman should have been grateful. She should have seen how much Vladan adored her! Still, he pitied the sobbing girl. Vladan offered her one wish, one gift. She could have had anything. Anything her vain little heart desired.

'I never want you to touch me again!'

Those words replayed in his mind. Still, he obeyed. He watched her run, knowing that he'd be able to find her. They were tied now. Vladan would give her time. He'd let her lull herself into feeling safe, then he'd strike. First a lover, then a few friends, then her children. Never did he touch his pearl, as she desired. He just ripped everything she loved apart. Eventually, she'd have no one left. No one left, but him.

All he had to do was keep going.

Vladan's blue eyes scanned the room. The home was small, but comfortable. Pity. Vladan noticed a photo. His eyes narrowed.

There she was again. The black woman he'd met in that little town. She was in at least one photo at every house he had been to. How peculiar. Her umber face seemed to follow him. Like an angelic presence.

    Vladan stood to look at the photo closer. The woman was younger in the photo. There was no gray in the woman's curls. No wrinkles on the woman's face. She had touched the many lives he had taken. Vladan tapped his claw against the glass. Age was something few got in his time. Aging beautiful was even rarer. This woman had grown with a grace Vladan would have likened to witchcraft. What was the woman's name?

    A groan made Vladan's eyes snap to the floor. The woman, who he thought he'd drained, was trying to crawl away. Vladan chuckled at her attempt. He took the photo off the wall. The woman let out a weak cry when she noticed him approaching.

    Vladan grabbed her by the hair. He placed the photo in front of her. "You remember her?" The woman didn't need to answer aloud. He searched her mind. Memories. Warm, bright, memories. Late night chats, study sessions, home cooked meals, hugs, cries, love, happiness, safety, home. Adelaide. Adelaide was her name. Adelaide was home.

Vladan was touched. A feeling he hadn't had in centuries. He let the woman's hair go. Her head thunked against the floor. Vladan looked at Adelaide's photo and tapped his nail against her face. He should visit the woman again.

Vladan turned the frame over and took the photo out. It was thick and glossy. Modern technology was so fascinating. He ripped Adelaide out of the picture. Next, he folded the picture and tucked it into his breast pocket. The woman on the floor was moaning in pain. Vladan crouched down and snapped her neck.

Fireworks went off outside. There were cheers in the distance. Vladan looked down at the cooling body. "Happy New Year!" he cheered, stepping over the corpse and out the house.

The girls would be back in an hour. Adelaide had been scrambling for the past week to get the house in order. Food was stocked. Extra blankets and sheets were washed. The smell of sex was aired out.

Adelaide collapsed onto the couch. Misha walked into the room, glass of water and muffin in hand.

"Here, beloved," the vampire handed off the items. Misha made sure the woman ate. There was tension in the air. Misha hoped the children would like her. She knew the air she gave off was…strange. People were either entranced or unsettled. On rare occasions, some were both. "Is there anything else to do?" she asked. The woman had finished scarfing down her food. It was cute how Adelaide's cheek protruded while eating. Like a chipmunk.

Adelaide chugged her water to wash down the muffin. "No, just waiting now." She relaxed against the couch. Everything Misha needed to start school was assembled. Schedule, paper, pens, books. The semester would begin in a couple days, hopefully it would be calmer than the last.

The clock ticked above the mantle. Adelaide sighed. Misha nuzzled into her side, head on her shoulder. That made the taller woman smile. She turned her head and looked at the vampire. Those emerald eyes were alight. "What?" Adelaide felt a warmth bloom in her chest.

Misha moved closer. "We won't be able to kiss, in here, for a while." She trailed her finger over Adelaide's chest. Misha licked her lips. "Maybe…" the blonde trailed off.

Adelaide bit her lip. Screw it. She locked lips with the vampire. The pair moaned simultaneously. Adelaide pushed the vampire down onto the couch cushions. Cool fingers slipped up her shirt and cupped her breast. Adelaide pulled back from Misha's lips. "Peaches."

Misha chuckled. "One last ride, Beloved?"

Adelaide groaned. Last night had left her sore. The vampire had Adelaide sit on her face for hours. The blonde cheekily cried, "Happy New Year!" as Adelaide's climax hit. "You're insatiable," Adelaide bit Misha's lip.

"Come on," the vampire urged. Who knew when they'd be alone again.

Adelaide rolled her eyes but kissed the vampire again. She dropped to her elbows and pressed herself against Misha. Their tongues danced, gently caressing each other. She reached down and pulled Misha's leg around her hip. The vampire groaned. Adelaide nipped at the woman's neck.

Misha giggled. "Oh, beloved," she moaned. She reached her other hand down and squeezed Adelaide's ass. "Harder," Misha growled. Those blunt, mortal teeth became rougher. They dug into the vampire's tough flesh. "Yes!" Misha cried, head falling back.

Adelaide moaned. Her jaw was beginning to ache. When she pulled away from Misha's neck, there were indents in her skin. Within seconds, the marks disappeared. Flesh, once again, became unblemished. "Pity," Adelaide whispered and pressed a final kiss on the spot.

Misha grasped Adelaide at the waist. Her fangs extended. Thirst burned her throat. "Beloved?" Her angel. Her beautiful, loving Adelaide tilted her neck in offering. Misha sank her fangs into that hot, umber skin. The blood awaiting her was sweet. Spiced with hormones and aged like a fine wine. Misha groaned as she drank.

Adelaide gasped, shivering above the woman. The bite felt incredible. Misha pulled back, Adelaide whined in loss. Till she noticed the vampire biting into her own wrist, offering it to Adelaide. The taller woman took it. Those fangs were then placed back in her neck. Adelaide's eyes fluttered. Misha was taking her time. Sipping from her. It was hypnotic. Adelaide could've fallen asleep right then and there. The blood on her tongue was rich. Her vision blurred, then it shined. Light was more intense. Colors popped. Sound was sharper.

Adelaide let go of Misha's wrist, which she hadn't realized she'd been clutching. The vampire released her neck in turn.

Misha watched as the wound she made closed. The blood she'd given Adelaide was pumping through her veins. The taller woman was swaying, unsteady. Misha sat up, urging Adelaide to rest against her.

"You're stronger than molly, peaches," Adelaide slurred with a dopey smile. She nuzzled into the side of the woman's neck. "God, you're so damn pretty. Pretty, pretty peaches." Misha's skin was so interesting. Flesh over marble. There was only a little give. "My Aphrodite," she whispered. Kiss after kiss was laid on Misha's face. Adelaide didn't realize she was the one laying them till Misha's lips captured her own. "Oh, hello," she giggled against the vampire's mouth. The blonde squeezed her backside again. It made Adelaide squeak. "Now, you listen here," she started but lost her train of thought, kissing the woman instead.

There was honking outside. "Oh, no," Adelaide whispered. "Mama!" Tracey called from the front porch, knocking loudly. The other girls began calling out as well. Adelaide was too high to greet the girls. Too high to keep her mouth in check.

Misha kissed her cheek. "I will help you, beloved," she whispered into Adelaide's ear. The blonde helped the woman stand.

"MAMA!" the girls cried.

"I'm comin!" Adelaide replied and staggered to the door. She giggled and turned the handle. The door didn't budge. Misha came up behind the confused taller woman and clicked the deadbolt open. Adelaide giggled and kissed Misha's cheek. "Thanks, peaches." The woman threw the door open. "Babies!" she greeted.

The girls poured into the house, exchanging hugs with Adelaide. Misha stepped back, letting the girls have their contact unimpeded. She had grossly underestimated the love Adelaide had for every girl that came through her doors. Guilt gnawed at her. It caused a deep frown to form on her face. She quickly smoothed it out in hopes of not attracting attention. It was too late however.

"Who are you?" Heather asked. She looked the strawberry blonde up and down. Adelaide normally maxed out the house with ten girls.

Misha opened her mouth to answer then closed it. Her throat felt too shaken to trust her voice to be steady. Thankfully, Adelaide answered for her.

"That's peaches!" the taller woman cheered. Adelaide got out of the hugging circle she'd been trapped in and went to the vampire's side. "She's startin' this semester and I expect y'all to help her." Adelaide hugged the woman. "Her name's Misha!"

All the girls looked at the new girl skeptically. Tracey broke rank and went to the newcomer. "Welcome to the house!" she hugged the blonde. "I'm Tracey, it's nice to meet you."

Misha smiled at the child. "It is nice to meet you too."

All the girls' eyes widened.

"She's foreign?" Monica blurted out. Wendy lightly smacked her arm. "Russian?" Dawn asked Tina, who was studying linguistics. Tina shook her head, "Crimean, maybe. Possibly Ukrainian." Heather huffed, arms crossed, "She just showed up?"

Adelaide frowned. "Now, Heather. Misha wants an education. No different from any of you." The high was finally dying off. Thank god. "Besides, we're the best sorority in town!" That got the girls to cheer. Adelaide sighed in relief. Misha was tense against her. "Why don't you girls unpack and get yourselves cozy? I'll start dinner." The girls all nodded and a thunderous chorus of feet went up the stairs.

Adelaide let out a breath she didn't know she'd been holding. "You okay?" she asked the vampire. Misha had an odd deer in the headlights look. "Peaches?" Adelaide touched the blonde's shoulder. That snapped her out of it.

Misha looked up at Adelaide. "Sorry," she whispered. The realization of what was going to happen to Adelaide's past students weighed on her shoulders. Instead of dwelling, Misha turned to her love. "What will we cook tonight?" she asked.

Adelaide giggled and snuck a quick kiss on the vampire's lips. "I was thinking some fried chicken, or maybe pork chops."

"I think they'd prefer chicken," Misha advised. She went to the kitchen, Adelaide trailed behind her. She swallowed her remorse and helped the woman cook a feast.

Justin rubbed his eyes. Classes would begin tomorrow. The anxiety of it all was making his eye twitch. So far, Rick had kept to his word. The murder in admissions was on the down low. Partially due to the poor boys found mangled in the church yard. Oh lord, why him? Why his town? Why his school? Rick burst through the door. Amanda, to the secretary's credit, tried to stop him. "It's fine, Mandy," Justin waved the red faced woman off. She closed the door behind her. "What do I owe the pleasure, Ricky?"

"He's killin em," Ricky said, throwing newspapers on the desk.

Justin frowned, examining the headings. All Margots or Margarets, all past students. His face went pale in an instant. "Oh, no."

"'Oh no' is a fucking understatement," Rick huffed, "We need to put out a warning and a statement."

"No!" Justin stood up in terror. "Jesus, Rick, the alumni-"

"Four families have been slaughtered, Foreman! Eleven people total. Eleven fucking people!" Rick picked up a paper. "This woman was murdered in front of her toddler and the baby was found gutted! Fucking gutted, Justin! Three Margarets, one Margots! All these people are fucking dead!" Tears pricked his eyes. He slammed his fist into the desk. The FBI was scrambling. The murders were happening all over the place. California. Tennessee. Maine. Fucking Alaska! How the hell was one man doing this? How could this be happening? It didn't make sense. Justin was stammering and sniffling out excuses. Rick grit his teeth. "How the hell can you sit there and not try to help these poor women?!"

"We owe them nothing!" Justin countered. "Legally, we owe them nothing!" He felt hysterical. Justin took out his handkerchief and wiped the sweat from his brow. "I can't risk my job, Rick. The donors, they-"

"FUCK THE DONORS!" Rick threw the glass paperweight on Justin's desk. It shattered against the wall. "Either make a fucking announcement, OR I WILL"!" Rick vowed.

Justin's face twisted. The officer was walking away. Before he reached the door, Justin blurted out, "I'll tell them!"

Rick scoffed. He looked over his shoulder. "Tell who what?"

Justin felt bile rise in his throat. "I'll tell them about you." A new tension entered the office. Rick straightened up. When his eyes met Justin's, the dean felt his heart stop. The unbridled rage in those steely eyes were enough to knock him into his chair. He'd seen that look before. It was one he'd gotten right before his nose was broken.

"Will you now?" Rick stalked up to the desk. He placed his hands on it, leaning in. The creak of the wood and the squeak of his boots harmonized and bounced off the walls. The pair were so silent, they could have heard a pin drop from the next room. "And how you gonna explain why you know, hm? Gonna tell 'em you bore witness, *personally*?" Rick leaned in closer, "Gonna tell 'em about *us*?"

Justin swallowed audibly. He knew that southern drawl meant Justin was one step away from knocking someone's lights out. He licked his suddenly dry lips. His threat was a shot in the dark and, god, had it backfired. "Ri-Ricky-"

"Either make a statement," Rick put his hands on his belt, "Or I will." The fear in Justin's eyes was satisfying. "I'll give you three days." With that, he walked out of the office, not bothering to close the door behind him.

Justin gasped. Tears flooded his eyes as he tried to catch his breath. He sniffled and wondered how the hell he was going to explain this to the donors. Three days. That would be plenty of time to get someone to shut Rick up. Justin practically ripped open his desk drawer and pulled out his book of numbers. The paper on his desk showed a family photo of a woman and her toddler. Justin turned the paper over and began dialing.

Heather didn't trust the strange woman who was refusing to eat Mama's cooking. She sat on the right of Adelaide, smiling up at her. Chair too close for comfort. In fact, Adelaide had accidently bumped the girl a few times while eating. "So," Heather started, "why don't you eat?"

Misha's green eyes snapped at the woman. Her hair was charcoal, with blue eyes, a pretty combination if her distrust didn't disrupt Misha's place. "I have," she looked at Adelaide and blinked innocently, "what is the word again?"

Adelaide smiled, "Allergies." She looked at Heather. "She has a very specific diet, otherwise she gets ill."

Heather pursed her lips. "How do you know?"

Adelaide frowned, "I saw it." She leaned back on her chair. The other girls' faces fell at the sight of hers. "It wasn't pretty," Adelaide explained, "There was a lot of blood."

Wendy shuddered, "Oh, shit." She ate her mashed potatoes. "I'm sorry, lil red."

Misha tilted her head in confusion. "Lil red?"

Monica rolled her eyes. "It's just a nickname." She pointed at Tracey, "Wendy calls Trace that too." Tracey nodded, mouth full. "Yep!" She swallowed and playfully scolded Wendy, "Come up with a new name!" Wendy rolled her eyes, "Fine, lil pink." Tina grimaced, ripping off a chunk of cornbread. "That sounds…" she trailed off. The rest of the girls agreed. Wendy scoffed, "Fine!" She thought for a moment. "Lil peach?" The rest of the girls nodded in agreement.

Adelaide sighed, "Just fucking call her peaches."

The girls all gasped. "Mama cussed!" Dawn cried, giggling into her hand. The others joined in, teasing the older woman.

Misha rolled her eyes. "Children," she teased the group.

Wendy scoffed, "You're like our age!"

Misha frowned, "I am not."

"Bullshit," Nicole chastised, "You're like what, twenty-two? Twenty-three?"

Misha huffed. She looked at Adelaide. A sly smile spread across the vampire's face. Misha looked at the awaiting girls. "I'm actually six hundred years old."

A silence fell over the table, before all the girls erupted in laughter.

"Never mind," Mabel giggled, "You're alright, lil peach!"

Misha smiled, "Why thank you, Mabella." She looked at Adelaide. The taller woman had a smile in her eyes that made Misha melt.

The girls all went quiet and looked between each other. Each wondered how the girl knew Mabel's full name. Maybe it was just a lucky guess. Probably was.

Adelaide noticed their unease. She asked them, "Who's suffering through Dobson?" All the girls groaned at the mention of the professor's name. Conversation began anew. Adelaide slipped her hand under the table. Misha's cool fingers entwined with hers.

The auditorium had hundreds of seats. It reminded Misha of an operating theater. Tracey was on her arm. The child was filled with an infectious energy. She seemed excited to have another redhead around. The pair sat closer to the front. Tracey's eyes were apparently weak. Misha wondered why the girl didn't get glasses.

It would be something for Misha to do with her later.

"Dobson is a creep, so I'm glad you're with me," Tracey whispered, anxiety in her voice. She didn't want to sit so close, didn't want to be noticed, but she had to. Glasses were expensive. She knew mama would have bought her a pair, but didn't want to impose. She already felt like she had done that enough. Tracey sat, Misha beside her. The woman had an air of authority to her, like she could snap anyone in half if she wanted. It was comforting. "Wendy said he sometimes makes girls stay behind. If he does, you'll stay with me, right?"

The girl reminded Misha of a frightened rabbit. "Yes, I will," she vowed. The professor in question walked in. He was a balding man, pipe between his lips. His mustache was thick, chestnut brown with gray hairs in it. His brown eyes scanned the room and landed on Misha and Tracey. He began leering at them.

"Welcome, new students," Timothy Dobson greeted. The pretty redheads in front of him were a welcomed surprise. "Take out your textbooks, we'll begin with chapter four." There was shuffling around the room. Dobson began writing on the chalkboard. The clock ticked as he talked.

Misha listened to the man's droning voice. Others around her wrote notes, Misha didn't need to. She'd memorized the textbook already, something the man was reading off word for word. How boring. Misha chewed on her pencil and decided to explore the man's mind.

It was a cesspit.

Misha quickly left his thoughts. He was worse than the girls had warned. A pig. She twirled her pencil between her fingers.

"Young lady?" Dobson stood in front of the redhead. He leaned down, "You seem bored." He noticed her textbook was closed, "Would you like to tell the class what was found in Ethiopia?"

Misha smiled, "Lucy of course."

Dobson pursed his lips. "And why was this discovery so important?"

Misha rolled her eyes. "Obviously because she was millions of years old. Meaning humanity's ancestors have existed far longer than previously thought. Walking around before stone was shaped." She leaned back. "Also, she caused a fire in the church. Upset that humanity was not as young and divine as they once thought." Misha tilted her head to the side. She reached out, flicking the cross around Dobson's neck. "Seems you've found peace with it though. Good for you." She gave the man a cheeky smile.

Dobson furrowed his brow. This little bitch. She wasn't the first know-it-all to cross his threshold. All of Adelaide's girls were snooty little prudes. Dobson missed when the girls were meek and submissive. There used to be so much power in teaching. Now, he couldn't even invite a girl into his office without the dean breathing down his neck. Ethics. Dobson rolled his eyes. He cleared his throat. Normally, he'd snap at the girl, but the redhead was strange. There was an aura around her that made him hesitate provoking her. Dobson trusted his gut. He stepped back. "Open your book," he instructed and went back to reading.

Misha did, just to humor him. Tracey was staring at her in shock. Dobson continued his drivel. The vampire was becoming bored. She hoped the other teachers would do more than just lazily read. Eventually the clock chimed. Class was over. Dobson instructed them to read more chapters. Misha got up and placed her book in the satchel Adelaide had gifted her. It smelled like the woman. Pomegranates and honey.

Tracey packed frantically.

"Excuse me," Dobson came up behind the strawberry blonde. Such a unique color on such a bitchy girl

"Class is over," Misha snapped. She took Tracey's hand and walked out of the room. The professor called after her, but the vampire kept walking.

Tracey giggled beside her. "You're insane!"

Misha shrugged, "I suppose."

The rest of the day was better. The teachers got more and more engaging. Misha actually learned something new. She ran into the other girls in different classes or passing through halls. College was something she'd never experienced before. It was thrilling.

Misha entered the library and inhaled deeply. All the books around her were young, but still had that unique smell only aged paper carried. The librarian at the desk eyed her up and down. Misha ignored her gaze and began to explore. She ran her fingers over the spines and hummed to herself.

"Oh, it's you!" Jamie said in surprise. It got him shushed by the librarian. Jamie gave her an apologetic look.

Misha rolled her eyes. "Hello, boy," she greeted with a smile. "What do I owe the pleasure?"

Jamie scoffed, "I wasn't looking for you." He lightly shook his books. "I got some reading to catch up on." Jamie looked the girl up and down. "You know, you actually look normal."

Misha huffed, "What is that supposed to mean?" Adelaide had helped her dress. The girls had helped her put on makeup. She looked like the other students.

Jamie put up a free hand in surrender. "I just meant, every time I've seen you, you've looked so otherworldly. You look like an average person now." He chuckled nervously. The girl was not average, not in the slightest, but Jamie could pretend. He leaned against the bookshelf. "So, how do you like school so far?"

Misha smiled, "I am pleasantly surprised." She then huffed, "I do not like Dobson."

Jamie grimaced. "Yeah, he's a bastard." The boy sighed, "I'm sorry you got him."

Misha shrugged, "I am glad, actually. The child is in his class as well. Would rather his lingering gaze be on me then her."

"Child?" Jamie tilted his head. Who the hell was the child? His eyes widened, "Do you mean Tracey Templeton?" That girl was what Tony labeled 'jailbait'. Jamie groaned. He hated that term. She was just a kid. Tracey was a well protected girl, for very good reason. There were many wandering hands and eyes. Jamie was happy Misha had joined the pack to protect her. He asked, "Is she okay?"

Misha narrowed her eyes at him. His thoughts were clean, unlike the awful teacher. Misha's face went placid. "She is fine," she answered, taking a book from the shelf.

"That's a good one," Jamie said, "Twain's a classic." He frowned, warning the blonde, "that one does have a few slurs in it though." Misha huffed and stuffed it back on the shelf. Jamie winced. "Sorry, just thought you'd want to know." He added, "It's still a good story! Just…a product of its time."

Misha simply replied, "I will not bring that into Adelaide's house."

Jamie couldn't blame the girl. He looked at his books. "Here," he offered her, "I've already read it twice. Good read."

Misha looked at the cover. "What is this Frankenstein? Is it a name?" she asked, turning the book over. The cover was lovely. Thick and black with gold lettering and edges.

"You'll have to read to find out," Jamie said in a teasing manner. The blonde seemed intrigued. Jamie was making some progress. Maybe Misha meant her offer of friendship. "Hey," he said to get the girl's attention, "Follow me. There's another book I think you'll like!"

Jamie walked out of the aisle, thankfully Misha was following him. He unnecessarily ran through the alphabet in his head. "N, M," he mumbled, then chuckled, "L!" He went into the section, snatching the book quickly and turned to present it to Misha. "This one is super cool! The Persian is awesome."

Misha took the book. "A ghost in an opera house, hm?" She added it to her stack. The boy's enthusiasm was adorable. Misha hoped the stories lived up to his joy. "Thank you," she said. Jamie's face lit up. A part of her felt foolish for being jealous about him. Adelaide was right, he was a boy. He still had that spark of childhood in his eyes. How blind had Misha been? "Do you have any more?" she asked.

Jamie beamed, "Absolutely!"

Chapter 15

Mike frowned at the site of the kids. All of them were unaware of the danger around them. Oh, to be young and innocent again. Mike only had a decade on most of them, but that decade was enough.

"Mikey," Rick said, trying to get the man's attention. He held their coffee in his hands. The man set them on the roof. There was chatter on the radio. Rick leaned in the window and grabbed the mic. "Come again, Nancy?"

Her voice cut through the air. "We need you back at the station, Rick. There's a visitor for you."

Rick sighed. He pressed the mic to his forehead. God, help him. At least it wasn't another body. Rick grabbed the coffees off the roof. "Mike!" he called, that made the man jump. "Get in, boy!" The younger officer hopped into the car. Rick drove leisurely, taking sips of his coffee. "Probably going to get an earful when we get back, so drink up."

Mike frowned, taking a sip from his go cup. "You shouldn't have threatened him." Justin was a sniveling manchild, one of the reasons Rick and him had a falling out. Still, there was one thing that gave the bastard a back bone, money.

Rick scoffed. The fact that Mike of all people was scolding him was a hoot. The man was usually so gung ho about protecting people and serving justice. "People's lives are at risk, Mike. Should I have done nothing?"

Mike scoffed, "I would've told the news first." He relaxed into the chair. "Catch that fucker off guard. Make them make a statement."

Rick pursed his lips. Now he regretted not taking that route. He hoped whatever was waiting for him at the station wasn't anything more than a headache. "That would've been smart," Rick groused out.

Mike chuckled. Rick was a good man, but he thought too small. For a long time, the town had been a little box. Everything could be solved interpersonally. Not anymore. "Should've asked me," Mike teased. Rick rolled his eyes. It made Mike smile.

The pair finally got back to the station and both rolled their eyes at the sight of the mayor's car. "That fucking little snitch," Rick growled. Mike laughed beside him. The pair left the cruiser and made their way inside.

Mayor Shepard was waiting in his pressed suit. He was sitting on Rick's desk and let his legs swing. His salt pepper hair was slicked back. There was a little bird toy on Rick's desk. Josiah dunked the little bird's beak in the water. He noticed the men walking in, "There they are!"

Rick rolled his eyes. Josiah Shepard had been the local car salesman and it showed. The man's teeth were too bright to be natural and his smile was too wide to not be forced. "Cut the shit, Jo. What do you want?" Mike chuckled beside him.

Josiah looked away and licked his teeth. The older members of town had never respected him. They remembered when he was a smooth talking wise ass. He still was, but now he was a politician. They could at least feign respect. "Listen, Foreman gave me a call yesterday and-"

Mike cut in, "Did he tell you a cross country serial killer is using his school records to murder women and their families?" He watched as Josiah's face fell. Mike huffed, "Didn't think so."

Josiah tugged on his ear. A nervous habit he never grew out of. Well, this was going to be more uncomfortable than he originally thought. "Listen, guys," he tried to find the right words, "The school is the beating heart of this town. You two know that."

Rick held up his hand. "Stop, just stop. What do you think will hurt the town more? Us taking action to stop a crazed killer or us doing nothing and then the public finding out later that we knew all along?"

Josiah's frown deepened. He looked at the poster of missing people. "You find Max?"

Rick shook his head. Max had taught Josiah everything he knew. They were as thick as they were thieves. "Please, Jo."

Josiah shifted his jaw side to side. Contemplating his next move. This wouldn't be a problem that would go away. It was one that would only grow and blow up in their face.

"A two year old," Rick said. Josiah furrowed his brow in confusion. "He killed a two year old. Ripped the baby apart," Rick explained. Josiah's eyes went wide, then welled with tears. It was a low blow. Rick knew for a fact Jo's grandson had just turned two. He hoped it was the right push. One that would get them help to catch the sick bastard on a rampage.

Josiah nodded. "I'll tell Foremen to contact the FBI about the records." He stood straighter, "We'll get the news on the radio and in the papers by Friday." A part of him wanted to go to the dean and wring his neck. A killer, a child killer no less! Josiah was disgusted by the blubbering man. "Hopefully it'll save someone."

Rick sighed in relief. Maybe Josiah wasn't the scumbag he thought he was.

Adelaide turned on the radio. It crackled to life. The girls were in class. Most were planning to hit the town in the evening. Some party at another sorority. Adelaide had said Misha should go, but the vampire declined the offer. Due to the kids coming back, orders flooded in. Girls and boys wanted new clothes for the spring.

Patterns and fabric littered the floor. First up was an Easter dress. The floral pattern was beautiful. The pink rose buds and white daisies littered the white fabric. Adelaide wondered if she should keep some for Misha. The vampire would be a vision in a little sundress. Oh, warm weather couldn't come sooner. Adelaide sat at her sewing machine and began to work. Fabric slowly took shape. The music cut out. It was time for news. They discussed the weather. The college warned against black ice. The Cornus murders were sweeping across the nation, nineteen bodies so far.

Adelaide paused her work. Her eyes widened in shock. Cornus. That was the name of the college. No. No, no, no. She raised the volume to hear it more clearly. Maybe she heard the name wrong? A trick on old ears.

The announcer had slowed his usual fast talking pace to explain the situation, "A series of strange murders has gripped the nation. Dubbed the 'Cornus murders' by law enforcement, these grisly cases have put every Cornus University alumni on edge. Nineteen bodies have been discovered so far. The FBI are saying the wives of the family seem to have been the main target of the killer. Anyone home with them are unfortunately caught in the crosshairs. Police have connected all seven women to Cornus University, located in Virginia. All the women graduated in different years, studied different majors, and attended for varying lengths of time. There are theories that the murders are being conducted by a satanic cult, since they span across the country. The savagery of the slayings and the college are the reasons the FBI believes them all to be connected. The dean of Cornus has issued a statement this morning-"

Adelaide stood up. No. She ran to grab her coat and wallet. No, no, no, no. She threw open the front door and raced down the street. Not her girls. Please, don't let any of them be her girls. The pit in her stomach grew. The awful feeling made her nauseous. It was obviously Misha's maker. Obviously, but God,

Adelaide prayed she hadn't sent the devil to any of her children's doorstep.

Guilt seized her heart. Adelaide hadn't prayed in decades, but she was making up for it now. Her legs ached and her lungs burned as she ran. The pain was sharp, but she pushed through. She needed to know. She had to know.

Adelaide threw open the drug store door. The bell above it rang loudly. The poor pharmacist behind the counter jumped. Adelaide went to the newspaper stack. There were multiple publications. All of them had the 'Cornus Murders' on the front page. Adelaide grabbed a copy of each. She went to the counter. "These, please." Adelaide's throat was raw.

The pharmacist, Dayl, cleared his throat. "Sure, Adelaide," he rang the woman up. "It'll be $1.75."

Adelaide threw two dollars on the counter. "Keep the change," she said and raced out of the store. Gone as quickly as she came. Adelaide sprinted back home. She ran into someone. "Oh!" Adelaide fell to the cold concrete of the sidewalk. It hurt like hell. The papers that had been in her arms littered the ground. Adelaide snatched them up.

Professor Dobson sneered down at Adelaide. "What the hell, Freeman!" he growled. He'd spilled his coffee on the front of his shirt. The woman was gathering up her papers. She seemed hysterical, frantic. "Adelaide!" he yelled.

Adelaide stood on her shaky legs. "Sorry Dobson, I need to go!" She tried to run off, but the man grabbed her. Adelaide ripped her arm away from him. "Get off!"

Dobson jumped back. He had never heard Adelaide raise her voice before. "Who do you think you're talking to, girl?" he hissed.

Adelaide looked the man up and down. "Get with the times, Timmy. It's not 1957 anymore." She raced back home. Dobson was screaming behind her, but she couldn't care less. Adelaide slammed her front door open then closed. Misha was waiting for her. Either a class was canceled, or the vampire had heard the news. Adelaide didn't know which option was worse.

"Where did you go?" the vampire asked, arms crossed. Misha noticed the panic on Adelaide's face. The sour smell of fear. Oh no. "Beloved?"

"HE'S KILLING THEM!" Adelaide wailed. She threw the papers on the ground. "He's killing them, Misha!" she wept. Oh god, she'd sent death to their doorstep. "He's killing my girls, Misha." Adelaide opened one of the papers. She pointed at a woman. "I had her in '66!" She pointed to another, "I had her last year!" Adelaide wailed, "I had her in '52." She collapsed to her knees. "He's killing them. God, he's killing them. He's killing their families." Adelaide covered her face. She tried to catch her breath. She felt like she was going to throw up.

Misha kneeled down and cupped Adelaide's face. "Beloved, breathe, my love. Please." The woman hiccuped and tried to stabilize herself. Misha pressed her forehead to the woman's. Adelaide's skin was scorching hot. "It's okay, you're safe," she reassured.

Adelaide looked up at the vampire in shock. "Me? ME?!" she roared. "Jesus Christ, Misha! I don't give a fuck if I'm safe. He's killing my girls!" She grabbed one of the papers. "You called them my children, Misha. How could you think I care about my own fucking life?!"

"I care about your life!" Misha yelled back. She grabbed the newspapers and threw them aside. "I care about your life."

Adelaide's eyes widened in horror. Tears streamed down her face. She asked, voice shaky and barely above a whisper, "Did you know?"

Misha's face twisted. "Adelaide."

The woman stood up. She walked out of the room. The world became muffled. Misha was pleading but Adelaide heard none of it. She walked up the stairs and to her room, slamming the door in the vampire's blood tear stained face. There was knocking. Pounding. Adelaide went to her bed and collapsed on it. Her mind felt like a television shutting off. Everything went black.

When her eyes opened again, it was dark out. Adelaide groaned in pain. Her body was aching. She didn't want to move. There was a dip in the bed. Her black eyes looked up at Misha. The vampire had been crying, was still crying. The woman was going to cry herself dry. "You knew," she croaked, throat raw.

Misha sniffled and nodded.

Adelaide frowned, "Why?" She choked on the question. The vampire had her head down, as if she was terrified to look into Adelaide's eyes. "You knew I loved them," Adelaide wept. "Is that why?" Was it like Jamie? Was Misha jealous? Was she glad her maker had slaughtered Adelaide's children?

"No!" Misha cried out. She finally looked at the woman. "Beloved, no. Please don't ever think that of me!"

"How can I not?!" Adelaide snapped. She sat up in a flash. "You knew he was going to kill them. You fucking knew!" Adelaide would have rather had Misha cheat on her than this. Hell! She'd take Misha stealing all her money and killing her to this! "Why didn't you say anything?!"

"You would have tried to stop him! I know you would have!" Misha cried, "It was you or them! I will not be ashamed for choosing you!" She cupped Adelaide's face. The woman tried to get out of her hold, but Misha held fast. "Beloved, listen to me," she begged. Adelaide tried to wrestle her hands away. "Beloved, he would have done awful things to you. He would have made a display of you."

"How," Adelaide seethed, gripping Misha's wrists like a vice. She tried to throw the vampire off. Misha was like a granite statue. She refused to budge, no matter how hard Adelaide tried. "How can you just fucking sit there and be fine with this? What if it was your children?!"

"It was my children!" Misha screamed. Ugly awful memories overwhelmed her. Her sweet, beautiful girls. She'd taken them from the streets. She taught them to dance. She loved them with all her heart and soul. For the first time in centuries, she had a family. All she wanted was a family. "It was my children!" she wept. "It was my lovers! It was my sisters! He's taken everything from me. Everyone I have ever loved. He strung them up. He set them ablaze. He drained them dry!" Misha lightly shook Adelaide, "I won't let him have you too! I can't lose anyone else." Misha wept, "I'd rather die. I will die. I'll throw myself on a pyre. I should have centuries ago." The blonde pressed her forehead against Adelaide's. "I love you. I'm so sorry. I'm so sorry that I love you."

    Adelaide paused her fighting. The confession was like a bucket of ice water on her head. It made her stock still, then shiver. "Misha…"

    "He killed my sisters when I denied his proposal. He ripped every lover I ever took to pieces. He slaughtered my children and set them around the dinner table to wait for me when I got home!" Misha hiccuped and finally let Adelaide go. "He'd wait for years to strike. Sometimes decades. Made me think he was finally gone, let me forge a life, let me relax, then he'd-" She ran her hands through her hair, tugging at it. "After my children, I came here. I wanted to lose him in your war. I buried myself. I slept. I wanted to disappear. I wanted to go where he couldn't find me." Misha laughed in misery, "Being comatose was the only time he could not hurt me." She let out a scream in agony. Misha tugged at her hair and wailed.

Adelaide watched as Misha broke down. Her body felt tingly. Pins and needles. Adelaide pulled the woman to her. She hugged the vampire to her chest.

"I can't lose you," Misha begged. "I can't. Please, beloved, I can't."

Adelaide buried her nose in Misha's hair. She rubbed the woman's back. "I can't let him keep killing them." Misha gripped her, face buried in her neck. "He's not a man we can reason with," Adelaide said gravely. "We need to kill him, Misha."

The vampire looked up at her. "Beloved, we-"

"Need to!" Adelaide said firmly. She sniffled. "We can make a plan. Lure him back."

"How?" Misha asked.

Adelaide frowned. How indeed? "We'll think of something." She kissed the top of Misha's head. "We'll think of something," she repeated.

Vladan showed the woman her photo of Adelaide. He soaked in the memories. The joy. The light. They held a love he had never gotten to experience. Vladan licked his lips, practically tasting the sweetest of the past.

Margo Smith was weeping, remembering happier times. She missed her Mama A. She missed her husband, who was dead by the front door. "Please," she whimpered.

The woman's voice snapped Vladan out of the memories. He hissed in rage and ripped her head off. It caused a mess, wasted good blood, but it did soothe his rage. Vladan sighed, dropping the woman's head in a huff. Pity. He was enjoying those memories. This woman in particular had received so much comfort from Adelaide. Hugs and kisses.

Vladan looked at the mangled dog in the corner, the foolish husband by the door, the headless body of the woman. There was nothing left to do here. He left the house, taking the man's car keys. Their vehicle was nice. He pulled out of their driveway and began speeding down the road. The list of names was nearing its end.

Vladan noticed the gas was low. He rolled his eyes and pulled into the next station he saw. The vampire didn't bother cleaning himself up. Whoever was behind the counter normally knew better than to ask too many questions. He slipped the man some money and went back to the car.

As he pumped his gas, he began to think. How many years had he known Misha? Six hundred years? The woman had never loved him. Never cared for him. He had been her mentor, her teacher, nothing more. Had he been trying too hard on the wrong person? It was starting to feel like it. Yes, Misha was physically perfect, but mentally? Vladan hissed. He placed the nozzle back to its holder. A true companion couldn't just be based on aesthetics. No, a pair needed to align mentally. Vladan wanted someone nurturing. He wanted someone loyal. Someone who could be kind and cruel. There was a darkness in Adelaide. A beautiful evil that could be nurtured.

Vladan reached into his coat pocket and pulled out the photo of Adelaide. She was a different type of beauty. The love she was able to radiate through a picture was staggering. Vladan pressed the photo to his lips. Maybe it was time. Maybe it was time to finally set his sights on someone worthy. Vladan snatched the records from the passenger seat.

He threw them into the trash and drove off. Only a cloud of dust was left where his car had been.

The girls were all in the living room. While they had enough space, it felt claustrophobic. The fireplace was roaring, crackling. There was a drop of water coming from the faucet in the kitchen. The television was on and the news was playing. The anchorman's voice was hypnotic in the worst way. He pulled them in with his shaky tone and the gruesome details. So many dead. Mutilated beyond recognition. A baby. Dear lord. The FBI were stumped. Aside from the names, there was only one common denominator. The college. Their college. It was terrifying.

All the girls were shell shocked. Their mouths hung open in horror. Some had tears in their eyes. Finally the news moved on. The room was left tense. No one dared to speak.

Adelaide's frown was deep. Tears streamed down her eyes. She knew every single girl. Half of them had been hers. Her children. Her girls. One, Morgot Jensen, had been from '47. Her first group of girls. Thirty years ago. Seven dead. Because of her. Pain exploded in her chest. It gripped her heart and twisted it. An invisible force choked her throat. She wanted to scream, but couldn't. Misha's hand was on hers. Those cool fingers were interlocked with hers. Adelaide had it in a death grip. She was shaking, visibly shaking.

    Tracey's eyes scanned the photos on the mantle, then to the photos on the walls. Some of the faces on the broadcast had been familiar, now she knew why. Tracey looked back at Adelaide. The woman looked like she was about to break. Tracey had never seen Adelaide look so vulnerable, so…weak. Mama was normally strong. A pillar of safety. Now, Adelaide sat there shaking and crying. She looked so young, no older than the girls around her. "Mama?"

    Adelaide looked at Tracey. Those big blue eyes looked to her for answers, for solace. The weight of her eyes made Adelaide's shoulders fall. She looked around. Ten pairs of eyes were looking to her. Normally, that drove her to find an answer. It made her want to fix and save. Now though, now…she wanted to run. "Girls," she began carefully, "I think you all should move out."

    Those ten eyes widened in shock. "Mama!" Heather stood, "we can't just fucking leave!" How the hell could they leave the older woman to fend for herself? She noticed the newcomer had her hand in Adelaide's. Heather's mouth twisted. "We're not leaving!" she insisted, tears spilling from her eyes.

"The last death was in Arkansa," Monica said, "Besides, why would he come here?" She hoped reason would change the woman's mind. Adelaide's eyes were hard. They held the stubbornness of a mother who wanted nothing more than to protect her children. "Mama, please," Monica sniffled. This was her home. It had been her home for so long. She couldn't just leave.

Dawn began to cry. Tina wrapped her in a hug.

"Where would we go?" Tracey asked. She looked around for an answer. Would she have to go home? Were there any rooms left in the dormitories? Sororities? She couldn't go home. She'd rather die than face the silence of her family and scorn of her peers. "Mama," Tracey crawled to Adelaide. "Please, don't make us leave," she wept.

Adelaide sobbed. God, what had she wrought? Her poor girls. She hadn't thought it would be so hard. Didn't they understand how much danger they were in? No, of course they didn't. None of them were named Margot or

Margaret. None of them were alumni. To them Adelaide was throwing them out over murders happening across the country. God, she wanted to tell them. Tell them all how the killer would most likely come back and she didn't want to risk their lives. They were too precious to risk. Adelaide buried her face in her hands.

Misha pursed her lips. She'd have to take over. The girls wouldn't listen otherwise. "The fraternity," she said. "Jamie's house. The rooms are all empty. I'm sure he would welcome the company." The girls all looked at her, confused.

"Wait, what house?" Heather asked.

Adelaide fought through her crying, "Tony's. All the boys, but one, have been murdered."

All the girls gasped in shock. "Are you fucking serious?! Wouldn't that place be more dangerous?" Mabel gripped at her hair. "This is fucking insane!" Nicole wailed.

Adelaide wept. "Girls, please. This place. This sorority is the problem. All the boys died out of the house. They were random-"

"You don't think these are random?!" Tina cried, pointing to the TV.

Adelaide could only cry. God, she wanted to explain, but knew that would only make things worse. They would demand to stay and protect her. God, Adelaide didn't know what to do. This was the hardest she'd cried in years. The type of full bodied sobs that left you nauseous. Hands were on her. They rubbed her back and shoulders. They wrapped around her and squeezed. Adelaide tried to speak but her words came out jumbled. "I can't- It's my fault- and I can't," she blubbered.

Misha couldn't take it anymore. She stood and clapped to get all of the girls' attention. "**You will move into Jamie's Sunday**," she compelled. There was a hiss under her voice, one that made the girls go still. "**You will live there for the rest of the semester. You know this is for your own safety and the safety of Adelaide. You will not question why. You will begin packing tonight and will not pester Adelaide anymore.**"

All the girls' eyes glazed over. They all nodded in unison. Misha sighed in relief. She collapsed onto the couch, her nose was bleeding. Compelling more than one person was always a struggle. She rubbed the blood off her face. "You all should go start getting your things together, then rest, it is good for all worries."

The girls nodded. Those left on the floor stood. Tracey hugged Adelaide close. The other girls followed her lead before trailing toward the stairs. Once the living room was cleared, Misha turned her attention to Adelaide. "Beloved-"

"That was smart," Adelaide interrupted, voice hoarse. She wiped her eyes. "I'm sorry," she looked at the vampire. It wasn't Misha's job to deal with her girls. Adelaide was normally better at this. She normally knew what to say and do. Tonight though, she felt weak. She felt like a child again. Helpless. "I should have-"

"Hush," Misha pulled the woman into a hug. "None of that, beloved." She kissed the woman's cheek. "You have every right to be upset." The woman relaxed in her arms. "I love you," she whispered into Adelaide's ear. The taller woman moved closer to her. Misha buried her nose in black curls. "We will keep them safe," Misha vowed.

Adelaide looked at the vampire. "I'm scared, Misha." She nuzzled into the blonde's neck. "I feel like a failure." Adelaide had sworn to protect her girls. They trusted her. They turned to her for comfort, for safety. Her identity was built on such shaky ground and now it was crumbling.

"You are no failure, Adelaide," Misha sternly whispered. "You are kind. You are beautiful. You are everything good in humanity." She kissed Adelaide's forehead over and over. "I will protect you," she swore. Misha pulled Adelaide's head to lay on her chest. The vampire's strange heartbeat seemed to sooth the woman. Adelaide fell asleep. Misha carried her to bed.

Chapter 16

    Jamie had accepted the girls easily and the girls accepted him. He was a good boy. The type that radiated out gentleness. He helped them with their bags and luggage. Tracey took a shine to him especially. He was the first boy not to act strange around her.
    Adelaide was relieved beyond words. She was grateful. Misha had finished helping the last girl carry in her boxes.
    Jamie noticed Adelaide leaning on his car. The woman's eyes were red. She looked exhausted. The woman must have been crying all night. The poor thing. Jamie walked over to the house mother. "They're all in," he announced with a half smile. Adelaide tried to force a smile, it refused to stick. She obviously didn't want the girls to go. Her lips were bright from being bitten and her face was twisted into

a frown. Jamie didn't understand why the woman was doing this. One of the girls mentioned the Cornus murders, but he didn't see why those mattered here. The woman knew something they didn't. "Adelaide?"

Said woman snapped out of her dissociation. "I'm sorry, baby." She winced, her voice was still raw. Jamie's concerned look worsened. Adelaide forced herself to smile, but her lips shook. "I'm okay," she lied. Her words didn't soothe the boy, but he also didn't press.

Jamie stood beside the woman. "You know, I had a massive crush on you."

That made Adelaide actually laugh. "I know, baby." The boy giggled beside her. "It was pretty obvious."

"You could have said you didn't go for-" Jamie gestured to himself. "Unlike the other asshats around here, I can take a no. I would've fucked off."

Adelaide frowned, "Like you said, most asshats don't. I've seen plenty of sweet boys flip on a dime." She nibbled at her thumb nail. "Besides, I didn't want you to fuck off. I like you." Adelaide reached up and ruffled Jamie's brown hair.

The boy chuckled, a blush spreading across his face. "Knock it off, Mama," he playfully pushed the woman's hand away.

Adelaide's heart sang. That was the first time he'd ever called her that. It was said so sincerely that it brought tears to her eyes. She looked at the old frat house. The sound of the girls shuffling around spilled from the open windows and doors. "I'm trusting you," she said, looking at Jamie again.

The boy nodded, "I know."

"You'll watch out for 'em?" Adelaide knew he would. "They'll look out for you too." She added, "I'll come by and cook for y'all every night."

Jamie frowned, "Doesn't have to be every night. You deserve time off too." He gestured to the house, "Besides, we're all adults here. Well, except Trace." Jamie shrugged. Misha's accented voice rang out. Jamie snickered, the woman was trying to wrangle the girls into actually moving in instead of chit chatting. Jamie leaned over and whispered into Adelaide's ear, "Also you and Misha should keep enjoying your quality time."

Adelaide was glad her skin was so dark. It was harder to tell when she blushed. Still, the heat in her cheeks caused a smile to tug at her lips. "Hush you," she scolded, trying not to giggle.

Jamie chuckled, bumping Adelaide's hip with his. "You both are lucky girls."

Adelaide rolled her eyes. "I'm not taking teasing from an English major!"

Jamie gasped dramatically, "Mama, I'm hurt!" He clutched his chest. "Thoust words are cruel!"

Adelaide finally laughed, a full belly one. It made her hold her knees. "You can't just say 'thoust'!"

Jamie teased, "Whomst is the English Major here?"

Adelaide shook her head and started for the house. "I can't deal with you!"

Nicole poked her head out of a window. "Mama, Misha's being mean!" she snitched with a smile. Tina chimed in, giggling, "She keeps yelling at us!"

Misha poked her head out of another window. "They are lying, beloved. The children are not listening!" Her accent was thicker with frustration. "They refuse to organize their boxes!"

Some of the other girls poked their heads from the window. They began to boo Misha.

"Your boos mean nothing to me!" the vampire snapped, "I have seen you cheer at monkeys in hats!" All the girls booed harder. Misha leaned out the window and playfully flipped them all off. The girls' jeers turned into full belly laughs.

Adelaide cackled. "I'm coming!" she jogged into the house. Jamie followed her and they tried to get the girls settled. When they finally sat down to eat dinner that night, Adelaide felt at peace.

It was the calm before the storm.

Rick looked at the sketch. It was the best one they'd gotten of the strange man. He turned to his fellow officers. Twenty other cops looked at him. "Alright, men . This is the bastard we're looking for! If spotted, arrest him on sight for suspicion. This suspect is incredibly dangerous." Rick set a stack of the sketches on the desk. "Everyone take some. We need to spread these around town. High traffic areas. Especially where the kids will see." Rick gave one of the sketches to Nancy, "Spread these to the surrounding towns. FBI already has it." The sketch had been a showcase on last night's broadcast, but it would still help to have the posters spread around.

Nancy sighed. "Alright." She took the sketch from him. "Pity," she said, "he looks handsome." Nancy wondered what made men turn into sickos. She stood from her desk and went to the fax machine.

"As handsome as a rattlesnake," Rick grumbled. He rubbed his tired face. "Alright, some FBI boys are coming here. Be prepared," Rick noticed Mike's pinched face. "What's wrong, boy?"

Mike sighed. He walked over to Rick and whispered, "I think we need to talk to Adelaide's little red haired girl."

Rick pursed his lips. They had talked to her. Hadn't they? Yes. They'd walked up to her multiple times. She'd said…something. Rick's brow furrowed. Wait… "We did," he said, it sounded unsure. He remembered walking to the woman then walking away. Why did they walk away?

Mike shook his head. "No, we keep saying we are, then we find her, and then nothing." Mike showed him his note book. "You know I'm meticulous. You know I write everything down. Look" Mike stood beside Rick. Every note at the top had the date, it had the name Misha, then nothing. No notes, no statement, nothing. Just a blank page. "Rick, I don't think that girl is right."

The older officer took the notebook. Mike wrote down every statement. Even the ones filled with lies, he wrote it all down. Rick bit his lip. His gut churned. He remembered their first encounter with her. The girl's porcelain face. Not even a pimple or pore. Her strange nails. The more Rick thought about her, the more he focused, the stranger she got. He looked at the stretch of the man. He'd been the same way. Pieces were falling into place.

"RICK!" Nancy screamed, "They caught sight of him heading into town."

All the men in the station immediately began to scramble.

"I want everyone out there. First sight of him you call. We go as one. If he doesn't comply, shoot him!" Rick ordered. All the men agreed in unison. The older officer turned to Mike. "Bring your shotgun," he whispered before heading off to his cruiser.

They were going to get that son of a bitch.

Adelaide pushed her cart through the grocery store. Everyone was in class. There hadn't been a murder in a week. Either the man ran out of names or he finally got tired of slaughtering innocent people. Adelaide didn't care which. She just hoped he'd fled back to whatever hole he crawled out of. Maybe he got scared of the FBI. They had him at the top of their list with his little sketch. Last night, Adelaide and the girls had watched as the news broadcaster struggled to say his name.

Vladan.

Adelaide went through the aisles. The fluorescent lights buzzed above her. The store was blissfully empty. It normally was right before 3pm. Adelaide was blessed to have a job that didn't tie her down to a strict schedule. She wondered what to cook that night. The girls and Jamie had taken to cooking for her a couple times. It was sweet, but tonight was a celebration! A whole week of peace. Adelaide wanted to make something special. Ribs? Pork chops? Meatloaf?

"Ribs are good."

Adelaide jumped. She turned to see…oh god. The man's icy blue eyes stabbed into her. They froze her in place. Adelaide bit the inside of her cheek to keep herself from screaming. Thankfully no one was around. She didn't want to get anyone else killed. The man was smiling down at her. His pupils were huge. Hungry. Adelaide shivered.

"I see you know who I am." Vladan smiled. He traced his knuckle along Adelaide's high cheek bone. To his shock, the woman didn't flinch. How curious. "Terrified for your life and yet still worrying about others." Vladan pinched the fat of Adelaide's cheek between his fingers. "So soft," he whispered in wonder. Next, he twirled one of the woman's curls between his claws. Her locks were black with scattered strands of silver. Yes, she was mature. A maturity Vladan had never appreciated before. She'd be a wonderful companion.

Adelaide sucked in a deep breath through her nose. The man didn't appear ready to pounce. Adelaide had dealt with men like him before. Maybe not as deadly, but still the same mindset. They fed off of reactions and attention. Adelaide let her shoulders drop. She nodded. "Ribs it is then," she turned and began to push her cart.

Vladan blinked in surprise. The fear in the woman went as quickly as it came. He chuckled, walking to keep up with her pace. She wasn't trying to run, in fact, she continued on with her shopping. Not ignoring him, but also not making a fuss about his presence. Never before had Vladan experienced someone so…calm.

Adelaide looked at the honey on the top shelf. She pursed her lips. She was tall, but not that tall. Adelaide looked at the man. "Can you hand me that?" she asked.

Vladan's eyes widened in shock. He looked at the bear shaped bottle. It was easy to reach up and take the item down. He offered it to the woman. Adelaide wasn't even phased at the chill of his skin. She merely took it and set it in the cart. They continued on with the shopping. Adelaide would sometimes ask for things on the top shelf. Aside from that, they moved in a quiet peace. It was fun. The type of fun Vladan hadn't experienced in decades. It was all so simple.

Adelaide paid for the groceries. At checkout, Vladan helped her bag the items. The girl behind the counter gave her a frightened look. Her eyes darted to the man then back at Adelaide. She must have seen the news last night. Adelaide nodded slowly. She took her bags and walked out, Vladan following.

Thankfully, Adelaide took the car. She used her key to open the trunk. Adelaide placed the groceries into the trunk. Vladan watched her move around. He still had that curious glint in his eyes. Adelaide wondered what to do next. She closed her trunk and turned to him. "Can you take the cart back?" she asked, pointing at the cart return. The vampire looked at her up and down. To her shock, he did as she asked. Adelaide slowly got into her car. A second ticked by. Adelaide locked the doors. She jammed her key into the ignition and slammed her foot on the gas. Adelaide refused to look into the rearview mirror.

Panic pounded her heart. Tears flooded her eyes. Adelaide tried to keep her breathing even. She gripped the steering wheel and slowed to the speed limit as she entered her neighborhood. Adelaide pulled in front of her house. To her shock, five squad cars were waiting for her. Adelaide sniffled and slipped out of her car. She felt like a robot. Rick was staring at her in horror. Adelaide furrowed her brow, then she felt it. The hairs on the back of her neck stood up. Someone was behind her. Adelaide slowly turned to see Vladan by her side. The redhead man was smiling. A smile that was too wide and showed all of his teeth. He was staring at the police.

"Put your hands up!" Mike ordered, pulling out his service weapon and pointing it at the man. The other officers followed suit. Six barrels pointed at the man. The redheaded man raised his hands in the air. Vladan looked at Adelaide and gave her a wink, flashing his fangs.

"Adelaide!" Rick called to the woman. He jerked his head to his side. "Come here." The redhead snapped his eyes to Rick. That icy gaze would've made a less hardened man shiver. Not him though, Rick was filled with rage. "Get on your knees!" he ordered the man. Thankfully, the monster heeded his orders.

Adelaide watched as Vladan sank onto the asphalt. That gave her little comfort. She knew how fast Misha could move without intention. How fast could Vladan move if he wanted something? She slowly walked toward the officers. For the first time, she felt safe with the police. Adelaide paused beside Rick. The man was a good sheriff. They'd grown up in the same town and only saw each other across the way. This was the closest they'd ever been. "Richard," Adelaide tried to warn.

"Get inside," Rick whispered to her.

Adelaide looked at him. She knew these men stood no chance against the beast they were unknowingly taking in. "Be careful," she advised. Adelaide kissed his cheek and whispered in his ear, "He's not human. Aim for the head." Rick looked at her from the corner of his eye, shock clearly on his face. Adelaide calmly went into her house.

Rick swallowed his fear and lowered his weapon. He took the cuffs off his hip. "You're under arrest," he informed the man and began to read off the beast's rights. The redhead let himself be cuffed. Rick led the man to a cruiser. "Call the big boys," he said, Mike scrambled to his cruiser. Rick got the man in the car and slammed the door. He looked at Adelaide, the woman was standing in her doorway. Her doe eyes seemed even more black.

Mike radioed into the station. "Nancy, we have the suspect in custody. Tell the feds." He climbed into his car. The other officers piled into theirs and started the engines. Sirens blared as the five cruisers sped down the road. The world seemed to come alive. Students were flooding the streets, classes had let out. Hundreds of eyes watched as the cruisers went by, like a funeral procession.

Misha watched the parade in horror. Her eyes locked with Vladan's. His smile was wide and twisted. Misha dropped her books in shock. As the sirens faded, so did the stupefaction. Misha ran down the street. Faster than a human could. She didn't care if anyone spotted her. It didn't matter. The only thing that mattered was Adelaide. Misha stopped in front of the woman's house. To her relief, Adelaide was there. She was whole. The woman seemed dazed, like she was under a spell. "Beloved!" Misha cried.

Adelaide snapped out of her stunned state. "Misha?" The blonde wrapped her in a hug. Adelaide looked down at the vampire. She wrapped her arms around Misha. "Hi, peaches." She buried her nose in the woman's hair. "He-" Tears flooded Adelaide's eyes. "He found me at the store and-"

"Shh, shh," Misha soothed the woman. "Come, beloved. Come." She pulled the woman inside. Misha looked down at the welcome mat. She snatched it off the porch and threw it into a closet. Adelaide was standing in the foyer, looking lost. The woman was biting her fingers. Misha gently took Adelaide's hands in hers. "Beloved?" Those doe eyes looked at her. "Are you harmed?" Adelaide shook her head. Misha sighed in relief. She raised up on her tiptoes and nuzzled her nose against Adelaide's. It made the woman giggle. The sound made Misha's dead heart race. By some miracle, her love was alive. That was worth more than all the gold in the world.

Adelaide melted under the contact. She hummed and rested her forehead on the top of Misha's head. "I love you," Adelaide whispered. Misha's cool hand rubbed her shoulder.

"Come," Misha guided the woman upstairs. They had a few hours. Maybe even more if her maker decided to strike during the dead of night. Misha pitied the poor officers who were no doubt going to meet their end at his fangs. She wasn't willing to start a fight, especially since Adelaide needed her. The men were on their own. Misha wanted to hold Adelaide for as long as she could.

Adelaide frowned, "He's going to come back." She realized she couldn't feel the coolness of Misha's hand. Adelaide realized it was because her own hands were cold. That couldn't be good. Why was she so cold? Fear? Adelaide normally ran hot.

Misha nodded, "We have until nightfall." She clicked on the heater in Adelaide's room. When they got there, the space would be nice and cozy.

Adelaide furrowed her brow. "How do you know?" she asked, allowing herself to be led down the hall. The empty rooms around her were both a comfort and curse. Her girls would be safe, but the house felt wrong. Adelaide blinked and they were in her room. She was sitting on the edge of her bed. When had that happened? She shook her head. The heater's hum was lulling. Adelaide wanted to sleep. The fog in her head was lifting, but the exhaustion from shock was settling in. Adelaide's eyes felt heavy. She blinked and Misha was standing between her legs. Adelaide looked up at the vampire. Those green eyes were filled with concern. "How do you know?" she asked again.

Misha frowned. She cupped Adelaide's face. The woman blinked slowly. Misha leaned forward and kissed Adelaide. The woman's plush lips took a moment to respond to hers. Misha forced herself to stop kissing the woman. She pressed her forehead to Adelaide's. "We are stronger at night," Misha whispered.

Adelaide nodded, that made sense. She captured Misha's lips again. "We need a plan," she whispered against those cool lips.

Misha frowned. "Rest first, beloved." She gently guided the woman to lay on the bed. "I will watch over you," Misha vowed. Adelaide smiled up at her. Those big doe eyes were full of love and trust. Misha wondered if she'd ever feel worthy of them.

Mike glared at the man. Calling all the departments and filling out paperwork took hours. The redheaded man sat in their drunk tank. Those piercing blue eyes were locked on the missing persons board. The bastard was probably admiring his handy work. Mike growled. He stood and went to find Rick. The man was standing in front of the station, practically inhaling a cigarette. "We need to talk," he said in lieu of greeting.

Rick finished his smoke and ground the bud under his heel. "You want to talk to Adelaide." It wasn't a question. He knew.

Mike nodded. Rick just started walking to their cruiser. The younger cop followed. "You think the guys will be okay?" Mike asked as he buckled his belt.

Rick gripped the steering wheel. The setting sun gave the world a hellish glow. It was like a fiery omen. A harbinger of the night to come. "You have your gun, right?"

Mike nodded, "Course."

Rick started the car. They sped to Adelaide's house. The woman had always been an enigma. She made waves without tipping the boat. She made friends without being the center of attention. She made change without a violent revolution. Rick never had a good read of the woman. Adelaide was strange, now she was even stranger.

Mike alerted his mentor. "Hey, Rick, left!"

Rick snapped out of his thoughts and slammed on the breaks. He made the turn and got to Adelaide's house without his mind wandering again. The house was dark. On the porch stood the odd strawberry blonde. The officers got out. They walked up to the porch. The woman's aura was the same as Vladan's. A predator. A killer. It was in stark contrast to how she'd been before. As if her mask had fallen off as the sun set. Her face was placid, curls perfect. Small inhuman things became magnified all at once. Her nails were claws, pupils too big, canines sharp. Rick noticed Mike's hand went to his gun. "Calm down," Rick advised. He looked back at the woman. "Evening," he said in greeting.

Misha's face twisted. "Get inside, before he comes." She turned and entered the home.

Mike and Rick exchanged looks. Would they dare enter the den? Rick took a steadying breath and walked up the steps, Mike followed him. The fireplace was lit and bathed the walls with a hellfire glow. There was a metallic click. Adelaide had weapons laid out on the coffee table. Two shotguns. A revolver. A handgun. A machete. An array of knives. "Didn't take you for a fighter," Rick said. He took off his hat and set it on the side table.

"Fighting comes in many forms," Adelaide explained, "I don't like violence." She snapped the barrel shut after loading two buckshots, "But needs must."

Mike came around and picked up the revolver. "This thing is ancient."

"Better to have it and not need it, then need it and not have it," Adelaide sagely said. She stood from the couch. "Got a smoke?" she asked Rick. The man nodded and gave her a cigarette. Adelaide hadn't smoked in decades, but if she was going to die tonight, she wanted to have one last ride on nicotine's high.

The last rays of sunset died over the horizon.

"Your men are being slaughtered," Misha told the officers. She took up one of the weapons. Two hundred years had given way to many advancements, especially for killing.

Mike looked at the woman in horror. "What?"

Misha frowned. "Vladan is on his way." She set the gun down. "He is slaughtering the station." The vampire bore her fangs. The men's breath hitched in fright. "Take up arms." Misha looked at Adelaide. The woman had a determined look on her face. "Beloved, I beg of you-"

"No," Adelaide stood, shotgun in hand. "He killed my children too, Misha."

Rick looked between the women. "Are you like them?" he asked Adelaide. The woman turned to him. She had none of the subtle inhuman traits. That made Rick's heart settle.

"She is human," Misha hissed.

"So what are you?" Mike asked, taking the hand gun and tucking it into his belt.

Misha huffed, "I am a vampire."

Rick hated that the answer calmed him more than upsetted him. He took the second shotgun. "Alright, so what's the plan? He shows up, we open fire?"

Misha shook her head. "You two, go get gasoline. We will need to burn his remains, otherwise he will get back up again. I will keep him engaged. When you get back, shoot him. A bullet to the brain will stun him and stunt his motor skills. That will be enough for me to rip him apart before we burn him." She then turned to Adelaide. "You stay inside."

Adelaide growled, "Misha-"

The vampire hissed, "I'm not losing you!" She took Adelaide's face in her hands. "Shoot out the window if you must, but you are safe in here, beloved. We must be invited. In these walls you are safe." Misha pressed her forehead to Adelaide's. "I need you to live. You must live. For me."

Adelaide's lips twisted in pain. "Misha," she began.

"I will kill him. This time, I will," the vampire swore. They looked into each other's eyes. Misha stood on her toes and captured Adelaide's lips. The woman leaned forward and wrapped an arm around her.

Rick watched the display. His heart swelled. Oh, it all made sense now. Mike seemed to be having the same reaction. Rick cleared his throat. "You're sure the station was wiped out?"

Misha set herself back on her feet. She nodded. "He can send me visions. He has eaten them all."

Rick scowled. Hot tears flooded his eyes. He gripped his keys. "We'll get the gas, then give him some lead to chew on."

Chapter 17

Jamie was sat on the windowsill. The girls were scattered on the floor, noses in their books. Living together did them all some good. Normally Adelaide would have been over to cook, but it seemed she'd forgotten. Jamie nor the girls wanted to pester her. They were all adults, sans Tracey, they could cook their own dinner.

All of them had missed Adelaide's presence. It was a special night. The killer had been caught! It made Jamie smile. The bastard was behind bars. The parade of cop cars had caused cheers to erupt in the streets. You would have thought Dorothy came down and crushed the wicked witch.

Jamie had seen the man in the cruiser. The bastard who killed his friends. Jamie bit his lip and tried his hardest to focus on his book. An anxiety was building in him. Why? The pit in his stomach grew. Maybe he should call Adelaide, just in case. Jamie sighed. Misha wasn't here, so that probably meant Adelaide was fine. Jamie didn't want to scare the woman. How would he open? 'Hey Adelaide, cops caught the serial killer! You still alive?' Jamie rolled his eyes at himself. He was worrying too much.

A chill ran down his spine. The hairs on the back of his neck and arms stood straight up. Terror gripped him. Jamie looked out the window. There he was, like a monster coming forth from the darkness. The boogeyman walked down the road, drenched in blood. His stomach turned. It was like watching a rabid animal. You knew someone was about to get bitten.

Jamie kneeled on the sill and looked at the direction the man was heading. His heart sank. "No," he whispered in horror, "No, no, no." Why was he free? Oh god. Where was he going? Jamie needed to do something..

Terror. Fear. What could he do? The man kept walking. Maybe he could stall him? Yes, get the girls to call the cops and hopefully get the man arrested again. Jamie looked back, the girls were all staring at the man too. They all shared nods. A silent agreement. Jamie bit his lip, alright then. He cracked the window open. "Hey!" he screamed at the man.

The redhead stopped. He turned. The house was a pale blue. He'd passed it before, but paid it no mind. The smell coming from the cracked window caught his attention. Adelaide. Vladan came closer, standing on the lawn. He tilted his head and inhaled. His pupils dilated. His fangs itched. "Is she in there?" Was she hiding from him?

Jamie frowned. He took in a shaky breath. This son of a bitch killed his friends. This bastard tore apart his first home. There he stood, covered in the blood of more victims. "Fuck you!" Jamie spat.

Monica came to stand behind Jamie. She gasped, "Oh my god." The man standing in the lawn looked like Carrie White after prom. Monica tried to force herself to believe the blood was fake, but something in her knew it wasn't. A primal fear filled her. "I'm calling the cops!" she screamed at the man.

Vladan laughed. "They are all dead~" he teased, raising his hands up and showing off the blood on them. "They tasted bitter!" He stepped forward. More faces came to the window. Little lambs for the slaughter. He wasn't particularly hungry, but he could always save some blood for later. "Come out, Adelaide!" Vladan called. He taunted, "Or will you be like Margosha and offer your children to me so you can run?!" Vladan knew Adelaide wasn't a runner, she fought. Fought and fought and fought. Vladan wanted to take her. He wanted to break her.

"Don't touch our mama!" Tracey screamed at the deranged man.

"Yeah, fuck off!" Dawn added. Heather told the man, "We're calling the cops!"

Monica ran to the kitchen and got the phone off the hook. "Operator!" she called. The line buzzed. She hung up the receiver and picked it up again. "Operator?"

"They are dead as well!" Vladan teased. He laughed, "You are funny little things." In a blink he was in front of the cracked window. He squatted down, placing his face near the opening. He hoped one of the little ones came closer. An inch outside the house was all he needed.

Vladan laughed, a cackling thing that made the children shudder. "Maybe I will keep you. Little pets to entertain Adelaide and I. I have missed having little ones around. I slaughtered my little dancers for Margosha. She was too distracted by them. She thought she was one of them. She thought she could run off with them! She didn't know those were meant to be pets! Our little dancing blood bags. She was supposed to be mine! Margosha refused her place. Adelaide will know her role. She'll know she's for me. If you give her to me, help me convince her, I'll let you live, little lambs. Just help me."

Wendy's face twisted in horror, "Dude, you're fucking nuts!"

Vladan hissed. The homely little blonde made his blood boil. "I'll drain you first!" He snapped his teeth at her, making the child jump in fright. Vladan laughed. He was riding the high of their terror. Acidic and bitter. It resembled the coffee Vladan used to drink as a human. The dark brew had been his favorite. He missed the taste when he was first turned, but quickly found a lovely replacement.

Jamie felt like a bucket of ice water was poured over his head. The monster in front of him was becoming more and more inhuman. His pupils were huge, only thin rings of blue were left. Those fangs were long and sharp, claws were digging into the window sill. He was crazed. Jamie hocked a loogie in the man's face.

Vladan was taken aback. His face turned placid. Never before had someone disrespected him like that. Even Margosha had never spat on him. The cold fury in him rose. "I'm going to skin you," his voice was even and calm. It was a stark contrast to his monologue from before.

Jamie smiled. The man couldn't come in. He was a shark swimming around the cage, invisible bars keeping him out. Jamie wondered what would happen if he got the man to cross the boundary. Jamie laughed, "Adelaide kissed me." The monster's mask fell again. His face twisted in rage and fueled Jamie's joy. The boy kept his distance but taunted, "Her lips are really soft. Too bad she'll never kiss you!"

Vladan screeched, making the children hold their ears. He forced his arm through the opening to grab the boy. His skin was set aflame. It peeled and hissed. Flesh bubbled and burst. Vladan howled in agony. A force projected him away. He landed on the lawn. The old laws were not to be trifled with.

The girls and Jamie screamed in horror. "Holy shit, holy fucking shit!" Heather wailed. Chunks of the man's flesh were on the floor. They moved and sizzled. They turned into flames and then ash. What the hell?! Monica screamed, "Phones are dead! What the fuck are we going to do?!"

Vladan collected himself. The price for his temper was high, but worth it to frighten the little bastards inside the house. One downside was the pain made his mind unfocused. He tried to find his second voice and hissed out, "**Let me in**."

Tracey's eyes turned glassy. While everyone else scrambled and screamed, she made her way to the front door. Her hand landed on the knob.

"Trace?!" Nicole practically tackled the girl. "What the fuck are you doing?!" She shook the girl, but Tracey seemed dazed. "Tracey?!"

Nicole panicked and slapped the girl. That knocked some sense into her.

"What?!" Tracey looked around in terror. "What happened?" Nicole pulled her to her feet.

"Upstairs!" Jamie ordered. He told the girls, "He can't get inside unless we let him. Get upstairs!" Most of the girls scrambled, protecting Tracey in a circle. Monica and Wendy stayed down. The pair gave Jamie a stern look. They weren't leaving. They were the oldest in the house. Wendy had a bat. Monica had a knife. They were ready to fight.

Jamie's heart swelled. He looked back at the window. The awful beast was back. "Wanna try again, dumbass?!" he roared.

Vladan laughed at the boy's fury. "You enjoy baiting my rage." He dragged his nails against the glass. The children covered their ears in pain. Vladan hissed again, "**Let me in!**"

"Fuck you!" Jamie screamed. The man's voice was wrong. So crazy fucking wrong. It was like there was a worm in his brain. It wriggled and writhed in fury. It demanded he open the door. Jamie fought it. He pulled his hair and closed his eyes, refusing the trance.

"Vladan!"

The air shifted. A new chill ran down Jamie's spine. The world tilted. Behind the monster, standing on the lawn, was Misha. The strawberry blonde was dressed down. Tight fitting clothes. Harder to grab, Jamie realized. The inhuman elements on her were on full display. He wanted to warn her of the danger, but the look in her eyes told him she knew it well.

Vladan turned around. The sight of his pearl was a shock. "Oh, Margosha," he cooed. The man hopped off the porch. "I've been looking everywhere for you, my love."

Misha snarled. The man advanced, but she held her ground. "I am not your love," she spat.

Vladan's eyes widened. He then began to laugh anew. "It's been so long since I've heard your voice!" Vladan bit his lip and looked her up and down. "I think I know why you always run, Margosha."

Misha's face twisted. "Because I want you to leave me alone!"

Vladan shook his head. "No, no. If you wanted that, you would fight." He leaned close. He'd forgotten how short she was, his poor little pearl. A small morsel he'd molded to perfection. "We are predators, my dear. You know that running," he hissed, "Only gets you chased."

Misha drew her fist back and smashed it into Vladan's face. The other vampire flew back into the porch. He landed with a sickening crack. Wood splintered and flew in every direction. The window exploded. The echo of the destruction rang through the neighborhood. Lights turned on and eyes looked out to the street.

Jamie was dragged down to the floor by Monica as the window shattered. Glass flew like shrapnel. The girls upstairs screamed in horror. The house shook. It sounded like a bomb going off. Jamie hoped no curious onlookers stepped out of their houses. He dared to rise to his knees. To his horror, the monster was dragging himself out of the hole that had formed at the base of the house.

Vladan's jaw hung limply. He grabbed it and snapped it into place. "Oh, my pearl. You broke our rule."

Misha furrowed her brow. "Rule?"

Vladan smiled, "I suppose I should not hold up my end any longer either." He crashed into the woman, sending her flying across the street and into a parked car. Misha howled in pain. Glass exploded and metal crunched behind her. The car's alarm blared. Vladan laughed. He ran to smash her deeper into the twisted metal, but Margosha was smaller. She was faster.

Misha dodged Vladan's punch. She kicked him in the ribs, sending him down the street. People began to come out of their homes. Door after door opened. Shocked faces lined the streets. Misha roared, "**GO INSIDE!**"

Vladan took advantage of her distraction and tackled her to the pavement. He smashed his fist into her pretty face. Blood splattered across the pavement. Her nose was broken. "Such a shame," he mocked, "Would have preferred to kiss this cheek."

"I'd rather fucking die!" Misha spat blood into Vladan's eyes. The man cried out. She got her legs under his stomach and kicked, sending him into the air. The bastard couldn't fly, he landed in a heap on the pavement. A sickening splat against the blacktop. Misha wiped the blood from her mouth. "You are a coward!" Misha ran over to him and kicked him again. Vladan's body skidded on the asphalt. "You kill my sisters," she cried. "You kill my children!" she wailed. "Yet you have never faced me!"

Vladan laughed. His bones began to snap back into place. "My dear, I merely did as you wished." He stood on his broken legs.

Misha frowned. The man was a well of confusion. She growled, "What are you talking about?!"

Vladan wiped the blood from his face. "When I made you. I offered you one wish. One promise I would never break." He stalked closer. "You wished I never touched you," Vladan was in front of her in a flash, "And I never did." Vladan punched the woman in the chest, sending her down the road with the force. Her body broke the asphalt, then she bounced and skidded.

Misha choked as blood projected from her mouth. She caught herself on all fours. Her claws scraped against the pavement. Vladan was charging at her.

A shot rang out.

Vladan wailed in agony. White hot pain exploded in his abdomen. Chunks of his flesh flew off. There was a hole in his side. Organs slipped out of his wound. He stumbled. Vladan turned to the direction of the shooter.

In the open doorway of the pale yellow house, stood Adelaide. Her shotgun was still raised, barrel smoking. She pumped it, the used cartridges fell to the floor.

Vladan smiled madly. "Oh, Adelaide."

"Shut up," Adelaide pulled the trigger again. Vladan's chest exploded next. The vampire wailed in agony and fell to the ground. His body shook, heels kicking against the road.

Misha was panting in shock. She stood and staggered to her feet. Misha looked at Vladan's mangled body. Warm arms wrapped around her. Misha's eyes widened in horror. Before Misha could speak, Adelaide kissed her. The blonde melted into the embrace. Oh, her sweet, foolish girl. Misha forced herself to pull away. "Get inside!" she cried and tried to push the woman away.

Adelaide furrowed her brow. The man was laid out on the black top. There was a hole in his chest for Christ's sake! "Misha-" Adelaide gasped as she was knocked off her feet. Misha screamed in horror. Strong, cold arms were around her, her feet dangled in the air. Adelaide turned and saw Vladan's bloody face. She tried to fight her way out of his arms, but she only had so much of a chance against a damn vampire. The man was like stone.

"Please, don't!" Misha begged. "You can have me! Just don't hurt her."

Vladan giggled madly. He buried his nose against Adelaide's neck and inhaled. The acidic fear in her blood was tantalizing. There were healing puncture wounds in her neck. Vladan hissed.

Adelaide wretched as the man licked a line up her neck. She struggled anew. "Get off of me!" she screamed, kicking back widely. That only got her a laugh from the beast.

Vladan looked at his creation. "I know why you ran," he spat at Margosha. "You're still a child," he laughed. "Still that foolish little dancer who snuck away to kiss her co-stars behind the curtain. A simple girl!"

Adelaide reared her head back and caught a chunk of the vampire's face between her teeth. It didn't give like human flesh, but it was enough of a distraction. Vladan gasped in shock, his grip loosening. Adelaide wrestled herself free, falling on the pavement.

Vladan laughed, "You bitch." Margosha tackled him.

Adelaide scrambled to get her dropped shotgun. The vampiric pair were back to throwing each other around. Adelaide looked at her car. People were coming out of their homes. Vladan would kill them. Adelaide knew the sick bastard would kill them. Enough people had been killed because of Adelaide. She threw her shotgun into the passenger seat and fired up the engine. The headlights illuminated the supernatural pair. "Hey!" she screamed out the window.

Vladan whipped around to look at the woman.

"Come fucking get me!" Adelaide screamed and peeled down the road. She looked in her rearview mirror. Vladan was chasing her.

Good.

Chapter 18

Adelaide raced through the streets. The vampire grabbed her driver side window. Adelaide tried to send the gas pedal through the floor.

"You can't out drive me, my love," Vladan mocked.

Adelaide laughed, "I'm not trying to!" She turned the wheel and smashed the vampire into a utility pole. The wood splintered and cracked. It broke in half and fell. Wires popped and snapped. Sparks flew and lit up the sky. Transformers exploded overhead and caused the streets to go dark. Vladan was swallowed by the blackness. Adelaide then cut the wheel hard into the other direction and sent the car barreling through the low fence that surrounded the church.

She grabbed her gun and raced to the large diggers. Work had resumed on the church's reconstruction. The hole in the center looked like a void. The night was suddenly silent. Adelaide swallowed. She couldn't see Vladan. It was like the darkness had taken him back to the depths of hell, where he belonged.

"How poetic," a voice teased on the wind.

Adelaide jumped. She raised her gun and scanned the area. Nothing. The only things around were the diggers and bulldozers. They loomed large underneath the moon. The shadows they casted were the perfect hiding spot for a deranged vampire to lie in wait. She pressed her back against one of the excavators. Adelaide felt her heart in her throat. The cross on the top of the steeple seemed to glitter. Adelaide wondered, could the devil set foot on hallowed ground?

Memories of finding Misha flooded back. Those lost green eyes. That tattered dress. Adelaide felt tears roll down her cheeks. If she could go back in time, she wouldn't change a thing. Adelaide would still take Misha home. She'd still kiss her. She'd still give her whole heart and soul to her. Even if she died tonight, even if Vladan ripped out her throat, Adelaide would die without regrets. She got to love.

That was more than he ever got.

"How sweet," Vladan spat.

Adelaide looked at him. The man stood a couple yards away. She raised her gun.

Vladan's eyes softened. "You're out of ammunition," he said. He waved his hand dismissively.

Adelaide looked down at her gun and grit her teeth. Even still, she kept it raised. The vampire smiled at her. Had she not known him, she would have thought it was kind.

"That's why I like you," Vladan explained, "You fight. You care. It's novel."

Adelaide sneered, "No it isn't." She widened her stance. "Why can't you just leave us alone. You have all the time in the world!" More tears flooded her vision. "Why spend eternity hurting people? Stalking people? What's the fucking point?!"

Vladan looked at her. His icy eyes seemed vacant. "There is no point," he said.

Adelaide's heart nearly stopped. "What?"

Vladan walked closer. "There is no point," he repeated. "We are animals, Adelaide. All of us. We live and live and live until we become dust." He ripped the gun out of the woman's hands. Her gasp was beautiful. "I may have more time than you, but that means nothing. Life means nothing. It's just pain and pleasure and pain again."

Vladan cupped the woman's face. "Don't you see, Adelaide? Don't you see that there's nothing. No reason other than what we give it. This life needs no restraint, no morals. I want, I take. I'm hungry, I eat. I create, I destroy." Adelaide's eyes were wide and reminded Vladan of a frightened fawn. "Don't you understand? I am offering you freedom."

Adelaide wanted to step back, but was met with cold unmoving metal. Even still, she tried to fuse herself with the vehicle. "You're not making any sense."

Vladan laughed. Adelaide was foolish, like Margosha had been, but what a beauty her folly was. He went on, "I need no reason for what I do, Adelaide. I do as I please." He took her hands. "You have been restricted, forced into smaller and smaller boxes your entire life." Vladan smiled, "Let me free you."

Adelaide wanted to wrench her hands away. "You honestly believe if you turn me I'll become like you? A selfish, deranged monster who consumes and kills with no remorse?" She wanted to spit in his face. "You claim I'm your love and yet it seems you don't know a damn thing about me!"

Vladan grabbed the woman's throat. She grasped his arm but didn't thrash like most would. Adelaide remained calm, even with a deadly grip around her neck. "I know you well. You have some much to avenge." He leaned closer. "The treatment of your family, of yourself, of your kin. There is so much anger inside of you, so much resentment you hide behind your kindness. A monster that lingers and is just waiting to strike."

Adelaide growled. She placed her feet against the bulldozer, which bought her a little bit of air.

Vladan smiled at her cleverness. "You would be a force to be reckoned with, Adelaide. You and I could even rip apart the queen. You can play the homely house mother all you want, but I see the same darkness in you I saw in Margosha. The same darkness my maker saw in me. We are meant to be the hunters of man. We were made and bred to be." Vladan elongated his fangs. "You are old enough. You have seen enough, my dear. Become my angel of death." He pressed his forehead against Adelaide's.

Adelaide looked into his eyes. "I may be a monster, but I'll never be yours." her breath was labored as her throat was constricted, but she kept going. "Yes, I want to kill. So many of these fucking bastards, I want to kill, but actions speaks louder than words. I have a deep hatred inside me, but I'd never take it out on the world just because I fucking could!" Adelaide reeled her foot back and swung it forward into Vladan's crotch. It was enough to get her dropped to the ground.

Vladan chuckled. He couldn't believe the woman would do that. "Fine." He watched as she crawled away. The woman grabbed her gun. Vladan rolled his eyes and set upon her. He straddled her and tried to go in for a bite. Vladan now realized the gun was a barrier, not a weapon. Adelaide pressed it longways against his throat, keeping his teeth at bay. "Once I turn you," he grunted, "You'll understand!"

Adelaide laughed in his face. "Un-fucking-likely!"

"Enough!" Vladan hissed. He reared back and grabbed the woman's wrists, then forced them to the ground. "**Lie still**," he ordered.

Adelaide paused her struggling. She looked into Vladan's eyes and relaxed. The vampire let go of her wrist. Her nails clawed at the thawed dirt.

"That's a good girl," Vladan cooed. He gently turned Adelaide's head. The mark

Margosha had left made a fire burn in his stomach. What an unruly child his once love was. Vladan opened his mouth wide.

Adelaide took a lump of dirt and smashed him in the face with it. She made sure it got in his mouth and eyes. The vampire wailed and Adelaide scrambled away. Her ankle was caught by Vladan's steely grip. She kicked back, getting him in the face, but it only seemed to piss him off and hurt her foot.

"You ungrateful bitch!" Vladan dug his claws into Adelaide's flesh, making her scream. "I-"

A gunshot rang out. Vladan's head went sideways. The bullet flew through one temple and out the other. There was a pause, then a cacophony of bullets reigned down. Adelaide screamed as she was dragged away.

"Beloved, beloved!" a frantic voice tried to soothe her.

Adelaide looked up to see Misha. She then turned into the direction of where the shots were coming from. Rick and Mike were pulling their triggers like madmen. Adelaide was surprised she hadn't been hit by accident. The girls and Jamie were there as well. Once the bullets finished, Wendy came in swinging with a bat. Knocking an already swaying Vladan to the ground. The others joined in.

Bike chains, knives, crowbars, more bats. They all took turns laying into the bullet riddled vampire.

Misha stood and walked over to the mob. They moved once they noticed her approach. Vladan laid in a crumpled heap. His body twisted and jerked, trying to force out bullets and soothe impact trauma. Misha noticed the hole in the church yard. The one she had buried herself in and the one she'd dug herself out of.

Adelaide watched as Misha dragged Vladan away. The man disappeared over the edge and into the pit. Mike and Rick came over with cans of gasoline. Adelaide tried to stand on her shaky legs. They collapsed beneath her and she let out a pained cry. The adrenaline was wearing off. Every part of her body was screaming in agony. The girls and Jamie all came to her side.

"It's okay, mama," Tracey reassured. She rubbed the woman's heaving back. Jamie hugged the woman. Heather hugged the woman's other side. A protective circle surrounded Adelaide. The embrace soothed her rattled nerves. They were alive. Her babies were alive.

A strange noise caused the group to jump. A screech rang out, then horrid garbled cries that made everyone wince, filled the air. All eyes fell on the inferno erupting from the pit. The flames reached toward the sky. Twice the size of a person. Mike and Rick stood a couple yards back.

Misha was near the edge. She stood before the mouth of hell and watched the devil turn to ash. Vladan was now dust. A wave of relief washed over her. The pressure of Vladan's existence lifted off of her shoulders. He was gone. Finally gone. Tears flooded Misha's eyes.

Adelaide watched as Misha turned toward them. The vampire's hair blended in with the hellfire behind her. She looked serene as blood trailed down her face. Freedom. That was the only word Adelaide could put to the feelings Misha projected. The fiery halo made her holy. The vampire was a goddess of chaos, of blood, of love, of death. She was ethereal. The edges of Misha shined. Adelaide's vision tunneled. All she saw was Misha. The darkness crept in, and in, before taking over.

Adelaide was swallowed and pulled into the abyss.

Rick watched as a power washer was taken into the station. The cleaning crew was trying their best, bless their hearts. The kids were out for a week due to the murders. Paperwork was hell. The interviews were worse. He barely remembered anything. Trauma, one of the shrinks had told him. Rick rubbed his tired eyes. A warm hand tapped his shoulder. The older man looked to his side. Mike was there. His eyes were just as dark with the weight of weariness. Neither of them remembered much. They'd gone over everything over and over again.

"Got you a coffee," Mike yawned. He took a sip of his own cup. The FBI were beside themselves. No body meant no real closure for most. All they had was a mound of ashes. Someone had the good sense to snap photos of Vladan's burning body and smoldering remains. Everyone was furious at the officers for 'helping a hysterical woman set the man on fire', but the pair didn't care. Vladan was dead. Dead. Dead. Dead. It was worth the possible consequences. If they weren't the only cops left in town, they would've been fired in a heartbeat.

Rick took the offered cup. Grief hadn't settled in yet. Everything still felt so dreamlike. It was all so fuzzy and unreal. Even when he walked through the station and saw the dismembered bodies of his force, it didn't settle in. Rick just wanted to forget. He was too old for all of this. "Thanks," he drank his coffee and watched as furniture was taken out and thrown into the back of a dump truck. What a waste. Rick asked Mike, "Any word from the kids?"

 Mike smiled. It was a small one, but it was there. "The girls are alright. Jamie said the house's foundation was damaged beyond repair, so they're all back at Adelaide's." He watched as one of the cleaners ran out of the station and vomited into the bushes.

 Rick nodded, "Moved them in, just to move them out." The coffee was terrible. He wanted a richer brew. Screw it. Rick dumped his cup out into the grass. He threw away the cup in disgust.

 Mike laughed. The noise felt so foreign, but it was nice. Mirth had been lost over the past few days. It felt good to have it back. "Foreman is stepping down as dean." He wanted to give the other man some good news.

 Rick huffed, "About damn time." He tried to keep talking. Talking helped to ban the horrors that crept in when all fell silent. "That boy, James?"

 "Jamie," Mike corrected.

"Right, right," Rick went on, "He got in with the paper. The kid sure knows how to write a story." He hated to admit it, but he had the boy's article framed on the wall. Not only was it a good piece of writing, but it also quelled some of the fears people had. Of course, Jamie had given the officers far more credit then they were due. Rick barely remembered what the hell happened. Apparently Misha threw some gas and he shot the man. The friction or something set the killer blaze. Rick didn't think that was what happened, but he didn't have any way to disprove it. All the girls and Mike said it happened that way, so Rick guessed it did. It wasn't worth the headache to think about it harder.

The town now adored him, which was nice. The police weren't viewed too kindly by the youths. Now though, Rick got a couple high fives when he walked down the street. It didn't feel earned, but it was still nice. Rick took the admiration in stride. Mike even gave him a toast at the bar, everyone had joined in. "You think the girls will be okay?" Rick asked. The poor things had given heartbreaking interviews.

Mike shrugged, "Don't see why they wouldn't be. Yeah, it was scary but they got to see the son of a bitch burn."

Rick snorted, "True." He did remember that. The pit had looked like Hell's entrance. Like if he jumped in, he'd meet the devil on the other side. Rick remembered the woman standing beside him. What was her name again? Adelaide's little red head? Rick pinched the bridge of his nose.

Mike noticed the pinched expression on Rick's face. The poor man had been running himself ragged. Hell, so was Mike. When was the last time they ate a full meal? Mike couldn't remember. That wasn't good. "Let's go get some grub," Mike lightly patted the other man's shoulder. He turned to get in the cruiser.

Rick agreed. The pair drove to Jimmy's, the local diner. They were greeted with cheers and happy hollers. Rick tipped his hat in acknowledgement. The pair sat in a booth. Rick placed his hat by his side. He looked out the window and saw tranquility. Something he hadn't seen in months. That same peace washed over him. He relaxed into the booth chair.

Mike watched as his mentor, his best friend, finally untensed. The man smiled. He waved at their waitress, Olive, who came to leave a pot of coffee at their table. They picked up their menus and looked it over. They were going to get the same thing they always did, but they wanted to pretend they'd get something new.

The bell of the front door jingled. Murmurs followed as two agents entered the diner. They were the stereotypical men in black. A pair of walking cliches. Their glasses-covered eyes scanned the room before landing on Mike and Rick. They swiftly walked over. The two were young, clean shaven, fresh out of the academy. This was probably their first job in the field.

Rick huffed. Out of all of the fuckers to send, the feds sent some newbies. Other agents had come and gotten statements, why were they back? What else could they possibly need? No one had a clear memory of the night. Maybe they were there to ask about the destruction on the street? Not that anyone remembered how that happened either. The town only got the phones back up that morning. They were still looking for more operators. Rick groaned. God, so many bodies. He stared down at the table in mourning.

A cough made Rick look up. The agents were standing at the edge of their table. "Can I help you boys?" Rick asked. He poured himself a cup of coffee, mostly to keep himself from rolling his eyes. The feds were the last thing he wanted to deal with at the moment. Rick poured his partner a cup too, pushing it across the table to the other man. Mike smiled and took it graciously.

The agents stood straighter. They looked between the men, mouths twisted. Obviously the cops didn't take them seriously, or they were that exhausted. "I'm agent Wright, this is agent Kent," the man, Wright, explained. "We've been going over your statements and would like to confer with the woman mentioned." The cops hadn't given the name of the woman who threw gas on the killer. That was strange to say the least. They would have assumed the men had been lying, if not for others confirming the woman's action. No name though. No name.

Mike rubbed his eyes. "We told you, don't remember." He could have pointed them in the direction of the sorority, but something held his tongue back. Something told him not to give anyone a lead. Hell, he didn't remember the woman's name. The strange redhead. He couldn't remember her face. Mike groaned and rubbed his eyes. His head throbbed.

"You can't try to?" Kent hissed.

Rick decided to ignore the pair. He hoped the agents would take the hint and fuck off. Unfortunately, they didn't.

Kent and Wright growled. "Can't stand you backwater hicks," Kent spat. That made the pair's head snap in their direction. Kent's mouth clicked shut.

"And we can't stand you yuppies!" Mike snapped back. He watched as the men flinched. It gave him a sick sense of satisfaction. The fuckers could do with a good fright. They'd been trying, for days they've been trying! How dare the agent try and claim they hadn't been trying! He wanted to slug the men in the face. "You fuckers haven't been worth the pot you piss in, so get the hell out of our town!"

The other people at the diner were now glaring at the agents. Some of the men at the bar turned on their stools. Fists were formed and scowls littered everyone's face. Wright read the room and cleared his throat. "We don't need them," he announced loudly to Kent. "Come on," he urged his partner out of the diner before the townsfolk decided to strike. Kent gave the cops one last glare before following Wright out of the diner.

Rick sighed in relief. "I swear they're getting dumber." Mike chuckled. Rick finished his coffee. He looked out the window again. Once again, peace settled in. He hoped it stayed that way for the rest of his life.

Jamie sat on his bed. Posters were hung, books were stacked, and clothing was put away. He was thankful that the college gave everyone a week to settle back in. The once extra room of Adelaide's house was now his. Twelve kids under one roof, well...that wasn't true. Misha was not a kid. Well, no. She was, but. Jamie furrowed his brow. Why did calling Misha a kid feel wrong? She was the same age as Monica. Right?

Heather stepped into the doorway. The brunet was on his bed zoning out. "You okay?" she asked him. The other night had been a mess. Everyone woke up in a daze. It was understandable, since they caught a serial killer. Still... Heather didn't want to deal with the headache that bloomed whenever she thought about that night. No use dwelling on it.

Jamie looked up at the woman. Heather was the intense one, but she also had a soft spot that Jamie was lucky enough to see. Jamie smiled, Heather reminded him of Misha. "I'm alright," he assured. He flopped back on his bed. There was a crack in the paint on the ceiling. "Just happy to be here, ya know?" It wasn't a complete lie.

Heather nodded. She walked over and laid down next to Jamie. This room had once been Evaline's. She'd graduated the year before. Now she worked for the government. There was something in the air of the house. An unspoken oddity. The strangeness of that night was still fresh. That monster had left a stain in her mind. "Misha set a serial killer on fire," she said in disbelief.

Jamie nodded, "Yeah, that was fucking nuts."

Heather couldn't help but laugh. She covered her face and tried to stifle her snickers. It was all so ridiculous. The semester had barely begun! Heather couldn't even hate the strange little russian any more. The strawberry blonde had saved who knows how many potential victims. That bastard could have gotten off for his crimes. Misha did the world a favor. Even though Heather didn't remember most of the night, she remembered the woman against the hellfire glow. Jamie was looking at her with those big blue eyes. "I'm going to Harvard next year," Heather randomly announced. It was more to change the subject than anything.

Jamie beamed. He was happy for the distraction. "You're going to do great!" he cheered.

Heather blushed, "Thanks." Jamie was a sweet guy. It gave her a bit of hope in the world.

"What'cha doin?" Tracey asked, coming into the room. She noticed them lying side by side and decided to take up a spot on the bed as well. "Misha said we should get take out." The other redhead was such a badass. Tracey hoped she'd be able to fight like the Russian some day. The woman set a guy on fire! It was like a movie scene.

Jamie groaned, "Is my room gonna become the hot spot again?" The girls had decided the living room at his frat sucked. They would instead congregate in his room, unless they wanted to watch some TV.

Heather shrugged. "If it's not broke, don't fix it," she teased.

Nicole popped her head in the doorway. "There you are!" She noticed Heather and Tracey. "Oh, are we havin' a Jamie party?!" Nicole cheered. She came into the room and flopped on the bed, partially landing on Heather and Jamie.

The boy groaned. "Noooo!" He got up and sat with his back to the headboard. Before he could say anything else, the other girls flooded into the room. Jamie let his head thump against the wall as ten girls crowded onto his bed. "Guys!" he whined.

"What?" Wendy giggled, "We're just sitting!"

Monica nodded, "I think we deserve a little hang sesh."

Heather wrapped an arm around Jamie. "You're one of us now, JJ! Welcome to the poindexters!"

Jamie rolled his eyes but couldn't keep a smile off his face. All thoughts of the other night were forgotten as they began to gossip and tease one another. Jamie was just happy to not be alone.

There was a hum. A low rumble. Sunlight streamed in through the curtains. The room was alight with a golden glow. Adelaide whined. Her eyes felt heavy. She forced them open. Dust danced above her. The room was cozy and warm. Her eyes became fuzzy, unfocused. She blinked them clear again.

Adelaide's throat felt dry. Parched beyond measure. Her body was like a dead weight. All her limbs wished to rest. There was a vague sensation of something on her right hand. It was odd, but not worth the energy to fight. Adelaide sighed. She opened her mouth. That was also a task. Her lips were dry and stuck together. Peeling them apart resulted in a strange sensation. Not quite pain, but also not pleasant.

Adelaide turned her head to see fire. That couldn't be right. She blinked rapidly, her vision focusing. It wasn't fire, but hair. Strawberry blonde hair. Adelaide smiled. It took a lot of effort, but it was worth it. "Misha," she croaked out. God, her voice was wrecked. The vampire's head snapped up in shock. Those green eyes stared into hers. Misha's pale face was stained with blood. There were crimson tear tracks that contrasted strikingly with her white skin. Adelaide couldn't stop smiling at the vampire. "Hi, peaches."

Misha gasped and lept into motion. She clambered up onto the bed, wrapping the woman in a hug. "Oh, beloved," she cried, "beloved, beloved." Misha pressed kiss after kiss on the woman's face. "My love. My light. Adelaide, Adelaide, Adelaide," she wept.

Said woman giggled. It was a soft sound. "Oh, Misha." Adelaide willed her arms to defy gravity and wrap around the vampire. "Are you okay?" she croaked out.

Misha nodded. "Yes, yes," she kissed Adelaide on the lips. The woman's heartbeat made her own soar. Adelaide was alive. She was alive. "I am healed. I know you may feel heavy. When you fainted, I panicked, and gave you my blood. Possibly too much," Misha admitted. She laid down next to Adelaide. Her hand went to Adelaide's messy curls. New tears flooded her eyes. They were alive. Alive! "Oh, beloved. My beloved." Misha pulled the woman into another kiss.

Adelaide went willingly. She sighed into it. Adelaide knew her breath was terrible, but the vampire didn't seem to care. Misha's tongue met hers. It was like an adrenaline shot. The fog over her body lifted. Adelaide cupped the vampire's face. The kiss went on and on. Misha pressed against her. The pair were wrapped together like ivy. Adelaide eventually had to stop to breathe. She shuddered at the sight of Misha licking her lips. "Oh, peaches," Adelaide whispered. Those green eyes stared into her black ones. "I love you," Adelaide rubbed her thumb over the vampire's cheek bone.

Misha sniffled, "I will love you forever, Adelaide." New tears fell from her eyes. "Forever and always." She took the woman's hand.

Adelaide's lip quivered, a tear rolled down her cheek. "I'm yours, eternally yours."

Misha scooted forward and caught the woman in another kiss.

Adelaide smiled, till reality hit her. "Wait!" She tried to sit up, but ended up falling back on the bed with a groan.

"Beloved!" Misha scolded. She searched the woman's scrambled thoughts. Oh, Adelaide was worried about the girls. "I have wiped their minds," Misha whispered. She hoped her love would understand. Thankfully, her answer made Adelaide relax. That was good.

"Of everything?" Adelaide asked the vampire.

Misha pursed her lips. "Just the supernatural. I have allowed them to remember pieces. To take everything would not be wise. A change of memory can only stick if it is believable. An entire night of multiple people erased may cause…" Misha trailed off.

Adelaide sighed in relief. Misha did have centuries of covering her tracks. The woman tugged at the vampire. "Come here," she begged. "Hold me." Misha wrapped her up in her lukewarm arms. Adelaide relaxed and buried her nose into the vampire's strawberry blonde hair.

Chapter 19

Dobson didn't know what to make of Adelaide sitting front and center in his class. He looked around in confusion. The strange woman and young girl that lived with Adelaide were on either side of her. "May I help you, Adelaide?" he asked.

Adelaide tilted her head. "Oh, did you not get the updated list?"

Dobson raised an eyebrow.

Adelaide went on, "I'm enrolled. I've heard so much about your class, Timothy. I wanted to see it for myself." There were snickers throughout the room.

Dobson frowned. "Aren't you a little old to be in attendance, Addie?" he sneered.

Adelaide smiled sardonically. "Aren't you a little old to be hitting on teenagers, Timmy?" The class erupted into laughter. It was such a happy sound. One that Adelaide hoped she could cause more of. Especially since it pissed off Timothy to no end. The man's face was turning a bright red. Tomato Timmy. That would be the new nickname Adelaide would use. It would probably make the girls hoot and holler.

Dobson huffed in rage. The chorus of laughter was getting to him. "Alright!" he snapped, thankfully the hall fell silent. "I'm not backtracking, Miss Freeman. Do try and keep up," he snarled and went to the chalkboard.

Adelaide smiled brightly. "Will do."

It was going to come up eventually. Adelaide knew it would. After her fifty-second birthday, they were laying in bed. Adelaide was recovering from Misha's 'gift'. Her face was hot and her blood was pumping. Some of her blood was on Misha's lips. Adelaide looked at her. Underneath the moonlight, Misha was a vision. There was a knot in Adelaide's stomach. The vampire would stay that way forever. Misha was frozen in eternal beauty. Adelaide looked at her hand. A new spot had formed on it. When had that happened?

"Do you want me to turn you?" Misha asked. The blonde could hear the woman's thoughts. She could feel her love's fear. Misha wanted to turn the woman, more than anything, but she'd never force it. Never.

Adelaide rubbed her face, banishing her depressing thoughts. She turned to the vampire. "What?"

Misha turned to her side and propped her head up, elbow on the bed. "Do you want to be a vampire?" she asked. Those big doe eyes went wide.

"You…" Adelaide turned to her side as well, "You can do that?"

Misha nodded, "Yes, beloved. I can, if you'd like."

Adelaide turned to lay on her back again. She thought for a while. The idea of living forever was daunting. How long even was forever? Would her forever last a decade or thousands of years. Was eternity worth taking at her age? She'd outlive her girls. Outlive her friends. Possibly outlive her country. How many nations had fallen and risen in front of Misha's eyes? Hell, a whole nation formed while the vampire slept in a church yard! Adelaide bit her lip and thought. A cool hand covered her own. Adelaide looked at Misha.

The vampire's eyes were filled with bloody tears. "I will not force you," she assured. Her voice was so broken and small. Misha tried hard not to show the terror she felt on her face. "I…" she let out a shaky breath, "I will hold you while you die. I will make it gentle and sweet." Misha guided Adelaide's hand to her lips and kissed the woman's hand. The gold band Misha had gotten all those years ago was firmly on Adelaide's finger. Her matching one met Adelaide's when Misha interlocked their fingers. The soft clink of them connecting made Misha's heart sing. "I will return with you to the dust," she vowed.

Now it was Adelaide's turn to cry. "You'd die with me?" she asked in disbelief. Why? Why would Misha do that?

Misha held the woman's hand tighter. "Beloved, I would die with you. I would live with you. As long as you are with me, that is all that matters." She pressed another kiss onto Adelaide's hand. The hand she took as her own. They couldn't get married officially, but they were in every way that mattered. Some day they'd have a ceremony. Someday Misha would get to see Adelaide in a bridal gown. Maybe not tomorrow, or in a year, but someday.

One day.

Adelaide sniffled and pulled Misha to her. "Come here," she urged. Her arms encircled the vampire. Misha returned the hold, burying her cool nose into Adelaide's neck. The woman pressed a kiss to the vampire's forehead. Adelaide then buried her face into Misha's hair. Pomegranate. "I want to graduate first," Adelaide whispered into strawberry blonde tresses. Misha squeezed her tighter.

Heather's room was empty. Monica's room was empty. Wendy's room was empty. They were blackholes along the hallway. Adelaide cleaned each one. She took down each plaque and closed their doors. Normally, she'd keep them open, waiting for the next girl to fill the space. Adelaide shut the last of the three doors. It just felt right to.

"You will not be accepting more?" Misha asked. Summer had begun and with it came hotpants. They especially looked mouth watering on Adelaide. Ogling could wait though, her beloved was currently contemplating something life changing.

Adelaide looked at the little handmade plaques. "I think," she began, "I think it's time. Don't you?" Misha tilted her head in confusion. Adelaide shrugged. "I mean, over thirty years running this place. Over fifty years staying here. I think it's time." Adelaide smiled at the little blocks of wood that held her girls' names. "Tracey will be my last," she said definitively.

Misha nodded. She gently pulled the woman into a hug.

One.

By one.

By one.

The doors lining the hall became vacant. A new black hole formed as the years passed and the seasons changed. Adelaide added more graduation pictures to her scrapbook. Little plaques were packed away. The scent of life slowly faded and faded. One summer, Tracey's door was shut.

Then, finally, there was only one left.

Adelaide closed the front door behind her. The moving van wasn't as full as she thought it would be. The house had always seemed so huge, until now. Misha was waiting for her. The vampire leaned against the box truck. Adelaide placed a final tote inside the bed and shut the rolling door, then secured it.

All done. All moved.

This was it. Adelaide looked back at the pale yellow house. The house she was raised in. The house that held both wonders and terrors. The house she'd found heartbreak and love. A tear rolled down her cheek.

It was time.

Adelaide turned to Misha. The blonde was patiently waiting. Adelaide sniffled. "Ready to go?" she asked.

The vampire nodded and got into the driver's side. Adelaide went to the passenger side. There was an odd leather case on the seat. She picked it up and hopped into the van. "What's this?" she asked.

Misha smiled, "Open it."

Adelaide did. It was her diploma. A fresh wave of tears flooded her eyes. They fell on the glossy protector and beaded over the signatures at the bottom

"I thought it deserved a better holder," Misha flippantly said as she started the van. The waves of love and appreciation Adelaide was giving off were going to make her cry if she focused on them for too long.

The rumble of the van reminded Adelaide of the heater. The setting sun reminded her of its fiery glow. Misha reminded her that home wasn't a place, it was a feeling, and after years of searching, she had found it.

Epilogue

Misha picked out a merlot. It was a good vintage. She took it to the counter. The pretentious man behind it pursed his lips at her. Misha wondered if she had time to eat him. No. It wasn't worth the risk of being caught on camera. She paid for the wine and left.

New York was as bustling as always. The sun had set long ago. Neon lights practically blocked out the stars. The billboards and flashing signs were mesmerizing. So many sights and smells. No wonder people got lost. There was confetti still lining the streets. New Years had just passed. There were even a couple of people still sporting their 2000 glasses.

Misha wove through the masses till she finally stood in front of her brownstone. Such a fun word. Brownstone. It made Misha giggle the first time she'd heard it, so of course, it was the home she chose. The vampire went inside, locking the door behind her. "I am home!" she announced.

Misha took off her wool coat and scarf. The crackle of the fire made her nostalgic. Music was playing softly from their stereo set. Technology had been exploding and didn't seem to be slowing down anytime soon. Photos lined the walls. Pictures from Rome, Athens, Kiev, Tokyo, London, and more. Misha put her keys in the bowl and noticed another set inside.

The vampire entered the living room. There, on the sill of their back window, sat Adelaide. The woman had built herself a little nook, lined with pillows and fairy lights. She was absorbed in whatever story she was reading. Misha set down the bottle of wine. The sound made the woman look up.

Adelaide's black eyes shined in the firelight. What once revealed a deep brown now showed a crimson red. Despite the change, Adelaide kept her wrinkles. They were softer, but still there. Her clawed nails released the page she was about to turn. "Welcome home, peaches," she greeted with a smile, showing her a glimpse of her fangs.

Misha beamed. She practically flew to the woman's side and captured her plush lips in a kiss. "I missed you," the blonde whispered.

Adelaide chuckled, "You were gone an hour."

"Too long," Misha whined and pressed kiss after kiss on Adelaide's cheeks, neck, and chest.

"You're a fiend," Adelaide teased, allowing her head to fall back. She opened her mouth and sighed.

A knock at the door made the women groan.

Adelaide huffed out a laugh. Misha pouted, "Ignore them." The blonde kissed her wife. Another knock. The pair groaned again. Misha got up. "Coming!" she called and stalked over to the front door. "This had better be good!" If it was a solicitor, she was going to drain them dry! Well, no, Adelaide wouldn't let her do that; however the woman would let Misha scare the shit out of them. It accomplished the same goal, just with less clean up. Misha ripped open the door, "Yes?!" The unneeded air in Misha's lungs were sucked out in an instant. She stood frozen. There, before her, was a creature unlike any she'd ever seen.

The being was tall, almost too feet taller than Misha. It was thin, sharp cheekbones and collarbones. In fact, it was all angles. Its eyes were larger and somehow blacker than Adelaide's. The nose had no nostrils and its ears were pointed.

This creature was old. Older than Misha. Older than Vladan had been. The ancient air around it was palpable and commanded respect.

"Who are you?" Misha asked it.

The being smiled, showing off it's row of sharp teeth. "I am Atropa," it answered in a gravelly, broken voice. Obviously, this being was not born to speak the tongue of man. It leaned forward, over the threshold. No invitation needed. The protection of the home did not stop it. Even Vladan had been bound to the old laws, but not this creature. "I have come with an invitation."

Misha gripped the doorframe tight, the wood creaked beneath her hold. "An invitation to what?"

Atropa smiled, "To join my Court."

Printed in Great Britain
by Amazon